Dear Readers,

Many years ago, when I was a kid, my father said to me, "Bill, it doesn't really matter what you do in life. What's important is to be the *best* William Johnstone you can be."

I've never forgotten those words. And now, many years and almost 200 books later, I like to think that I am still trying to be the best William Johnstone I can be. Whether it's Ben Raines in the Ashes series, or Frank Morgan, the last gunfighter, or Smoke Jensen, our intrepid mountain man, or John Barrone and his hard-working crew keeping America safe from terrorist low lifes in the Code Name series, I want to make each new book better than the last and deliver powerful storytelling.

Equally important, I try to create the kinds of believable characters that we can all identify with, real people who face tough challenges. When one of my creations blasts an enemy into the middle of next week, you can be damn sure he had a good reason.

As a storyteller, my job is to entertain you, my readers, and to make sure that you get plenty of enjoyment from my books for your hard-earned money. This is not a job I take lightly. And I greatly appreciate your feedback—you are my gold, and your opinions *do* count. So please keep the letters and e-mails coming.

Respectfully yours,

William Johnstone

WILLIAM W. JOHNSTONE

THE FIRST MOUNTAIN MAN: BLACKFOOT MESSIAH

WAR OF THE MOUNTAIN MAN

PINNACLE BOOKS
Kensington Publishing Corp.
http://www.kensingtonbooks.com

PINNACLE BOOKS are published by

Kensington Publishing Corp.
850 Third Avenue
New York, NY 10022

All Kensington Titles, Imprints, and Distributed Lines are
available at special quantity discounts for bulk purchases for
sales promotions, premiums, fund-raising, and educational or
institutional use. Special book excerpts or customized print-
ings can also be created to fit specific needs. For details, write
or phone the office of the Kensington special sales manager:
Kensington Publishing Corp., 850 Third Avenue, New York,
NY 10022, attn: Special Sales Department, Phone: 1-800-221-
2647.

Pinnacle and the P logo Reg. U.S. Pat. & TM Off.

ISBN-13: 978-0-7860-1902-1
ISBN-10: 0-7860-1902-6

First Pinnacle Books Printing: August 2007

10 9 8 7 6 5 4 3 2 1

Printed in the United States of America

THE FIRST MOUNTAIN MAN:
BLACKFOOT MESSIAH
7

WAR OF THE
MOUNTAIN MAN
293

THE FIRST
MOUNTAIN MAN:
BLACKFOOT MESSIAH

1

Preacher had to go east to travel west, he discovered, when he decided to accept an assignment from the U.S. Army. Times had been lean for a while. Trapping was a thing of the past. Only a handful of men clung to the old ways, trapped and traded pelts to a market with little demand. Not so the legend called Preacher. Wisely he had salted away ample gold and silver coin, even invested some, most recently in what sounded to many like a fool's venture; Mr. Fulton's steamboat works.

As the smoke-belching paddle wheelers proliferated, so did Preacher's profits. Although ten years of only investment income had severely drained his reserve, he could no more leave the High Lonesome than many of the mountain men. Which meant he had to take whatever he could get to stay in supplies and keep afloat. Thus it was that he grudgingly considered accepting a commission from the War Department to act as trail guide and scout for a regiment of Dragoons. Preacher read again the letter that had accompanied the commissioning papers that had yet to see his signature.

Word has come out of the Northern Rocky Mountains of the Unorganized Territory that the Blackfoot are gathering in great numbers. The savages are being agitated by some holy man, who claims to have the way to bring back the White Buffalo and drive the white men out of the plains forever.

It is vital in these unsettled times to secure our northern flank. A conflict with Mexico seems imminent and our nation could ill afford an Indian uprising when our attention shall be directed southward. To which purpose, it is the decision of the Secretary to dispatch a battalion of Dragoons to the area of the Bighorn Mountains in the northeast part of the Territory to serve as a presence in the area.

The battalion is to depart Jefferson Barracks in Missouri, and proceed up the Missouri to the North Platte River, and from there into the high country of Wyoming where they will establish a fort. The purpose of this post will be to oversee the Blackfoot from a discreet distance, and to show the flag to the Cheyenne and Sioux.

What a stupid idea, Preacher thought. Then, as was the habit of many men who lived alone in the stunning quiet of the High Lonesome, he spoke his ruminations aloud.

"That'll only cause trouble where there's none now. What's got in ol' Quincy's head?" Preacher was referring to Quincy Vickers, an old friend. "He lived out here, and trapped, and knows the Injuns. Maybe it ain't his idee at all. Might be he needs his irons hauled out of the fire."

Knowing the striped-pants crowd from past experience, Preacher was well aware of their propensity for overreaction and . . . for stupidity. He was to sign the papers and take them to Bent's Fort, where two copies would be sent by fast messenger to Jefferson Barracks and Washington City. There he would pick up the first installment of the fee offered him. After a heavy sigh and an idle scratch of his thick, yellow-brown hair, Preacher picked up a quill pen and dipped it in his ink pot. With meticulous care, he formed the letters of his name.

Preacher shut and latched the door to his wintering place, careful to poke the latch string back inside. He'd be busy all summer, most like. He curled a dally of the lead rope of his packhorse around the overlarge horn of the Mexican saddle and swung atop his most recent acquisition, a crossbreed Morgan stallion which had a sturdy mountain mustang for a dam. Preacher had named him Tarnation. He shook the reins and drummed heels into stout sides.

"Well, Tarnation, we'd best be eatin' miles. I reckon I can find some companionable fellers down Bent's Fort way to accompany me on this commission as they called it."

In his letter, Quincy Vickers had told Preacher that he was authorized to hire on up to four men, at a rate of three dollars a day. Leave it to the government, Preacher mused, to offer enough money for some men to kill over it.

Big Nose Harper and his sidekick, Algernon Bloore, had gotten roaring, stumbling, falling-down, crap-in-their-drawers drunk the previous night. Now, some seven hours later, they didn't fare much better. Still too soaked in alcohol to suffer hangovers, they nevertheless sought some "hair of the dog." Their source, no matter how ill-advised, was William "Nifty" Bates, who had recently opened a trading post and road ranch saloon at the summit of Trout Creek Pass. Nifty was frankly afraid of Big Nose.

Big Nose Harper was a bear of a man, with a barrel chest, long, thick arms, tree-trunk legs, and his most memorable feature which gave him his nickname, an overlarge nose that had been smeared over his face. He held in contempt all "shopkeepers," to which subspecies he considered Nifty Bates belonged, and he went out of his way to make their lives miserable. Nursing his alcohol fog, Big Nose now went about tormenting Nifty.

"This whisky tastes like frog pee. You waterin' it down again, you cheat?"

"N-n-no, not at all, Mr. Harper," the barkeep stammered. Bates would soon sell out, inspired in part by the events of that afternoon.

Harper slammed his pewter mug on the pine-plank bar hard enough to make dust rise. "I say yer waterin' it. An' m'name's Big Nose."

"No I'm not, Mr. . . . er . . . Big Nose."

Harper's mean, close-set eyes narrowed. "Are you makin' fun of my honker?"

"Oh, no. You—you told me to call you Big Nose."

Big Nose looked offended. "I never said no such thing. Any man calls me that's lookin' for a killin'. A pantywaist like you's good for a knuckle-drubbin'."

A shadow fell across the toes of the boots worn by Big Nose, cast by a figure that filled the doorway. "Why don't you pick on someone nearer your size, Big Nose? Or should I call you blubber ass?"

Harper spun to face his detractor. "Who in hell are you?"

"They call me Preacher."

"Folks say he's a mean one, Big Nose," sniggered Algernon Bloore, who was more than a few biscuits shy of a plateful.

"Shut up, Algie," Harper snarled. He sized up Preacher and found him wanting. Whisky had so clouded his reasoning that he failed to see the hard, deadly glint in the gray eyes of the raw-boned man in the doorway. "Now, if you'll oblige me by gettin' the hell outta here, I'll have another drink. Barkeep, make it snappy."

Emboldened by the presence of Preacher, Nifty Bates

took a stand. "No, sir. You've had too much. The bar is closed to you."

Harper cut his eyes to Algie. Surprise registered on both their faces. No man ever spoke to Big Nose Harper that way. Growling, Big Nose reached across the plank bar and balled the front of Bates' shirt in both hands. With a yank that looked effortless, and was, he hauled the proprietor off his feet and across the bar.

Taking quick, mincing steps, which caused his long, greasy black locks to churn in protest, Big Nose Harper crossed the room and threw Nifty Bates out into the dusty dooryard. He then dusted hamlike palms together and snarled a reply to Bates.

"I say who drinks an' who doesn't around here."

Preacher took exception to that. "Like hell you do."

Glee brightened the pig eyes of Big Nose. "Mr. Preacher, prepare to meet yer maker."

With that, he came at the living legend of the mountains, arms widespread for his favorite bear hug. It had crushed the life from seven men before this. Big Nose saw no problem in making it eight. Which proved to be a terrible mistake.

Preacher crouched and duck-waddled out of the grasp of those powerful arms. When Big Nose blundered past, Preacher popped up and slammed an open palm into the side of the brawler's head, cupping it over the ear. If not for the thick ropes of greasy hair, the blow would have burst the ear drum of Big Nose. All it did, though, was set up a furious ringing and made him even angrier.

Big Nose whirled and swung at Preacher's chin. Preacher pulled his head back a few inches and let the big knuckles swish past. Then he went to work on the exposed ribs of Big Nose. Soft thuds sounded clearly enough to be heard by Nifty Bates. Dull-witted Algie Bloore decided to get in some licks on Preacher to win favor from his companion. He got a solid kick in the stomach for his efforts, flew backward with a hefty grunt and smashed into the bar. At once he began to spew up the liquor he had consumed.

By then, Big Nose had rallied and again grappled to encase Preacher in a bear hug. Preacher would have none of that. He backpedaled and swung a short, hard right to the face of Harper. Big Nose's most prominent feature got a little bigger when Preacher connected with the much-broken bridge. Preacher followed with a left hook that snapped Harper's jaw shut with a loud click. A second later, arms and legs twined around Preacher from behind.

Always a sneak, though not bright enough to profit by it, a somewhat recovered Algie Bloore had maneuvered to where he could leap on Preacher's back. "I got him, Big Nose, I got him!" he yelled gleefully.

Instead of struggling, Preacher simply flexed his knees and rammed himself backward into a six-by-six upright that supported part of the roof. Algie's shout of triumph turned to a squeal of pain.

"B'god, b'god, I think my back's broke."

"You'll git over it," Harper growled. Then he came for Preacher.

Always obliging, Preacher stepped away from the post and let Algie fall limply to the floor. He met the onrush of his opponent with a series of fast lefts and rights. A small grunt came from Harper with each impact. Half a dozen and he staggered sideways, his vision blurred. Fresh rage welled up inside him and he reached for a knife.

A shaft of sunlight through the open doorway made the keen edge a streak of fire. Harper advanced on Preacher, who produced his Greenriver and took a couple of swipes through the air. When Harper lunged, Preacher cut him across the back of the hand. The knife fell from pain-filled fingers. Preacher kicked it aside.

"Yeaaaaah!"

Preacher whirled to find a revived Algie Bloore hurtling at him, a knife extended in one hand. Preacher parried and sidestepped. He kicked Bloore's feet out from under the slightly built, ferret-faced man and Bloore went sprawling on the plank floor. His face was gouged by the rough boards; his knife skidded across the room. Preacher paused to take stock.

Both men looked fairly well whipped. Big Nose Harper stood, slope-shouldered, his breath harsh and irregular, head bowed. He tried, clumsily, to wrap a bandanna around his wounded hand. Preacher strode to the bar and pulled a beer for himself.

"Look out!" The warning shout came from Nifty Bates in the doorway.

Preacher spun on one heel to see Algie Bloore pull a long, single-barrel, caplock pistol from his waistband. Now, Preacher had been willing to oblige when the pair of frontier trash yanked steel on him, but he figured this was going too far. Recently outfitted with a pair of .44 Walker Colts, Preacher unlimbered one. He smoothly cocked the hammer as the muzzle cleared leather and snapped his elbow inward to elevate the barrel and level it on the target.

For all of his getting started last, Preacher's bullet reached the target first. Algie Bloore's head snapped backward from the impact of the 200-grain ball. A fist-sized chunk of his skull erupted from the left rear and showered the wall with gore. Reflex triggered his pistol and sent a ball into the front of the bar, close by Preacher's leg.

Enraged beyond caution by the swift death of his partner, Big Nose Harper dragged out a pair of double-barreled pistols. He thumb-cocked one awkwardly and swung it in the direction of Preacher. His first barrel discharged and put a ball into the wall beside Preacher's head a split second after Preacher put a .44 slug from his Walker Colt in the center of Harper's forehead.

Ears ringing from the confined detonations, Preacher examined his handiwork. Thick layers of powder smoke undulated in the cool interior of the saloon. Shakily, Nifty Bates entered. He walked over to Preacher and wrung his hand in gratitude and relief.

"I ain't never seen such fancy shootin' in my born days. Drinks are on the house, Preacher. Dinner, too. This pair's been nothin' but a misery and torment to me the past three days."

Up in the Blackfoot Mountains of Montana Territory, a huge gathering of warriors whooped it up around a large fire. The entire carcass of a bison, cut into quarters, turned on green-wood spits over separate cookfires. Off to one side, three Blackfoot braves handed out shiny new rifles from wooden crates at the back of a wagon. Each man gifted with one of these received a bag of a hundred lead balls and a horn of powder. For the time being, they would not be given the percussion caps. Four older men, seated around a large drum, hit the final double beat and concluded their song. The warriors stopped dancing and gathered in a wide semicircle around a startlingly white buffalo-hide lodge.

A young-looking man stepped out of the entrance and struck a pose before them. Although in his mid-thirties, he had the look of a man in his early twenties. His coppery face was elastic and unlined. He wore ankle-high moccasins, beaded and quilled in traditional Blackfoot design, a knee-length loincloth and an abbreviated, soft, pliable, elkskin hunting shirt. Over that was a most unusual item of garb, which lay in turn beneath a second, larger hunting shirt. Hair-pipe bracelets adorned his forearms and a breastplate of bison teeth, hair-pipe beads and brass cones covered his chest. He raised his arms above his head to command attention. The silence, immediate, became profound.

"My brothers, there are many among you who say Iron Shirt is too young to make strong medicine. You say that I have been a medicine man for only ten winters. Yet, I say to you that I have the strongest medicine. I received it in a vision when I visited among the Paiute. My spirit guide appeared to me and showed me a hidden valley. 'Dig here' the spirit said, pointing at a low mound. 'You will find the power of White Buffalo. You will learn the ways of making the medicine that will bring back White Buffalo and drive the white-eyes from our land forever.' I dug there, and I found what the spirit wanted for me. Then I was shown the dance we have just danced, and much more. It makes me safe from any white man's bullets. It will work for you also. The day is coming soon when the white men will fall to the earth like soft hailstones. I bring you rifles, the newest and best. Plenty of bullets, too. When you have finished the ritual of Iron Shirt, you will be stronger than any bullet."

"You say the white man's bullets cannot harm you, Iron Shirt. Prove it and we will follow you," a doubter among the experienced warriors challenged.

Iron Shirt looked at his detractor contemptuously for a moment, then forced an amiable expression on his face. He was, after all, selling something. He pointed with his chin at one of his earlier converts.

"I ask Bent Trees to step to the far side of the fire. Take your gun in hand and point it at my chest." Bent Trees did as bidden. When he was in position, Iron Shirt continued. "When I say so, shoot me."

Gasps of surprise and shock arose among the Blackfoot. "He will not aim at Iron Shirt," one brave stated flatly.

"The gun is not loaded with a bullet," opined another.

"It is a trick."

Another convert sought to disabuse them. "No, it is the power of Iron Shirt's medicine. Watch and see."

"Now, Bent Trees."

With a sharp crack, the .60 single-shot pistol discharged. A black hole appeared in the outer hunting shirt worn by Iron Shirt a split second before he violently rocked backward, his face twisted in pain. Several Blackfoot rushed forward. Iron Shirt held up a hand to stay them.

Carefully he reached into the hole and worked his fingers a moment. He came out with a flattened .60-caliber ball. Yips and whoops of victory broke out among the spectators as he held it high and slowly turned full circle. When the jubilation subsided, he spoke again.

"You will be shown the secret of this medicine when you complete the ritual to become part of my Iron Shield Strong Heart Society. Death to all white-eyes!"

Seated inside the lodge of Iron Shirt were three white men, dressed as Blackfoot. One, Morton Gross, with thinning, mousy brown hair and eyes that looked like chips of blue ice, smoked a cigar. All three looked inordinately pleased with the progress being made. The nominal leader of their cabal nodded to Gross.

"It's fortunate that you have important friends in high places, Morton. Nice to get advance warning that a regiment of troops is on the way, and that it would be guided by an experienced frontiersman."

Morton Gross made light of his informant's importance. "He's only a clerk. The really important ones are so high up they don't dare make direct contact with us, but my informant was able to read the letter sent to the former mountain man, Preacher."

Praeger beamed as he bragged to his companions, "And now, if the men we sent to watch the Santa Fe Trail only do their job, our goal is in our hands."

2

A day's ride from Bent's Fort, Preacher sipped from his first cup of coffee in night camp. Orange shafts slanted over his right shoulder and the night birds and katydids were gradually tuning up for their serenade. They suddenly went silent and Preacher stiffened a moment, then moved with studied casualness as he set aside the tin cup and draped a hand over the butt of his right-hand Walker Colt. A moment later a man's voice rang out from among the trees.

"Hello, the camp. We done smelled coffee."

Preacher looked up in that direction. "Howdy to you, stranger. If you be friendly, come on in. There's plenty for both of us."

"We be two if that's all right by you?"

"Fine as frog hair. Come sit a spell."

Two men entered the clearing on foot, leading their horses. The one in front had a broad, ample girth, chubby arms and legs, and a moon face. The one behind him had a skinny frame, gaunt as a scarecrow's, with flat, dull eyes and big ears. He wore his hair in a boy's "soup bowl" cut, Preacher noticed. The friendly voice came from him.

"They call me Fat Louie, though I can't for the life of me figger why. Ain't put on a single pound since before my voice changed. This lump o' lard be my pard, Yard-Long Farmer. I reckon you can work out why the name," he concluded with a wheezing cackle.

Yard-Long Farmer joined in the laughter. "Yup. When I was ten I had me the biggest tallywhacker of any kid under fifteen in our town," he offered in the event Preacher could not puzzle through the nickname.

"Name's Arthur," Preacher responded evasively. He had heard of this pair and kept alert. "Sit a while."

He poured coffee around and broke out some cornbread and a pot of molasses. While they munched and sipped, Fat Louie spoke flatteringly to Preacher.

"I tell ya, Arthur, you're the very best we ever saw. We didn't cut no sign of you whatsoever. We wouldn't have found this camp if we hadn't near stumbled right into it. You been in the Big Empty long?"

"Since before my voice changed," said Preacher dryly, mocking Fat Louie's earlier turn of phrase.

Fat Louie seemed not to notice. "It certain shows. Say, that's a mighty fine horse you've got. Looks like he could go a long ways, rid hard and put up wet, an' not be harmed. Must be worth a pretty penny."

"He's out of a shaggy mountain mustang," Preacher deliberately belittled his sturdy stallion.

Over the next half hour the conversation went much the same way. When Preacher came to his boots to pour more coffee, Fat Louie cut his eyes to Farmer. The chubby thug nodded slowly. Fat Louie agreed. They had this Arthur off his guard. At once, both rogues whipped out pistols and drew down on Preacher.

"Don't get goosey, Arthur. We'll just be takin' all yer gear an' yer horses an' those fancy irons yer wearin'."

Having been credited with inventing the words *gunfighter*

and *fastdraw,* this did not faze Preacher in the least. He had known of this pair's reputation for years, knew them to be cowardly trash who would kill him in a hot tick. He slowly turned toward the louts threatening them.

He spoke in a soft, flat tone. "I don't think so."

Fat Louie smirked over the barrel of his pistol. "Oh? What makes you say that?"

"Because you've got yourselves a little problem here. Most folks don't call me by my given name. They call me Preacher."

Yard-Long Farmer's eyes went wide and he let his jaw drop before he gulped out a frightened, *"Oh . . . hell!"*

Between the *Oh* and the *hell,* Preacher unlimbered a Walker Colt and shot Fat Louie in the center of his breast-bone. Louie's pistol bucked in his hand and he put a ball through the side-wing of Preacher's long, colorful *capote.* Then his legs went rubbery and he sank to his knees.

Preacher immediately turned on Farmer and put a .44 ball in the hollow of his throat. Yard-Long went down, gargling his blood. His finger twitched and he fired one of the pair of pistols he held, sending the ball into his left calf. Pain sounded through his gurgles.

"Why? Why me?" he managed to choke out.

Preacher stepped over to him and removed the unfired pistol from his hand. Right then he heard the click of a caplock mechanism. Fat Louie had not yet gone off to meet his maker. Ignoring the question for a moment, Preacher turned to his right and fired in an almost casual way. His bullet went in one ear and out the other, ending forever the nefarious career of Fat Louie LaDeaux. Then Preacher dropped to one knee beside Yard-Long Farmer.

"You know, it's too bad you and yer partner chose the wrong path to walk. Best you make your peace with the Almighty. You ain't got much time."

* * *

When Preacher reached Bent's Fort, he encountered two old friends, Antoine Revier, a half-breed Delaware, and Three Sleeps Norris. Former mountain men who, like Preacher, could not leave the mountains after the fur trade collapsed, they moved like ghosts from one old haunt to another. Three Sleeps Norris burst out through the stockade gate with such animation that dust boiled up around his moccasins.

"I'll be danged if it ain't Preacher. Still got his hair, if he has growed a little potbelly."

Preacher dismounted and they embraced, then danced around and around. "I don't have a potbelly," Preacher protested. "And I keep my hair by stayin' on the watch for those who would lift it." He stopped their caper and held Three Sleeps out at arm's length. "I will say that you have grown a mite rounder since I last saw you."

Three Sleeps faked a pout. "I ain't no rounder. It's these clothes."

"Sure, sure, of course it is. Anybody else around from the old bunch?"

"Antoine Revier is inside now. Also Pap Jacobs is mendin' from a broke leg. Nobody else at home but a couple of stuffy soldier-boys."

Preacher frowned. This was embarrassing. "They're waiting for me."

Three Sleeps cocked his head to one side. "What? Preacher hangin' with soldier-boys?"

"Not exactly hangin'. I got some papers for them. To be delivered. Back in Washington City."

Three Sleeps gave Preacher a knowing wink. "Couldn't be that you're signed up to actual work for the Army?"

Preacher swallowed hard and rushed his words. "We'll-talk-about-that-later. Now I want to wash the trail dust out of my throat."

"Wal, come on. Old Turner has him a new spring house where he keeps his beer barrels. Like to crack yer teeth it's so cold."

The Bent brothers had long since departed from the private fort named for them. Currently a man named Ransom Turner occupied the trading post and saloon, and the immigrant's store. The fortifications had deteriorated badly. The Arapaho were no longer a threat, and the Kiowa raided farther east. Turner, more a businessman than a frontiersman, had not bothered with repairs. One of the gates, Preacher noted, hung from a single huge iron hinge. They strode across the small parade ground to the front of the saloon to encounter another warm welcome for Preacher.

Seated at last at a table in the plank-floored saloon, Preacher drank contentedly from a large stein of beer, which he used to chase swallows of some whisky of dubious origin. He easily saw why his present companions preferred the beer. Across from him, Antoine Revier leaned toward Preacher. Beady, black eyes glittered with merriment under Revier's thick mane of black hair and bushy brows.

"*Sacré nom,* it is good to see you again, Preacher. When was the last time?"

Preacher studied the traces of gray shot through Revier's hair at his temples and in his luxuriant mustache. A lot of time had gone by. "The 'twenty-eight rendezvous, as I recollect."

Antoine slapped a big hand on the tabletop. "You are right. It has been at least that long. What have you been doing of late? Met any of the other trappers?"

"Not in awhile. I did get crosswise of Fat Louie LaDeaux and Yard-Long Farmer jist the other day."

Revier scowled. "Those two are bad business. They rob the dead—people they have just shot in the back."

Preacher's eyes sparkled. "Not anymore. They tried their game on the wrong feller."

Revier and Norris sniggered. "Now that 'wrong feller' wouldn't happen to be called Preacher, would he?" Revier prompted. At Preacher's nod, he went on. "Good riddance."

Three Sleeps Norris tapped the side of his long nose. "I don't mean to pry, but what brings you this far south, Preacher?"

"Like I said, Three Sleeps, later."

Before Preacher could be asked more, the soft thumps of moccasin soles in the doorway drew their attention. A grizzled mountain man, one not known by any of the three. He nodded to the trio and crossed to the bar.

"Whisky," he ordered. "You hear the latest, Ransom?"

"What would that be, Ev?" asked the proprietor.

"There's word on the wind that a wagon train of pilgrims have been led astray somewhere up to the northeast. They was last seen along the Platte River." Evan Butler turned to include Preacher and his companions. "What do you think, boys? I say we've got more than enough flatlanders shovin' in around here. Present company excepted," he added over his shoulder to the relative newcomer, Ransom Turner.

With his tongue, Preacher worried a scrap of jerky that had caught in his teeth. When he freed it he spat it on the floor. "I say half of those who have come into the High Lonesome are more than enough. Why, them that don't want to tear up the sod and plant crops are Bible thumpers and Psalm singers. Most of them can't button their trousers of a mornin' without retraining, nor know which foot their boot goes on. Give me another beer, Mr. Turner," Preacher said in an aside. "Them lost pilgrims out there can rot for all I care." When the beer came, he quaffed a long draught and smacked his lips.

Quinton Praeger arose from the fragrant pile of pine boughs on which he had slept and stretched his long, lean frame, toughened by years of living out of doors. He was of an age with Morton Gross, yet he knew himself to be in far better shape. Years as a mining engineer had conditioned him to sleeping on the ground, and for him, unlike the ro-

tund Gross, the Blackfoot bed of buffalo robes and boughs
was a luxury. He reached down for his clothing and nudged
the bare flank of the young woman who had pleasured him
the previous night. She turned on her side and opened blue
eyes. When she focused on Praeger, her expression registered disgust. But, as a slave to the Blackfoot, this white
woman had no choice, Praeger knew.

Although he would have preferred a young, barely nubile
Blackfoot girl, his host had offered this one and he would
have offended by refusing. She'd been good, though, he had
to admit. At least once he had gotten her suitably warmed
up. They would be moving on today. Iron Shirt's Traveling
Medicine Show, Praeger reflected with amusement. Three
more bands of Blackfoot to visit, then they would go to the
Cheyenne. Before long they would have the entire frontier
aflame.

Over a rack of open pit-roasted bison ribs, Preacher finally
acknowledged that his earlier assumption had been correct.
He could not nursemaid a battalion of baby Dragoons all the
way to the Big Empty alone. He indeed needed someone to
come along. So he began to fabricate an elaborate tale to
spin for his friends. Licking grease off his fingers, Preacher
tossed away one rib bone and cut off another.

"Now that our bellies are full and we're feelin' good, I'll
tell you all about what I come here for. Three Sleeps is right,
I gave them papers to the soldier-boys. An' . . . though it
galls me to admit it . . . I done signed on for a job with the
Army. You see, there's this new-formed battalion of Dragoons . . ." Preacher went on to describe what he expected to
find when he reached Jefferson Barracks. After talking of
the well-known hazards of the vastly unforgiving mountains,
he concluded with his sales pitch.

" 'Course I knowed right off that it was gonna take men
of courage and powerful wisdom to shepherd those green

soldier-boys to Wyoming. I'll have to be real careful and choosey as to who I pick."

"Why, that's the stupidest thing I've heard," Three Sleeps Norris exploded. "Them greenhorns would be out there all alone. The nearest white settlement is more miles away than I can count, even if I take off my moccasins. Wyoming, plumb crazy."

"Oh, I agree. No man in his right mind would pick that wild and wooly country for putting up a solitary fort. 'Course the government is gonna pay in gold, and plenty of it. They wrote me that I could pay three dollars, gold, a day for any who sign on."

"Three dollars?" Norris and Revier chorused.

"Yep. That's right. The way I see it, it'll take the entire summer to get the job done. That comes to a total of two hundred seventy-six dollars."

Antoine scratched his head. "Well, now, they sure are generous. Out here a man can live a whole year on that and have some left over. And it beats competin' with a dozen other fellers over every dinky little bit of work that comes up. If you'll have me, Preacher, I think I'll come along."

Three Sleeps nodded in agreement. "What you said about the competition for jobs out here is right, Antoine. Seems as how Preacher has got himself into a bear cave the first day of spring. Might be a couple of good fellers, like ourselves, could save his bacon for him. Count me in." He extended a hand to Preacher, who shook on the bargain. Then Norris signaled for another round.

Preacher beamed at them with sincere gratitude. "I've done seen the soldier-boys, and they took off lickety-split back east. We can light out first thing in the mornin'."

3

Night swiftly came on again at the edge of the Wyoming Bad Lands of the Great Divide Basin. Eve Billings hugged herself with tired arms. They ached from driving a team of six mules all day. Only two days previously had they found a way out of the Medicine Bow Mountains, at least that's the range in which she believed them to have been. Eve teetered on the verge of losing her battle with despair.

How much more must she endure? How much could she ask her children to take in stride? First the loss of her husband, killed a month and a half ago by a war party of Sauk and Fox in Iowa Territory. Next, their captain and his trail guide had led the wagon train into a blind canyon in the Medicine Bow range. There the scoundrels had robbed and abandoned the settlers. When at last the party had found their way out of the mountains, this stark desert rolled over to the horizon to daunt them.

Resolutely she spoke aloud her foremost thought. "We have to move on."

There was scant water for the stock, blistering heat, although it was only the end of May, and terrible chill at night.

However could they find their way? In the distance, a coyote called for his mate, to be answered by half a dozen yaps and yelps. Eve shuddered and tightly clutched the barrel of the Model 40 Bridesburg Arsenal rifled musket her husband had so prudently provided as a necessity. A thin sliver of moon hung in the east, while the western sky still was washed in orange and magenta by the afterglow. Her eldest child, Charlie, came up to her and tugged at her apron as he had done as a babe.

"Mom—Momma, I'm hungry. Anna is cryin' again and wants to eat. What are we goin' to have?"

"There's some bacon, and a few potatoes left."

Charlie wrinkled his nose and twisted his ten-year-old face into a mask of repugnance. "Ugh! The bacon's all green and slippery on the outside."

"I'll trim it. That's all we have."

"Why can't we just go back?"

Eve's heart ached at the misery and pleading in the expression of her son. "We can't, Charlie. It's two months' journey back to New York State. In two months we'll be in the Oregon Country. A new home, a new life."

Charlie rubbed one bare foot over the other. "I don't *want* a new home. I don't want a new life. 'Sides, who's gonna lead us to Oregon? Mr. Tate? Mr. Labette? They can't find their way to the outhouse."

A scowl formed on Eve's high, clear forehead. "That sort of talk will get your mouth washed out with soap, young man. You are not old enough to fail to show respect to your elders. Mr. Pruitt seems to know what he is doing. At least he can hitch his mules without someone showing him how to do it."

"Big help that is," Charlie jeered, then dodged the swat Eve aimed at his rump.

"Back to the wagon, Charlie." When she turned back, the stars shone brightly in the bowl of the sky. Maybe tomorrow help would come.

* * *

Twenty-four naked Blackfoot warriors stood in a solemn rank on the bank of the Bighorn River. Monotonously, two drummers struck the surface of the big drum with their milkweed and sacred pollen padded buffalo-hide strikers. *Thummm* and *thummm* the skin stretched over a large section of hollowed tree trunk sounded. The close-by walls of the Bighorn Mountains reverberated with the drumming. Before the men stood Iron Shirt, stripped of his loincloth and moccasins. For a man of such ambition and power, he had surprisingly average endowment. He raised his bare arms above his head to capture the initiates' attention.

"My brothers, you are about to learn the mysteries behind my great medicine. First you must be purified. Part of that has already been accomplished in the sweat lodges. Now your fear of the white man's bullets must be washed from you so that you are reborn into the society of the Iron Shield Strong Hearts."

Here he paused and stepped backward into the shallows of the river. His bare feet found purchase among the rocks that lined it. The water was aching cold, though he showed no effect. He beckoned with both arms to the first two in line.

"You two come forward into the water." When they did so, his instructions continued. "Turn around and face your brothers." Once in position, four of Iron Shirt's closest followers joined the Blackfoot. Tipping them backward, they lowered each candidate into the water until fully immersed.

Iron Shirt raised one hand over each in benediction and solemnly intoned, "I command all wickedness and fear to abandon you, for you to renounce the power of the white man's bullets, and I baptize you in the name of the three-faced god, the Father and the Son and the Holy Ghost. Arise my brothers in Iron and go forth to be warmed by the coals."

Obediently, the pair waded clear of the river and walked to where a long, narrow trench had been prepared. The air above it shimmered with distortion from the heat given off by a deep bed of coals. They stood near, letting the radiant waves warm their chilled bodies. While they did, Iron Shirt continued until all the remaining initiates had been baptized. Then he joined them at the firepit. Again he spoke the ritual words.

"To walk safely through the blaze of the white man's bullets, you must first walk through this earthly fire. Prepare your bodies and spirits for this ordeal by praying to the Great Spirit for the strength of the Sky Legend; Firewalker. When you are ready, I will lead you across the abyss of flame."

Iron Shirt waited a hundred heartbeats, then positioned himself at the lip of the trench. He stuck out one foot and made contact with the bed of coals. With a firm, unhurried tread, he walked the length of the shimmering embers. On the far side, he strode ten paces from the pit and raised first one foot, then the other, to reveal not the least damage. The candidates had followed close on his heels and emerged now in the same condition, until the twenty-second in line.

Suddenly that unfortunate warrior let out a pain-wracked shriek and leaped to one side. He fell to the ground to reveal feet of a cherry-red hue, puffed and badly blistered. He had not enough faith. Iron Shirt turned to him. He made a gesture of sympathy.

"Go and have Red Elk dress those feet with bear grease. Know that you did not gain dishonor for your failure. When your faith grows stronger, come again and make the sacrifice, that you may join us." When the injured man had been helped from sight, Iron Shirt gestured to the others. "Come, my brothers of Iron Shield, gather around. It is time for me to reveal the mystery of my medicine's power."

They did, eager as small boys around a strange animal. Iron Shirt reached down and pulled up the hem of his outer hunting shirt. It revealed a complete set, front and back, of chain mail. Although dented in places and rusty in other spots, its sturdy construction and latent protection awed them all.

Iron Shirt turned slowly so they could examine the all-encasing war garment, then lowered his shirt and retrieved his loincloth and moccasins. The initiates did likewise, silent throughout. At last, Iron Shirt addressed them again.

"And would you now like to test your new power?" To their enthusiastic agreement, he added. "To the south and west of us, there can be found many rolling lodges of the whites. We shall ride there and kill them all. It is a true thing, I tell you. Not a one of us will fall."

They had circled the wagons for the night. Asa Wharton peered out into the ruddy glow of the setting sun and wondered at what fools they had been. To believe that they could make their way to the Oregon Country on their own should be enough to put them in the asylum, he thought with chagrin. We are too far north, his musings prompted. We always have been. It had been as much his fault as anyone else's. Worse, his voice had been one of the loudest, insisting that the brothers not bring along any firearms.

"We are the children of God," he had declared. "We must show that we come in peace."

A lot of good that will do. There are Indians out in the hills all around us. He could feel it in his bones. He strongly doubted the savages would spend much time listening to anything they had to say. For the first time since childhood, Asa Wharton wondered what it would be like to die. He shuddered when he recalled the hoofprints he had seen in the loose soil.

He had been riding ahead of the slow-moving wagons when he came upon them. They angled down one slope and crossed the trail. From there, they disappeared over the ridge to the south. By the time the first wagon arrived, a stiff breeze had wiped out any sign of them. *Why had he not told the others about them?*

Because he did not want to create panic. Now it was too

late. Asa sighed and turned away. He had taken only one step when the eerie, seething hiss of an arrow registered on him before the projectile winged between a pair of nose-to-tail wagon boxes and buried to the fletchings in Asa's back. The bloody point protruded, dripping, from his chest. Blackness engulfed him.

Iron Shirt led his Strong Hearts silently across the scrub-studded plain. They came within fifty feet and loosed a flight of arrows. Screams of terror and shrieks of pain followed moments later. Young Blackfoot boys, apprentice warriors, held the horses while the braves streamed forward on foot. The only shots fired came from the rifles in the hands of the Blackfoot. They had devastating effect. Seven men fell in the seconds after the death of Asa Wharton.

Whooping Indians broke through the barricade and rushed toward the stunned people. With tomahawks and war clubs they slammed into the helpless whites huddled beyond the fire. Iron Shirt stood back and watched with growing satisfaction. Given another moon, he would have an invincible force. The Cheyenne would join. The Sioux would be next.

Then, he thought, his mind filled with darkness, he would deal with the white men who masqueraded as Blackfoot and run the war against all whites his own way. How good that would be. Beyond him, within the circle of wagons, the slaughter grew terrible. Children, he contemptuously labeled the men and even the women who fell without offering the least resistance.

When the last white died, Iron Shirt came forward. A quick check showed him that there had been no survivors. And better still, the Blackfoot took no losses.

Early the next morning, Preacher and his companions set out together along the north fork of the Santa Fe Trail. Hard-packed and rutted from much past use, it let them make good time. Near mid-morning, they came upon a packhorse trader. He had three animals on lead, their packsaddles heaped with tin pots and pans, shielded tin lanterns; one loaded with patterned pressed panels for ceilings.

He hailed the trio enthusiastically. "Howdy, fellers. Good to see a friendly face. I'd be obliged if you'd ride along a spell. You're more than welcome."

Preacher considered it odd the peddler was headed the same way they were. "Don't mind if we do," he responded. "M'name's Preacher. These two are Three Sleeps Norris an' Antoine Revier."

"Pleased to meet you. I go by the name of Tinman, but it's really Morris Lorson."

"If you don't mind my saying so, them goods of yours looks like something bound for Santa Fe," observed Preacher.

"It is—it is. I just came from there. I got turned away, you see."

Three Sleeps gave him a puzzled look. "How's that, Tinman? I thought those Mezkins was all-fire hot for American goods."

"They are, usually. Only lately things aren't so cordial for Americans. Not since the Texicans won their independence back in 'thirty-six."

Preacher furrowed his brow as he thought this over. "That's old news, and didn't have anything to do with us Americans. What's got into 'em now to get riled at our people?"

Tinman Lorson gave Preacher a knowing look. "Didn't you hear? For the last couple of years there's been talk about the Texicans wantin' to join up with the United States. An' the folks in Washington City are pushin' for them to do it. You can see how that don't sit well a-tall with the Mexicans."

"That a fact?" Preacher responded, then tuned out the peddler's chatter.

They made camp late in the afternoon. Around coffee, after ample plates of broiled grouse—provided by Antoine with his delicate, slender-barreled shotgun—fatback and beans, Tinman Lorson studied his impromptu fellow travelers. After several moment's consideration he hesitantly explored a subject of great interest to him.

"If you don't mind, I surely don't wish to pry, but would you tell me how you got that name—Three Sleeps?"

"Wal, it ain't nothin' much. It happened a long time ago."

"No, really, I'd like to know. I . . . ah . . . collect nicknames and the stories behind them. It's something to pass the long hours shared with others along the trading path. Please, indulge me if you will."

Preacher inserted himself in the conversation. "Three Sleeps is too modest to brag on hisself. I'll be happy to enlighten you."

Lorson brightened. "Yes, do."

Preacher thought a while, then began his tale. "Like Three Sleeps says, it happened a long time ago. He was a youngster then, hardly old enough to wet his throat with good whisky. As it happened, he was doin' just that one fine day when this notorious brawler slammed into the tradin' post where young Archibald Norris stood at the bar. As it happened, this bear-wrastlin' lout was spoilin' for a fight. Hadn't thumped on anyone for a couple of days and was feelin' out of sorts.

"So he eyes Arch here and says, 'Who let this skinny little puke in here?' Now Arch happened to be sensitive about his size at the time," Preacher went on with a chuckle. "He turns to face . . . ah . . . what was his name?"

"Travers. Meat Hook Travers," Three Sleeps provided quietly. He gave a little shudder.

"Yep. That's the one. Meat Hook Travers. Anyhow, ol' Meat Hook stomped up to the bar while Archibald formed the words he would say. Meat Hook thumped Arch on the chest and bellowed to the barkeep. 'Somebody answer me.' Archibald had his words gathered by then and decided it was up to him to speak. 'I brought myself in on my own two legs, and I reckon to leave the same way.' For Meat Hook, that was too hard to chew, let alone swallow. So, he rears back and bellows at Archibald. 'You'll go out of here on a plank.'" Preacher paused for a swallow of coffee.

"An' that's where ol' Meat Hook got a big surprise. Young Archie came at him like a buzz saw. He walked up Meat Hook with his fists and down t'other side. He booted that tub of muscle and lard in the butt and when Meat Hook turned with a roar, Arch mashed his lips with a solid left—or was it a right? Never mind, he moved fast as a wasp with a busted nest. Archie was quick and he was sneaky. He landed five punches for every one Meat Hook connected. Then Meat Hook tried to catch Archibald in a bear hug.

"Archie was havin' none of that. He danced back and kicked Meat Hook in the belly. That did it. Meat Hook sank to his knees. Arch here waded in. When he got done, Meat Hook was stretched out on the dirt floor, cold as an iced-over lake. Arch rubbed his sore knuckles and stepped back to the bar. 'You'd best put some distance between the two of you,' the bartender advised. 'Not a problem. I think I'll finish my whisky and have a little brew,' Archibald responded. The fellow in the apron had good advice. 'He'll come after you for sure.' All calm and collected, Archie swallowed down his whisky and gestured for a beer. 'There's plenty time to make tracks. The way I see it, he's good for about three sleeps.' And, by jingo, if the name didn't stick. I know for certain it happened that way because I was the only witness beside the barman."

Slack-jawed, Morris Lorson stared into the fire. He did not know, for all his experience at collecting names and legends, if he was having his leg pulled or not. Then something that had been nagging at him all day went off in his mind. He looked up at the weathered features of the narrator of the tale.

"Are you the same Preacher who single-handed cleaned a nest of thieves and cutthroats out of a trading-post saloon a decade ago?"

"Friend, it's been at least a dozen saloons I've cleaned out by myself," Preacher enlightened him. "Not to count the Injuns I've fit and the personal squabbles with other mountain men. You've got the right one, sure enough, if your claims for me are a mite more modest than some."

Lorson beamed. "Then it's a pleasure to be counted among your associates, if only for a short while. And I have me a new nickname and the story behind it. I'm obliged." He rocked back on his heels.

"An' I'm for gettin' some shut-eye," announced Preacher. "Daylight comes mighty fast in these parts."

Along about what Preacher judged to be ten-thirty in the morning, he and his partners parted company with Tinman Lorson. They spurred their more lightly loaded mounts and rode ahead, to soon lose him from sight over a ridge. Shortly after that, Preacher began to pick up sign of an Indian presence.

A trimmed, decorated eagle feather stuck an inch or two above the ridge to the south. Bird calls, which had been plentiful moments before, had dwindled to a few. Those that came did not sound entirely true. A tiny puff of dust drifted upward suddenly from beyond the swale to the north. Preacher reined in abruptly and dismounted. His friends did likewise.

After a quick look around, they formed a close square with their mounts and the packhorse. Antoine cut his eyes to Preacher. "I noticed them, too, *mon ami.*"

A second later, a small party of howling Kiowa warriors broke the southern horizon and thundered down toward the white men behind the improvised barricade.

4

"Watch our backsides, Three Sleeps," Preacher instructed calmly while he sighted in and cleaned one Kiowa from the saddle with his rifle.

Quickly, Preacher reloaded. He changed his point of aim and put a .54-caliber ball through the shoulder of another warrior. Beside him, Antoine fired his trusty .36-caliber squirrel rifle and plunked a ball through the center of a screaming Kiowa's forehead. His war whoop ended mid-yelp.

Behind them, Three Sleeps Norris downed another warrior with a gut shot. "You were right, Preacher, they're comin' from the north now."

By then, Preacher and Antoine had reloaded. It would be their last rifle shot for this charge, they knew. The Kiowa braves had come within twenty yards now. Preacher fired first. He split a buffalo-hide shield and shattered the forearm behind it. The warrior ignored it, his left arm flopping uselessly amid a shower of blood. Antoine ended the life of another savage with a ball through the throat. Then Preacher drew one Walker Colt. He made a quick check of the percussion caps, found them secure on the nipples. Then he raised the heavy revolver and eared back the hammer.

A fat cloud of smoke enveloped the defenders when the big .44 fired. Preacher quickly recocked the revolver and got off another round. A shout of pain answered him. The light breeze slowly blew the obscuring cloud away. Another round from Preacher's Colt took a warrior in the side. With that, they had enough.

A shrill bark turned the Kiowa and they swung away from their target. They quickly galloped out of range.

"They'll be back," advised Preacher.

Several minutes passed in an eerie silence. Then the Kiowa came again, this time from the east. Preacher had counted twenty warriors at the outset. Now four lay dead on the ground and three had been severely wounded. That left a baker's dozen. Three rifles spoke with deadly authority and reduced the number to ten.

Still the Indians would not leave off. Their blood was up, their friends killed or wounded. They badly wanted these white scalps. Once again they recoiled from the blaze of Preacher's six-shooters.

Running Bull could not understand it. Had they come upon a party of the Texicans called Rangers? He knew of no others who possessed the fast-shoot hand rifles. If so, why did the others not use theirs? From the reverse slope of the rise to the east, he studied the besieged white men with keen eyes.

They are only three, he thought with confusion. How could they kill so many so quickly? A quick glance left and right showed his warriors poised for another attack. He also detected signs of nervousness. They, too, could count.

Running Bull raised his voice in exhortation. "This time we do not turn away. Ride over them, wet your lances in their blood. Are you women that only three frail white men can stop you?"

Blood lust boiled over and the Kiowa set the mounts to a fast trot up and over the ridge, to thunder down the incline. Ahead waited the fiery death of the white men. Not a one of them lacked fear; yet they knew it to be a good day to die.

"Sacre-bleu! Here they come again," Antoine spat out as he raised his rifle to take aim.

At extreme range, Preacher sighted in with his Hawken and put a ball in the chest of a warrior, piercing the right side. Undaunted, the Kiowa raised his lance and charged on. Preacher set aside the .56-caliber rifle and put the slender buttstock of his French Le Mat to shoulder. The finely made .36 sporting arm had served him well before. Now he honed the sights in on the face of his enemy.

Hair-fine, the second of the double-set triggers let off the round with ease. Smoke belched and blew away in time for Preacher to see the black hole that appeared where the tip of the warrior's nose had been a moment before.

At once, his lance sailed skyward and the Kiowa did a back-roll off his laboring pony. He hit with a thud and bounced only once. Preacher reloaded swiftly, only to be caught with the ramrod down the barrel of his Le Mat when the distance between him and the warriors closed to less than twenty feet. He lowered the muzzle against Tarnation's heaving flank and drew the reloaded Walker Colt. With what precision he could muster he emptied it into the mass of Indians in front of them, and yet they came on.

A lance thudded into the ground so close to his leg he felt the pressure of the shaft. Preacher holstered the Colt and drew the second one. He spent two rounds before the Kiowa warriors reined around and beat a hasty retreat. A quick count showed Preacher that only five remained alive.

"Stubborn," he told his companions. "Plain damn stubborn. They coulda quit a long time ago. I'd been willin'. What about you?"

"Oui. Without a doubt," Antoine panted.

Preacher turned to the horses. "We'd best be movin' on. We don't want them to work up the spit to make another try."

One fine afternoon, three days later, Preacher and his two friends rode along the trail with the sparkling waters of the Arkansas River to their right. Chubby barrel cactus and wicked-tipped Spanish bayonet abounded on the rolling sand hills ahead of them. Abruptly, Preacher raised his hand for a halt.

From a distance ahead came the dull thumps of gunshots. They all had heard them, and had halted to try to make out what they meant. With the recent Kiowa attack fresh in their minds, Preacher and his companions suspected a war party.

It had to be a large group under attack, or both sides had firearms, Preacher decided a moment later when the rate of fire escalated. This country did not lack for human trash that would prey on the law-abiding. He drummed heels into the ribs of Tarnation and rushed forward. Antoine and Three Sleeps came right behind.

Over the next rounded dune, the sounds of shots grew clearer. Preacher drew his revolver. Antoine and Three Sleeps loosened pistols in the holsters slung over their saddlehorns. Dust mingled with powder smoke had risen high enough to be clearly seen before they topped the grade. Preacher halted them again.

"Let's not blunder in, boys. I'll take a peek first."

He dismounted, removed his floppy summer hat and approached the ridge in a crouch. Slowly he raised his head. A moderate-sized freight train came into sight first. Preacher raised up a little higher and focused on some twenty white renegades, several of whom fired on the teamsters from an outcropping of boulders south of the trail. Others milled back and forth on horseback, apparently prevented from circling front or rear of the caravan due to concentrated fire at those points. It looked to Preacher like those freighters could use some help.

Quickly he returned to the others and explained the situation. Mounted again, he led the way up and over the ridge. Pistols in hand, they dashed down on the unsuspecting outlaws. The surprise arrival of three more fighting men cleared four of the ten saddles before the bandits knew that help had come for the teamsters. Quick to realize that relief had arrived, the teamsters began to rally. Preacher heard a voice raised over the tumult, singing in a sweet tenor.

" 'At the risin' o' the moon, at the risin' o' the moon, the men and bies will gather at the risin' o' the moon.' Give 'em hell, bies, there's help on the way. C'mon, ye soldier-bies!"

That galvanized the outlaws. Those who could whirled away and ran a murderous gauntlet along the length of the stationary wagons. Those afoot in the rocks turned and tried to make a stand. Preacher sighted in on one and reined sharply to send a .44 messenger on the way. The letter it carried was death.

Shot through the mouth, the highwayman fell backward in an awkward sprawl. Preacher emptied the last round from the Colt into the stomach of another hard case. He changed weapons quickly and sought another target. A ball cracked past close enough that he heard its ominous moan. The shooter died an instant later, shot through the heart by Antoine Revier. To his left, Preacher heard the sound of increased resistance.

Bullwhackers fired and loaded and fired again. Rifle balls snapped through the air, whined off rocks and brought forth screams from human targets. Several more outlaws died in this withering fire. Ahead of Preacher, wounded men crawled toward their horses, desperate to escape. Churned-up dust began to obscure the scene. Preacher fired at a fleeing man and missed. He turned Tarnation and sprinted to the head of the wagon train.

He reached his goal in a growing silence. Gradually the crackle of gunfire had diminished. At the lead wagon Preacher saw half a dozen highwaymen spurring frantically until they disappeared beyond the next swell.

A big, red-faced man came out from between two wagons and walked Preacher's way. He was a bull of a man, with bulging muscles and ham hands. When he spoke, his mouth became a black hole in his heavily bearded face.

"Right on time, lads, that ye are. Good work. Sure an' where's the soldiers you're scouting for?"

Preacher gave him a curious look. "At Jefferson Barracks. We haven't joined up with them as yet."

Momentarily stunned, the lead bullwhacker worked his mouth soundlessly. Words returned with a sputter. "Y-y-you mean there's just the th-three of you?"

"That's right."

"Well, truth is you fight like a whole company of soldiers. They call me Big Tom Lawson. This here is my strong right arm, Brian O'Shea, en' we're obliged to you."

Preacher gave them a nod. "Big Tom, Brian, my pleasure. I answer to Preacher, and these be Three Sleeps Norris an' Antoine Revier. Any idea why those road agents picked your train to raid?"

"None that make sense. What we're haulin' is too heavy to take off on horseback and these wagons would leave a trail a blindman could follow." Finally Preacher's name registered. "Say, you ain't *that* Preacher are you? The one in the penny dreadfuls?"

Preacher's cheeks carmined. "To my eternal torment, I be. What foolishness them idiot writers can dream up would gag a maggot. What you read in them things ain't true a-tall. Except I may have been in some of those places at the time they said I was, and I may have had something to do with what happened to some of those fellers they claim I done for. Jist may have, mind you."

Big Tom made a wry face. "Sure an' I don't buy none of

that at all. Never mind. You are a gen-u-wine legend in yer own time. A living hero, you are. We'd be overjoyed to have you join us in our trading expedition, full share for all of you. Lord knows, you just earned it."

"No," Preacher replied politely. "We have to push on to Jeff Barracks. Gave my word. In writing, at that."

Big Tom looked greatly disappointed. "I understand contracts right enough. The least you can do is stay a spell and take supper with us. We'll lay on a right regular feast. Why, we even have a fruitcake along. All sopped up in brandy." He gave a big wink. "I figgered to use it to mellow the Governor General in Santa Fe. What ya say, Preacher?"

Patting his flat, hard belly, Preacher produced a euphoric smile. "I never could resist fruitcake. 'Special if it's got itself drunk."

Once started out onto the Great Divide Basin, after long, heated debate, the wagon train ran into disaster after defeating disaster. Mr. Ledbetter had three mules die. After acrimonious exchanges, in which accusations of selfishness flew like snowflakes in a blizzard, it was decided to draw straws to see which two wagons would "voluntarily" give up a mule so that Ledbetter could keep up. Eve Billings drew one of the short straws.

No sooner had that predicament been solved than another sprang up. One day five precious water barrels had sprung leaks or broken apart. The next day, three more became useless. With much shouting and gesticulating, the decision was made to turn back. Eve had nothing to tell her children.

"Mom, are we really going home?" Charlie asked eagerly when it became apparent to him that they were retracing their steps.

"Only part way, dear," Eve told him tiredly.

"But why?" His button nose wrinkled in the effort to understand these adult mysteries.

"We aren't ready to go on as yet. We need a guide, someone who can take us out of this wilderness. Without water, the livestock will die, like Mr. Ledbetter had happen." She did not add the obvious, that people would die as well.

"I want to go all the way home."

"Don't start on that again, Charles Ryan Billings."

Charlie instantly lapsed into silence. He always knew when he was in trouble; his mother used his proper first name. When she used his middle name, too, he knew he was up to his neck in it. Charlie heaved a defeated sigh and scampered over the rumps of the mules to his favorite spot on the back of Jake, the lead animal.

Eve watched her son move with agility and assurance and then lifted her gaze to the horizon. She estimated they had another day of travel, back to the old camp.

A storyteller's high, singsong voice rang out across the camp in the Bighorn Mountains. He related an ancient tale of the grandfather times. One in which the Cheyenne and the Blackfoot were allies. It had to be a long time ago, Cloud Blanket thought as he watched the historic meeting from his place in the Cheyenne council circle.

Less than a moon ago, he would not have believed this gathering could happen. The Blackfoot had come under a white belt of truce. They had a great story to relate. About a young medicine man and the power he possessed. When the council gathered, the talk quickly turned to war against the whites. That greatly disturbed Cloud Blanket, though he could not name the reason why. All he could say was this was not the time to fight the white men. Suddenly he found the talking stick offered to him. He took it and came to his moccasins.

"You say that this prophet's medicine is so strong none of you fell in the battle which was described to us?" Two Moons nodded in the affirmative. "That may be so. It could also be that the whites did not carry long guns with them." His eyes twinkled with secret knowledge. He might have seen forty winters, might be past his prime, but he was not helpless or ignorant. Cloud Blanket had his sources of information, and one of them had told him of the attack on the unarmed whites. How odd, he thought, that anyone would not carry weapons. Did they not know there were tribes hungry for war? He suddenly realized the Blackfoot named Two Moons had responded to his jibe.

"The great prophet will come among you soon," Two Moons repeated when he saw the Cheyenne chief's attention had returned. "He will show you his medicine. It is true that he cannot be killed by normal bullets. His medicine is strong, the most powerful. We have been given his shield," Two Moons stated emphatically.

Cloud Blanket remained unimpressed. "I have seen far too often what the bullets of the white men can do."

Too hot in his zeal, Two Moons snatched up a rifle that lay beside a Cheyenne. "If you doubt me, take this, shoot me. Go ahead. I will not be killed."

"If I believed that, I would shoot you." Cloud Blanket shook his head resignedly. "I have heard of such medicine before. It has always failed its user. Leave us now, the council will reach a consensus and let you know. I am but one man, my voice is not listened to as much as it once was. Perhaps you will win an ally after all."

After the Blackfoot delegation withdrew to eat and nap through the afternoon, the Cheyenne spoke heatedly about the issue. Several agreed with Cloud Blanket: it would be a bad idea to make a pact with the Blackfoot. Had they not been enemies for longer than the storyteller could remember? In the end, Cloud Blanket prevailed on that point. He lost on the other. He felt obliged to take the word to the Blackfoot. He found them in the lodge that hosted them.

"Our council has come to a consensus. We will not ally with you at this time. You can send your prophet, Iron Shirt; we will listen to his message."

5

Preacher, Three Sleeps and Antoine spent the night at the Cottonwoood Crossing on the Santa Fe Trail. There, they underwent inspection by two disreputable characters, one with wispy strands of mustache that drooped below his jawline in Oriental style. His brown skin marked him as a Mexican. His partner had wild-straw hair that stuck out at all angles, buck teeth and pale, hollow cheeks. The pair slouched into the saloon of the trading post shortly after Preacher and his companions arrived.

Preacher nodded in their direction. "Now there's a pair to draw to."

Three Sleeps sniffed the air. "I wonder if they know what the word *bath* means?"

Antoine nodded agreement. "How about 'soap'?"

Preacher chuckled, a low, throaty sound, and leaned closer to them. "Way I rec'llect it, ain't neither of you could lay claim to bein' in the Every Saturday Night club." He drew in a lungful. "Though I will admit they've got a certain ripeness about them."

For the next hour, the surly pair nursed pewter mugs of

beer and paid considerable, though covert, attention to Preacher and his friends. Then they settled their tab and stomped out. Preacher watched them through the open door as they settled down some distance off from the tavern and inn that had sprung up at the crossing to accommodate stagecoach travelers.

"Not overwhelming sociable, are they?" Preacher observed to his partners.

"I ain't gonna lose any sleep over it," remarked Antoine.

Preacher stroked his chin. "I wonder which way they're goin'? That's a pair it would do a body good to keep track of."

Three Sleeps narrowed his eyes. "You thinkin' they're trouble, Preacher?"

Preacher nodded. "That I do. I could smell it on them plain as that sweat stink. I may be wrong, but I could almost swear I saw the towheaded one with that bunch what attacked the freight wagons."

Although up well before dawn, Preacher noted that the unwashed pair had already departed. He saw to making a pot of coffee and was soon joined by Three Sleeps. The frown on the forehead of Norris indicated that he had noted the absence of the human trash.

He gestured with his chin. "They ain't gonna be missed. Not by this mother's son."

"Like I said, it'd pay to keep them in sight, or know what they might be up to."

"You've been alone too long, Preacher. That makes a man suspicious for no reason."

"You turnin' womanish on me, Three Sleeps?"

"Nope. C'mon, I'll lend a hand with that packsaddle. After we eat we can take right off."

"Now that's a good idea."

After a plate of fatback and beans, Preacher downed the

last of his coffee, used the dregs in the pot to quench the fire and scuffed dirt over it. In the saddle, they made their way eastward. The trail ended at Independence, Missouri, but there were supposed to be good roads through the state. At least as far as Jefferson Barracks, Preacher had been told. Two hours down the Santa Fe, Preacher's keen hearing picked up what sounded like thunder.

He looked around at a clear sky and produced a puzzled frown. "D'you hear thunder, Antoine?"

"Yep, sure sounded like it, but there's not a cloud up there."

Yet, the sound persisted and grew louder. Then the creak of wood on leather springs and the jingle of harness explained it to Preacher. Laboring up behind them came a six-up of spanking bays. Foam lathered their flanks and around their collars. Seated above them the driver sawed on the reins and called to his team.

"Gee up, there. Keep it brisk or no corn for you tonight."

Clouded in dust, the stagecoach grew in Preacher's vision. They must be closer than he thought to Muddy Creek Crossing, the mountain man thought to himself. Otherwise that feller would not be runnin' them horses like that. He turned in the saddle to watch the team draw up alongside. A scowling man, armed with a Purdey percussion shotgun, eyed the three mountain men with suspicion. Preacher removed his slouch hat and gave a cordial wave. The express guard acknowledged it with a curt nod.

"Well, he ain't bein' paid to be friendly," Preacher opined to his companions.

"You got the right o' that, Preacher."

"How long's it been, Three Sleeps, that the stage lines have had to run a guard on their coaches?"

Norris scratched the top of his head. "Leastwise ten years. An' it's gettin' worse, I'm told."

Preacher pondered a moment. "It's types like those yesterday that's behind it. Law's too easy on them."

"They still have hangings, don't they?"

"Oh, yeah, Three Sleeps. Used to be a man kept the law himself. Now, with law dogs mixed up in it, if a man shoots a thief, likely he'll be the one winds up in jail."

In the Black Hills of the Unorganized Territory, a young Red Cloud refused to even listen to the emissaries of Iron Shirt. Little good it would do. Since he had not yet seen twenty winters, he would not have been listened to anyway. Oh, the elders on the council would have made a show of hearing him out, but their ears might as well be plugged with wax from a bee tree. So frustrated had he become that he jumped on his favorite pony and rode out as the council gathered to hear the message of the prophet. Red Cloud sat atop a knoll and looked down into his village.

He knew every lodge. There, the one of his friend, Runner. Over close to the big drum lived White Knife. They had grown up together, hunted, then gone off to war the best of friends. White Knife had lost a little finger to a Pawnee war club while fighting at the side of Red Cloud. Now he added his voice to those clamoring for the council to approve bringing Iron Shirt and his medicine to the Lakota.

Red Cloud spat on the ground. A great shout reached his ears. The council had decided. From the looks of it they had decided in favor of the cursed Blackfoot and his iron medicine. Drums began to throb, and from every lodge, the women brought pots and baskets of food to feast the Blackfoot men. Red Cloud's lip curled in disgust.

What hurt most was his grudging admission that the time would soon come when the Lakota would have to fight the white men, but the time was not now.

A week and a half had passed since their first disastrous attempt to cross the Great Divide Basin. Fear of the unknown and indecision had kept the abandoned wagon train stranded at the same small spring that had previously provided their scant water supply. Eve Billings opened her flour barrel, and a momentary bolt of panic shot through her. She could see the bottom in places.

Provisions had run short for everyone. Eve knew she wasn't alone in this predicament. So many people had killed or run off the sparse game in the area, the men had to ride for miles to get even a few rabbits. She crumbled yeast into the bowl and began to add water to the flour. When she looked up, there stood Charlie.

The thin film of perspiration on his bare, sun-browned shoulders and sides under the straps of his overalls made his skin glow. He fixed big, cornflower blue eyes on her face. She wondered if her worry lines had become permanent. From the looks of Charlie, they must have.

"Mom, what are we having for supper?"

"Fried bread with molasses and potato soup," she answered, painfully aware of how inadequate that sounded.

Charlie's usually smooth, childish features twisted into an expression of misery. *"Again?* That's what we had last night."

"And the night before. Be grateful we have that. And that Mr. Tate shared his rabbits with us on Sunday."

"I want meat tonight!" Charlie stubbornly insisted.

"Well, we simply don't have any."

Charlie took on a coy, wheedling expression. "I could get us some. At least some rabbits. I'm a good shot, you know that, Mom. Please, let me take my rifle and go after some rabbits. I won't go far, and I know better than to shoot in the direction of the wagons."

He had already robbed her of her two best arguments. She swore that the boy would become a lawyer, or a politician some day. Or worst yet, both. What could she say to counter his intentions, good though they might be? Carefully, she framed her sentences.

"What horse would you use? The grass is so scarce that your pony's too weak to carry you."

Bright enthusiasm lighted Charlie's face. "I can always use Jake."

"A mule? One not broken to saddle at that, Charlie. I don't think it would be safe."

"I ride his back every day we're on the trail. An' when I take the others out to graze. He knows me an' he don't mind. Really, Mom."

Eve sighed. Rabbit would taste mighty good. A deep, vertical furrow formed between Eve's brows. "If you go—and mind, I said if—you would have to stay within sight of the wagons."

"Mo-oom," Charlie enunciated with exasperation, small fists on hips. "There aren't any rabbits within sight of the wagons. I'll be all right. After all, you said I would have to be the man of the family now. Please let me prove I can do it."

What could she say? What could she do? With a suppressed sigh, Eve swallowed her mother's fears and relented. "All right. But you take your father's pocket watch with you, and you be back here in two hours exactly, or you'll never go again."

Charlie abandoned his mannish stance and leaped up to wrap arms around his mother's neck. "Oh, Mom, thank you, thank you. I'll bring us rabbits, I promise. Enough we can share."

"And wear your boots," Eve added as Charlie turned from her.

When the boy scampered off to get the watch and his rifle, powder horn and bag of balls, Eve stood staring after him. Her son complaining about small portions and the lack of real meat. His little sister with a slight fever and runny bowels. What more could she endure? A sudden thought came to Eve.

Could it be the water? Painfully aware that they were far from the established trail, the specter of everyone falling victim to some terrible sickness arose to haunt her. Surrendering to a moment of despair, Eve began to suspect that no one would ever come along to lead them out of this desolation.

While Eve Billings battled with her dejection, Preacher and his companions took their nooning at Muddy Creek Crossing. The coach that had passed them had also stopped there. While the hostler changed the horses, Preacher watched the passengers descend to take their meal in the shade.

A chubby, moon-faced Osage woman, wife of the stage agent, and her gaggle of youngsters, stair-stepped from about thirteen to seven, brought out heaped platters of fried chicken, bowls of baked squash and beans, stewed onions swimming in butter and cold, boiled potatoes. All this bounty came from a large, well-tended kitchen garden that Preacher saw behind the ramshackle stage station. For the hefty sum of ten cents each, Preacher and the mountain men also sat down to the feast.

For that purpose, the relay station had trestle tables set out under a large, gnarled old cottonwood. A young woman passenger took note of Preacher's handsome features. Pursing her lips, she fixed her violet eyes on his profile and batted long lashes flirtatiously.

Antoine nudged Preacher in the ribs. "You got an admirer, I see."

"Huh? Who'd that be?"

"Over to your left. There's a purty young thing givin' you the eye."

Preacher cut his eyes quickly to the left and caught a flutter of long, black lashes. The woman brought a fan up to cover her face and uttered a brief titter. Preacher looked away. For several minutes he dedicated his attention to a chicken leg. Three Sleeps kicked him on the shin. Preacher jumped as a result.

"She's at it again. Givin' you the big ol' come-on eye. A right toothsome lass, you ask me."

"Then you flirt with her," Preacher grumbled.

Three Sleeps Norris sniggered. "Wouldn't mind at all."

Suddenly the older woman with the flirtatious one caught her at it. This ample-bosomed dowager took an abundant pinch of forearm and hissed loud enough to be heard by Preacher and his friends.

"Agatha, for shame. I'll thank you to conduct yourself like a lady."

"But he's sooo handsome."

Her visage turned to stone, the elder companion took another pinch, this time of cheek. "You disappoint me, Agatha Sinclaire. That frontier trash isn't fit to shine your shoes. If you cannot behave in a refined manner, I'll see that you return to the coach." That said, she turned her acid tongue on Preacher. "And you, you unwashed barbarian, I'll thank you to keep your lustful eyes off my ward. It's your kind that have sullied this beautiful country. Those uncouth louts with you are no better. Have they no shame? It's scandalous the way they smirk and waggle their heads. Why . . ."

Her invective slid off Preacher like water ran off a duck. When the older woman finally ran down, Preacher removed his floppy hat and scratched his head, as though looking for lice. He ran his tongue around the inside of his mouth and came to his boots.

"Well, now, ma'am. I allow as how the girl is a toothsome bit, right enough, but me an' my friends have important business at Jefferson Barracks and I can't take the time to dally."

With a squawk of indignation, the dowager abandoned her meal, grabbed the wrist of her charge and hauled the two of them off to the coach. Seated at another table, the same two scruffy ragbags from the previous day took in all that transpired. They exchanged meaningful glances and rose to silently slip away.

Preacher took note of that and stored it for later. He stared long after their rapidly retreating backs. They, too, were headed east. He and the other mountain men finished their food and started off for the Lost Springs Station. Something told Preacher it would be a long afternoon. One he might live to regret.

A grinning Charlie Billings returned to the wagon train with four plump rabbits strung over the neck of Jake. His slender-barreled .36-caliber squirrel rifle lay across his thighs. For all her elation over the fresh meat, Eve still noticed with irritation that Charlie had ignored his boots. He had also fastened a length of rope around his waist and slipped off the shoulder straps of his overalls, so that he rode bare-chested as a wild Indian.

"Charles Ryan Billings, you put up the bib of those overalls right this minute. You're a scandalous sight. You look like a heathen red savage." Part of her irritation came from the memory of the four reports she had heard distantly from beyond a hill.

She had bitten her lip at hearing each shot. Worried that Charlie had injured himself, that he lay bleeding and near death, she could hardly contain herself, remain at the wagon and knead her bread dough. Now he shows up, looking like a brown-skinned imp of Satan, grinning and showing off his hunting skill. Abruptly her irritation fled and an ocean of love swelled up in her chest.

"Look what I've got, Mom! It was easy."

It took all her will not to run forward and embrace him, and she failed to keep from blurting her thoughts. "My wonderful boy. We'll share them with the Tates and the Warners."

Charlie produced a pout. "I thought we'd smoke 'em and have meat for all week."

Eve put her hands on her hips and glowered at her son. "We have been gifted by others, now we can return their generosity. I'll fix you a hind leg and a chunk of loin."

"All right," Charlie agreed. He reined Jake to the right and rode to the Tate wagon.

Eve nearly called him back; he had done nothing about adjusting his clothing. "I swear, that boy would go buck-naked if he could get away with it," she said aloud to herself.

"Why, Mommy?" Anna asked from the spot of shade under the wagon.

Startled, Eve turned to her. "Because he has your father's orneriness, sweetie. Now, do you feel strong enough to help make dough balls with me for the fried bread?"

"Yes, Mommy, but my tummy hurts some."

"Oh, Anna, Anna," Eve spoke through a tight throat as tears welled in her eyes.

6

Preacher and his mountain man friends decided to spend the night in the dormitory-style hotel east of the stage station at Lost Springs. The Spanish had named the location during the Coronado expedition in the sixteenth century. The climate had been entirely different three hundred years earlier. The springs they had located and marked with tall stakes and flags had disappeared on their return from a fateful encounter with the Pawnee. They had called them The Lost Springs. Preacher explained the reason behind his suggestion to stay over a sit-down meal in the tavern.

"We're gettin' into country where people get suspicious of fellers campin' under the stars. Makes 'em edgy. So we might as well start gettin' used to a roof overhead."

"Sounds reasonable," Antoine Revier agreed. "Say, the feller who owns this place has got himself one powerful good cook. Who would have ever thought someone way out here could do a proper soufflé?" He smacked his lips in appreciation. His spoon paused over the gold-brown dome of the fancy corn pudding, which chose that moment to collapse.

Three Sleeps sniggered and Preacher pointed at the soufflé disaster with his chin. "It supposed to do that?"

Defensively, Antoine dug into the dish. "It's the thought that counts. My pappy. Now there's a man who could cook a perfect soufflé."

Preacher raised his brow. "That's right, your pap was a Frenchie, a *voyageur.*"

"Mais oui. He was also a great cook. A chef. A master in the kitchen."

Three Sleeps Norris waggled his head. "Cookin's women's work."

Antoine bristled. "Not so! The world's greatest cooks are men. Why, back in the days of knights and noble ladies, women were not even permitted to serve the food, let alone cook it. My friends, you are entirely too limited in worldly experience. Now, leave me to my soufflé in peace."

Three Sleeps sounded wounded. "It's part ourn, too."

Nose rising in the air, Antoine passed judgment on that. "You haven't the taste to appreciate it."

"Even if it is flat?" Preacher inquired.

Antoine relented, at least a little. "Awh, dig in, Preacher, it's ruined anyway."

After their evening meal, Preacher and his companions staked out floor-level, straw-stuffed mattresses and then went in search of distraction. Antoine and Three Sleeps found the bar, where a curious fellow worked fast and skillfully at charcoal sketches of some of the patrons. They watched in fascination while the features of a stolid Osage seated at one table emerged on the stretched canvas. Antoine nodded toward the Indian and his likeness.

"Right clever. D'you mind if I ask what yer doin' that for, mister?"

The artist looked up from his work. "I am preparing my canvases to do the subjects in oil."

Three Sleeps gaped at him, unbelieving. "You're gonna boil all these fellers in oil?"

Chuckling, the artist disabused him of that idea. "Far from it, my friend. I am going to paint them."

That set Three Sleeps back a bit. "Oh, oh, yes. You're an . . . an artist?"

"Just so. Would you like me to do you and your friend here in oil?"

"How long'd it take?"

The artist took a second to consider that. "An evening to do the sketch. Two, three days to finish the portrait. Then you could take it with you."

"Hmmm. Sorry, we got to keep movin' east. Be gone at first light tomorrow."

"That's a shame. Perhaps another time. My name is Catlin. If we meet again, I hope you have the time for me to paint you."

For Preacher distraction turned out to be a gaming table. Five men sat around the green baize circle when he approached.

"Evenin', gents. I answer to Preacher. Oh, no," he hastened to add when one man produced a black scowl. "I'm not going to give you a sermon on the evils of gamblin'. Matter of fact, if there's room, I'd be obliged for an invite to join the game."

Abandoning his scowl, the pudgy, soft-handed man produced a welcoming smile. "The name's Jessup. I own this place. These gentlemen are noble followers of the bullwhacker calling. Sit right down, Preacher. Your money is as good as any man's."

Jessup had his hair slicked down and smelled of bay rum. He had small, close-set eyes that missed meanness due to a warm, friendly twinkle. He and the others completed the hand while Preacher dumped a stack of gold pieces on the table. Jessup passed the deck to the man on his right, who nodded to Preacher.

"Among the teamsters, I'm known as Long Tom. What's yer pleasure?"

Preacher did not lack in card-playing etiquette. "You name it, Tom." Introductions went around the table, and Preacher met Billy Green, Hank Lupton and Frank Spence.

Long Tom shuffled and announced, "Five-card stud."

Preacher played tight and smart. He folded after the third card. Jessup stayed to the bitter end with a bluff, Preacher noted. The next dealer called for five-card draw. Preacher was dealt a pair of queens, a ten, eight and deuce. He stayed and drew two cards. That gave him two pair. Jessup ran another bluff, raising the bet every time. Hank Lupton folded the first time Jessup did that. Billy Green's hand hovered over his stack of coins before he saw the final raise. Again Jessup lost. Preacher had the winning hand.

It soon became apparent to Preacher that Jessup should keep to his trade of tavern-keeper. He proved to be a terrible gambler. In one complete round at the table, he'd failed to take a single pot.

When it came Preacher's turn to deal again, he leaned forward and prefaced his call of game with an explanation. "There's a game I learned off a river boat captain up on the Platte one time. It's called seven-card stud. Played jist like five-card, but with three down cards, stead of one. Makes for an excitin' game."

He dealt it, watching Jessup closely. The man had a terrible hand, not even a pair or good face cards showing after two up cards. Why didn't he fold? He was truly awful. Someone real good could come along and clean him out, Preacher speculated. No matter, Jessup kept calling the bets. After the third card, he had a possible flush. A straight flush at that, Preacher noted. The bets, raises and cards went around. Preacher blinked.

Jessup had bettered his hand. This time he raised the bet. The final card went around, down. Only four players remained. Preacher had folded on his third card. Billy Green held the high hand in up cards. He bet a five-dollar gold piece. Jessup doubled it. When the pot was right, Jessup turned over his cards to reveal the straight flush.

Looking much relieved, he raked in the pot. Play resumed with Jessup dealing. He played badly over the next two hours. Preacher made it a habit never to count his stack of gold until the game ended. He did not like the idea of playing to scared money. This night proved his habit unnecessary. When he left the game, his poke bulged considerably more than when he had entered.

"Thank you, gents, for a right entertaining evening. Now I need some shut-eye before the sun catches me by surprise. Good night."

"Have a nightcap, Preacher. On me," Jessup offered.

"Thank ye kindly, but no thanks. I do need my sleep."

Makepeace Baxter had been badly misnamed by his doting parents. As a child, he had made war on small animals, tormenting them until they died. He loved to pull one wing off of several flies and watch them crawl around in circles until they dropped over from starvation. Another favorite was to pull the legs from frogs and toss them in a water trough to drown. His absolute favorite was to catch a cat on the tines of a pitchfork and watch as it writhe to a horrible death.

When he entered his teens, his tastes had become more refined. He tortured children smaller than himself, and threatened to kill them if they told. Once, at the age of fourteen, he went too far. A child died and he ran away from home, to live the next three months in terror of being caught and accused. Makepeace never went back. Over the ensuing years, he had found his niche among the lowest of the low, in the ranks of criminals.

He robbed, and often maimed, drunks for what money they might have. Lately, in this forsaken part of Indian Territory, he had taken up with the pair who sided him tonight. Now a hulking eighteen, he crouched in the sagebrush at the edge of the clearing on the southeast side of the creek created by the lost springs, which flowed sweetly from clefts in the rocks which formed a portion of the bank. With him were his best friends. His *only* friends, truth to be told. Youthful louts actually, who could stomach his sadistic ways. Lights had been lowered in the hotel portion of the stage station and the only sign of life came from the tavern.

Makepeace literally slobbered with anticipation. A bright, tall rectangle bloomed when the door to the tavern opened and out came that salty mountain man. "Him. He's the one," Makepeace Baxter whispered to Nate Glover and Wally Slaughter. "He won big in that game."

Preacher turned in the direction of the hotel and was striding toward the entrance when the three pieces of human debris made their move. They rushed at him, visions of gold discs filling their undoubtedly deficient brains. This would be easy. Their target looked completely unsuspecting. Makepeace Baxter growled like a dog when he leaped at the man in buckskins. He had not even made contact when he ran into a fistful of knuckles and learned that their victim had not been as unsuspecting as they would have liked him to be.

Makepeace landed on his butt. He dimly saw the man he attacked raise a leg. Pain exploded as Preacher kicked him square in the chest.

"Lookin' to bushwhack me, boy?" Preacher hissed, his face close to the pain-wracked one of his attacker. That was when Nate and Wally joined in, grabbing hold of Preacher by both arms.

An instant later they went flying as Preacher flung his arms wide. They fared somewhat better than Makepeace. Preacher slammed a fist into the side of the lout's head, which made his ear ring. By then Nate had regained his balance and gone for the mountain man again. Preacher met him with a grin on his face, dodged a wild left and put a looping right into the pudding face of the twenty-year-old thug. Nate came to a sudden stop. His arms sagged and Preacher gave frightful punishment to his ribs. When the man from the High Lonesome decided his opponent had been softened up enough, he went back to work on the face.

Blood spurted from Nate's broken nose. His lips stung as Preacher mashed them into his teeth, loosening two in the process. Nate tried to raise his arms to cover his head only to have his ribs explode in exquisite agony. He flailed wildly at Preacher to no avail. Preacher finished him with a sharp uppercut that clapped Nate's mouth shut with a loud ring. Nate sighed softly and settled in the dust. By then, Wally Slaughter had screwed up his courage and come at the wildcat they had cornered. Preacher let him approach, then sidestepped and whacked Wally in the side with his forearm. Next, Preacher grabbed the youthful bandit by the hair, which was long, blond and greasy, and yanked backward.

Wally's feet went out from under him and he went down hard. A screech of pain came when his tailbone fractured. Whimpering, he crawled aimlessly around on the ground like one of Makepeace's flies. Preacher paused and looked around himself, well pleased. That's when Makepeace Baxter got back in the fray. He came at Preacher with a knife. Moonlight gave the edge a wicked, blue glint.

Preacher had his own Greenriver in hand in an instant. The knife fighters squared off. Makepeace lashed out, a testing gesture. Preacher ignored it and began to circle.

"C'mon, stand still an' fight like a man."

"I am, you little bastard. You ever been in a knife fight before?"

"N-no."

"What's your name?"

"Why you wanna know?"

"So I have it right on your gravestone."

"It's Baxter. Makepeace Baxter, an' you're the one who's gonna die."

Preacher chuckled. "I reckon you'd best make some of that peace with the Almighty, 'cause you're gonna meet him real soon."

Makepeace could no longer contain himself. He launched forward. He swung his knife, now a blur, in front of him, left-right, right-left. Preacher backstepped and circled in the other direction. Makepeace followed him, his breathing harsh gasps, born of desperation as much as exertion. Preacher's moccasin landed on a loose pebble and caused him to stumble. At once, Makepeace rushed his opponent. He made a powerful slash and sensed the contact his blade made.

Preacher grunted and took a backstep, then plunged his Greenriver to the hilt in the chest of Makepeace. An expression of utter surprise formed on the suddenly pale face of the boy. He dropped his knife and closed his hands, gently as a lover, around Preacher's, which held the haft of the Greenriver.

Baxter's attempt to speak brought forth a river of blood. Then he gained enough of an opening. "You killed me."

"You didn't leave me much choice."

"Who . . . who are you?"

"They call me Preacher."

A mournful groan escaped the bloodied lips of Makepeace Baxter. "Oh, Jesus. I . . . I been done in by the best."

"That you have," Preacher told him without false modesty. He turned the blade slightly to break it free and pulled it from the dying youth's chest. Makepeace fell to the ground.

Preacher watched the young thug's dying throes, then turned away. He felt a lightness at his waist and reached down. During the brief fight, Makepeace had slashed open his money pouch. Half his winnings lay scattered in the dusty station yard.

"Damn, oh, damn, now I'll have to crawl around and pick it up like a beggar." Tomorrow, he speculated fervently, just had to be better.

7

Eve Billings tried once more to reason with the hard-headed men of their wagon train. "We must move on. Several children have taken a fever from some unknown source and even more are likely to."

"Fever's fever. We don't have to know what caused it," Gus Beecher stated stolidly.

"If we knew what caused it, we could avoid it. I suspect the water is tainted somehow. I have been boiling all of mine before giving any to my children. Little Anna is improving rapidly. No more stomach pain and the fever is lower."

Beecher remained adamant. "I say we should stay where we are. No one knows what's out there."

"Yeah," Enos Throcker inserted. "Look what happened when we tried. We got plum lost."

Eve was ready for that. "Send out scouts."

Throcker shook his head stubbornly. "They'll never find their way back."

Determined, Eve pressed her point. "There are several older boys and young men who are levelheaded enough.

They can tell north from south and read sign. They could mark the trail for us in piles of stones."

Gus Beecher rejected her suggestion. "Wouldn't do. What if we wandered off between the piles of rocks?"

Eve thought that over a moment. Somewhere she had read something that might work. What was it and who had done it? It came to her after a long pause in which the men began to hope they had silenced her.

"There is a way. Do any of you know the story of the Llano Estocado? The Staked Plains down in Texas?" She received no answer and went on. "When the Spanish explorers first went there, they found a vast desert. Not a tree to guide one, no way to lay out a trail for others to follow. The leader had an idea. He had soldiers ride back to the last stand of tall, young saplings. They cut poles from them, hundreds of them, oh, maybe fifteen feet high. To these they attached big flags. The leader had one set up at the edge of the rolling area of sand and rocks. Then they started off, taking the other poles with them.

"When they reached a spot nearly out of sight of the first pole, they erected another. Then they moved on and put up more flags." Eve paused, to make certain the men followed her. "Each staff was numbered, so if they wandered, and came upon one, they would know where they were and which way to go. And it worked exactly like the leader said it would. They crossed that barren, waterless wasteland and went on to found Santa Fe."

Enos Throcker was not buying any of that. "When'd they do that?"

Eve had her answer ready. "Almost three hundred years ago."

Throcker snorted in derision. "There, you see? Old-fashioned ideas like that won't get us anywhere."

Unable to abide such stupidity, Eve let go. She stomped her tiny, booted foot. "That's plain crazy. If we sent out the older boys and some young men, with arms to protect themselves and a wagonload of poles and flags, they could mark the trail the same way. Even come back if they needed more, or if they ran into trouble. After a couple of days head start, the train can load up on water and any game we can get, and follow the markers."

Silence answered her. Eve looked around, her features set in grim determination. "What about you, young Honeycutt? Do you think it would work?"

The adenoidal sixteen-year-old cut his eyes to his father, who shook his head in the negative. Then David Honeycutt took a deep breath and made his bold first venture at independence. "Yeah—yeah, I do. And it would be a great adventure." He turned to a cluster of his peers for support. "What do you think, fellahs?"

"It'll work, Davey, I know it will," a defiant Eb Throcker encouraged. His father took a menacing step in his direction. "Leave it be, Paw. We ain't gettin' anywhere just sittin' here eatin' up our supplies."

It quickly got out of Eve's hands. With the prospect of something, anything, to do besides sit around, the young men clamored to go. The decision made, those who would take the risks decided to set off that afternoon to find and cut a wagonload of lodge-pole pines. Meanwhile, their mothers and sisters would fashion flags from any bright material they had at hand. They would start off within two days, taking the wagon and three saddle mounts.

Hunkered down in a tall stand of wild mulberry, the spikey-haired lout who had dogged the mountain men along the Santa Fe Trail stared out at the deeply rutted roadway. Any time now, Amos Scraggs reckoned, the excitement growing. He itched. He twitched. Uneasily he cut his eyes left and right. His ace-boon runnin' pard, Miguel Lopez, sheltered behind a fallen tree to the right. Five others were closer in by the road.

Strung out on both sides of the trail were the surviving dozen of the gang that had attacked the freight wagon train. They had been paid well to locate and kill the mountain man known as Preacher. They had attacked the wagons out of greed, but their specific charge had been to see that Preacher, and anyone with him, never lived to reach the Missouri side of the river of the same name.

Now their chance had come. Only the three mountain men had broken up their raid before, Amos Scraggs recalled. Could it be they could do it again? He stiffened when he heard the distant thud of hooves. Four horses, he figured it to be. It had to be them. Amos saw the one called preacher come into view first. He lined up his sights, as he tried to quell the quiver in his hand. Slowly he squeezed off a round.

A loud crack shattered the pastoral calm of the morning. Big mistake! the mind of Amos Scraggs shouted at him as in the next instant the mountain men exploded into a deadly fury.

Bright sun no longer slanted into Preacher's eyes when he reined in. Shadows had grown so short they had become pools around the bases of the objects that made them. He estimated their morning's travel had brought them close to Diamond Springs Crossing. Another four days should see them in Missouri. He had traveled the Santa Fe Trail three times before and felt confident with that assessment. He turned to share that with his friends when a shot blasted to silence the warbling of the meadowlarks. Preacher put heels to the flanks of Tarnation as he slid his Hawken from its scabbard. The words that left his mouth had nothing to do with their destination.

"By dang, we're bein' ambushed!"

Three Sleeps Norris grumbled agreement. "I figgered that out for myself. I see some of 'em over there." He fired as he spoke, sent a ball in among the high stand of wild mulberry, and went for his powder horn. Preacher loosed a round. A scream answered. To his right, Antoine emptied his Hawken into the screaming face of a pasty-skinned outlaw who broke from cover, confident that their numbers and surprise would carry the day.

He died without knowing the flaw in his judgment. Antoine quickly drew one of his single-barreled pistols from the saddle holsters and chopped a hole through the underbrush with a double-shotted load. His second pistol brought a groan and an enemy ball discharged skyward. Quickly Antoine holstered the empty weapon and drew one of two double-barreled pistols from the wide, red sash around his hard, flat middle. He cut his eyes to his companions and saw Preacher unlimber one of his wicked Walker Colts.

Three fast shots downed two more of the ambushers. Preacher looked at Antoine and nodded. They worked well together, the gesture seemed to say. With a roar, a squat, ugly thug stormed at Three Sleeps Norris, who had a cap fail to fire. Preacher wheeled around in the saddle and put a .44 ball into the jaw hinge of the attacker. He staggered three steps closer, enough so that Three Sleeps dropped him with a butt stroke to the top of his head.

"Obliged, Preacher."

"My pleasure."

By then they had ridden in among those who had laid the ambush. Preacher struck one down with the barrel of his Colt, then shot another who sprang upward to fire wildly. The bullet cracked by Preacher's cheek and struck a resin-slicked pine a foot away. A shower of amber moisture slapped the back of Preacher's neck. He'd play billy hell getting that out of his hair, he thought crankily, while he exchanged Colts.

Stunned by the incredible firepower of the mountain men, the border trash fell back as their intended victims kept coming. In rapid order, their number had diminished to a mere seven. Yet, they still outnumbered the men they had come to kill by two to one. Preacher and Antoine quickly reduced that advantage by two.

Antoine pulled a sad face as he advised Preacher. *"Par hasard,* I have shot myself dry, my friend."

By chance, eh? Preacher thought. "You got a war hawk ain'tcha?"

Antoine brightened and brought forth a wicked-looking iron-bladed tomahawk. The thug in front of him paled and threw a wild shot. The ball made a red line along Antoine's ribs, but failed to prevent him from splitting the skull of the hapless bandit. Preacher heeled Tarnation to one side, and fired one of his remaining three loads.

Mouth puckered in a soundless howl, the ruffian who took that .44 ball bent double and toppled to one side. A second later, Preacher held his fire as a fear-stamped face popped out of the underbrush. He was not surprised to recognize the straw-haired rascal who had been dogging their trail since Cottonwood Crossing.

"Don't shoot. I give up. I'm hurt bad," wailed the young outlaw.

Another disreputable creature crawled into the open. His usually coppery complexion had turned a sickly gray-green. Thin wisps of mustache were matted around his face by sweat. He dragged a bloody leg with a bullet-shattered thigh-bone. *"Yo también.* Don't kill us, *por favor."*

Preacher and his friends surrounded the defeated pair. Preacher chuckled softly. "Now ain't this something?" He leaned low in his saddle. "Haven't we met someplace before?"

Groaning, the towhead with the spiky hair licked dry lips. "You know damn well we have. You gonna stop this bleedin'?"

Preacher examined the wound in the side of the ruffian without moving from his horse. "We might, if we get some straight answers. Like, to start, do you have a name?"

Anger flared a moment. "Of course, everyone has a name.

Mine's Amos Scraggs. This is my pard, Miguel Lopez. But, we don't know nothin' about nothin'."

Preacher pursed his lips. "Now I believe that."

"You do?" a surprised thug blurted.

"Yep. Back some years we had us what we called the University of the Rockies in the High Lonesome. I learned me a lot of grammar there. What you did was use a double negative; 'don't know nothing' you said. Well, what rules we've got for English says a double negative is a positive. In other words, you small piece of buffalo dung, you know a whole lot we'd like to hear from you."

"What if we don't tell you?"

"We leave you here to bleed to death."

"You'd never do a thing like . . ." Then Amos Scraggs read the deadly message in Preacher's steely eyes. "What do you want to know?"

"This jist another fling for you? Like that freighter train?"

"N-no. We—we were sent to see that you never reached Missouri."

"Who's we? That include that scruffy lot you rode with?"

Scraggs' eyes strayed from Preacher's face. He forced a tone of indignation into his voice. "No. We weren't no part of them," he lied. "Ask Miguel. That bunch was pure trash. Miguel an' me joined up for that raid on the freight wagons only to make more money."

Miguel, who believed incorrectly that the artery in his thigh had been severed, and he was about to die, sought to absolve himself before he met his Maker. He motioned to Preacher. The mountain man dismounted and squatted down beside the Mexican bandit.

"What is it?" he asked.

Heat flared in Amos. "Don't tell him nothin'!"

Miguel whispered urgently, his eyes alight with the fear of death. "I will tell you the truth, Señor Preacher. The whole gang had been paid well to keel you."

"Who paid you?"

"Three men. They are called Gross, Praeger and Reiker."

"You done good, Miguel. I'm sure the Almighty will take that into account."

"Por favor, please, I want a priest. I want to make my confession."

"We'll see if we can find you one. First off, we've got to bind up that wound and fix your partner."

Sergeant Stalking Elk of the Osage Tribal Police rode up to the Diamond Creek Crossing relay station. That young Ryan boy had come like a whirlwind. Had two prisoners and a whole passel of bodies to take care of. Stalking Elk wondered how Finn Ryan and his boys, both under fourteen, could have stood off so many as made up the pile of corpses outside the tavern door. He supposed he would find out soon.

Three tall, lean men in buckskin stepped out into the dooryard. The one in the middle, with a square jaw and a far-off look in his eyes, introduced himself as Preacher and named his friends. Stalking Elk nodded toward the bodies.

"Do you want to tell me about it?"

"Don't mind if I do." He went on to describe the ambush, eliminating only the purpose. Then he added, "There's two inside who need medical treatment, if any's available."

Stalking Elk pulled a wry expression. "Our medicine man is all that's near."

That'll have to do. I've been put back on the rosy side of health more than once by a medicine man. If these two don't cotton to it, tell 'em they can walk to the nearest white doctor."

Stalking Elk studied the toes of his moccasins for a moment. "From what you tell me, they're due for a hanging under white law."

"That they are."

"White man's law does not apply out here. We don't have courts or hangmen. When an Osage kills another of his tribe, he is beaten and turned out of the camp. That is most likely what will happen to this pair."

Preacher puckered his lips and worried his tongue around his mouth a while. He didn't like the idea of exile. "It'd be a shame if they died of their wounds, then."

Sergeant Stalking Elk cut his eyes to the pile of corpses once more. Thoroughly impressed with the fighting prowess of the mountain men, he offered up a bit of embarrassing news. "I read a book once about the legendary mountain man called Preacher. Never thought I would meet him in person."

Preacher blushed hotly. "Aw, shucks, them things is pure fancy. I've never done half the things they put in there. It's jist stuff and nonsense."

"We will see to your living pair. I don't suppose they will go adventuring again. Mr. Ryan can bury the dead. There is money from your government for such needs."

Preacher extended his hand. "Thank you, Stalking Elk. We'll stay and lend a hand."

"May I ask where you are bound for?"

Keeping a straight face, Preacher saved himself from a lie by only a light exaggeration. "We're set on seein' Independence, then go on to Jefferson Barracks."

"Safe journey, then."

Takes Rain and Gray Eagle looked downslope at the laboring of the draft animals. A mixed train of mules and oxen trudged through the roiling red-brown dust of a sage-choked basin near the banks of the Yellowstone River. Soon they would stop to take food, Takes Rain knew. That is when the Blackfoot would take something else. A cold smile lifted the corners of his mouth. Before long his Bison Eaters society would test the power of the medicine given by Iron Shirt.

"Wagons . . . Whoooooa-UP!" came faintly on the light breeze that blew from the direction of the train toward the Blackfoot warriors waiting to strike.

Those words had no exact meaning to Takes Rain. He only knew that it was what they said when the leader wanted the wagons to stop. Obedient to them, the rolling lodges began to slow and swing into a half circle. Women dismounted and their birdlike chatter lifted on the wind. Time to strike. Takes Rain cut his eyes to Gray Eagle and nodded. Both men came to their moccasins and released their ponies. Swiftly they mounted. Thirty other warriors did the same. Takes Rain raised the new rifle he had been given by the followers of Iron Shirt and waved it over his head.

"Ki-yi-yi-yi!" he keened to sound the attack.

Startled white faces looked up at them. Then the warriors hidden around the wagons, in the thick covering of sagebrush, opened fire with bows and arrows. Rifles cracked also. Three men went down, one gagging and clutching at the arrow that stuck out from his throat, front and rear. A woman shrieked and dropped the pot of beans she had saved from breakfast. A red stain spread on her ample bosom around the gruesome exit wound a .56-caliber ball had made.

Shouting their war cries, and profane insults, thirty Blackfoot warriors thundered down the slope to flow through their comrades and bring more death and destruction. Several oxen went slack in their harness and sagged to their knees. A mule erupted in agony, its rump pierced by two arrows. Stunned by the suddenness of the attack, the immigrants finally began to react.

Several men grabbed up rifles and returned fire. Their bullets seemed to avoid all the mounted Indians. Another volley had as little effect. Five men died before they could reload. Children screamed and ran in panic. Whooping warriors rode in among them, oblivious to the crack and moan of white men's bullets. The Blackfoot bent low and scooped small boys and girls off their feet, then whirled away from the scene of battle.

Seizing a flaming brand from a cookfire, Gray Eagle hurled it into the rear of a wagon. Screams of terror came from within. The flames quickly licked up. A woman with graying hair and two barely nubile girls tumbled out. The woman died from a lance thrust, the girls were dragged aside to provide later amusement for the aroused warriors. Unable to reload in the swirl of battle, Takes Rain slung his fine new rifle over one shoulder by a rawhide thong and drew his tomahawk.

Horror filled the face of the white man who watched the grinning warrior with the war axe descend on him. Blackness quickly replaced the sight of the savage as the keen edge of the 'hawk blade sheered through the pilgrim's forehead and mangled his brain. Then a man with a shotgun found one howling savage within range and gave out a load of buckshot. Five of the nine .32-caliber pellets pulped the chest of one Blackfoot, after shattering his hair-pipe bone war vest.

Dismayed, the warriors nearest him looked on in disbelief while he slumped dead over the neck of his horse. This wasn't supposed to happen, Takes Rain thought, his stomach churning. Maybe the medicine was not good against the many-balls guns. Sensing the loss of faith among his companions, Takes Rain signaled for the braves to follow him as he streaked away.

They took the young women and small children with them. Only two adults had survived the attack. They stood in numbed despair as flames licked at four wagons. Slowly they looked around at the scene of slaughter. From over the rise they heard the shrieks and wails of the young women and girls as the savages used them in cruel and lustful ways. Helpless to do anything about it, the man and woman could only hug each other and weep.

The torment went on for a long time. At last the Blackfoot had been drained of their urgent sap and split the skulls of their abused captives. Then they rode off with the children. Silence slowly returned to the banks of the Yellowstone River.

8

At an isolated trading post on the North Platte River, Praeger and his partners received a message from Washington City. Instructions written on the outside had told the proprietor to hold it until called for. Praeger, whose aggressive qualities and dominance had propelled him without dissent into leadership, split the wax seal, and opened the thick, threefold paper. He read it quickly and then raised his mottled-blue eyes, the slight cast in the right one disconcerting as always, and smiled.

"It is short and sweet, gentlemen. We are informed that arrangements have been completed for stage two. Those involved will be on their way within . . ." He consulted a calendar on the wall beside the bar. "A week from now."

Morton Gross rubbed pudgy hands together. "Wonderful. How long will it take them to get out here?"

Praeger considered that. "I would imagine six weeks to two months. Unless they take the mail packet or some other steam-powered riverboat."

Gross worked his thick, rubbery lips in and out. "And our little . . . ah . . . impediment?"

"You mean Preacher? By now I assume he has been taken care of. Come, this calls for a celebration. Barman, do you have any champagne?"

Mouth a black O in his thick, ebony beard, the bartender blinked in disbelief. "Any what? I ain't seed no champagne since I moved out here." He pronounced the word champ-agnee. "Never saw none before that neither."

"Do you have a good rye?" Praeger asked suspiciously.

"I got a small barrel from the Cumberland Gap country."

"That will do quite well." To the others, Praeger said, "We have to get Iron Shirt to move faster on enlisting the Cheyenne. They are the key to the whole thing."

Across the Missouri now and drawing nearer to Jefferson Barracks each hour, Preacher felt downright uneasy. He spared no effort putting his discomfort into words.

"It's too crowded around here. Why, there's actually more than one house per' mile. Not fittin' nor healthy for folks to live all shoved up against one another like that."

Intrigued, Three Sleeps chimed in. "What do you consider comfortable living space, Preacher?"

Preacher did not even hesitate. "I reckon one per ten or twenty miles. That be the absolute limit I can tolerate. Among white folk, that is," he elaborated.

"Don't keep them from being ornery," Three Sleeps observed as he indicated a group of armed men who sat astride the high road. The bulk of their horses blocked the advance of the mountain men.

A big, ugly brute, with orange-red hair and matching beard, in the middle of the ragged formation, raised a hand and pointed one thick finger imperiously at Preacher. "What you fellers' business?" he demanded.

Preacher gave it a moment's thought and decided what he had told Sergeant Stalking Elk would serve in this case equally well. "Why, friend, we're on our way to . . . ah . . . Independence."

Thunder clouds writhed in the scowl produced by their interrogator. "It be back the way you came. So, you'd best turn around an' light a shuck out of here. There ain't no room for frontier riffraff the likes of you three among civilized folk here in Missouri."

Preacher had heard all he needed to. He worked his mouth a bit and produced a cud of Redman Premium Braid. "Well, then," he observed as he spat the wad of tobacco at the hooves of the delegation's horses, "we'll just have to make room."

In a flash the fight was on. Preacher leaped like a panther from the back of Tarnation. His powerful arms looped around the leader of the welcoming party and dragged the bigger man from the saddle. With a lithe twist, Preacher turned them in midair so that the carrot-topped brute landed on his back, with Preacher atop him.

Wind knocked from his lungs in a loud grunt, the unfriendly lout went cross-eyed while Preacher sawed the lapels of his hairy cowhide vest across his throat.

"Gah . . . gah . . . yer chokin' me."

Preacher smiled down at him, his expression conveying that he was fully aware of that. "Now, we might not be the most sartorially splendid fellers you've ever seen, that I'll allow. But you an' yer friends are no prize winners yerselves. I'd appreciate it if you could find it in your heart to be more cordial in your greeting."

While this exchange went on, Three Sleeps Norris let out a whoop and sprang toward the pair nearest to him. His point of aim was a space between them, which he swiftly filled by a quick reach and grab. Then Three Sleeps swung his arms inward and filled the opening with their noggins, which made a loud *clunk!* as they met in midair. On the opposite side of Preacher, two of the local, lowbrow social arbiters had decided on the use of deadly force.

Their hands barely touched the stocks of their rifles when they heard the double click of hammers. They looked up, startled to see the twin muzzles of a double-barreled pistol pointed levelly at them. Antoine Revier gave them a wide, knowing smile.

With a roar, the huge man under Preacher heaved upright and freed himself. He drove a fist into the face of his opponent, which caused stars to explode in Preacher's left eye. Preacher let the force of the blow carry him up and over. He hit on heels and shoulders and bounded upright.

By then the brute who had dislodged him came at him with ham fists. Preacher dodged backward, only to come up against one of the pair Three Sleeps had dealt with. The groggy man stirred and then reached out with both hands to cling tightly to Preacher's ankles.

"Get him, Red," he urged.

"Thanks, Barney." Red came after Preacher with punishing punches to the mountain man's face.

Preacher's lips stung and swelled. His tongue explored and felt several loosened teeth. His left eye was almost closed. Then Red shifted weight to put a finish to the interloper. Preacher seized his chance.

He put his shoulders and hips behind each smashing blow he drove into Red's chest and gut. Although padded by fat, Red felt each one, and with increasing intensity. His arms drooped slightly. Enough so that Preacher could go to work on his face. Red's lips split and his nose became a rose blossom before the bully could draw a refreshing breath. Knifelike pains filled his chest.

Preacher sucked in air and spoke lightly to his friends. "I'd appreciate it if one of you would unwind this snake from my legs."

Three Sleeps sprang to the task. He hauled the slighter built Barney away from Preacher's legs and spun him. His moccasin collided with the seat of Barney's trousers and propelled the leech back down the road in the direction of home. Stumbling, Barney recovered quickly and turned on Three Sleeps.

Norris set himself for the rush. When it came, he side-stepped and smacked Barney on the side of the head. Staggered, Barney turned in the wrong direction. Preacher popped him in the mouth and sent him on around to Three Sleeps.

Laughing now, Norris pegged Barney on the left hinge of his jaw and the Missourian went rubber-legged. He collided with the flank of his horse when he went to the ground. Red roared again and reached for Preacher, while Three Sleeps walked over to one of the mounted men and yanked him from the saddle.

"Reckon I can put this away," Antoine speculated aloud.

He released the hammers and did just that. Then he dismounted and hauled the other thug from his horse. Knuckles met flesh and a new brawl was on. By then, Red had brought himself upright and planted a fist between Preacher's shoulder blades. It staggered the mountain man, who turned as he jolted forward.

"Some fellers never learn," he grumbled as he blocked a punch and answered with a short right.

It gradually dawned on Preacher that fists would simply not do it with this brute. When Red bore in again, Preacher flexed his legs, cocked the right one and slammed the heel of his moccasin into Red's exposed belly. Eyes bulging, Red did a pratfall that jarred his teeth. Preacher turned slightly and kicked Red in the side of his head. Bells and birdies went off inside Red's skull. His eyes rolled up and he fell backward, arms widespread. His body stirred up puffs of dust, and he let out a soft snore.

"Welcome to Missouri," Preacher panted and the trio of mountain men chuckled sardonically. Then, "Think they've had enough?" Preacher asked his companions.

"Just about," advised Antoine as he drove a hard left to the jaw of the last standing Missourian. His target flopped onto the ground and lay still. "Now they have."

* * *

It worked for them like it did for the Spanish on the Llano Estocado. Eve Billings thrilled at the sight of the fifteen foot shafts, their colorful cloth pennants fluttering in the hot breeze that blew across the sandy soil of the Great Basin. From the ridge where her wagon rested, she could see a line of them leading back to their starting place and on into the distance beyond. Progress had been slow at first.

They'd barely made seven miles a day the first three days because the neophyte scouts frequently dashed back with alarms that proved unfounded. Such a misgiving had stopped them at the saddle of this ridge not half an hour ago. Davey Honeycutt had galloped a lathered horse back, his eyes as enlarged as his mount's.

"Injuns!" he had shouted. "Injuns not five miles ahead."

From the color of his face one would suspect they were the ghosts of Indians. A party of armed men rode forward to investigate. Eve could see them returning now, small, black specks against the blasted earth. Beside her, Charlie stirred on the seat and shifted his rifle.

"They're not wavin' a red flag, Mom." Charlie sounded disappointed that the agreed-upon signal to warn them of hostiles was not fluttering above the riders.

"We can thank the Lord for that," his mother responded.

"Aw, Mom, I want to shoot an Injun."

Shocked, Eve almost slapped the boy's face. "No you don't, Charles Ryan Billings. You don't want to shoot any human. Hunting for food is a necessity, killing someone is a horrid crime."

"Even if they are tryin' to kill you?"

That left Eve speechless for a long moment. "You're just a boy, Charlie. Leave those sorts of things to grown men."

Some of the less alarmist among the travelers started their wagons out toward the approaching men. There would have been shots, after all, had there been Indians. Overall, Eve remained highly pleased at their progress. Even better, the game which had been absent on their first attempt now seemed to have come back in abundance. Anna was growing stronger every hour, and Charlie had become quite an expert shot, adding to his credit deer and antelope as well as rabbits. She put the Bridesburg Arsenal rifle aside and turned to Charlie.

"Put your rifle up, Charlie. We're heading out."

"Can I take Star out and hunt a little?"

"No need today, son. Remember those plump rabbits Damion Brewster brought us?"

Charlie did not sound enthused over that. Damion, an acne-riddled youth with a crush on his mother, was a pain in the butt. "Oh, yeah, those."

Charlie replaced his rifle in the wagon bed and scampered out to his usual place, astride Jake. His bare heels bounced with the churning rhythm of the stolid animal. Once again Eve surveyed her world and found herself entirely at peace. Then she looked up from the rumps of her team to see a solitary Indian sitting on top of a close-by mound.

Sudden cold clutched at her heart. Could he be the forerunner of the Indians the Honeycutt boy thought he had seen? If not, where had he come from? She tensed and reached for the rifle at her feet when the Indian slowly began to raise his lance. Extended to full arm's length, the Indian moved his lance from side to side.

Fearing that to be the signal for an attack, Eve filled her lungs for a cry of alarm, only to realize that it was only a friendly wave, backed up by a broad smile.

At Jefferson Barracks at last, Preacher found the situation and the troops even sorrier than he expected. The Dragoons turned out to be raw and green, barely aware of what was expected of them. While Preacher and his companions walked their horses through the gate, sergeants bellowed at the hapless soldiers, their faces scarlet with their fury.

"No, damnit, Mallory! Far the love of Jazus, how many times do I have to tell ya? Ye mount so yer facing the same direction the horse is, ye do."

Mallory made the mistake of whining. "I don't know why I get so mixed up, Sergeant Muldoon. Honest I don't. Maybe I ain't a horse person."

Battalion Sergeant Major Terrance Muldoon threw down the riding crop he carried and strode to Mallory's side. He shoved his face to within an inch of Mallory's and bellowed. "It's Sergeant Major, ye dimwit. It is. Ye'll go get yer knapsack. Ye'll fill it with rocks, ye will. An' ye'll report back here to me on the double."

"I know what's gonna happen then, Sergeant Major," Mallory recited, his stupid face alight. "I'm gonna run around this big ol' field here."

"Parade Ground goddamnit! Parade Ground."

Mallory looked puzzled. "Ain't seen no parades go by since we been here."

"Yer a sorry son of a . . . Aw, what the hell. It's no use, you're no use. Sure an' sometimes I think I'm of no use, I do. Get that knapsack."

"Yah, sure, Sergeant Major."

Preacher approached the infuriated noncom. "Excuse me, Sergeant Major, could you tell me where I can find Colonel Danvers?"

BSM Terrance Muldoon turned to Preacher with a sour expression. "In Saint Louis."

"May I ask what he is doing there?"

"Who be ye?"

"They call me Preacher, this be Three Sleeps Norris an' Antoine Revier. We are reporting in as guides for this battalion through the Injun country."

Fists on hips, feet wide apart in a belligerent stance, Muldoon introduced himself. "Battalion Sergeant Major Muldoon. An' fer yer information, the good colonel and those young gentlemen officers of his wanted a last fling among the ladies an' the sparklin' wine before makin' their great sacrifice fer God and country."

"They left you in charge?"

"No, Mr. Preacher. We've got us one officer with his brains in his head, not in his pants, we do. Captain Edward Dreiling is commanding at present, he is. Ye can find him at battalion headquarters. Across the parade ground there, it is."

"Thank you, Sergeant Major." Preacher turned to leave as Mallory returned.

The knapsack bounced viciously against his shoulders and back as he began to run. The black visor of his flat-topped bill-cap slid slowly down his forehead until it obscured his eyes. Preacher stared at him as though seeing a creature from another planet. Then he began to laugh. At his side, an amused Three Sleeps questioned BSM Muldoon.

"Does it do any good?"

"Does it now? Not with that one, sure an' it doesn't. There's some's fine lads, smart and quick to learn. But that one has to take off a boot to count to eleven, he does. I fear what will become of him out there." He gestured to the west.

Preacher and the other mountain men walked to the head-quarters building. Inside, an orderly told them that Captain Dreiling could be found on the firing range on the far side of the cantonment. Preacher got exact directions and led the way to the sound of erratic firing.

Seated on a canvas-backed camp stool, an officer observed while sweating, swearing sergeants conducted firing exercises. The captain wore the split-tail, regulation blue uniform coat with thick, shaggy, brass epaulets at the shoulder points, matching insignia of rank—three horizontal strips—on the high, tight collar. His trousers, with the gold stripe down the seams, covered the high tops of his black boots. His shako style hat, of black, patent leather, complete with horsehair plume that drooped over the front, sat squarely on a round, blond head.

Somehow he managed to seem cool and comfortable, while the NCOs and enlisted men showed wide rings at their armpits and long wet smears down their backs. Their appearances made even Preacher feel uncomfortable. Captain Dreiling had no difficulty in recognizing the newcomers. He rose and extended a hand.

"You must be our guides. And, I would say that you are Preacher." He unerringly picked the right man.

"That I am. You'd be Captain Dreiling?"

At six feet, the broad shoulders, full chest and narrow hips gave Dreiling a handsome cut by anyone's standards. He answered Preacher with alacrity. "Yes. However, on informal occasions, you may call me Edward."

Preacher prefaced his remarks with a softening smile. "An' you can call me Preacher. I don't mean to pry into Army business, Captain, but may I ask why you did not join your associates in the pleasures of Saint Louis?"

For an instant, Preacher thought the expression of contempt that darkened Captain Dreiling's face was intended for him. "Bloody damned children, you ask me. Most of these rabble cannot yet tell right from left foot, let alone conduct themselves as soldiers, and the ones with the responsibility to hammer them into shape go off skirt-chasing."

To emphasize his point, a Hall Model 43 rifled carbine discharged loudly in their direction. The ball from the breechloading weapon cracked past close enough for Preacher to feel the wind. Immediately a sergeant burst forth in a flurry of profanity.

"You goddamned idiot! You'll get the effing lash for that. I said to clear all weapons before leaving the line." A fist lashed out and knocked the offender sprawling. The sergeant kicked him in the ribs twice.

"Excuse me," said Dreiling politely before turning to the sergeant. "Enough of that, Sergeant Peters. Extra duty for Emmons and four punishment tours should suffice. No one was injured."

Suddenly rigid in the position of attention, Sergeant Peters saluted smartly. "Yes, sir. Very good, sir. It will be done as ordered. Now, you worthless reprobate, keep that muzzle downrange at all times, you hear."

A fair-minded man, as well as conscientious, Preacher thought to himself. The rest of the day's tour of the battalion established some strong opinions in Preacher. At the stable area, soldiers tried rear vault and running side mounts, most falling in the dirt over and over. Sergeants screamed and cursed. Those who could ride, Preacher soon learned, could not hit a bull in the ass with a bass fiddle, let alone score on a target from the prone position with their weapons.

Which left him with a rather dim view of Colonel Arlington Danvers, the battalion commander. If the other officers, save Captain Dreiling, are as ill-concerned about the readiness of their men, they could all be in for a hell of a time out in the High Lonesome. Instinct told him to seek out the Battalion staff in St. Louis at once. Logic told him to wait here, lend a hand where he could and hope for the best when the errant officers returned. Whatever came of this, Preacher promised himself, he would sure as hell never take a job with the Army again.

9

Lieutenant Colonel Arlington Danvers and his officers returned to Jefferson Barracks five days later. To the expert eyes of Preacher and his mountain-man friends, they all looked powerfully hungover and sadly dissipated, an all-around surly lot. By the lights of the mountain men, based on the harshness of the noncoms and the appearance and deportment of Lieutenant Colonel Danvers, the colonel was a martinet and thorough popinjay. This opinion was reinforced when they reported to Danvers in a borrowed office, intended for some of the permanent staff. The colonel looked up and his lip curled with contempt and disgust.

"You're a scruffy-looking lot, I must say. Do you ever take baths? You'll have to in this Army."

"Pardon me, Colonel," blurted Preacher. "But we ain't in 'this Army.' We're just hired to guide you to where you want to go in the Big Empty."

Nattily dressed in a freshly pressed uniform, Danvers looked Preacher up and down. Preacher had a classic shiner, all purple, yellow and blue. He had a cut on his chin, and a red mark on one cheek. Danvers worked his mouth as though he wanted to rid himself of some foul-tasting object.

"You have obviously all recently been in some sort of drunken brawl. From now on, until the completion of your employment, you will all refrain from spirits—liquor of any sort—and you will clean up your clothing and present a well-washed appearance at all times. Your hair is to be cut to regulation length, and all facial hair is forbidden.

"You are to ride out before dawn each morning, scout the territory ahead and send back reports." Danvers' arrogant tone continued while he ticked off each point on long slender fingers. "You will not fraternize with the officers, noncommissioned officers or the enlisted men of my command. You will negotiate safe passage for us with any savages you encounter. You are to make certain that the path we take is wide enough to accommodate mounted troops—four abreast, with our field piece at the center of the column—and wagons, two wide to the rear."

Preacher bristled. He'd heard all of the "You will" and "You are" that he could swallow without getting a sore stomach. He raised a hand to cut off the tirade.

"Now whoa up there a second, Colonel. Exactly who are to be the guides for this expedition?"

Danvers blinked. "Why, you three, of course."

"Well, then, don't the colonel think that the men in charge should have some say in how the soldier-boys will march?"

Lieutenant Colonel Danvers countered at once. "Regulations cover that quite nicely, I believe."

Fire fanned in Preacher's eyes. "Ain't no regulations out there in the High Lonesome. An' as for the trail, dependin' on which way you intend to go, there ain't no real trail at all. We just have to find the best way through, over or around the rocks, rivers, gorges and hills as we can. And do it without breaking every wheel or upsettin' any loads.

"Now, marchin' four abreast might be well an' good on a

wide street or grassy meadow, but not out there. There's cactus with thorns long and sharp enough to pierce a horse's hoof to the cannon bone. There's prairie-dog holes jist waitin' to bust a leg." Preacher paused for a breath, which he took, swallowed deeply and went on. "Then you have bison who'll stampede at any loud sound, and rattlesnakes that can fell a horse as easy as a man. Not to mention Injuns by the thousands. Nope, two men to a file, an' they alternately walk and ride their mounts. Another thing. No horn tooting or drum banging. That's the surest way to attract some unpleasant Injuns. Those fancy sabers yer so fond of has got to be padded and tied down so they don't rattle, an' all tack and loose gear also. An Injun can hear the noise they make a mile away."

Filled with equal parts of bluster and indignation, Danvers protested hotly. "We absolutely must have trumpet calls and drums to convey orders. Typical civilian ignorance," he summed up.

Preacher cocked an eyebrow. "Ever hear of arm signals? The Injuns have used 'em for ages and get along jist dandy."

Danvers continued his resistance. "And field music is essential for morale."

"I wonder how serious you are about getting there and getting your fort built before you take on the hostiles? If you have your soldier-boys practice arm signals while we're still in friendly country, they'll know them when they need 'em. Me, I say it's the smart thing to do."

"They are Dragoons, Mr. Preacher. Dragoons."

No matter what Preacher proposed, Lieutenant Colonel Danvers balked at adopting. At last, Preacher had reached his limit. "Here's my final word on this, Colonel. We're gonna do it my way, or I quit the job and hand the money back to the government."

Realizing that this assignment was his last hope of providing for his future, Danvers knew he had no choice. He had been passed over for promotion too many times, so his career would soon be at an end. If this did not go the way he had been told it would, the years ahead would be bleak indeed. Mustering his will power he suppressed his outrage and caved in.

"Very well, it will be as you say."

With a single drum marking time, the column moved out early the next morning. To Preacher's surprise, the troops had improved greatly. They sat their horses straight and tall, all of them required to be no less than five foot ten to six foot two in height. Not a one fell off his horse. Not even simple-minded Mallory mounted backward.

On the highroad outside the barracks ground they rode four abreast. For all their smart appearance, Preacher sensed something odd. He rode in a relaxed slouch with Three Sleeps and Antoine some two hundred yards ahead of the battalion commander and his staff and flag bearers. Cardinals warbled and woodpeckers kept up a steady *rat-a-tat* on hollow trees. Preacher glanced constantly behind them, his gaze resting long on the files of men and horses. At last, he decided to confide in Three Sleeps.

"D'you feel it, too? I got me a strong sensation that something is mighty wrong."

Three Sleeps Norris showed indifference. "I don't follow you."

"I don't know exactly how, but these greenhorn soldier-boys—er, excuse me—Dragoons have done messed up the works somethin' powerful."

"We'll find out eventually." Three Sleeps stifled a yawn, then swatted at a huge horsefly that had lined up an enticing spot on the neck of his horse.

Preacher cut his eyes to the column again. "I certain sure hope it's soon enough."

* * *

"Sure, an' what do you mean they were left behind, Hadley?!" roared BSM Muldoon.

Preacher and his companions turned to see what caused the outburst. Slanted backward from the glowering, red face of the Battalion Sergeant Major, who leaned over him, the Quartermaster Sergeant, Hadley, gulped hard before answering. "That's what happened, Sergeant Major. Four of my teamsters reported to sick call this morning and there was no one to drive the wagons."

"An', why wasn't I told of this?"

"Y-You were. I reported four men confined in the infirmary."

BSM Muldoon poked a thick finger into Hadley's chest to emphasize each word. "But . . . you . . . didn't . . . tell . . . me . . . four . . . wagons . . . didn't . . . have . . . drivers!"

Sergeant Hadley looked like he was about to be sick all over his shiny boots. "I . . . I thought you'd figure that out for yourself, Sergeant Major."

"Yer flirtin' with insubordination, Hadley, b'God ye are. "An', Lord love us, we'll have to send men back to recover them." He spun on one heel. "You there: Collins, Masters, Pickerel and Sawyer. Can you drive a wagon?"

"Yes, Sergeant Major!" they chorused.

"Then mount up and ride like hell back to the barracks. Ye'll find four of our supply wagons there. Bring them up with the column right quickly, lads."

"What about evening chow, Sergeant Major?" Corporal Collins asked.

"Take food enough with ye for two or three meals."

Sergeant Hadley tugged urgently at Muldoon's sleeve. "Bu-but they're not teamsters."

"Sure an' I don't give a damn if they're old-maid schoolteachers. We need those supplies."

Preacher turned away in disgust. "Here we are; haven't made fifteen miles the first day and we have lost half of the supplies. At this rate, we'll make the North Platte come December."

* * *

Far from the foothills of the Ozark Mountains in Missouri, at a large, well-tended trading post on the North Platte River, Quinton Praeger sat at a table with his coconspirators and their chief henchman, Blake Soures. All four men lapsed into silence when a large platter of roasted bison hump arrived at their table.

They ate heartily, pleasurably chewing slabs of the layered meat and fat along with boiled turnips and onions, squash and chili peppers, all washed down with tankards of beer. Not until the last morsel disappeared did Praeger bring up business.

"Everything is going according to schedule. The money is starting to roll in from back East. The Dragoons are to have left Jefferson Barracks yesterday." He paused and wiped greasy lips with a soiled napkin. "We should have us a tidy little Indian war before too long."

Always a blunt, direct man, Blake Soures spoke his mind. "Exactly what is behind this plan to stir up the Indians? That is, after all, a dangerous thing to do."

Morton Gross looked amused. "How is that, Mr. Soures?"

"A feller can be their friend and ally one day, an' the next they'll lift his hair. They're . . . changeable, moody."

"The idea is to get rid of them once and for all," Praeger explained patiently. "And the best way to do that is to get an Indian war started. We can count on the Indians doing their part through Iron Shirt. He has tremendous influence among the Blackfoot, and now with the Cheyenne. His power grows daily."

Soures frowned. "That's the part I don't like, what I'm tryin' to warn you about. I've got seventeen good men ridin' with me. Then there's you three. Twenty-two guns don't amount to a fart in a windstorm if Iron Shirt decides he don't need us anymore."

Aaron Reiker gave Blake Soures a condescending smirk. "I think you are overestimating his capacity for duplicity. We provide him with rifles and ammunition and we brought him out of obscurity and made him famous. No, friend Soures, we can trust Iron Shirt."

"But why get rid of the Injuns at all? That's what I want to know."

Morton Gross answered, his voice sugary, as though talking to a dolt. "The East is getting crowded. The land these Indians occupy will be valuable in any westward expansion. Certain high-placed interests in Washington City have a desire to lay claim to that ground. At least, once the savages have been eliminated."

Soures produced an expression of concern. "But, ain't it Injuns' land?"

Praeger turned a condescending gaze on their chief gunman. "Our friends in Washington City are paying exceedingly well to see that it no longer is. Well enough to assuage any conscience."

Soures frowned. "What's that mean, ass—assuage?"

"To pacify, Mr. Soures, to calm."

None of the conspirators mentioned the presence of gold in the mountains of Montana. Instead, they directed him to an assignment as backup to the men sent to stop Preacher.

"There is only one impediment, one man who might be able to prevent an all out war of extermination," Praeger pressed on. "His name is Preacher, and he is known and respected by both sides. Only, if all went well, he should be out of the picture by now. If he is not, it will be your job to remove him."

True to Preacher's prediction, a whole lot was wrong with the expedition. Trouble began before the troops got out of Missouri. After the four supply wagons joined the column, they made better time. A lot of good that did them.

BSM Muldoon came to Preacher one evening in camp. A harried-looking Dragoon had just ridden in on a lathered horse. He must have galloped the animal for a good ways. What he revealed, sent Muldoon to seek help from the mountain men.

Now Muldoon stood contemplating the three rugged guides, his bristly red hair and florid complexion making a torch of his head. "Gentlemen, I come to you with a . . . wee problem, it is. Now mind, I could send some of me sergeants to deal with this. But then it would become an official matter, it would."

Preacher laughed softly. "Spit it out, man."

"The thing is, it is, that some of the lads have taken it to mind to slip off from our encampment and indulge themselves in some spirituous waters." Muldoon's perpetually rosy nose gave testament to his own fondness for such diversions. "In the process, so's to speak, they have got themselves afoul of some of the local citizens." He paused and cleared his throat, as though the words bore thorns. "The fact of the matter is, there's one hell of a fine brawl goin' on between some eight Dragoons and some sawyers from a nearby mill, that's what."

"And you would appreciate some small gesture of aid from the three of us?" Preacher got to the point.

"Sure an' it would avoid the messiness of a court-martial and the need for punishment."

Preacher gave him a hard eye. "We'd not be taking sides. We'll bust anyone who gets in our way."

"It's skinnin' yer knuckles on all comers, is it?" Muldoon clapped his hands together in approval. "Then, so be it. I'll be accompanyin' ye buckos. Though not in an official capacity. Thing is, we don't need any floggin's before we get beyond civilization. That's how I see it."

" 'Floggings'?" Preacher echoed.

"Aye. That's the usual for such infractions. Six of yer best, laid on with a will."

A thunderous frown creased Preacher's brow. "By damn, I'll not be party to any of that."

"So it's the four of us, is it?"

Preacher gave a curt nod. "Right, Muldoon. We'll head out now."

Screams, curses, and the crash of furniture could be heard from two hundred yards off when Preacher and the cleanup squad reached the tavern. They trotted up to the tie rail outside and looped reins over the crossbar. Preacher looked up at a particularly loud, tinkling crash and saw a man fly bodily out through a window. He grunted and cut his eyes to take in the others.

"Looks like we have a lot of work on our hands."

Three Sleeps nodded enthusiastically. "Yer not lyin' there, Preacher."

With determination, the four men stalked to the door. It flew open in their faces and two men, wrapped in a mutual bear hug stumbled out. Being nearest, Preacher reached out and grabbed both miscreants by the hair and slammed their heads together. They went down like heart-shot elk. BSM Muldoon bent and separated the Dragoon from the lumberman and dragged him to the hitch rack. The three mountain men entered the establishment.

It had been a nicely appointed place, Preacher noted, before the fight began. Now splintered tables and chairs floated like driftwood in a tidal pool of beer which had come from a ruptured hogshead. There had once been a mirror behind the bar. It lay in diamond spears of brightness amid overturned bottles and small casks. One of the ceiling supports had been snapped in two, the roof sagged dangerously above it. Showing even worse signs of wear, eight men remained on their feet, flinging fists with wild abandon.

One of those went down as the mountain men gained the doorway. Preacher stepped through and took the knuckles of a huge sawyer at the under edge of his right eye.

"Aw, hell, now it's the other one," he grumbled.

Then he set his feet and pile-drivered a steady rain of

punches to the sturdy frame of the sandy-haired man who had hit him. It seemed all too easy to Preacher. The man went down and was out at the first pummeling Preacher gave him. Three Sleeps and Antoine waded in behind him and the three started picking Dragoons off their opponents and hauling them toward the door.

"Take yer damn hands off me," one snarled.

Three Sleeps released the complaining soldier and raised both open hands, in a gesture of surrender. "All right, all right." Then he swiftly closed his right hand into a fist and popped the Dragoon flush in the mouth.

With all the rolling muscle of his powerful shoulders behind it, the blow decisively felled the private. His boot heels bounced off the rough boards of the floor. Three Sleeps grabbed him by the collar and dragged him out into the dooryard. Then, with a grin, he turned about and went back for more.

"By Jaazas, those mountain fellers sure love a fight. They must be Irish," Muldoon said to the unconscious Dragoon. Then he added the young soldier to the stack growing by the tie rail.

Preacher hurled another protesting Dragoon out the door and Muldoon saw the spitting, cursing lout stumble toward him, then quickly corrected that with a hard left to the jaw.

A furious bellow came from the mill workers inside the tavern. "You let us at those soldier-boys. We'll tear them limb from limb."

Preacher's voice sounded. "Calm down. We're takin' 'em all back where they belong."

His words were followed by the loud click of a hammer being cocked and the sharp report of a single-barreled pistol.

10

Following instinct and training, the remaining Dragoons dropped to the floor the instant the shot went off. Preacher and his companions did not. Antoine reached down and felt a hot, burning gouge along his ribs that oozed blood. That made both sides. Damn, he'd be sorer than a fresh-gelded hound dog for more than a month. He reached for one of his double-barreled pistols, but Preacher beat him to the draw.

A big Walker Colt appeared in Preacher's hand and the hammer dropped on a percussion cap. The fat ball sped across the short distance and pinwheeled the belligerent sawyer in the breastbone. "Yer lucky to be alive, Antoine. He was a lousy shot."

None of the Missouri lumbermen had ever seen a revolving pistol before. They stared at it in wonder. One, who had gone for the butt of a small pocket pistol, let go of it with all the speed of a cat making contact with a cookstove. Preacher cocked the weapon and put a menacing look on his face.

"Unless any of you is eager to argue with my friend, Mr. Walker here, I'd advise you forget all about tearing anyone limb from limb."

"You kilt Tucker Blake," accused one of the less intimidated mill workers.

"Didn't know his name. That don't matter. What matters is, your Mr. Blake drew first. What's more, he shot a friend of mine. I don't take kindly to that. Though I will say I'm sorry your friend is dead."

Unmollified, the talker challenged. "You won't get away with this. We'll get the sheriff on you."

"It was self-defense, any fool can see that."

Three Sleeps Norris stepped up and touched Preacher on the arm. "Not any Missouri fool, Preacher," he said tightly. "I suggest we send for the sheriff ourselves and let him hear both sides of the story."

Preacher eyed the mouthy sawyer. "How far off is your sheriff?"

"He's right here," came a hard voice from the doorway. "I'd put that smoke-pole up if I was you."

The man who entered the tavern was a size with Preacher, though he carried authority and power with him enough to make him ten feet tall. "Bill Parker." He introduced himself as he gave the corpse a casual glance. "What happened here?"

All of the lumber company men began to speak at once. The one who had challenged Preacher overrode his friends. "This stranger came through the door, bold as brass, and shot down Tucker Blake in cold blood."

"Yeah, that's right. That's what he did, all right." A chorus of agreement.

Shrewd enough not to be deceived by men whose thick noggins he had thumped more than once, Sheriff Parker pursed his lips, eyed the scene again and then spoke. "If that's the case, George, what accounts for the pistol in Tucker's hand?"

Stunned at having his version disputed, and by a fellow Missourian at that, George gaped a moment before he could find new words to butter his lie. "He . . . uh . . . one of his friends put it there. Ain't that right, boys?"

Sheriff Parker turned and eyed Three Sleeps and Antoine. "Was that before or after this feller got his ribs skinned?" He whirled back to face the sawmill men. "My maw didn't raise any stupid sons. What do you take me for? That's Tucker's pistol, I've had to take it off him enough times when he got drunked up. I was on my way here when I heard the shots. Kylie Burks came by to tell me there was a big fight goin' betwixt you boys and some soldiers. I'd have been in here sooner if I hadn't stopped to have a word with the sergeant out there."

"That's Sergeant Major, if ye please, Sheriff. Battalion Sergeant Major Muldoon," said that worthy from the doorway. "Now, if ye don't mind I'll be takin' my lads and our brave frontier guides back to our camp."

Sheriff Bill Parker made a mock bow. "Go right ahead, Sergeant Major Muldoon." Then, to Antoine, "I'd get that patched up right quick. Might fester."

Antoine cocked an eyebrow. "Thank you for good advice, Sheriff."

Outside, Muldoon surveyed the subdued but conscious, and the unconscious Dragoons. "Thank the Virgin an' all the saints, their horses are right at hand. Be a thankless task rousin' them all to walk that far."

"We'll lend a hand getting them across their mounts," Preacher offered.

"That won't be necessary. There's enough of them with their wits about them to do that."

Not to be denied the last word, mouthy George stood in the doorway and shouted to them. "If I was any of you, I'd get me as far and as fast out of Missouri as I could. We've got friends."

No sooner had the errant Dragoons been returned to the camp near Sedalia than Lieutenant Colonel Danvers summoned the necessary members for a drumhead court-martial.

Having been assured that he had acquired a second shiner and more sore ribs for the purpose of avoiding this very event, Preacher had his curiosity piqued. He went along to witness. Naturally, his companions accompanied him.

Preacher could not believe the abrupt nature of the proceeding. All eight of the disobedient Dragoons were hauled before a lantern-lighted barrel head, over which Danvers presided. He read off a list of charges, including desertion, absent without leave, public drunkenness and inciting to riot. He did not ask how the accused pleaded.

"Now, as regards Corporal Evers, and Privates Fields, Smith and O'Banyon, the charges of desertion and absent without leave are dismissed. On the counts of public drunkenness and inciting to riot, the above-named soldiers are fined two-thirds of a month's pay for three months. Now, Privates Babcock, Upton, Venner and Killeen, you are sentenced to be stretched upon a wagon wheel and given six strokes of the lash."

"Are ye not givin' them a chance to plead their case, Colonel, sor?" BSM Muldoon burst out, unable to bridle his umbrage.

"Contain yourself, Sergeant Major," Danvers said in an aside.

"But, Colonel, sor . . . it's . . ."

Lieutenant Colonel Danvers snapped at him in black humor. "Would you like to join them at the grate?"

Captain Dreiling leaned close to Lieutenant Colonel Danvers and whispered in his ear. "Regulations, Colonel. You are always saying that. And in this case, regulations will not allow you to flog the Battalion Sergeant Major without a full general court-martial."

Lieutenant Colonel Danvers swelled and seemed ready to burst, then sighed until deflated. "Yes . . . yes, you are right, as usual, Captain. Much to my regret, I might add. He should never have gone after those fools." Then back in his judicial role, "Sentence to be carried out at once."

Although outraged by the barbarity of the punishment, Preacher remained to watch it carried out. Afterward, he fetched a jug from a parfleche on his packhorse and, regulations be damned, got riproaring drunk along with his friends and BSM Muldoon.

Two wagons had broken down that day. Eve Billings was beginning to have second thoughts. After the past three days of soul-searching, she had made up her mind to go to Isaac Warner, who had been elected captain for their attempt at crossing the basin. She put aside the last of the dishes from supper and walked reluctantly to his wagon. Eve had hardly begun when Warner interrupted her.

"I have an idea what it is you want to say. And I want some of the other men to be here to hear it." He gave a wave of one arm to Damion Brewster to summon him from his family cookfire a third of the way around the circle of wagons. When the youth arrived, Warner gave him curt orders.

In short time, Renard Labette and Hiram Tate ambled up. They were immediately joined by Gus Beecher and Cecil Brewster. Tate gave a polite nod to Eve and asked, "What's up, Isaac?"

"The Widow Billings here has something she wants to tell us. Now, go ahead, don't be shy," he prodded Eve.

Cheeks crimson and hot from his patronizing manner, Eve glanced at each man in turn. "You know about the breakdowns. Not only those today, the others. They are taking a heavy toll."

Warner jutted his chin defiantly. "Yep. Said that was what would happen. Go on."

"Also, game and water are growing scarce again. I feel . . . it seems to me the time has come to examine our decision to try making a crossing."

"What you're gettin' at is?" prompted Warner.

Eve wanted to shout. Out of pure spite this pompous man

was forcing her to say every bitter word. Nervously she cleared her throat. "Those of us who favored the attempt had no idea how strenuous it would be. It is perhaps time to consider the possibility of turning around and following the stakes to the edge of the basin and then going beyond to fresh water and plentiful game." There, she had said it and they could smirk all they wanted.

To her utter frustration the same men who had stubbornly insisted upon that course of action from the outset now objected to the idea with perfectly straight faces.

"I say it's the wrong thing to do," Isaac Warner snapped.

"Yes. We've come this far, there can't be much more like this," Gus Beecher added with a taunting smirk.

Eve's torment and humiliation lasted a long time, while the men wrangled over what should be done. Her patience at last exhausted by their circular reasoning, Eve slipped away. Dredging up new hope, she went to seek out the wives. The first was Hattie Honeycutt, to whom Eve recited what she had pointed out to the men.

"We have to make them see reason," she summed up to Mrs. Honeycutt. "There has to be a way."

"But we're mere women. Our menfolk have total sway over us."

An idea forming, Eve countered quickly. "Not in all things."

"Name me one," came the challenge.

Eve leaned forward and whispered in Hattie Honeycutt's ear.

Eyes wide and mouth in an O of astonishment, the portly woman sputtered a while before regaining her tongue. "That would never work. Why, they would just . . . just . . ."

"No they wouldn't, not if we all stuck to it. And not if we slept with a loaded gun at hand."

"My word. It's such a strange idea."

Eve went from wife to wife, explaining their womanly rebellion. Whenever she was told it could not possibly work, she smiled enigmatically and dropped the final gem of her argument.

"It has worked before. It happened back in ancient times. There was this woman named Lysistrata . . ."

After that it became easy. One by one the women approached their husbands and whispered in their ears.

"You'll what?" bellowed Isaac Warner. His wife told him again.

Several other men repeated Isaac's shocked response on being informed, only to be assured that their wives meant what they said. Visibly shaken, by nooning the next day, they began to admit that maybe that pushy woman, the Widow Billings, might be right for once. If they did return to the foothills, they would have graze for the livestock, fresh water and a chance to hunt for their food.

Independence, which they had skirted on the way to Jefferson Barracks, teemed with people. Droves of wagons appeared to be bound for destinations at every point of the compass. Men, women and a surprising number of children swarmed the streets, bustled in and out of stores and shops. Few of them took time to stop and stare at the column of Dragoons who rode their mounts at a walk down the main street to the distant docks. Only the night before had Preacher learned that he and his companions were in for a rare treat.

Lieutenant Colonel Danvers had summoned Preacher to his tent, yet he would not directly meet the eyes of the mountain man. "Due to the delays," Danvers began, clearing his throat frequently, his embarrassment clear in his posture, "I have decided that we shall negotiate this portion of our journey by riverboat. It will cut a month off our travel time."

Hiding his surprise and pleasure, Preacher spoke sincerely. "That's mighty smart thinkin', Colonel. I'd never have come up with it myself, what with bein' used to crossin' the mountains by horse or shanks' mare."

"No . . . no, I suppose not. Advise your assistants and be prepared to board tomorrow when we reach Independence."

Now they did just that. Two by two, the Dragoon horses went aboard a livestock barge, to be towed by the rearmost of six steam packets requisitioned by Lieutenant Colonel Danvers. They had been paid for by voucher drawn on the Department of the Army. Danvers, who oversaw the operation from beside Preacher, turned to the mountain man.

"Due to your positions as scouts, you hold ranks equivalent to a captain's and to lieutenants'. Therefore you will be billeted aboard the lead vessel with myself and the other officers." His expression told how little he liked that.

Preacher beamed with insincerity. "That's plum considerate of you, Colonel."

Danvers's expression became pinched. "It is not out of consideration, believe me. It's—"

Preacher stifled a guffaw. "Yeah, I know. It's *regulations*."

"Well put," Danvers replied tightly.

"It'll be a pleasure for all, I'm sure," Preacher concluded as he turned away.

Steam Packet *Prairie Spirit* shrilled a lively blast on its tall, brass whistle and pulled away from the dock in Independence at three-thirty that afternoon. On board were the battalion commander, his staff, the captains commanding the four squadrons and the three scouts. Also one company of Dragoons. The blunt prow nudged into the Missouri River's brown water and began to struggle to overcome the current to make way upsteam. The huge side-mounted paddle wheels thrashed the water and sent off a fine mist of spray. Rainbows formed in a nimbus around each churning wheel.

More steam-whistle blasts and then everything began to settle down. The fifteen civilian passengers left the rail and went to their staterooms to open trunks and prepare clothing for dinner. Several of the men made their way to the Gentlemen's Salon. Preacher and his companions located their accommodations and dumped their belongings in the corners.

Preacher confided in his friends. "I don't know if I'm gonna like this. Outside of the time it will save, of course."

"Why is that, Preacher?" Antoine inquired.

Preacher studied his moccasin toes. Embarrassment pinked his cheeks. "I've never felt entirely comfortable on the water. Nothin' I can put a finger on, but it jist don't seem . . . natural. Water's for fishes and beaver."

"What about small boys?" asked Three Sleeps. "Didn't you like to swim when you were young?"

Preacher looked up at them. "Tell you the truth, I was over twelve an' livin' with the Cheyenne before I learned how to swim right proper like. Up to then, I jist paddled around like a spaniel after ducks. An' not likin' it much, either." He sighed. "It's funny. I put money in Mr. Fulton's steamboat works, an' this is only the third time I ever rid one of the contraptions."

Antoine turned an anxious face to Preacher. "I have heard that the boilers blow up sometimes."

Preacher nodded, which did little to allay Antoine's worry. "That they do. Usual it's because the stokers overfill the fireboxes or the metal is old."

"How does one tell if the metal is old?"

"Antoine, my friend, I don't know. I jist have to hope the captain and the engineer have some idea."

They changed into cloth suits and boots and took dinner at seven o'clock, an hour before the sun went down. That only served to amplify Preacher's uneasiness. The truth that Preacher would not admit to was that prolonged travel over water made his stomach queasy. Although he did not suffer dizziness and nausea, it did make him develop gas. Preacher soon found himself out on the foredeck, a hand gently pressing his belly.

He was still there, the rumbles somewhat subsided, when a conversation among three fellow travelers advised him that there were card games in the Gentlemen's Salon. Despite his precarious internal state, the lure of the pasteboards drew him like a dead critter attracted flies.

After sitting in for an hour, Preacher's situation made it understandable to a reasonable person that he grew increasingly edgy when an oily fellow with a remarkable deck of cards made deep dents in his "government money," paid in advance for services rendered.

Beauregard Calhoon, still slim and dapper, with a thin, pencil line of a mustache and manicured fingernails, gave a shark's grin as he raked in yet another pot. He laid a particularly offensive sneer on Preacher, who had lost steadily. Preacher allowed as how he must keep an eye on Calhoon and discover the source of his unusual luck.

"Y'all seem to be havin' a terrible run of luck," the fashionably overdressed Calhoon observed to those at the table. "I learned to court the lady at a tender age an' I never fail to pay her homage."

Preacher's words had a coating of ice. " 'Pears to me that her favors have been phe-nom-inal."

Calhoon gave Preacher a fishy eye. After three more hands, two of which were won by Calhoon, Preacher deliberately discarded an ace of clubs during the next, which he discreetly creased with a thumbnail. Sure enough, Calhoon won again. His full house of aces and tens contained the ace of clubs.

Before Calhoon could pick up the hand with which he had won, Preacher came to his boots, leaned across the table and clamped a hard hand over Calhoon's wrist. His composure broken, despite his oily, black hair neatly parted in the middle and his fancy, shiny boots, the gambler could only splutter.

"See here, there's nothing to be gained by this sort of conduct. Release me, my man."

"I ain't yer man, nor any other's. I find it right interesting you won that hand with the ace of clubs. 'Special since I discarded that same card in the draw."

"You can't prove that," Calhoon gulped.

"Oh, yes, I can. You see, gents," he addressed the entire table. "I took the trouble to crease that card with a thumbnail before I dropped it on the table. By that time I had got myself the idee that this particular deck had a special set of marks Calhoon, here, can read."

Preacher squeezed tighter as Calhoon began to squirm. It caused the voice of the tinhorn gambler to rise two octaves. "I must protest. You'll not find a crease on that card, suh."

Preacher shook his head. "Nope, I don't reckon I will. But, I am willin' to bet I'll find the crimped one up your sleeve, or in a vest pocket. Somewhere anyway. You saw what I was gettin' rid of an' couldn't resist the urge to put another one into your hand to improve it."

"Are you calling me a cheat, suh?"

Preacher's eyes bored deeply into those of Calhoon, while his free hand delved into the sleeve of the fancy suit Calhoon wore. Deftly he produced the card in question. "That's exactly what I'm sayin'."

"Then, I demand immediate satisfaction." With these words, Beauregard Calhoon thrust his left hand under the wing of his coat and came out with a small, .36-caliber, double-barreled pocket pistol.

11

Preacher responded with the speed of a puma. His open hand, still holding the evidence, flashed across his body. Preacher's shoulder rolled when he made powerful, backhand contact with the exposed cheek of Calhoon. The impact could have been a thunderclap. Beauregard Calhoon shot back from the table, spun slightly and reeled drunkenly toward the bar. At the last moment, before he made violent impact, he remembered the pistol in his hand.

Fighting to control the movement of his body, Beauregard swung the small .28-caliber, four-shot, revolving-barrel pistol to bear on Preacher. One hammer fell on a cap. A thin stream of smoke spurted from the nipple an instant before detonation of the small powder charge. Several gentlemen gasped as the little ball made a loud *thock!* when it struck the wide, thick, bull bison-hide belt Preacher wore around his middle. Immediately Beauregard rotated the barrels and fired again. And hit Preacher again.

Concussion from the two slugs bulged Preacher's eyes and stabbing pain doubled him over. Air shot from his open mouth. For a long, spellbound moment, no one moved. Then

Preacher straightened shakily, erased the agony-drawn lines from his face, and extended his right arm. The hand at the end held a Walker Colt, its hammer full back and ready to drop. This gun Preacher pointed steadily at the center of Calhoon's chest. He fought for air and, at last, spoke in sepulchral tones.

"You done played yer last hand."

Stunned by the incredible staying power of his target, Beauregard Calhoon only then recovered enough of his wits to turn, cock and aim the third barrel. This time, Preacher beat him to the mark.

Flame lanced from the muzzle of the .44 Colt, as it bucked and snorted in Preacher's hand. The round, two-hundred-grain ball sped across the small distance to the center of the exposed chest and smashed bone and tissue with destructive force. Flattened slightly now, it ploughed a wide furrow through the aorta, only slightly off center, and into back loin muscle, before blasting one of Beauregard's vertebrae into fragments.

Reflex jerked the trigger of the pistol in Calhoon's hand. The woefully underpowered ball shattered the glass chimney of a wall-mounted lamp and rang musically off the inside of its brass shade. Gleaming shards tinkled to the deck in the silence that followed. A thick layer of powder smoke undulated in the space between Preacher and the dead cheat. Slowly, Preacher reached down and plucked one of the little balls from the thick leather of his belt. A worried player hurried up to him.

"Neither one got all the way through," Preacher informed him. "But I'm gonna be sore as hell for a week. Awful bruise, you can bet."

Awed, the well-dressed man spoke for everyone in the salon. "You've been saved by a miracle."

Preacher shook his head. "Nope. Buffalo-hide belt. That little popgun didn't have a chance."

Another of the men who had been at the table spoke from where he crouched beside Beauregard. "He's dead."

"I didn't aim to only tickle him some."

A cluster of onlookers at the doorway gave room for the first officer to enter, buttoning his jacket as he crossed the room. "Someone tell me what happened?" he commanded. "Oh, and put away that revolver."

Preacher complied while the man at his side made explanation. "I'm Norton Babbott, Babbott Bobbin Company. This gentleman caught a cheat in our game. The scoundrel pulled a gun on him. Shot him twice. The rest you can see for yourself."

"I know this man," the first officer declared. "It's Beauregard Calhoon. We've had complaints about him before." He paused, cut his eyes to Preacher. "You're a brave man to have faced him down . . . or a fool."

Preacher winced and unconsciously touched his aching middle lightly. "Right now I feel more the fool."

"It happened as Mr. Babbott said?"

Preacher shrugged. "More or less."

"How did you manage to detect him cheating?"

"I spend as much time watching the players as I do the cards in a game. Calhoon had a marked deck and he used hold-out cards, too."

Turning to look at Calhoon, the first officer spoke over his shoulder to Preacher. "I'll explain to the captain. He may want to speak with you. You're not planning to disembark soon, are you?"

"Nope. Not until I get these baby soldiers to the upper North Platte."

"And your name, sir?"

"I'm the one they call Preacher."

Eyebrows rose. "So that's why you're standing and he's not. Yes, I see, now. Very well, Preacher, from here on, it's merely a formality."

* * *

Far up the North Platte River, after an uneventful passage, the squadron of Dragoons disembarked. While the long, tedious process of unloading the horses, wagons and equipment progressed, Preacher consulted with the captain and river pilot. The latter showed Preacher a map of the river's course. With a stubby finger he pointed out their present location. Preacher nodded with satisfaction.

"This is where we are now. It's not much of a town, called North Platte. End of the line this time of year. I reckon you'll be heading northwest, through the small settlement of Scottsbluff. Nice folks there. Last trip, we brought them five ton of flour in barrels. You can resupply there without any problem."

Preacher studied the sparse details on the map. "Don't see why you can't get on up there. The map shows the river runnin' all the way into the Wyoming country."

"Too shallow. Why, by August, most of the river west of here will be dried up into a series of mudholes connected by a foot-wide trickle. No, sir, this will be our last run this far. Next trip will be no farther than the town of Grand Island. There's two hundred folk livin' there now. Makes for profitable hauling when the river's up."

Preacher matched the map's representations to images in his mind. They would still have close to two weeks travel to reach the part of the Bighorn Mountains Danvers had selected for his fort. He thanked the river men for their assistance and strode off onto the dock.

A small warehouse fronted the river at North Platte. In its tiny office, Preacher approached the factor. A portly, baldheaded man with an open, friendly face and jolly manner, the manager greeted Preacher affably.

"You came with the soldiers?" he inquired.

"That I did. Anything goin' on in these parts that I should know about?"

"Nothin' much. Except that the Pawnee have been kicking up their heels a mite."

"Do tell. Never could abide nor trust a Pawnee. Go on, if you please."

"They've made periodic attacks on the trail. Burned a small settlement west of here. Scared hell outta the folks in Scottsbluff. Matter of fact, they did a good bit of scarin' around here."

"When's the last time they hit?"

In an unconscious gesture left over from when there was something to scratch, the factor rubbed fingertips on his bald pate. "About a week ago. Least, that's the last we've heard of here in North Platte."

Preacher split his darkly tanned face with a grin. "That sounds good. Don't imagine they'd be eager to take on a squadron of Dragoons."

"I wouldn't say so. You be settin' up a fort around here by any chance?"

"Nope. We're headed way northwest."

"What? The whole frontier is on the verge of a massive uprising and those idiots in Washington City send troops clear the hell and gone into where?"

Preacher answered him, his voice somber. "Northeast corner of the Wyoming country. Someone's got a wild idea that a fort out in the middle of nowhere, supported by nothing, will scare the breechcloths off the Injuns."

"You ask me, mister, a person has to be certified to have no brains at all to qualify to be a politician. I mean them all, an' I can say that 'cause I'm neither Whig nor Democrat."

Preacher clapped a big hand on the factor's shoulder, and winced at the pain in his bruised belly. "I have to agree with you there, friend. What else can you tell me?"

"There's talk flyin' around about some hotshot medicine man amongst the Blackfoot talkin' a holy war against us whites. Though I doubt you need to be told that. Part of the reason they're puttin' that fort out there, ain't it?" He gave Preacher a conspiratorial wink.

Preacher replied in kind and added, "Government secrets. Ask our illustrious squadron leader, he'll tell you it's to show the flag to the Sioux and Cheyenne. Whatever that means."

They jawed over other matters for a while and then Preacher departed to rejoin the column of Dragoons. He found them on the edge of the tiny village of North Platte. As usual, Lieutenant Colonel Danvers was in a foul mood.

"I have heard that the Pawnee are raiding in this area."

Preacher cocked his head to one side. "I hear the same, Colonel. We'll likely find evidence of their prowlin' before long."

"Such as what?"

Studying the officer closely, Preacher drawled an answer. "Oh, broke arrows, burned buildings and wagons, bones. The usual Injun leavings."

"Would they attack us, do you think?"

Preacher raised an eyebrow. "Not unless they've plum taken leave of their senses. We're too many and we have that little cannon."

Not entirely convinced, Danvers took on a belligerent posture. "I'll remind you of that in the event the need arises. For now, head out and scout ahead of our line of march." Danvers emphasized his order with a crisp snap of his riding crop.

"I'm sure you will," Preacher muttered, stung by the implied lack of confidence.

"What's that?" snapped Danvers.

"I said, I'll get the long view from the top of that hill." With that he wheeled Tarnation and sprinted off, leaving the colonel with an open mouth.

"Forty miles a day on beans and hay," turned out to be more than a boast Preacher soon discovered. The first day on

the trail, the Dragoon squadron made twenty-five of that. Even burdened down with eight huge freight wagons and a field piece, the column covered fifteen miles by midday. They also found the first sign of Pawnee raids.

A well-established trail paralleled the North Platte River, which some were already beginning to call the Oregon Trail. It being wide enough at this point, Preacher relaxed his double-file formation rule and let the troops move along four abreast. In a hidden defile, which kept them from sight on the rolling prairie, Preacher and Three Sleeps came upon the blackened remains of three wagons, along with the bones of the owners.

"Look over here, Preacher," Three Sleeps called to his friend. "Arrow shafts. Most broken, some with the feathers burned. They've had the heads removed."

"Thrifty folks, those Pawnee," opined Preacher.

He studied the ground a while. He estimated the attack to have happened at least a week ago. With that established, Preacher remounted and rode back to report to Lieutenant Colonel Danvers.

The colonel heard of the attack with mounting fury. "We have a treaty with the Pawnee," he exploded. "It has been in force for twenty years. Their chiefs should have stopped this outrage."

Patiently Preacher explained. "Among the Injuns, the chiefs have no absolute power. They ain't rulers, Colonel. They lead, give advice, represent the tribe or band with others. An' yes, make treaties. But the folks they represent don't have to obey them or hold to any agreement made in their name by the chiefs."

"Why . . . why, that's preposterous. What sort of leadership does that represent? The Army would get nothing at all done if the troops were not required to do as I order them."

"There might be somethin' good in that," Preacher observed in a muttered aside.

"What did you say?" demanded Danvers.

"I said, there's more to it than that. Most likely the chiefs who signed that treaty are dead now or replaced by someone else the folks are more willing to follow. And so, the people are free to decide whether or not to continue to honor the treaty."

"But they can't do that!"

Preacher could no longer stifle the guffaw that climbed his throat in a rush. "Oh, but they can and do, Colonel. They have always followed their way—it's their law, for want of a better word."

Colonel Danvers made it clear that he was unimpressed and definitely not amused. He addressed Preacher with dismissive authority. "We'll push on. The scene of this massacre would be too depressing a place to camp."

Hump Jaspar had survived the fury of the mountain men by the simple expedient of running like the devil was after him when the ambush failed. He had headed north, robbing folks occasionally to build up a stake. When he reached the North Platte, after running three horses to the ground under him, he took passage on a riverboat for as far as it would take him. Then he started out West on horseback.

Jaspar stopped in his quest only long enough to inquire at trading posts about Praeger and his partners. He had to find them. No matter that the news he brought would probably send them up like July Fourth rockets, he knew he might receive some benefit from it.

Hump had never heard of the old tradition of kings killing the bearers of bad news. So, when he found Branson Naylor, one of his friends who had joined the gang run by Blake Soures, at a trading post far up the Platte, he learned that Praeger could be found in a Blackfoot camp not far from the Bighorn Mountains and rode there with all speed. Only to face the fury of Quinton Praeger.

"You got away? Only you? How many men did you say sided with Preacher?"

"Two." The smallness of his voice startled Hump Jaspar.

"Impossible! Three men killed twenty-five?"

"Yeah. But it was in two fights."

Sarcasm enveloped Praeger's words. "Only two fights? Only two? Why in hell did it take more than one to finish off three men?"

"The first fight wasn't against Preacher."

"Then kindly tell me about its purpose?"

"We . . . ah . . . we decided to rob this train of freight wagons."

Quinton Praeger went white. "In the name of all that's holy, what in hell possessed you to do that?"

"We . . . thought we'd make some quick money."

Praeger could not suppress the shudder that came from a foretaste of doom. "I see. Yes, I really do. But you said you fought Preacher there?"

"Yes, sir. He and these two fellers came along and broke up our attack on the wagons. Only at the time we did not know it was him."

Eyebrows arched, Praeger ran a finger along the knife scar on his left cheek. His voice purred with feigned reasonableness. "That explains it all. And the next time you met, he finished off all the rest, right?"

Hump Jaspar forced an expression of wide-eyed innocence. "Yes, sir. All except me."

"Thank you, Mr. Jaspar. Now that everything is in a shambles around my feet, I feel constrained to correct the one error Preacher made."

Puzzled, Hump Jaspar asked a fateful question. "Uh, what's that, Mr. Praeger?"

Praeger drew a compact .60-caliber, Miquelet Spanish pistol from under his coat and cocked the hammer. "Killing you," he replied a moment before he squeezed the trigger and shot Jaspar through the heart.

* * *

Praeger was still furious when he reached the council lodge. Iron Shirt showed his usual irritation at being summoned forth. He stood with arms folded over his chest, face black and in a glower.

"I was discussing important matters. What is it you want? We hear soldiers are coming. Is this true?"

"Yes. They are all a part of the plan. Right now I must speak with you and the war chiefs. It is an important issue."

"We will meet with you when we are ready."

Anger flared again in Praeger's chest. "Listen to me. I made you what you are. I gave you that iron shirt. I made up the ritual you use. Without me, you are nothing. When I want a meeting you will see that it happens. Is that clear?"

Iron Shirt's lips curled in contempt. "White man, you are a flea trying to bite a bull bison. When we are ready to listen, we will send for you." He turned on the heel of one moccasin and stomped back inside the lodge.

White, shaking with rage now, Quinton Praeger fought back a hot burst of profanity. Slowly he realized that his time with Iron Shirt had come near the end. Every day, every hour, had to be balanced with utmost care. Starting with regaining the dependency of Iron Shirt, he acknowledged. So, he smiled and waited.

Three hours went by before a young warrior came to summon him to the council. When he entered and went through the formalities, Praeger quickly explained the situation with Preacher. He concluded with a suggestion that when Preacher arrived with the squadron of Dragoons, the Blackfoot kill him themselves. To their credit, Quinton admitted, the war chiefs listened politely and with interest. Then they began to respond.

To his surprise, Praeger soon began to understand that the ferocious Blackfoot did not seem the least eager to face the living legend. When the last speaker's words had been translated for him, Praeger could not contain his profound exasperation.

"But we can't let him interfere with your war to drive out all whites," he blurted.

Two Moons rocked forward and came to his moccasins. "Why is it," he asked, "that you and the other two white men are so anxious to stir up war between our two peoples?"

Praeger worried that question a while, then made an oily, evasive answer. "I have learned your ways and have come to love and respect them. I wish to live as one of you after the whites are gone from this land."

Two Moons, as did the other chiefs, carefully kept his features neutral, in order not to reveal that they did not believe a single word of what they had heard. If it is true that ignorance is bliss, Quinton Praeger left the council lodge a misinformed but happy man.

12

Lieutenant Colonel Danvers had even less reason to be happy the next day. Antoine Revier came fogging back to the column at a quarter past ten with news that electrified the battalion commander and his officers.

"Colonel, we cut sign of a Pawnee war party about three miles ahead."

Danvers blinked and took a backhand swipe across his forehead. "Preposterous. We are at peace with the Pawnee." The last thing he wanted was to have a hostile force at his back when they settled in to build a fort.

Antoine gave him a mischievous eye. "Maybe this bunch don't know that. Preacher recommends that the tro—ah-Dragoons be mounted 'til this is worked out."

"We shall proceed afoot," Danvers decided aloud, ignoring the good advice. "Please inform Mr. Preacher that I wish him to extend his scouting activities over a much wider area."

With that dismissal, Antoine rode back to the point. The colonel waited until he had ridden out of hearing, then turned to call over his shoulder. "Captain Dreiling, flankers out, if you please."

"Yes, sir. Lieutenant Brice, take Sergeant Holcomb and twenty men to form flankers."

"Yes, sir. Holcomb, divide the platoon. You take the right flank, I'll take the left."

"Right, sir. First and Third Squads, follow me."

Lieutenant Brice wasted no time. "Second and Fourth, you're with me. Platoon . . . prepare to mount. . . . Mount."

With a flurry of dust from two hundred hooves, the flankers moved out smartly. Danvers watched them go in grim-lipped silence. He did not want to stir up trouble with the Pawnee. His orders were explicit. They were to proceed to the Bighorn Mountains, avoiding hostile engagements, and establish a cantonment area sufficient to house a regiment when completed. He had other orders as well, which he preferred not to think of. Sighing, he took up his reins, raised his arms and signaled for the column to advance. The Dragoons remained on foot twenty minutes later when the Pawnee raised up, seemingly out of the ground, and attacked the column.

Blind Wolf looked to the west, down the shallow slope of the rolling prairie. How foolish these white men. To go afoot when they had perfectly healthy horses to ride. More so for doing it in this country where death awaited them at every turn. This would be easy. Once his hidden warriors had them halted and confused, he and the rest of his brave Pawnee would sweep down on them at a gallop and ride the length of the column, killing many. He squinted to see the lead soldiers start up the next swell. He raised his feather-decorated rifle and gave the shrill call of a hunting eagle.

Responding to the signal to attack, Pawnee warriors came out from under their dirt-covered blankets and quickly sent a flight of arrows into the unsuspecting whites. Here and there a rifle cracked. Other braves, risking certain death, rushed forward to flail with their blankets and bison robes to frighten the horses of the white men. Even at his distance of a quarter mile, Blind Wolf saw several mounts' forehooves pawing the air.

Two even broke free of their owners' hold and bolted away from the noise—war whoops, shots—and the ghostly song of arrows. Any time now, he thought. Some of the soldiers had recovered and began to fire at the attackers. Blind Wolf knew he could wait no longer.

Raising his rifle again, he looked left and right, then brought it down smartly. At once he and twenty-five mounted warriors streaked forward. Swiftly, they closed on the wagons at the rear of the column.

An arrow made its uncanny moan past the ear of Lieutenant Colonel Danvers. Another thudded into the valise cover behind the cantle of his Grimsley saddle. A third bounced off the pommel of his adjutant's saddle. Instinct drove Danvers to take cover behind the stout forequarters and neck of his horse. This gave him a clear view of his holster, with its sheepskin cover.

To his credit, the Dragoon commander was the first to get off a shot. He threw back the tube of sheepskin and drew one large, unwieldy .44 Dragoon pistol and fired two fast rounds, one of which entered the screaming mouth of a Pawnee warrior who rushed at the horses with a flopping blanket.

Off went the left rear quarter of the brave's head as the flattened ball, now approximately .60-caliber in size, burned through brain and blew away bone and scalp. A Model 43 Hall, breech-loading carbine went off close by and Danvers flinched involuntarily. The hot wind of expanding gases from the foreshortened rifle brushed his cheek. Another flight of arrows seethed through the air.

One found a home in the forearm of Private Sawyer, who screamed as the point pierced the skin of his inner arm and protruded toward the forestock of his Hall. Corporal Collins, who'd gone back for the wagons left behind, came quickly to Sawyer's side, Danvers noted.

Deftly, the NCO broke off the shaft of the projectile and pulled the remainder through the wound. He quickly had Sawyer bound with a light blue neck scarf he had pulled from the open collar of his uniform jacket. Seemingly unfazed, Sawyer calmly reloaded his weapon, seated a percussion cap on the nipple and took aim on another screaming savage. Sergeant Simmons and the other lead NCOs bellowed commands to restore order among the milling, confused troops.

Gradually more of the Dragoons unlimbered their weapons and returned fire. For a moment, the Pawnee rush faltered. Then the thunder of pounding hooves attracted the attention of everyone to the rear of the column.

Gunfire crackled out as another swarm of hostiles raced along the eight freight wagons, rifles blazing. Unable to reload on the run, the Pawnee slung their rifles over their shoulders and resorted to more conventional weapons. Now the teamsters and their swampers plied their firearms. At a rate of fire three times that of muzzle-loaders—three per minute—the breech loading carbines poured a steady stream of lead in the direction of the Pawnee attackers. In a short time, the scene became obscured to the Dragoons and their enemy alike.

Blind Wolf had seriously underestimated the firepower of these flashily dressed soldiers. He had never encountered a breech-loading weapon before, had no idea of the speed with which they could be loaded and fired repeatedly. When the moan and crackle of balls thickened, and the reports of the short rifles grew to a deafening volume, he gave the signal for his warriors to pull back.

"We have hurt them. We will come again," Blind Wolf

told his son, Tall Raven, a boy of sixteen winters, who rode at his side.

Fired with the excitement of his first raid as a warrior, Tall Raven showed his disappointment. "Why not now, Father?"

"They are too many. They have shoot-fast guns we know nothing about. But, see, two of them are down, never to rise again. I count two hands of those who have felt the sharp teeth of the Pawnee. Soon again they will be off guard. It is then we will hit them."

Lieutenant Colonel Arlington Danvers rode the length of the column, inspected the damage and spent a minute with each of the wounded. Upset over the losses and the speed and surprise of the attack, he wore a deep frown. Beyond him, the flankers appeared over the swells to north and south while the Pawnee streamed away to the east. Danvers watched with mounting anger as the security details drew closer.

When Lieutenant Brice reported, the colonel icily cut him off in mid-recitation. "Explain yourself, mister. Why did you not get here in time to strike the hostiles from the rear?"

Brice stiffened. "No excuse, sir. But, for the record, we were pretty well spread out, screening for hostiles, sir, and it took some while to regroup and return, sir."

Realizing the correctness of this explanation, though loath to admit it, Danvers delayed his response. "Quite right, Lieutenant Brice. We will maintain flankers, only this time, they are to remain within visual contact of one another, and work in teams of two."

"Yes, sir. We'll go out at once, sir."

"Keep a sharp eye. Those savages caught us quite by surprise the first time," he grudgingly added.

"You expect them to come again?"

"Oh, yes, Lieutenant. Indians never give up with a single attack."

Brice and his platoon of flankers rode off to their assigned areas. A moment later, Preacher and Three Sleeps Norris cantered over the rise ahead of the column and located Lieutenant Colonel Danvers.

"We heard the ruckus, Colonel. Thought we'd best come see what went on."

"We were attacked by hostiles. Pawnee, I believe."

Preacher bent and retrieved an arrow. "That's what this says. Pawnee markin's right enough. They're fierce devils. Can't figger why they broke off so soon."

Danvers produced a satisfied smirk, recalling the surprised and confused expressions of the enemy. "I imagine they had never encountered breech-loading weapons before. We put out a volume of fire nearly triple that of older arms. I have flankers out. I think we can expect a return call from the Indians."

"Oh, yes, that you certainly can. You want us to stay back with you, Colonel?"

Danvers considered it. "The warriors seemed to rise up out of the ground. Total surprise for us. I think it best if you do stay with the column, work out to the edges. Maybe you can detect another such shock tactic."

Preacher had more bad news. "One thing sure, Colonel, they won't play the same trick twice. The Pawnee have a whole bag full."

Blind Wolf bided his time for the second attack. The soldiers had made another five miles before the mounted Pawnee rushed over the lip of a ravine to the left of their route. Driving hard, they rushed down on the flank of the column. From his vantage point, Blind Wolf watched with satisfaction as the soldiers once again reacted slowly.

Faint shouts in the white man's language, which Blind Wolf understood only poorly under the best conditions, came to his ears. The soldiers wheeled left and lifted short rifles from where they hung on the saddles. A faint smile lifted his full lips and flickered momentarily. Then he raised his arm and waved it left and right.

A flight of arrows soared upward from beyond the edge of a high creek bank to the right of the mass of soldiers. Before they landed, the left flank disappeared behind a wall of smoke. A moment later, another volley crashed across the prairie. Blind Wolf's lips compressed and his eyes narrowed. He had expected this. Yet, he ached for each of his brave men who fell in the withering fire.

Short of the soldiers by only three pony lengths, the Pawnee reined in, those with rifles fired, then they wheeled and galloped away. Another flight of arrows went aloft from the creek bank. Orders shouted in a thin, high voice, turned half the mounted troops in that direction. Two heart-stoppingly fast volleys ripped into the verge and chewed chunks out of the bank. Rifle in hand, Blind Wolf extended his arm and pumped it up and down.

Again his mounted warriors charged. Their ponies pounded down on the stationary ranks. Shrill whoops came from strong, young throats. The short rifles crashed again. Several braves flew from their saddles. Inexorably, the opposing forces grew closer together.

Then three buckskin-clad, white demons cut diagonally across the advancing warriors. Their gunfire rippled across the waving grass, the aim incredibly accurate. First one, then a second of Blind Wolf's leaders slipped from the backs of their ponies. In a flash, the surprisingly disciplined charge of the Pawnee warriors dissolved into a confused, milling mass.

With hardly any pause, the soldiers changed the shape of their defense. Alternating groups turned their horses left or right and began to move toward their attackers at a walk. In five heartbeat intervals, the walk became a trot, then a canter, then a gallop. With a raw roar from parched throats, the Dragoons charged.

* * *

By sheer volume of fire, the Dragoons stopped the Pawnee in their tracks. Then, while the men reloaded, Preacher and his companions dashed between the contesting forces, firing with their multiple-shot weapons. Preacher downed a leader, then wounded another. Antoine Revier killed a second sub-chief. That did it. The leaderless warriors turned, scattered. Cursing the showoff stunt of the mountain men, Lieutenant Colonel Danvers suddenly realized that it gave him the opportunity he sought. Now he could bring a decisive end to this. He stood full in the stirrups and issued commands in his high-pitched voice.

"By alternate companies, form as skirmishers, left and right. Draw pistols. Prepare to charge. Trumpeter, sound the charge!" As the crisp, tingling notes sounded, Danvers drew his saber. *"Chaaaaarge!"*

Haunches flexed, the big Dragoon horses bounded forward. Clods of turf flew in the air around them. Snorting and grunting, they increased their pace with each step. Quickly the Dragoons closed on their enemy. Suddenly, frightened faces turned toward them. Isolated islands of resistance formed here and there. The big, broad-shouldered soldiers in the two-tone blue uniforms grew huge in the eyes of the Pawnee. At extreme pistol range, the chilling order came.

"Take aim . . . fire! Take aim . . . fire! Take aim . . . fire!" On they thundered. "Fire at will!"

At that point, the flankers returned and struck the enemy in the rear. Quickly the huge, six-shot Dragoon pistols turned the tide. The Pawnee held fast for a moment, then broke in wild disarray, to be swept from the field. Within minutes, the battle ended. Silence settled over the field, save for the groans of the wounded. Abruptly, Preacher stormed up to Danvers.

Seeming furious, he lashed out verbally. "I thought I said no damn trumpets." Then he grinned broadly. "But it sure was a sweet, purty sight."

Danvers relaxed his usual brittle, disapproving attitude toward Preacher. "Yes, it is. A full-out, Dragoon charge is awe-inspiring." Then he frowned. "I see only one advantage coming out of this fierce, protracted fighting. It has bloodied these green troops." He had not finished with that.

"This skirmish could have been, should have been, avoided. I want a plan drawn up that will insure we are not delayed by such actions. Those savages are supposed to be on friendly terms. What can we expect when we encounter real hostiles?"

It had been intended to be rhetorical, but Preacher took delight in answering. "More'n likely you'll git yer hair lifted."

Despite himself, Danvers cut his eyes to Preacher and acknowledged the remark, which made it more to the point. "That is not amusing. Any more delays like this will make us seriously overdue on our arrival in the high country."

Preacher considered the colonel's upset over the raid to be excessive. Yet, he bided his time for the present. What would come, would come.

Early in the afternoon, the forsaken wagon train arrived in what was seen as a safe haven tucked into a fold of the northeast slope of the Medicine Bow Mountains, a lush, gentle valley spread along a buttress of the foothills. The clear water of the Platte River ran in front of their hidden vale. Their tired eyes explored the bounty and found it good.

Isaac Warner halted his wagon at the entrance and repeated his instruction to all who came by. "Go on in, find a likely space and settle in. We'll organize a hunting party soon as everybody is unhitched."

Each family quickly staked out areas of the belly-high grass for their draft animals and saddle stock to graze on. The women set about preparing firepits and rigging lines to air out long-confined clothing and blankets.

With her chores completed, Eve Billings ambled over to the site selected by the Honeycutts. Eve spoke her innermost thoughts to Hattie as she approached. "What a pure delight, all the water we want."

"And pure, too," Hattie added with a shake of her gray-streaked auburn hair. She had started the trek with uniformly coppery tresses.

"There will be plenty of game. And the chance for our livestock to fatten up for a long haul." She saw the older woman strain to move a boulder that she wanted elsewhere. "Here, let me help you with that."

They worked together for the better part of an hour. Eve soon noticed that neighborliness had once more come to life all over the encampment. Gone was the bickering and petty spite of the trail. It took far less time than usual to establish comfortable living areas. With the work out of the way, and the animals at graze, everyone seemed to decide at once that the time had come to wash away the dust and grit of the sun-blasted Basin.

While the adults and older youths decorously washed themselves in the shallows of the North Platte River, Eve watched as Charlie joined the other boys under fourteen and, along with the others, gleefully threw off his clothes and leaped into the chill water of the river. Eve could only cluck her tongue and shake her head. Not a streak of modesty in the lot of them. How like his father as a boy Charlie is, she thought.

Sudden tears sprang to her eyes at thinking of the man she had loved so dearly and who had died in her arms. She lowered her head to conceal her private grief from the others. Slowly her suppressed sobs, changed from gulps to sighs, and at last into long, slow, deep breaths. Eve looked up to see a sparkling, naked Charlie leap from a slippery boulder into the water in an awkward dive. A worried mother's words escaped her before she could cut them off.

"Charlie! Look out!"

A deep rumble of thunder came from the northwest to

drown out her appeal. Swiftly, the temperature dropped fifteen degrees. The children ran from the water shouting to hurriedly wipe themselves down and dress. Eve chuckled softly. At least there was something that would get Charlie into clothes without an argument. If only Howard could see him now, she thought with fierce pride. This time, fond, loving tears filled her eyes.

She glanced up to see a blurry figure on horseback across the river. Curious, and wary, Eve wiped away mistiness to discover the same Indian she had seen nearly a week before. Behind him were foothills and huge columns of boiling black clouds. Again he raised his lance in a salute and smiled at her. Mystified, Eve stood, the hem of her dress dripping, and watched him until he turned and slowly rode away.

13

Celestial keglers made strike after strike ahead of the route of march. From north to south, the horizon had turned a boiling black. Skeletal fingers, edged in orange, lanced through the obsidian stew. With a swiftness known only to denizens of the West, the towering, anvil-headed cumulonimbus arched out to engulf the whole dome of the sky.

Preacher had been watching the approach of the storm. He prudently exchanged his hunting shirt for one of faded green flannel and his fringed buckskin jacket for an oiled-skin *capote*. His floppy felt went into his saddlebag along with his skins. A spanking new, stiff-brimmed one took its place. Preacher used a fist to punch the crown into a faint resemblance of its original shape.

While he industriously made these alterations in his clothing, the thunder rumbled, increasingly louder. To his dismay, when he looked back at the column, the Dragoons appeared to ride along in blissful ignorance.

"Them fellers is gonna get a first-class soakin'," he confided to Three Sleeps.

Norris nodded. "I reckon so. They've got them those

fancy India-rubber *capotes* they use for ground sheets. I wonder why nobody's given the order to break them out?"

Preacher's face twisted into an expression of sudden enlightenment. "Now, that's the entire trouble with the Army. Somebody's always got to tell you what to do. They yell and cuss at a body until he forgets how to think for hisself, an' then they don't let them anyway."

Three Sleeps removed his coonskin cap and scratched at a thick thatch of silver-blond hair. "I *think* I understand what you jist said, but I ain't gonna answer any questions on it."

Preacher started to make a wounded reply when the light breeze that had been in their faces dropped to dead still. That held for several heartbeats; then a strong, cold blast rushed at them out of the east. At once, the temperature plummeted ten degrees and continued to fall.

Preacher tightened the chin strap of his hat; the brim fluttered wildly. "B'God, here she comes."

A tremendous peal of thunder came right on the heels of a searing, white tongue of lightning that slammed into a pile of boulders a hundred yards from the trail. The ground shook with the violence of it. Despite the powerful gust of wind, the air tingled with the scent of ozone.

Insubstantial shouts came from the column. Preacher looked down to see the Dragoons halted, dismounting now, and digging into the cylindrical valises behind their saddles. From them, the troops hurriedly took their water-proof ponchos and donned them.

"That seems to have got their attention," he said dryly.

Widely spaced, huge, fat drops made silver streaks in the air. Another blinding flash and boom. The thunder erupted directly overhead and continued to grind and growl across the sky. Echoes of its passage bounced from the sun-baked ground. More rain fell, thicker now, with the main downpour close behind. It arrived with a seething hiss and swept like a giant's broom across the ridge where Preacher and his friends sat their mounts.

Tarnation made wall-eyes and twitched his ears. His hide followed suit when the heavenly cannonade fired another battery of forked electricity at six wide-spaced places in rapid succession. Down below, Preacher saw the Dragoons had a lot of trouble with their horses. Having dismounted, they could barely control the animals in the fierce teeth of the storm.

"Those boys are gonna lose some horses," opined Antoine Revier.

Preacher nodded agreement. "I reckon they will." Another near miss by a sizzling bolt put Preacher in motion. "Let's quit playin' target for that stuff."

Halfway down the grade toward the column, the rattle and drumbeat of swiftly approaching hail reached the ears of Preacher. He drubbed heels into Tarnation's ribs and streaked for a low, spreading plain tree that stood in valiant isolation in the shelter of a gully. He reached it only seconds behind his companions.

Shredded leaves fell in green confetti around them, while out in the open, the Dragoons did not fare so well. Two horses, painfully pelted with fist-sized ice stones, squealed and reared. Rain-slicked, the reins slipped through the hands of the Dragoons who held them. At once, the frightened, hurting animals bolted.

In spite of orders to the contrary, their hapless riders ran after them. In no time, the Dragoons and their mounts disappeared over a low swell. Preacher spat on a fallen leaf.

"There goes a couple of damn fools."

"You got the right of it, Preacher," Antoine Revier agreed.

"Any bets as to who'll have to go after them?" Three Sleeps Norris put in.

Preacher grimaced. "None at all. Soon's this downpour ends, we'd best be making tracks."

* * *

For all its violence, the storm had been a welcome sight for the unfortunate members of the wagon train. Eve Billings had hurried back in time to gather in the bedding and clothes she had out to air. The rain, when it came, was warm and inviting. At the insistence of her children, Eve relented and erected a screen of spare wagon-top canvas. Within its confines, Charlie and Anna cavorted, bare as the day they had been born. The only protest the youngsters made was when Eve produced a bar of soap.

"Mind you do your ears, Charlie Billings," she admonished.

Smiling and humming an old tune, she sat out the tempest in the shelter of the wagon box. Blue-lipped and shivering, Charlie and Anna had held out to the last drop, then had oohed and aahed over a rainbow that formed on the northern end of the storm's back. At last, they climbed, dripping, over the tailgate. Eve toweled them dry.

"Ow, Mom, that hurts," Charlie complained of the stiff, prickly cloth.

"Yeah, that hurth," Anna lisped.

Another sacrifice of the trail. Eve had been able to wash clothes in the water of streams they had passed, many of which were rich in lime and iron particles. Her supply of bluing had long since run out, and she regretted the stiffness her efforts put into the items she had washed. She would have given anything to capture barrels of that marvelously soft rain water.

Now that the tempest had rolled away to the east, the leaves of beech and oak, and pine needles, dropped, as if doing a slow dance, into puddles that had formed on the long-dry ground. The pioneers began to stir in their wagons. Eve reflected on her mystery Indian as she laid a fire from dry wood that she'd sheltered from the elements in a net sling under the floor of the Conestoga.

Obviously he was not hostile, she told herself. Why was it he only appeared to her? She had mentioned him after the first sighting, but none of the men had admitted to seeing the lone figure. Gus Beecher had even snidely suggested that she was seeing things. Maybe she was, her mind mocked.

Dismissing that, she knelt by the pyramid of sticks and pulled a tuft of oily wood tinder from the brass box. She struck sparks from flint and steel and gently blew an orange spot in the kindling into lively flames. Careful not to burn her fingers, she shoved the lintwood in under a mound of shavings. They reluctantly ignited and sent larger, hotter tendrils of fire among the larger pieces of wood. She looked up as Charlie approached. He was dressed as usual, shirtless, in his one-piece overalls, bare toes squishing in the mud.

"Mom, I want to go with the hunters. I'll get us something good."

"I'm sorry, but no. It's not safe. Some of the men can't . . ." Eve cut herself off short. She had admonished herself not to criticize the men in the group after Charlie had repeated her scathing evaluation of their abilities weeks ago. It did little good this time, as Charlie provided her opinion of their marksmanship.

"Hit the broad side of a barn."

Mad at herself more than the boy, Eve spoke hotly. "Charles Ryan, what have I told you about speaking ill of your elders?"

"Oh, boy, am I in trouble?" His lower lip protruded in a pink, wet pout.

Eve looked down on his sweet face and could only shake her head in the negative. Then she had to turn away to keep from breaking out in gales of laughter.

After two hours of searching, Preacher had nothing to show for it but some muddy hoofprints. Again he cursed the Army, and Lieutenant Colonel Danvers in particular. The muddle-headed nincompoop had insisted that at least some of the guides remain with the column. His idea of some turned out to be all save Preacher. Well, Mrs. Houghton's little boy Arthur had not turned out dense.

Preacher figured it was Danvers's idea to get him killed by the Pawnee, which likely had happened to the idiots he attempted to track. He sighed heavily and urged Tarnation forward. While the miles ticked off, he grumbled about the stupidity of officer-type soldiers or gnawed on a strip of jerky which he had softened between saddle and blanket.

With only three hours of daylight left, he at last found the missing men right enough. A big cloud of bluebottle flies led him the last fifty yards to a dry wash that cut like a knife slash across the prairie. They made quite a sight, one that wrenched even as experienced a stomach as Preacher's.

They had been stripped, staked out, mutilated, killed and scalped. Though not necessarily in that order, Preacher noted. One had been slit from sternum to groin, and had his private parts stuffed in his mouth. The other had been cut deeply from crotch to ankle of both legs and armpits to wrists. It had been done slowly, Preacher reckoned from the contorted condition of the unfortunate fellow's muscles.

Cautiously, Preacher looked around the scene. His keen eyes took in everything. First, he noted that there was no sign of their uniforms, weapons or gear. There was plenty of sign of Pawnee warriors. Oddly enough, one of the dead men's horses placidly chomped grass at the bottom of the ravine. It had been stripped of all equipage.

"Damn an' double damn," Preacher swore aloud.

Moving with care, he walked to Tarnation's side. There Preacher fetched a short length of rope from a latigo tie and fashioned a crude hackamore. He approached the Dragoon mount with patience. When the creature's bulging eye first registered his presence, Preacher began to coo to it and speak softly.

"There now. There, nobody's gonna hurt you. Good boy. Stand still, ya hear?"

Step by mindful step, Preacher's moccasined feet took him up to the heaving flank of the horse. He touched the animal lightly, ran his hand along the curve of its back to the neck. Another pace forward, a second. Murmuring platitudes, he raised the makeshift halter. Then, with a deft movement, Preacher slipped it over the muzzle.

Only a slight jump came from the creature. Preacher patted his arched neck firmly and blew gently in a cocked ear. Then he carefully led the beast away from the patch of grass.

"Come on, boy, you've got an unpleasant task to do."

After adding a lead rope to the hackamore and fixing that to a ground anchor, Preacher cut free the dead Dragoons. He wrapped them in his ground sloth and an old blanket and slung them over the back of the captured horse. A nervous twitching rewarded his efforts. With a grunt of acceptance of a bad job done the best he could, he mounted Tarnation and took up the lead. Mindful of the bodies he brought, he put the noses of the horses in the direction of the column. He did not relish making a report to Danvers on what happened.

Preacher had predicted the result accurately. Lieutenant Colonel Danvers stomped back and forth in his tent, cursed and railed, then concluded his tirade with a wholly uncalled-for accusation.

"Why did you not get to them sooner?"

Preacher cocked his head to one side. "I don't put up with that kind of talk from you or anybody. What did you expect me to do? I counted sign of fully sixteen Pawnee warriors around them bodies. I ain't fool enough to ride in among 'em and pass the time o' day, or bargain for the release of those idiots what ran after their mounts in hostile country. Besides, I don't think it would have done much good. They looked to have been dead since shortly after the storm passed by. Now, *Colonel,* I'll accept your apology, or I'll demand satisfaction right here an' now."

Surprise painted Danvers's face. "Duel with you? Why, you're not even a *gentleman.*"

Preacher looked astonished. "I didn't intend on no duel. Death's a serious matter." He turned abruptly and started for the front flap of the tent.

"Then what did you have in that primitive brain of yours?"

"I jist figgered to tom-turkey stomp the shit out of you, Colonel. But I've cooled off some. We'll forget it . . . for now. Good night, Colonel."

"Wait!" Danvers started after Preacher. "What are we going to do to stop these treaty violations?"

Preacher stared coldly and levelly at the colonel. "These incidents will continue unless the Pawnees learn not to mess with us. The best way to do that is to raid their villages, burn their lodges and supplies, run off their ponies, kill a few warriors."

"That's madness, man!" Danvers went on to protest vehemently. "There is a treaty. These are not the Indians we came out here to fight."

Preacher's amused expression turned to one of intense curiosity. "What Injuns are you supposed to fight? The way I understand it, we didn't come out here to fight any Injuns. Jist to 'show the flag,'" he tossed the pet phrase of Arlington Danvers back in his face.

Danvers paled, cognizant that his mouth had overstepped his reasoning. "Yes . . . yes, you're right about that. The fort is to enforce the peace, not incite war. Yet, I must maintain that nothing can be gained from pushing a dispute on the Pawnee."

Preacher grinned and gave the colonel a wink. "I can think of something. It will provide excellent trainin' for yer baby Dragoons, that it will."

Grudgingly, Danvers saw the sense in that. Reluctantly he

agreed to allow Preacher and one other guide to observe any Pawnee camps or villages in close proximity to their route of march.

Over the next two nights, Preacher and Antoine Revier scouted many Pawnee villages. Preacher had reasoned correctly that such a large number of warriors could not come from a small raiding band on the warpath. It took him only to the second night to find what he sought. He would make a third foray to verify what he had learned.

Preacher squatted behind a stunted, wind-twisted bristle-cone pine and looked down into a village. Flickering firelight turned the scene a Dantesque orange. His ears soon picked up the spine-chilling throb of drums and the eerie, wailing of the Scalp Dance, a song he'd painfully learned long ago and had lived to remember. From the gyrating shadows projected onto lodge covers, he estimated that at least six of the marauders lived in this community. At the time, he did not realize he had missed the count by ten.

After half an hour of careful study, Preacher slipped away into the night to rendezvous with Antoine. The first thing the French-Delaware mountain man said was: "You saw it, too?"

"Yep. The Scalp Dance."

"I counted eleven of 'em got the hoop with the scalps on it passed to them."

"You did? I marked it as six. My eyes must be goin' bad. Or I left too soon."

"May have. From the other side I could see real clear. Made my blood run cold."

"We'll check that other village tomorrow night, then tell the good colonel where to hit."

"I'm for that."

Together, they turned their mounts to the south and started for the trail of the Dragoon column. On the way, Preacher began to formulate a plan of attack.

* * *

After the third night's visit, Preacher completed his strategy on the ride to the Dragoon camp. He explained it to Lieutenant Colonel Danvers and to his utter surprise, the constantly critical officer agreed entirely. He did make a couple of changes and offered a suggestion.

"Standard Dragoon tactics call for keeping one element of one's force in reserve. In this case, I think they should be deployed. They can act as a screen, at some distance, to see none of the hostiles escape us."

"You're sure gonna make life hard for those Injun folk. I reckon we can work it out right smart."

Shortly before dawn the next day, the Dragoons eased into position to attack the slumbering Pawnee village. When all was in readiness, Danvers gave the signal. Howling like banshees, the Dragoons stormed in among the lodges. Some of these they set afire. Others they pulled down. Rearing horses trampled firepits and cooking pots. Yapping dogs bristled in challenge, only to be shot down by Dragoons. Preacher took his own course to enter the encampment.

Shocked, he felt a tangible chill along his spine when he saw the horse herd had disappeared. Sudden premonition caused Preacher to try to shout a warning. The first words had barely left his mouth when disaster struck.

Suddenly the tables turned on the Dragoons. Howling Pawnee warriors attacked them from outside the village. Whooping war cries and screaming insults, they charged into the bewildered soldiers.

14

Panic struck the green troops on the outer edges when the Indians appeared so suddenly. It rippled inward to those still occupied with trashing the village. Entire companies milled about in confusion. Who was it shooting at them? There weren't any Indians. Those furthest removed from the Pawnee menace had no idea of the terrible death that threatened them.

Preacher put heels to the ribs of his stallion and drove a wedge through some Dragoons paralyzed by fear. "Spread out an' get them weapons workin', damnit! There's Injuns right over there." He pointed the way and his calm, purposeful demeanor broke the spell.

First by ones and twos, the Dragoons opened space between one another and brought their Hall carbines into action. An arrow hissed past Preacher's ear and he jinked his head to the side automatically. A Walker Colt filled his right hand, and he fired almost point-blank into the chest of a Pawnee warrior. With a final shriek, the brave rolled backward off the rump of his pony.

Preacher sought another target, to find himself face-to-face with Three Sleeps Norris. "Muldoon is over on the other side, tryin' to organize some sort of defense."

Preacher assimilated the information and nodded. "Antoine is right over there. I'll send him to Muldoon. You an' him can keep us in touch."

BSM Terrance Muldoon found himself alone in the command structure. Two young lieutenants had gone down in the first bevy of arrows to descend on the unsuspecting troops. Both officers took only wounds, but one was serious. No sign of Captain Dreiling, the most reliable and steadiest of the company commanders. None of the others had been on this side of the village. After the initial shock of the swift, swirling assault, Muldoon shouldered his mount into that of one Dragoon after another and shouted loudly enough to break their glazes of shock.

"Get that damn rifle to workin', soldier!"

"Bu-But the Indians," one had blathered back at him.

"Sure an' they ain't bulletproof, ye idiot."

By the time he had bullied enough of the wild-eyed troopers into a passable defensive formation, with every other man dismounted, the Pawnee had disappeared into the tall grass to prepare for a second rush. When the seed clusters at the tops of the stalks began to weave in snake-like patterns, Muldoon spoke low and reassuringly to the men he commanded.

"Easy now. Let 'em come to us. Be ready, stand fast, lads. Standing men kneel. Prepare to fire by volley. Hold yer fire. Take aim . . . Kneeling rank . . . fire!"

Lighted by the muzzle flash of fifteen carbines, the predawn murk turned to orange sunrise. "Reload. Mounted rank . . . take aim . . . fire!"

Again the sun rose in the south for the Pawnee. "Reload. Kneeling rank, take aim . . . fire! Reload. Steady, lads, steady.

Mounted rank, take aim . . . fire! Reload. Kneeling rank, take aim . . . fire!"

Seemingly oblivious to the hail of balls that snapped through the air in their direction, the warriors came on. At each volley, ten to twelve Pawnee fell in the grass, killed, stunned, or wounded by the Dragoons. After the third volley, the distance between them and the soldiers had narrowed enough that the Dragoons did not have time to reload their carbines.

Muldoon judged the situation well. His voice rang calm and clear over the defenders. "Replace carbines. Draw pistols . . . Fire at will."

A wave of staccato reports rippled along the file of Dragoons. The sheer volume of fire sent dread through the swarm of warriors. In disarray, they thrashed their way back into the concealing grass.

"Keep it up, bies, that grass can't stop a bullet," Muldoon cheered on his rag-tag band of soldiers.

"Muldoon's checked them on the north," Antoine Revier reported to Preacher after he rode up in a fog of dust.

Preacher gestured to the empty plain that stretched from the village to a deep gully. "They ain't showin' themselves so free and easy over here. I found a couple of the company commanders. They got their troops outta their daze and blasted hell outta the Pawnee a short while back." He beckoned to Three Sleeps. "Git yerself over to Muldoon, take some of this surplus of officers we've got here with you. Tell him I expect the next charge will come at this side any time now. I'm gettin' tired of runnin' this show for the Army. Time to let the one's supposed to do it." He paused and looked around, a puzzled frown creasing his powder-grimed brow.

"Speakin' of which, where in daylights is Colonel Danvers?"

"Don't see him anywhere," Antoine remarked.

Then Preacher replayed the first moments of pandemonium when the Pawnee attacked. He pursed his lips and slapped a thigh with an open palm. "As I recollect, when the hostiles fu'st hit us, Danvers disappeared into one of the tipis still standin'. Funny thing, I ain't see him since."

Antoine was full of helpful suggestions. "Let's go see if we can find him."

"We will, soon's I figger out which one he went to."

Preacher and Antoine drew blanks on the first two lodges. At the entrance flap of the third, Preacher found a private standing post as though on garrison guard duty. He poked his head inside and found Lieutenant Colonel Arlington Danvers.

Seated on a camp stool that Preacher sometimes thought must have grown out of his ass, Danvers directed his officers by way of messengers. One of the latter saluted smartly and stepped hurriedly in Preacher's direction. Taken aback by the unreality of what he witnessed, Preacher stared in disgust. At last he found control of his vocal cords and stomped into the lodge, Antoine right behind. Danvers's high-pitched voice elevated more in complaint.

"I don't understand why we have not heard from the north side of the village. Has Captain Dreiling taken leave of his senses?"

Preacher stepped in front of the colonel then and spoke with an obvious effort to control his loathing. "Might I suggest, Colonel, that if you were out there, where the fighting is goin' on, you could learn firsthand what is going on and why. You might even be able to personally direct your subordinates, which would free up all these messenger-boys to take part in the battle."

Danvers tried to wither Preacher with his most contemptuous stare. "That's what company commanders and platoon leaders are for," he told Preacher coldly. "Company commanders are supposed to observe, supervise and direct."

That he failed to intimidate became immediately obvious. Preacher turned partway from the prim, icy-eyed colonel, then swung back, fists balled and eyes turned to steel. "My point is, Colonel, that you sure as hell can't see much cringing inside a tipi like a yeller-bellied cur."

He stomped to the entrance to the lodge and was bending to exit when a shrill roar came from Danvers, only to be drowned out by war cries and explosions of Hall carbines from outside. Preacher made for the fight at once.

Warriors from the other villages had to be in on this, Preacher reasoned correctly. Even if all sixteen of the braves involved in the torture and killing of the Dragoons lived in this camp, there simply weren't enough lodges to account for the number of Pawnee who surrounded the troops. A man usually figured three warriors to a lodge. By count of tipis, this village should account for some fifty-four warriors.

Hell, Preacher thought, that many had already been killed or knocked out of action. And, he recalled, the other two villages had been larger by half than this one. Ruefully he acknowledged that the sneaky Pawnee had gotten one up on him again. Time to worry about that later. Preacher took aim and shot a lance-wielding warrior off his pony. Quickly he reloaded his Hawken. There had to be a better way of ending this, he told himself.

During the next assault, an idea came to Preacher. When the lull that followed the charge extended far longer than the previous ones, he decided to put it to use. To do so, he sought out Antoine Revier. He found Antoine standing in the shade cast by a lodge, loading his pistols.

"Antoine, ol' friend, I think we're overdue in bringin' an end to this mess. Get that long-range Frenchie rifle of yours an' let's go out an' change the odds."

Antoine turned a beaming countenance on Preacher. "I think

I know what you have in mind. We should have done this sooner."

"They hadn't settled down enough. I'd say they was gettin' some grub right about now. Should work perfect."

Ten minutes later, Preacher and Antoine Revier slipped out of the besieged village and headed due east. A mile from the circles of lodges, they turned north, skirted the Pawnee flank and worked their way to within half a mile of the enemy. Both mountain men spent a tense fifteen minutes in concentrated study of the hostiles through long, brass telescopes. Satisfied that they had identified the proper individuals, they moved in a bit closer.

Being long-range sporting arms, both Preacher's Le Mat and Antoine's Alouette had been fitted with simple, unsophisticated telescopic sights. At ranges up to six-hundred yards, they could reasonably be expected to hit a man-sized target with every shot, and cause a fatal wound three out of five times. At least, in the hands of these expert marksmen that was possible. They used Y-shaped metal barrel rests that came with the weapons, carried in the stock, behind hinged buttplates. After easing their way into suitable prone positions on a gentle upslope, they settled in and sought their targets.

Preacher found one first, took careful aim and pressed the set trigger. Then his finger curled around the firing trigger, and he fined his sight picture. A gentle squeeze and the .36-caliber rifle fired. At that range, he had the weapon clear of the stand and the old cap off the nipple before the head of a tall, wiry Pawnee with a face split by black and white war paint, snapped backward slightly and a geyser of gore spurted from the back of his crown.

Preacher had the powder charge rammed home by the time the other Pawnee reacted to the startling sight. Muffled by distance, the report of his Le Mat did not reach them until nearly two seconds after the ball that killed one war leader. A stiff crosswind had disbursed the powder smoke. Confused as to how and from where this blow had come, the Indians milled about, providing Antoine a target as easy as Preacher's had been.

His man went down rubber-legged a moment before Preacher fired again. A third war leader died. "I reckon one more each and we'd best get out of here," he advised Antoine after the latter had fired his second shot.

"Mais oui. Or we will leave our hair with the Pawnee."

Their guns reloaded, they sought out fresh marks and fired simultaneously. Another pair of war leaders clutched their chests and keeled over, their hearts pierced by deadly metal. Quickly, Preacher and Antoine folded up their gear and crawled off through the tall grass to where they had left their mounts on the far side of the low swell.

Six most important men killed in less than three minutes did it for the Pawnee. Muttering darkly about bad medicine, they abandoned the fight and rode off toward the other nearby villages. Even the inexperienced Dragoons knew that the battle had ended long before Preacher and Antoine rode into the battered encampment.

Iron Shirt stood before the assembled councils of the Northern Cheyenne. Many had journeyed far to hear the message of the Blackfoot messiah. Not all, though, were captivated by his promise to drive out the whites and bring back the old days. Some, including Cloud Blanket, privately believed, like the Crow, that some means must be found to live alongside the whites in peace. Cloud Blanket had heard appeals such as Iron Shirt's before.

They had failed to impress him then, and still did. He winced as Iron Shirt reached the part about how his secret medicine would make ordinary red men bullet proof against the white man's bullets.

"Not a man shall die of white bullets after joining in the ritual of the Iron Shield Society. Some of you may have heard of how some warriors died from the white man's many-balls gun. Recently the Spirit who guides us revealed to me what needs to be done to make my medicine proof against even these."

What nonsense, thought Cloud Blanket. At close range, a shotgun—yes, he knew the proper name for it—could bring terrible destruction. An old friend among the whites, Preacher, had once told him that it was the awful shock to the body from being hit so many times at once that killed. Unless, the mountain man had added, a man took a load in the heart or got his head blown off. Iron Shirt had reached the climax of his boastful speech, the exhortation to join.

"I want ten double-hands of brave Cheyenne warriors to step forward and become brothers in the Iron Shield Society. All is in readiness for the ritual. Those who do not join us are asked to leave now."

It heartened Cloud Blanket to see so many turn away. Yet, some eighty stood as though enchanted by the words of Iron Shirt. This would be a bad thing for the Cheyenne, Cloud Blanket admitted to himself. He turned to an old friend, Four Bears.

"I am thinking of moving my band toward the Black Hills. Iron Shirt is like a stick of green wood in a fire. It spits and pops and throws sparks in the air. But sparks are not a blaze . . . unless they land in your sleeping robes."

Four Bears nodded thoughtfully. "You are right. I will ask my people to do the same."

Back on the march again, the Dragoons seemed more confident and at ease, though somewhat subdued. Five of them had been killed; more than thirty took wounds. Most bore only minor injuries, and wore their white swatches of courage with noticeable pride. The six serious cases rode in wagons, under the care of Major Claire Couglin, the company surgeon. Troubled by the condition of his charges, Major Couglin left the wagon in which he tended three of them, and on his dapple-gray mare rode to the head of the cavalcade.

"Colonel, I am greatly concerned for the recovery of the seriously wounded men. I urge you to slow our pace. At this rate of march, the wagons are doing more harm than the Pawnee did."

Danvers snorted. "Nonsense, Doctor. We need to put as much distance between us and the Pawnee as we can, in order to avoid any more such . . . incidents."

The balding Major Couglin raised his eyebrows in astonishment. "I'd hardly call a pitched battle an 'incident,' Colonel."

Danvers gave him a hard, level stare. "Officially, that is what it has to be. Otherwise, we might be charged with violating the treaty."

Couglin scratched his chin. "Preacher has given me to understand that it is highly unlikely we will have a repeat of hostilities."

Snorting, Danvers glared in disdain. "Preacher? What does he know about it, *Major* Couglin?"

In a quiet voice, the doctor added his clincher. "He's lived out here for thirty years."

It had little effect on Danvers. "I regret to inform you that we cannot slow the pace, Major Couglin."

The major bristled. "Need I remind you that in matters of the health and well-being of the troops, I have authority to supersede your decisions?"

Fire flamed in the eyes of Danvers. "Your objection is noted—and rejected. In the presence of hostiles, my decisions alone are binding."

Defeated, Couglin tried one final appeal. "At least, let me have a suitable escort so that the wagons can proceed at a rate consistent with the best interests of the wounded."

Lieutenant Colonel Danvers relented. "Very well. You may have two platoons. This discussion is concluded."

From a short distance away, Three Sleeps Norris had overheard the entire exchange. He muttered to himself his heartfelt opinion of Lieutenant Colonel Arlington Danvers: "Heartless, miserable son of a bitch." Had he heard it, Norris knew, Preacher would have agreed.

15

Blooding the troops had side benefits born of their increased confidence. Preacher soon noted that the Dragoons' smart deportment made the old saw about forty miles a day solid reality. On one fine afternoon, he found the Medicine Bow Mountains on his left. He had seen their matte-black ramparts over the previous three days. Now sure enough they had gained the red-orange pinnacles covered with tall stands of lodge-pole pine, juniper and fir so dense that had the Black Hills of Lakota country not been seen first by white men, these would have borne that name. What Preacher did not expect was to come upon a mounted white man, who appeared suddenly out of one of the deep folds on the northeast face of the Medicine Bows.

A cry of surprise reached Preacher's ears a fraction of a second before the stranger energetically waved his arms in a show of peaceful intent. He spurred his horse and came on fast. Preacher urged Tarnation toward the approaching rider. Face alight with hope and relief, the newcomer reined up in a shower of turf.

"Mister, am I glad to see you. Thank the good Lord you've come at last. How many in your party?"

Preacher blinked and studied the man in an attempt to determine if he was addle-pated. "There's nigh onto two hundred."

That startled the stranger. "Lordy . . . lordy, that's the biggest wagon train I've ever heard of."

"Not a train. I'm guide for a squadron of Dragoons. Folks call me Preacher."

Face glowing with joy, Isaac Warner introduced himself, then added, "You have no idea how grateful we are to see you. Many of our people have given up hope."

Preacher rubbed his chin. "Maybe I should ask how many there are of you folk?"

"We number seventy-three souls, Mr. Preacher. Two of those are in danger of departing if we can't get medicine."

"It's jist plain Preacher, no mister about it. An' we've a surgeon along, so your sick can get help."

Warner raised his eyes to the sky. "Praise God, Preacher. Now we have a chance."

"That'll depend more upon Colonel Danvers than on me, I'm sorry to tell you, Mr. Warner."

Warner looked perplexed. "Surely he is a compassionate man. He'd not leave children stranded in this wilderness?"

Preacher pulled a long face. "Oh, it's entirely possible, Mr. Warner. To put the best light on it, he could be said not to have much use for what he calls 'civilians,' present company included."

"He's a harsh man?"

That had been amply proven with the flogging of the four Dragoons, to Preacher's way of thinking. "That's about the right of it."

"Wh-what sort of man can he be?"

"I'd say you would most likely say he resembled the north end of a southbound jackass."

That left Warner without a reply. After a moment, he broke the strained silence. "I had better show you to our encampment. Everyone will be so excited."

Preacher pulled a droll face. "Oh, I've no doubt of that. Even Colonel Danvers."

On the ride into the lush valley, Isaac Warner explained to Preacher how they had come to be abandoned in such an, as the pilgrim saw it, unforgiving land. When the perfidies of their guides and captain had been revealed, he concluded with a plaintive remark.

"So, we're not sure where we are, or how to get where we were going."

"Where might that be, Mr. Warner?"

"Why, the Northwest Territory, of course, to Oregon."

Preacher sighed regretfully. "You're about two hundred miles too far north for the Northwest Trace."

Warner frowned. "What's that?"

Preacher called on all his patience. "The trail you should have been on. The one folks are takin' to callin' the Oregon Trail."

"We're that far off?"

"Yep. And intentional, I'd judge. It's an old game. Lead a party out into nowhere, rob them and leave them for the coyotes and buzzards. I'm surprised they didn't take your livestock as well."

Warner shrugged. "I suppose we were too many, too well armed. They snuck away in the dead of night."

Preacher turned philosophical. "No accountin' for some folks." A moment later, the sheer volume of cheering, waving and hugging that greeted him left the mountain man utterly speechless.

"Absolutely not!" High as his voice might be, Lieutenant Colonel Danvers still managed a bellow. "Civilians," he spat out the word like an epithet.

"Complaining, dragging their feet, whining, they'll hold us back, make us a month late reaching our goal."

Preacher tried calming words. "Come, now, Colonel. We're only five to seven days from where you want to build that fine fort of yours. Even if they cut our daily advance in half, that's only two weeks."

Danvers slammed a small fist on the table. "I say leave them to their fate. They were fools enough to come out here without proper guidance, they should get what they deserve."

Chillingly, Preacher heard his own words thrown back in his face. He'd said the same thing at Bent's Fort. Coming out of the mouth of Arlington Danvers they sounded dirty and mean. That served to make him more determined.

His eyes narrowed as he pressed his argument. "Am I correct in believing that part of your purpose in being out here is to protect settlers moving through?"

Danvers paused before he fired off another hot retort. "Yes, yes, we have that assignment. It is secondary to keeping the tribes at peace."

Preacher cocked a brow. "Wouldn't it serve your purpose better to protect this partic'lar group of settlers? If you leave them here an' there's a massacre, the howl that's sure to go up back East will light a fire that'll singe your fingers way out here."

The colonel could not deny the truth in that. With a visible exertion of will, he toned down his demeanor. "Perhaps you are right, Mr. Preacher. Like it or not, I don't suppose I have any choice. Say, I thought you had short shrift for these immigrants?"

Shrewd ol' pup, Preacher thought silently. "Now, that's true. I've had me more'n one belly full of pilgrims. Damn fools the most of them. But that was then, and this is now. An' we got them on our hands. It's up to you an' me to do the best for them we can."

Danvers threw his hands in the air and walked away. Outflanked and defeated, he didn't want to admit it. Preacher spent no time gloating over his victory. Instead, he went directly to Isaac Warner. With Warner, he found a young woman. A particularly good-looking young woman.

"Preacher, this is Eve Billings. She and her two children have a wagon in our train."

Remembering his parlor manners, Preacher removed his hat and extended a hand. "Pleased to meet you, ma'am."

"Please, it is Eve. I came to find out what the colonel has decided."

Preacher found himself liking what he told her. "We're gonna escort you as far as we're goin'. When the fort is built, you can winter there and go south toward the Oregon Trace next spring, join another train."

In a gesture that harkened back to childhood, Eve clapped her palms together and did a couple of dance steps. "Oh, that's just wonderful. You're a . . . ah . . . minister?"

"No, that's jist what they call me in the High Lonesome." Preacher seemed uncomfortable to his friends. Three Sleeps sniggered.

"This calls for a celebration. I'm going to cook a regular feast for you and your fellow guides, Preacher. My son got us a deer today. You'll meet Charlie and Anna and . . ." Eve realized she was chattering and cut it off abruptly. "You'll be there? Good. An hour before sundown."

While his companions whooped and slapped each other on the back, Preacher stripped to the buff and entered the water of the Platte to wash away his accumulated grime. Following his ablutions, he dried, donned fresh, clean buckskins, tied back his hair with a strip of tanned rabbit hide, the fur still in place, and slid into his fancy pair of beaded and quilled moccasins. Three Sleeps and Antoine howled with laughter. They found his preparations uproarious.

Preacher did not share their mirth. "You two could stand a good douchin' off, ya know," he grumbled.

"Me?" Three Sleeps gasped. "Why, I smell sweet as a May flower."

"Road apple's more like it," grumped Preacher.

Eve Billings greeted them warmly, an apron around her slender waist, a big spoon in her hand. "We have venison stew, and I made pot pies from the kidneys and sweetbreads. You must take some along for your nooning tomorrow. Ah, here are the children," she gushed, then gulped back her flow of words and proceeded at a slower pace. "Preacher, Mr. Norris, Mr. Revier, this is Charlie. He turned ten two months ago. This is Anna. She's eight. Children, these are our guides, who are going to find a way out of here for us."

"I hope they're better than Mr. Beecher."

"Charles Billings, you watch that mouth of yours," his scandalized mother cautioned.

Preacher squatted to put himself on Charlie's level. "Don't you think it'ud make a body cross-eyed, watchin' his own mouth? Without a lookin' glass, that is."

Charlie had a giggle fit, and Eve surrendered in the presence of these carefree men who obviously knew this country so well. By the time she served up supper, with the help of Anna, Preacher and Charlie were fast friends. Eve exerted constant efforts to curb her babbling. To his companions, it soon became obvious that Eve had eyes for Preacher. She batted them at him throughout the meal. While totally oblivious to this, the object of her attentions enjoyed himself thoroughly.

During the next day's nooning, Lieutenant Colonel Danvers summoned Preacher back from point. "I trust you are aware we are making only half the speed today we did in the past two weeks," he said.

"Yep. That's what I said before. Half the pace will take us two weeks to make the Bighorn Mountains."

Danvers had a dire prediction. "It will get worse, mark me on that. With these wagons hanging on our backs, we will have all the problems and delays of any of their kind."

Preacher considered a moment. Ten miles a day would be disastrous for the pilgrims, too. Not to count the effect on the morale of the troops. Too many good-looking gals among the civilians. But not enough to go around.

"I can go to them and force more speed, but not a whole lot. And I think I can avoid a slowdown to ten miles a day. There are ways to trim time off all sorts of things."

"I certainly hope so," Danvers snapped.

Preacher went to where the immigrants cooked and ate at some distance from the soldiers. Several looked askance at him. Puzzled, he found a stump near the center of the circle of wagons. He jumped up on it and raised an arm to draw attention.

"Gather around, folks. There's some strips of stringy meat we've got to chaw on." When those who had finished their meal and those who had not started the cleanup had formed a semicircle around him, Preacher went on. "I've been told by the colonel that we're not makin' good enough time. He feels that the blame falls on you. Now, I don't take to that entirely. But there are some things you could do to speed us up."

Fully expecting it, Preacher at first absorbed the torrent of complaints and excuses that rained on him. "Our wagons will break down," Renard Labette objected.

"We can only move faster if we lighten our wagons."

"That means we'll have to abandon precious possessions," Martha Brewster blurted, near to tears.

Gus Beecher came up with what he thought to be the clincher. "It'll be too hard on our livestock. They'll start to die off."

Isaac Warner took a more personal outlook. "The soldiers will just have to move at a pace we can keep up with. It's their duty to protect us."

Preacher waited out the storm, arms across his chest. Then he jutted his jaw and laid out the alternatives. "Fact is, the soldiers do not have to do more than leave a small escort with you. They have their orders from the War Department. They have to carry them out. Colonel Danvers wants to leave you behind. He has every right to do that. If you can't keep up, if there are more delays, it will result in you being abandoned again. If that is the case, the Indians will find you. You won't be able to defend yourselves. Not even if the colonel leaves a company behind. On the other hand, if you exercise some imagination you will be able to keep up."

Fists on hips, Gus Beecher spat truculently. "Says you."

"Yes, says I. You have two choices; adapt and keep up, or be left behind."

Beecher wasn't ready to leave it alone. "Somethin' tells me we were better off before you came along. Might know you'd side with the Army."

Suddenly Eve Billings appeared beside Preacher. "Listen to him. He's fought hard against the colonel's determination to leave us to our fate. He must know lots of ways to help us save time."

Good girl! Preacher wanted to hug her. "That I do. For instance, buildin' fires and cooking meals at noon slows the whole column. From now on you might try cooking enough in the morning, or the night before, to provide for the noonin'. In this climate, meat cooked over a smoky fire will last several days. Biscuits will hold a week or more. If you have any cornmeal along, or dried corn that can be ground into meal, you can make mush.

"Warmed on a hot rock," he went on to explain, "it can be mighty tasty dipped in a little molasses at noon. Another thing, I see you have firewood slings under yer wagons. Send your kids along the route of march each day and have them collect deadfall. Stow it while yer rollin'. Then you don't have the hankering to stop early to gather wood. Those of you with spare draft animals, change 'em off at the noonin'."

"We still can't move as fast as the soldiers," Gus Beecher objected.

"Not unless you lighten your loads. An' I've already heard all the sad stories about grandma's treadle organ half a hundred times. For instance you, Mr. Beecher. I notice you have a whole lot of heavy iron things in your wagon."

"Of course. I'm a blacksmith."

"Thing is, it makes you lag behind the other wagons. I'd suggest you dump yer anvil and a lot of other stuff. They can be had off the ships that call on the Oregon country."

"I'll do no such thing. My life's work is in there."

Preacher planted a glower on his face and bent forward so he came eye to eye with Gus Beecher. "Mr. Beecher, you can either voluntarily lighten your load now, or you can have it done later by the soldiers at gunpoint."

Beecher turned red-purple. In a blink, he swung at Preacher's jaw. Preacher blocked the blow with steely fingers coiled around the offending wrist. He pivoted with the force of the swing and carried Beecher past him. All the while he squeezed tighter on the wrist. Beecher's hand opened and turned the same dark color as his face.

"Mind yer manners, friend. I've got no reason to give you real grief, unless you insist."

For all his great strength, the blacksmith could not take control of the situation. Defeated in mind as well as body, when Preacher let him go, he stumbled through those gathered to listen and headed to his wagon.

"Sorry for the little interruption, folks. Like I was sayin', it's up to you. If you have any questions me an' my friends will be proud to help."

Snaking silently through the aspens, a large party of Blackfoot and Cheyenne, armed with the mystical power of Iron Shirt and aided by his modern rifles, closed on an Arapaho village. Located in the foothills of the Bridger-Teton Range, along Little Sandy Creek, the Arapaho band had long enjoyed a peaceful existence. That ended suddenly in the keening war cry of the Blackfoot leader.

Swift and deadly, the warriors swarmed in among the lodges to take women and children for slaves, horses to build their importance in their tribes. Only belatedly did the Arapaho men begin to offer resistance.

16

Screaming, a portly Arapaho woman ran behind a brood of frightened children. She shooed them before her like a flock of chickens. Suddenly she stumbled and lurched forward when the head and half of a lance shaft entered her back between the shoulder blades and burst out her chest in a welter of scarlet droplets. Yipping his triumph, the Blackfoot warrior who had run her down yanked his weapon free and turned to overtake another fleeing Arapaho.

"This is easier than we thought, Black Hawk," he shouted to a companion.

Black Hawk agreed. "The Arapaho have become women. They do not fight."

"They do not have these fine new rifles, Gray Otter."

Gray Otter's face clouded a moment. "Yes. That is true, but the fancy-dressed soldiers have even better weapons than we do. They load without a ramrod, and fast, too. They punished us badly three suns ago."

Black Hawk copied Gray Otter's frown. "Men died. Is the medicine of Iron Shirt not as strong as he claims?"

Gray Otter spoke what would, under other circumstances,

be considered blasphemy. "I do not think his is good medicine at all. For all its power, it seems to follow the way of the dark spirits."

Black Hawk looked worried. "Do not let Iron Shirt hear you say that. He will have you stripped of the medicine and made a target for all men."

For a moment Gray Otter could not believe what he heard. "Do you mean he would have me killed?"

Nodding thoughtfully, Black Hawk revealed something else to the new recruit. "It is possible. Iron Shirt has three white men for council. They wear our clothes, but they are white. I have seen them."

"Then what do we do, Black Hawk?"

"Fight, and watch. The Great Spirit will show us what to do when the time comes."

More screams attracted their attention, and they turned to join in the final roundup of the children. In the distance, the stolen pony herd kicked up a dense fog of dust. Flames flickered from several lodges. Moments later, a sharp, clear peal of brassy notes alerted Black Hawk and Gray Otter to an unexpected danger.

Preacher sent back word when he first heard the rifle fire. There should not be anyone out here, he reasoned. Twenty minutes later, he topped the ridge he now sat upon and looked down on what appeared to be an Arapaho village. What were they doing this far north? Never mind that for now, he decided. Another, bigger problem faced him.

Someone had attacked the Arapaho. Preacher could do nothing. He and the other two scouts could not turn the tide. A large force had swarmed into the village to kill, loot and carry off captives. In the distance he saw a large cloud of dust that had to be the pony herd. This would be a matter of waiting it out, or taking the entire battalion in to drive off the raiders.

To his credit, Lieutenant Colonel Danvers brought the column up smartly and wasted no time in bluster or examining options. "We'll deploy as skirmishers and charge. From the sound of those rifles, I'd say we have encountered some of the renegades we've been informed of."

"I reckon you're right, Colonel."

"Very well, Mr. Preacher—"

Preacher winced. "It's jist *Preacher,* Colonel."

"Yes, as I was saying, Mr. Preacher, take your fellow scouts and reconnoiter our route of approach."

"Which will be?"

"Straight down this slope and have at them."

A fleeting smile turned up the corner of Preacher's mouth. "Sounds good. The sooner the better, they're stealin' the children down there."

When it came, Preacher saw the charge to be every bit as awesome as the first time he'd witnessed it. It caught the looters and slavers by surprise and riveted many in place, their hands coiled in the braids of small girls and boys. Several died that way before the spell dissipated and the survivors raced for their ponies. A dozen courageous ones formed a rear guard while their companions removed the captives. Then they swung astride their mounts and whirled away across the prairie. For once, Preacher found Danvers ready for continued battle.

"We should go after them, chase the savages down."

"That's not all that good an idee, Colonel," drawled Preacher. "When troops split up and go in pursuit of a war party that size, there's good odds they'll be ambushed. Injuns love to run away, only to spring a trap. No, sir, if you don't want to wind up staked out like those fools who chased their horses, you'd best let the Blackfoot get away with their new slaves."

Three Crows Walking, a young Arapaho war chief, came up to the gathering of officers. He recognized the cut of the buckskin-clad trio, if not their faces. Accordingly, he addressed himself to them.

"The Blackfoot do not fight like themselves." Then, in the best English he had, he repeated himself to make certain they understood. "The Blackfoot fight like crazy men. Not afraid of bullets, not afraid of arrows. Fight like Great Spirit watch over them. Crazy men."

Preacher nodded and cut his eyes to Danvers. "What is it you had on this Iron Shirt feller?"

"He is promising to drive out all whites, bring back the white buffalo. He is supposed to have some sort of magic that makes him bulletproof."

Not 'magic,' Colonel. Medicine. Powerful medicine," corrected Preacher. "An' I'm willin' to bet he's told his followers that if they keep to his ritual, maybe eat an' drink certain things, or don't eat or drink some others, they'll be jist like him. It's big stuff among the Injuns."

Danvers made a puzzled frown. "We've killed them, haven't we?"

"We've been fightin' Pawnee. These are Blackfoot, accordin' to . . . ah . . ."

"I am called Three Crows Walking."

Preacher nodded. "Accordin' to Three Crows Walkin'. And, accordin' to these here . . ." Preacher bent to retrieve two arrows with red paint markings. "There was some Cheyenne mixed in among 'em. This thing is spreadin', Colonel. I think you've got your first job already cut out for you."

More than you know, Lieutenant Colonel Danvers thought to himself. "Are you suggesting we interrupt our march to pursue, round up and punish these renegades?"

"New, Colonel. Nothin' like that. Partic'lar we got these pilgrims with us. We'll jist go along, keep a sharper eye and see what develops."

What about the behavior of these Blackfoot in the face of armed resistance? Have you ever encountered anything like that before?"

Preacher considered a moment. "Nope. Not personal. I've heard of Injuns chargin' into the mouths of guns like that some while back. Comanche, it was, down south in Texas. They had them a war chief name of Iron Shirt, jist like this one, who wore one of those Spanish iron breastplate things."

Captain Edward Dreiling stepped up to provide the correct term. "Cuirass. It's called a cuirass."

"Whatsomever, he could stop a ball from a flintlock musket, even some of the earlier caplock rifles. Feller who stopped him, he was a Texas Ranger, shot him right betwixt the eyes. His medicine didn't work too good against that."

Captain Dreiling had a question, which the colonel should have asked. "Preacher, do you think that is the answer in this case?"

"Sure enough. If you can get these grass-green youngsters to hold steady and hit what they aim at. Now, we'd best be doin' what we can for the survivors. Most special, that includes a big pot of coffee."

"Very well. Then we will push on in the morning."

Eve Billings hastily removed her stained apron and dabbed at a smudge of flour on her nose. She rinsed her hands and walked quickly to where the guides had their small gathering, putting on her best smile and patting back a stray strand of auburn hair. When the men looked up from the coffee they shared with two fierce-looking Indians, she repressed a shudder and spoke lightly, trying not to reveal in her tone the importance the invitation held for her.

"Preacher, it would greatly please me if you would take supper with my children and myself this evening." Before he could make reply, she stumbled on. "There will be another guest. Captain Edward Dreiling has graciously accepted an invitation."

Preacher rolled that around in his head a moment. "Well now, there's a couple of things I'd like to take up with him, he bein' the only officer in that outfit with a lick of sense. I thank you for the invite, and I'll be pleased to be there. What time?"

"Oh, say an hour before sundown. I've made a dried apple pie."

"Yer a treasure, Miss Eve. I'll bring along a little jug to wet our whistles." Preacher gave her a big wink.

After she departed, Three Sleeps Norris and Antoine Revier rolled on the ground, holding their sides in merriment. "Well, lah-di-dah! Formal invites from the little lady," Norris choked the words out over laughter.

"Best look out," advised Antoine. "She's set to make you the rooster in her henyard."

For a moment, Preacher looked thunderstruck, contemplating the future *that* promised. He rejected the notion out of hand. "I don't believe that for a minute. Naw, sir, not for a minute. She's only bein' friendly."

Antoine would not let it go. "Last time, when we all went, *that* was being friendly. Mark me, Preacher, she's got her cap set for you."

Preacher remained adamant. "Not by a long shot. You wait and see. That gal's jist bein' nice."

Preacher timed his arrival at Eve's wagon to coincide with that of Captain Dreiling. Eve greeted them warmly, showed them to straight-back chairs she had dug out of her household goods and had had Charlie dust to a suitable turn. Playing the good hostess, she accepted a very watered-down whisky from Preacher. The mountain man and the Dragoon officer took theirs straight and tall.

"Are we far from where you are going?" Eve asked to make conversation.

"Only a week or so, give or take a few days," Preacher responded, distinctly uncomfortable after the ragging given him by his companions.

"I must admit, I am grown quite weary of living in a wagon. What will it be like going on to the Oregon Country?"

Edward Dreiling smiled weakly at Eve Billings. "I'm afraid I can't help you there. Army travel is quite different."

"As I have observed," Eve answered, then added to soften the snippy sound of her words, "Riding free and easy on a horse, living in a tent. It seems so . . . romantic."

"Believe me, Miss Eve, it is far from that," Dreiling felt compelled to advise her. "Even for us, accustomed to going on horseback, it took a week after leaving the steam packets to rid ourselves of saddle sores."

Eve's light laugh rang musically. "My, sir, the image that presents. Should I be scandalized?" she asked rhetorically. "No, I think not."

As the evening progressed, Eve flirted with them both outrageously. She secretly wanted to strike sparks of jealousy from Preacher. To all outward appearances, her plan failed miserably. Preacher was charming and gracious, and entertained all present with tall tales of his trapping years. When the time came to end the gathering, Charlie asked permission to accompany Preacher to his fireside.

Once the boy had the mountain man out of earshot of his mother's wagon, he crooked an index finger to draw Preacher down to his level. Preacher hunkered down. Then Charlie spoke earnestly, in a low whisper.

"You'd best look out, Preacher. My mom's tryin' to kindle the fires of romance in your heart. I know so, 'cause I heard her tellin' Mizus Honeycutt."

A low chuckle came from Preacher's throat. "Why, shucks, son, I know that. Women have been hatchin' such schemes since the first Eve kissed a snake."

Charlie widened his eyes in shocked indignation. "But, don't you just hate it? How can you abide a woman who'd sneak about and plot behind yer back?"

"No problem at all. Truth is I sorta hanker after the affection of a pretty woman now and again. That ain't all that bad, is it?"

Hesitant, Charlie studied his toes. Given his age, his first response was predictable. "Girls ain't good for anything."

He paused, considered a moment. "No . . . I guess not," he replied. "If—if you don't mind."

"How about you, son? Would you object to my bein' around your momma somewhat?"

Feet forgotten, Charlie glanced up with a bright, happy expression. "Oh, no, sir. Not at all. I'd like to have you around more."

"Well, then, don't let all of it fret you. Ol' Preacher can manage for himself right enough. Now, good night."

Early the next morning, the Dragoons prepared to move on. The wails of the mourning Arapaho women, those few who were left, trembled in the air. Tight-faced, Three Crows Walking and five braves, one slightly wounded, came to Preacher.

"If you would have us, we would come with you, help to scout. Maybe we find the ones who did this."

Preacher hid his smile behind a pensive pose, hand over his mouth. "Now, I don't know about that. You'd have to provide eats for yerselves. Army won't feed you. Won't pay you, either. But, I might find a few coppers, some silver you can rub together when this is over."

Comprehension brightened the face of Three Crows Walking. "You would pay us? White man's wampum?"

"You do a good job, I sure will."

Three Crows Walking explained to his fellow Arapaho and they all produced expressions of eager approval. With that settled, they mounted the ponies they had managed to save and fanned out ahead of the column which was forming. They rode out of sight to the northwest.

Preacher gave them half an hour, then he and his companions mounted, ready to set off. But not before Lieutenant Colonel Danvers had his say. "Mr. Preacher, I trust you have made it entirely clear to the immigrants that the same fate as befell these peaceful Arapaho will be theirs if they fail to keep up?"

Preacher could not keep his disregard for Danvers out of his expression. "They've got eyes. I didn't need to put it quite that way. They'll keep up, be sure of that."

For all his assurances, by nine o'clock in the morning, a considerable gap had developed between the Army freight wagons and the civilian train. Something about the specter of the Arapaho village must have influenced Isaac Warner. He became more aggressive in setting the pace for the cumbersome vehicles. Constantly, he urged greater speed. At times his shouts to his mules could be heard far ahead by Preacher, in the stillness of the high plains.

By the nooning, it took only ten minutes for the pilgrim train to catch up to the Dragoons. After stretching their legs and working the kinks from their backs, the civilians ate in the shade of the Conestogas and drank water to wash down the food. Warner actually had his charges ready to depart before the soldiers had completed their meal.

To Preacher's surprise and satisfaction, he calculated they had made fifteen miles. Shortly after Preacher and Antoine Revier took their places ahead of the column, which had gotten under way without complaint or delay, a faint ripple of gunfire came from the rear. Preacher had a sinking sensation that it was not hunters out to bag fresh game for the evening meal. His suspicion was verified shortly when a messenger came pounding up from the head of the column.

"The Blackfoot. They've come back."

17

Warriors of the Iron Shield Society raced their ponies along the high-sided wagons of the immigrants. Fired with confidence by the medicine of Iron Shirt, they abandoned any of their usual caution. It came as a total surprise to two of them when young Davey Honeycutt leveled his side by side, 10-gauge Greener and pumped thirty 00 buckshot pellets into them.

Instant fire erupted in the lungs and belly of the first Indian Davey shot. Shock-borne blackness swept over him and he slumped forward onto the neck of his churning pony. The right side of his chest and face shredded, his jaw hanging from a single hinge, the other Blackfoot flew off his mount when Davey loosed his second load.

Ahead of the Honeycutt wagon, rifles began to crackle as the well-armed Blackfoot poured a stream of lead into the stout vehicles of the immigrants. After several confused minutes, it appeared the hostiles would buy an inexpensive victory. Eve Billings had been caught up in the middle of the fighting. Huddled low behind the three-inch-thick oak sideboards of the Conestoga, she made good use of the Model 40

Bridesburg Arsenal rifle and a shotgun. Hunkered beside her, Charlie industriously reloaded and handed the weapons to his mother as she fired at the Indians.

"Faster, Charlie, there's a whole lot of them out there."

"Sure, Mom, I know that." He paused in the act of ramming a ball home in the Model 40 as a warrior leaped at the open front of their wagon.

Swiftly, Charlie snatched up his .36-caliber squirrel rifle and popped a cap on the invader. A small, black hole appeared in the left side of the Blackfoot's chest and his grip on the dashboard relaxed. Screaming, he fell under the steel-tired wheel on the right front.

"Oh, sweet Jesus, Mom, I shot him," Charlie wailed.

Eve didn't consider this the time for commiseration. "Good boy."

Control came out of the confusion as Preacher and his companions, accompanied by Captain Dreiling and some of his company, turned back and fell on the Blackfoot. The hostiles saw them coming and those in the lead on both sides of the column reined in sharply. Several fired at the soldiers, while others reared their mounts and turned about. Few cared to run the gauntlet of the settlers again, yet the prospect of clashing with the soldiers held even less appeal. Preacher quickly pointed out their apparent milling confusion and hesitation.

"We got 'em bottled up betwixt us," he shouted to Captain Dreiling.

"Looks like it. I only hope those amateurs know enough to shoot at the Indians and not us."

Preacher quickly allayed his concern. "We'll be pushin' the Blackfoot hard. Likely those pilgrims won't have time to shoot at anyone."

Within a breath's span, the mountain man and those with him clashed directly with the hesitant Blackfoot. Their faltering ceased abruptly when face-to-face with the white troopers. Unable to reload, the Blackfoot soon discovered themselves to be at a terrible disadvantage. Armed with a dozen immediate shots each from the big Dragoon pistols, the soldiers blazed into the faces of the enemy. Preacher, too, unlimbered his Walker Colt and fired point-blank into the eagle wingbone breastplate of a screaming warrior.

Another came at him, screaming defiance, tomahawk raised. Preacher turned to meet the threat.

Short Tail and three others took the brunt of the Dragoon charge on the opposite side from Preacher. Led by Three Sleeps Norris and Antoine Revier, the soldiers under the command of Lieutenant Brice swept along the rear of the Army column and caught the Blackfoot by surprise. Short Tail made to swing away, only to find his way blocked by a grinning man in buckskin.

"Gonna run out on yer friends, eh?" Three Sleeps asked Short Tail in incomprehensible words.

"May your mother's Entrance to the World, through which you came, rot and fall off," Short Tail cursed back in Blackfoot.

Three Sleeps knew only enough Blackfoot to catch the drift of the insult. "I love you, too, you horse's patootie." Then he shot the tomahawk wielder through the breastbone.

An expression of consternation and disbelief washed over the warrior's face. How could this be? He is a white man, his bullets can do no harm. A moment later Short Tail learned that the truth ran radically contrary to his belief.

Three Sleeps sidestepped his mount as the Blackfoot fell dead at the side of his pony. He turned in the saddle and triggered off the second barrel of his pistol. The big, .60-caliber ball shattered another brave's shoulder joint, rendered his left arm useless and sent his pony in a frightened sideways dance ending in a frantic dash away from the sounds and smells of battle.

Two Moons witnessed the swift, sure deaths of eight of

his warriors. Quickly the number of wounded mounted to thirteen, with another two dead. He could not believe that this could be happening. What of Iron Shirt's medicine? Had the shaman lied to them, deceived them as to how much power his rituals, dances and dunkings in the river contained? In a tortured half minute, fanatic belief changed to repudiation. Hooting the recall signal, Two Moons rallied his warriors and led the way from the sure and certain death that prowled among them at the hands of the bluecoats and their plainsfolk allies.

Charlie Billings stood on the outside edge of the night camp, legs widespread, body bent forward and down. His stomach cramped, lurched and shot forth another spew of bitter, slimy liquid. Tears of shame and misery coursed down his face. The misery came from his appalling sorrow over having taken a human life. The shame came from his reaction to what he had done.

He had actually killed one Blackfoot, shot him right through the heart. He had wounded two others; one of them had spewed blood from his mouth as he fell away from the wagon.

God, this is awful! Whimpering like a sissy, Charlie thought desperately. How could he ever face himself, or anyone else, again? He tensed as he heard the rustle of a footfall in the leaves behind him.

"Takin' it hard, are you, son?" The warm, gentle voice of Preacher flowed over the boy who fought to hold back a sob of relief.

Misery returned in an instant. "Don't look at me."

"Why not, Charlie? D'you think you're the first and only man who's been upset by killin' someone?"

Preacher's praise—he had called Charlie a *man*—was unmarked by the boy. "Yeah, but, I'll look like a sissy to everyone, *especially you.*"

" 'Yeah, but,' "—Preacher put the words back on the boy—"do you think I didn't puke my guts out the first time I killed a man? An' I was four years older than you."

Amazement arrested Charlie's anguish for a moment, "You did? You were?"

Preacher took a slow step forward, reached down and put an arm around the boy's shoulders. Gently, he raised him to an upright position. "Yes. You might not believe it to see me now, but I went through everything you're experiencing. Trust me, it's never an easy thing. You saved your mother's life, and your sister's. You should stand tall Charlie, be proud. Yer a man now."

Charlie blinked his dark eyes. "I am? I mean . . . I am. I really am. I . . . I . . . ah . . . thank you, Preacher. I was so scared. I wanted to throw up all the time we were fighting. I wanted to run away and never hear a gun go off again."

"That's natural."

"But I . . . thought there wasn't that much difference between killing an animal or a man. That it would be easy."

Preacher patted him affectionately. "You had best thank yer God it wasn't easy for you. Those what find it like snappin' their fingers are plum crazy. They're bound to meet a bad end."

"Really?"

"Yeah. I oughta know. I've brung more of 'em to that bad end than I care to count. Now, come on, yer maw has supper ready."

After the meal, Eve confided in Preacher. "That was the worst thing that's ever happened to us. Those . . . those Indians didn't seem to care. They kept coming, no matter how many of us shot at them."

"They believe themselves to be bulletproof. It's some crazy, Injun medicine thing." He dismissed the fanaticism of the followers of the Blackfoot messiah.

"Please, don't misunderstand, Preacher. It's not that I fear for myself. It's only . . . only if some harm came to my children I could not bear that. I've heard the stories. H-How the savages use children in horrid practices. They have their way with girls as young as seven. Anna is eight. Some, I've been told, even use boys in the same manner."

Keyed to the intensity of her emotion, Preacher could still not refrain from being truthful. "I've never seen or heard of such-like happening to the younger children. An' it's only a few tribes practice such vile things. Mostly, the younger ones, like Charlie and Anna, are used as slaves, or to take the place of a child who has died for one reason or another. Especial if the kids show some spirit. Why, the way Charlie fought off those warriors, he'd be a prize to them Blackfoot. One of them would adopt him, certain sure, an' have him in a loin-cloth and moccasins, with a pony of his own, an' his hair in a braid in no time."

That prospect registered more horror on the face of Eve Billings than the possibility of abuse and eventual murder. Quickly, she put her emotions into words. "What a terrible fate! How could he possibly endure such a miserable life?"

He'd take to it like ducks to water, Preacher wanted to tell her, but refrained from doing so. "You gotta understand, men are kings amongst the Injuns, even when they're little kids. Most boys who are captured don't want to give it up when they've got the chance. They have ponies of their own, which makes for how rich a body is among the savages, and they learn to use a bow, set snares, all sorts of things civilized folk have forgotten how to do."

In a sudden shift of mood, Eve nervously tittered, then spoke. "That's not exactly reassuring, Preacher. You've described my Charlie exactly."

Preacher showed surprise; then his lips turned down. "Well, I was only tryin' to show you that somethin' else could be at hand in such an event."

"And bless you for it. It's only . . . only that I—I'm so frightened for my children."

Although he still did not fully understand, Preacher recognized her position and acted with alacrity. When tears brimmed in her eyes, he took her protectively into his arms to calm her trembling. Eve let go then. She stifled harsh sobs against his broad shoulder. Unconsciously, she pressed her body tightly against his.

Awkwardly, Preacher stroked her long, auburn hair, circled her trim waist with a strong, reassuring arm. Instead of tensing, as did so many women in the arms of a powerful man, Eve melted into his chest. Slowly her sobs diminished, grew less violent, to finally cease. She gasped for air and fought inwardly to regain composure.

Her eyes still shone from the recently shed tears when she tilted her head upward to gaze into Preacher's eyes, alight with concern. At a loss for words of appreciation, Eve rose on tiptoe and placed her lips on those of Preacher. It started out as an expression of gratitude, then quickly changed into a long, hungry kiss that sent tendrils of fire through both of them.

When it ended, both were breathless. Eve said not a word, only freed herself from Preacher's embrace and hurried into her wagon. His lips tingling, Preacher walked off to his blankets, thoroughly confused. That had been the best kiss he had shared in . . . what? Maybe ten years? Yeah, that was it. There had been that Cheyenne gal . . .

Camped alone for the first time in six months, Praeger, Gross and Reiker experienced an overpowering sense of relief and safety. They paid little attention to the splendor of the Bighorn Mountains. What commanded their concentration glowed dully in the light of a coal-oil lantern. Its main attraction centered on size. Fully as large as the third knuckle of Praeger's middle finger, the gold nugget lay on a square of black velvet that perfectly set off its splendor. Praeger reached out and caressed its smooth, warm surface. Then he nodded to the chunk of gold.

"It weighs a bit over six ounces."

Avarice glowed in the eyes of Morton Gross as he spoke. "Where did it come from?"

"The area I told you about before. It came out of the Lolo Range of the Rocky Mountains, near the Continental Divide. There are more like this, lots more," Praeger assured his partners.

A sudden rustle at the tent flap drew their attention and Quinton Praeger quickly concealed the nugget. Blake Soures, dressed in Blackfoot garb, entered. "The men are ready to ride out, Mr. Praeger."

"Where this time?"

"There's a clutch of Psalm Shouters nestled down to the east of here. Near the headwaters of the Tongue River. I figgered we ought to pay 'em a visit. We'll leave enough living behind to swear it was Blackfoot who did it."

Praeger beamed and came to his boots to shake the hand of Soures. "Excellent. Be sure that no one knows you are white men. That could be a disaster."

Brother Frankel could not sleep. He sat alone by the dying embers of the central fire in the circle of wagons. Behind him, the mules and horses of their wagon train milled about in drowsy stubbornness. None wanted to lie down and sleep. Like himself, the good brother thought.

Not a man familiar with the ways of horses, Brother Frankel failed to note when the animals became silent at the soft whuffle and stamp of hoof from the most dominant beast. Two more laid back ears and stomped the ground in warning. Still it went unnoticed by him. Reacting as though to an invisible pressure from beyond the circle, the livestock began to move inward. They exerted increasing pressure on the single strand of rope that restrained them.

At last, Brother Frankel looked up, affected by the unrest that emanated from the usually placid creatures. A yellow-orange streak suddenly arced through the blackness of night. A shooting star, Brother Frankel thought at first. While he was in the process of eliminating that due to its closeness to the ground, three more arcs of fire fluttered through the air. Two struck a wagon's side and the canvas top burst into flame. Jerkily, Brother Frankel came to his boots. Throat churning, he fought to get out the words.

"Indians! We're under attack. God protect us."

For two long minutes nothing happened. Brother Frankel continued to cry the alarm, though with little response. Then six burning brands shot through the night and struck two wagons. Shouts of alarm came from the three burning Conestogas. From beyond the crude stockade came raw yelps—war cries— followed by a steady stream of war paint-decorated savages who flowed into the unprotected center. One, armed with a rifle, took time to aim and fire a bullet at Brother Frankel. It pierced his skin low in the belly. He went down with a shriek of incredible agony.

By then, his fellow evangelists had roused from the stupor of sleep. Yelling in fright, the men and women poured from their rolling homes to spill onto the ground. There they cowered in the dirt, quaking in absolute terror. They died that way, cut down by arrow, tomahawk or bullet. Screaming children, the younger ones, peered out over tail gates to have their brains dashed out by war clubs and already bloody 'hawks.

Only at one point did some resistance show. The train captain, scouts and cook took up firearms and fought a desperate, no-win engagement. By the light of burning wagons they clearly saw their enemy. The attackers looked to be Blackfoot, the experienced frontiersmen agreed. Three of the savages died in less than a minute after the trained men returned fire.

"Stupid goddamned fools, I told them they needed guns out here," the captain spat out in useless anger.

"Lot of good that would do," the cook retorted. "Chances

are, they'd try to pray these heathen scum into peacefulness."
He took careful aim with a Hawken and shot another Blackfoot off his feet.

"Ain't no prayin' gonna get us out of this," a surly guide
scoffed.

More howling Blackfoot shoved into the melee. The
horses and mules had broken free and added another hazard
to the confused struggles of the nonviolent missionaries. It
did not take the invaders long to subdue the wagon folk. The
slaughter was fierce and methodical. When it ended, the only
evangelists left standing consisted of the nubile girls, those
newly ripe, and those not long in that state. Under the rough
direction of one big, burly savage, they were herded aside.

Once the livestock had been gathered and corralled
again, the raping began. The screams and wails, sobs and
moans of the young victims filled the night, bearing witness
to the unending horror of the brutalized girls. Unnoticed,
one of the guides, the cook and the captain slipped away into
the night while the raiders wallowed in their lust. One of the
rapists, who would be heard by no one in the attacked party
who would be left alive, commented on the object of his bes-
tial attention.

"Mighty sweet. I sure do thank you, Blake, for lettin' me
be first to pleasure myself with this one."

"Think nothing of it," Soures responded. "You did a good
job, you deserve a reward."

When the gang of murderous whites had expended their
churning appetites, they fired all the remaining wagons, took
the livestock and rode off. Blake Soures made certain that
ample items of Blackfoot manufacture remained to be discovered by those who found the remains of the unfortunate
missionaries.

18

Lieutenant Colonel Danvers counseled with Preacher and the mountain men at noon the next day. "We are to turn northward after our mid-day meal and head for the Powder River. Our objective, as I have explained before, is where the Powder cuts through the lower foothills of the Bighorn Mountains."

One long, soft, artist's finger pointed to a spot on the crude map. "Right here. There's supposed to be an ideal bluff on which to build the fort."

Preacher knew the country well. He studied the indicated location, gave it several moments' thought, then shook his head. "Nope. I wouldn't recommend it. Trees are scarce in those parts."

"Why, I've been assured the trees grow right down onto the bluff."

"May well be true. But, after you build your fort, you'd be required to go outside every day or so for firewood. An' another thing. From what this map shows, that bluff is exposed to higher ground on all but one side. Well, one side, an' part of a second. A feller could fire right down into the fort.

Won't matter much for a while. Only consider this: what happens when the Cheyenne get their hands on some of those new rifles like we took off the Blackfoot t'other day?"

Danvers raised his voice. "That is not your concern. Your job is to see we get there."

"True. Only pointin' out some things. Like for instance, unless you don't want to dig a well down sev'ral hundred feet, you'd have to take the livestock out daily to water at this little creek that feeds into the Powder, an' haul more water to have some for people."

"That's nonsense. You don't know what you're talking about. I've been given assurances from the United States Survey Office, backed up by the highest authority. They have assured me there is ample wood for lumber—and for cooking and heating—lush grass and easy access to water."

Preacher agreed readily. "Sure, so long as you don't rile the Injuns. That's Cheyenne country, an' the land of their cousins the Sioux. Now, they don't look on owning land the same way we do, but they're mighty territorial jist the same. An' I ain't even mentioned the Crow and Blackfoot."

Danvers loftily dismissed that argument. "Savages are savages. We will be prepared to take them in stride. Let it suffice that this is the location chosen at the War Department, and it is where we will build."

All through the next day, Preacher and his companions found plentiful Indian sign. It took little time to come to the obvious conclusion. They were being watched. Three Crows Walking returned to the column to report the same.

"What do we do now?" the Arapaho war chief asked.

Preacher had an answer ready. "Make real certain of every lump you see on the ground. Some of them might breathe." Three Crows nodded knowingly. "Also, I'd have my weapons at hand ever' minute. Never can tell."

"My thoughts exactly. We already keep watch on dust clouds in the sky."

Preacher reached over and clapped the Arapaho on the upper arm. "Good man, Three Crows. With you as our eyes out front, we don't need to worry."

For the rest of the afternoon Preacher rode along in higher spirits, though not oblivious to the plentiful sign of a Blackfoot presence. After camp had been made for the night, he walked away from the bustle of soldiers and pilgrims to find a little solitude for himself. He had only pulled a twisted, black, dry-cured cigar from the pocket of his buckskin shirt when he looked up and spotted three Cheyenne warriors on horseback. Silhouetted against the ruddy ball of the setting sun, they sat at ease, one bent forward with a hand on his bare knee. Preacher's eyes narrowed as he studied them.

Each wore two feathers at the back of his head, the frizzed and fox fur-trimmed tips pointed upward, a sure sign of being on the war trail. Slight motions of the watching Indians revealed that they both carried lances. Preacher jerked his gaze away from the Cheyenne at the sound of a footfall behind him. He turned cat-quick, with a hand on the butt of a Walker Colt.

Little Charlie Billings stood there, eyes wide with shock at the swift movement of Preacher. He swallowed hard and rubbed a bare foot against his overalls leg. "It's only me," he squeaked.

"Sorry, Charlie. Somethin' out there spooked me."

For the first time, the boy looked beyond Preacher. His eyes went round and white, and his jaw clapped shut. Before he could speak, he had to swallow hard.

"Are those Injuns Blackfoot?"

"Nope, Charlie. They's Cheyenne. An' done up for war. No reason to keep the truth from you. Yer man enough to handle it, an' I trust, man enough not to spread alarm amongst the rest of you pilgrims."

Charlie nodded solemnly. "Yes, sir."

Preacher clapped the boy roughly on the shoulder, nearly dislodging Charlie from his feet. "Good. You do me proud." No one who observed them, except his mountain man cronies, would have suspected how much discomfort Preacher experienced relating to small children. "Now, Charlie, what did you come out here for?"

"Mom told me to ask you to come to supper tonight." Charlie looked unhappy. "But now, with those Injuns out there, I don't suppose you can."

The prospect of a good meal, and good-looking companionship, pleased Preacher. "I don't see why not. Only, if I were you, Charlie, I'd sleep with your shotgun beside you tonight."

Dressed in white men's suits, Quinton Praeger, Morton Gross and Aaron Reiker sashayed into the most elegant saloon that graced a large, prosperous trading post on the south fork of the Powder River. All three paid token deference to current custom with the wide, brightly colored sashes around their middles. That the red one worn by Praeger, the green cloth strip on Gross, and the electric blue chosen by Reiker concealed at least one pistol each was a given. Several roughly dressed individuals at the bar gave them cold, inhospitable stares as they took a table to one side.

"Friendly sort, aren't they?" Morton Gross observed fastidiously. "Two months back they fell all over us, offering to buy the drinks."

Praeger shrugged. "We were dressed like they are then. I doubt if they recognize us, let alone remember how hard they tried to be hired on to work with Soures."

Reiker sighed. "We had us some times then, didn't we?"

A huge man with greasy, long, black, curly hair and a matching mustache pushed himself away from the bar and turned in their direction. He had thick, rubbery lips that shone wetly and made it obvious he had been drinking heavily. Waving a huge, ham hand, he encompassed the well-dressed trio.

"Hey, fancy-boys, this here's a man's bar. They call me Dandy Spencer, an' I want you to know we don't allow no prissy Eastern folk to come in and spoil the at—atmos . . ."

"Try *atmosphere,* my good man," Praeger suggested.

Spencer's face flushed dark red. "I ain't your 'good man,' nor any other's. I'm my own man and proud of it. Talk like that could get yer head busted out here."

"Are you challenging me, Mr. Spencer?" Praeger asked, his voice suddenly cold and menacing, although the tone went unnoticed by the bully.

Dandy Spencer rose on tiptoe and began to rock back and forth. "You goddamn' right."

"Well, then, since I'm the challenged one, I have choice of weapon, time and place, right?"

A puzzled frown creased the bull head of Dandy Spencer. "That's a mighty useless way to go about it, ya ask me. Around these parts, we jist open the dance and set to clawin'. You ain't got sand for that, turn tail and light out of here."

Quinton Praeger maintained an air of amiable civility. "Oh, I can understand the faint customs of such drunken louts as yourself without explanation, Mr. Spencer. My point is that I wish to make clear the terms of our duel."

"D-Duel? What duel?"

"Why, the one you challenged me to," Praeger tossed out lightly. The whitish cast in his right eye gave him a piratical mien.

Dandy could only splutter. "I didn't challenge you to a duel. I said I wanted to rip your sissy head off."

"Good enough. Same thing. You want to fight with me, I have agreed. Thus, the choice of weapons, place and time are mine. It's only fair."

Insulted, Dandy Spencer set things straight. "Ain't never fought fair in my life."

Praeger appeared unfazed. By far the toughest of the

three partners, one more than willing to kill when necessary, the cold glint in his eyes betrayed to all but the dullest, which included Dandy Spencer, the hidden strength he possessed. "I can believe that. You want a fight, I accept. Now, I pick how we fight and when. I see you have a pistol, so I choose pistols. And for the time and place; right here and now!"

With which, Quinton Praeger snatched a short-barrel, fifty-caliber pocket pistol—made by Deringer and Sons in Philadelphia—from inside his sash, cocked it and put a ball into the right elbow joint of Dandy Spencer. Dandy, whom fate had decreed to be left-handed, completed his draw in spite of the pain that flared up his opposite arm. Gritting his teeth, he swung the muzzle in the direction of Praeger and triggered a round.

His ball went wide. Quinton Praeger let his empty pistol drop to the tabletop and whipped out a second deadly Deringer. This ball he put between two ribs, low on the left side of the chest of Dandy Spencer. A stentorian roar came from the huge man, who absorbed the fatal shot with all the outward sign of having been bitten by a mosquito. His coach gun hit the floor and Dandy groped for another one.

"This one's a bit hard to finish," said Praeger in an aside to his companions. By then, they had come to their boots and drawn pistols to cover the rest of the room. Praeger took a third pistol from partway around the sash and brought up the barrel.

By then, the message sent by his body reached the tiny brain of Dandy Spencer and informed him that he was dead. Shot through the heart, he went slack-legged and flopped forward over the table occupied by the conspirators. Praeger returned the pistol to its proper place and hailed the bartender.

"I say, we need someone to remove this trash. And I'll stand a round for the house."

"Yes, sir, anything you say, sir."

* * *

Dawn found everything safe and sound. The Cheyenne did not attack. Accordingly, the column set out again on what could best be described as an uneventful journey. So confident had Lieutenant Colonel Danvers become that he urged Preacher to ride at his side. Preacher found that not at all a pleasant prospect. While they rode along, Danvers waxed almost eloquent. Waving a gloved hand at the fluttering grass on the uptilted prairie slope, he drew a deep breath and launched into his theme.

"Those Cheyenne did not attack us, as you can now see. They sat quietly and watched us, without any show of hostile intent. Perhaps they were curious. With their childlike minds, that could be expected."

Knowing it to be rude, and not giving a damn, Preacher interrupted. "Them 'childlike minds' you refer to have planned and carried off some of the slickest ambushes you'll ever see. As to their 'hostile intent,' Colonel, them braves had their feathers upright. Those feathers are symbols of their valor. They're fixed in a beaded disc, and are worn in different directions for different reasons. Down, toward their left shoulder, means they're lookin' for no trouble. Down, to the right, says they're lookin' to do some courtin'. Up, like they had 'em, means they're ready for war.

"The biggest mistake most whites make about Injuns is that since they live different from us they ain't got any smarts." Preacher cocked his head to one side. "Never fall into that pit, Colonel. It could be the death of you."

Danvers had a pensive look. Albeit he spoke stiffly, his tone lacked the icy sarcasm of earlier exchanges. "Believe me, I've learned that lesson already. I still can't find a reason why the Pawnee were so hotheaded."

Preacher sighed. To him it was entirely obvious. "Because the Blackfoot and Cheyenne are worked up. There's war talk—and raids all over the high plains. For all their lack of modern communication, word gets around the tribes mighty fast."

Danvers retreated to his orders for inspiration. "Our purpose in being here is to induce a calming effect."

Preacher shook his head. "Seems to me we're doin' jist the opposite." For a long time, he could not fathom the meaning behind the enigmatic smile with which Danvers answered him.

In the short term, Preacher soon found himself with a lot more to occupy him. By midmorning, the column had made ten miles, a new record since adopting the abandoned wagon train. It had been accomplished with no end of grumbling by the pilgrims. When Gus Beecher cantered up to the head of the column for the third time, Preacher knew he was in for more.

"Blast and damn, this pace is killing my mules," the burly blacksmith complained. "You have to slow down."

The colonel would not deign to address whining civilians. Instead he cut his eyes to Preacher in a silent order to the mountain man to handle the situation. Preacher sighed and made reply.

"We don't have to do anything of the sort. I can't see a reason to have to explain this again, but here goes. This is a military expedition. It is under orders to git along the trail at the convenience of the Dragoon Battalion Commander. That be Colonel Danvers here. He says we gotta make better time, we make better time. You may not like. it, I may not like it. But we ain't got any say in it. I told you before, Mr. Beecher, to get rid of some of that heavy load yerself or do it at gunpoint. If I was you, I'd hightail it back to that wagon and start heavin' heavy things out as you go."

"You can't do this to me. I—I'll protest."

Finally, Danvers bestirred himself to partake in the exchange. "To whom?"

"Wh-why to the War Department."

"Go right ahead," Danvers challenged in a brittle tone. "I

estimate the next post will run through here in about fifty years."

Gus Beecher muttered that he would hold a meeting, circulate a petition. Lieutenant Colonel Danvers put on a nasty smile. "Oh, you do that, Mr. Beecher. I *love* to read petitions."

Instantly deflated, Beecher uttered a muffled curse and turned away. He had ridden halfway down the column when, suddenly, a force of over a hundred Blackfoot braves in war paint rushed down on the cavalcade from one side and the rear. Women and children, out gleaning deadfall firewood along the way, dropped their bundles and ran, screaming in terror. Rifles cracked among the Indians and a slight-built boy of twelve went sprawling. At once a shrill howl of anguish came from the rear of a wagon.

"My boy! They've killed my Jimmy."

An arrow thudded into the tail gate in direct line with her body and she was violently thrust back out of sight. Nearly every Indian had a rifle, which they fired at once, with much enthusiasm, albeit little accuracy.

19

Whooping and howling, the Blackfoot rode just inside range and loosed a flight of arrows. Commands had been shouted up and down the files of Dragoons and the troops immediately responded with a furious volley.

"Reload!" More order came to the troops as their unseasoned officers gained control. "Volley by Companies! . . . Company A, take aim . . . fire! Reload. Company B, take aim . . . fire!"

So it went, down the line of the four companies. Forty rifles crackling in answer. Then, yipping, the Blackfoot rode away. A final volley raced after them. A dozen rifles fired a parting shot from the rear of the column and the Indians departed. Silence returned to the cavalcade, except for the sobbing of the woman whose son had been killed.

Their respite lasted only a short while. The hostiles swarmed down on their white enemy once more. This time the discipline drilled into them by Iron Shirt and his closest followers dissolved when six warriors toppled from their saddles. Hooting and shrieking war cries, the braves turned their charge into a scramble for individual honors.

It became a pigeon shoot for even the most inept Dragoons, a source of deep disillusionment for the Blackfoot as one after another of the braves fell dead from their ponies. Time enough had gone by to calm troops and civilians alike. They now brought withering fire on the hostiles. Preacher took time, while reloading, to pose a question to Danvers.

"Might be none o' my business, but I wonder why you didn't put out flankers today."

For an instant, the colonel stiffened; then he forced geniality into his voice. "You're right, it's none of your business. The truth is, I grew overconfident. Are these some of your friendly Cheyenne?"

"Nope. Blackfoot, though I'm damned if I can come up with a reason for them to be so far east. Unless . . . that prophet of theirs got them all riled up and is out smokin' the war trail."

Danvers spoke darkly, as though privy to some secret. "That had better not be the case."

Dangerously close to the wagons, within twenty-five yards, the Blackfoot lost their nerve at last. They scattered up a red-orange slope, so many coppery leaves in a whirlwind. Bullets followed them, though only Preacher's, his companions', and BSM Muldoon's scored in flesh. Not to be daunted, Danvers issued fateful orders.

"First and Second Platoon, C Company, pursue the enemy. Lieutenant Brice in command. Move 'em out!"

"I woul—" Preacher made to dissuade the Dragoon commander, then cut off his words at sight of the wild light in the colonel's eyes. Stubborn man, Preacher thought, let him learn the hard way.

With a full platoon at left and right, Lieutenant Brice led the charge from the middle. The big, powerful Dragoon horses churned up the rise and hesitated only a fraction of a second before plunging down the reverse slope. They had barely gone out of sight when all hell broke loose.

Preacher did not wait for the realization to come over

Danvers. Driving heels in the ribs of Tarnation, he shouted to Captain Dreiling. "Come on, Cap'n, bring the rest of yer company. Let's go get your men back."

With Danvers sputtering alone at the head of the column, the entire Dragoon battalion broke ranks and charged over the rise. In the lead, Preacher took encouragement from the continued crackling exchange. It had to be a small ambush to keep the troops alive so long. The big-chested, Morgan-cross, Tarnation, ate ground at a dazzling pace.

Preacher and the two remaining platoons of C Company slammed into the surprised Blackfoot war party before the Indians could react. The thunderous crash of Hall carbines drowned out their shrill war cries. To Preacher's right a Blackfoot swung around and fired his rifle one-handed. For all his lack of accuracy, the ball moaned past Preacher's head close enough for the mountain man to feel its wind. Preacher rode low now, the reins in his teeth, and the Hawken bucked in his grip. His shot hit the Blackfoot high in the chest, on the center line. Knocked to one side, the warrior disappeared under the hooves of his companions' horses.

With the Hawken dry, Preacher shoved it into the scabbard and pivoted at the waist to find another target. Plenty presented themselves. The Walker Colt spat lead and creased ribs on a youthful Blackfoot not yet out of his teens. Bone and meat flew in a welter of blood, and Preacher reckoned that the man-child would have a fist-sized depression on that side for the rest of his life. Preacher cocked the hammer as another Blackfoot swung his empty rifle at the head of the mountain man.

Powder smoke obscured the scene, so Preacher could not see the results of his hasty shot. The rifle butt did not meet his chin, so he rightly assumed he'd scored a good hit. Suddenly, the remaining Indians swung away from the onslaught of so many soldiers and rode swiftly out of range. Preacher took quick count.

Six Indian bodies littered the ground, and only one soldier had been killed. Seven had suffered minor wounds, though. Lieutenant Brice, his youthful face begrimed by greasy powder residue, dismounted and surveyed the scene. Then, Danvers cantered up, his saber drawn, and glowered at Preacher and Captain Dreiling.

"I demand to know who ordered that charge."

Dreiling cut his eyes to Preacher, who winked at him. "I do not know, sir. I did not. It . . . sort of . . . just happened."

Danvers surveyed the scene. "We'll not go after them. Mr. Preacher, your point about ambushes is noted and stored for reference." He turned to the Battalion Sergeant Major. "Sergeant Major Muldoon, return the men to the column."

Talking Cloud was decidedly unhappy. The medicine of Iron Shirt had deserted them. Of the number of warriors with which he had started—one hundred and seventeen—he had five hands killed and seven hands wounded. He directed the survivors to the big war camp to the west. There he went directly to Three Horses who listened to his complaints with obvious indifference. It only served to inflame Talking Cloud more.

"How could Iron Shirt's medicine have failed us?" Talking Cloud demanded hotly.

"They did not believe enough in the medicine, or they would be alive," Three Horses concluded about the dead. "Or they were not purified enough."

"You did not hear me. Twenty-five men killed, thirty-five wounded. Not that many could be impure or doubtful at the same time. That means we will not be able to guard our village from the Shoshoni this winter."

"Then take your people to the Bighorn Mountains."

Not satisfied in the least with this, Talking Cloud went in search of Iron Shirt. He found the visionary medicine man in the process of initiating a group of twenty-five Cheyenne. Talking Cloud viewed the proceedings with far less conviction than before. When the rite had been concluded and the mail shirt exposed, Talking Cloud took Iron Shirt aside. He wasted no time on diplomacy.

"Why is it that your rebirth in water and the gauntlet of coals did not purify the warriors killed so far?"

Iron Shirt cocked his head to one side, to show his disbelief. "You have had men die?" he asked in a chiding tone.

"Twenty-five," Talking Cloud shouted. "In one battle. They went down like aspen in a whirlwind."

Iron Shirt nodded thoughtfully, then gave Talking Cloud essentially the same answer Three Horses had given. After so doing, he suggested, "I think another Strong Heart ceremony is needed." He took on a cheerful expression. "Gather your men and we can do it while the coals are still hot. Then you will see."

That evening, when the nervousness and strain of the attack had eased, Eve Billings sought out Preacher, who sat with his companions, a plate of fatback and beans in his hands. She looked at the concoction with unease and forced a smile.

"You didn't come to supper tonight. I know Charlie relayed my invitation."

"Yep. That he did. An' nope, I did not. Too much good cookin' makes a man soft." He set the tin plate aside and pinched his flat, hard abdomen. "Why, I reckon I've gained five pounds spongin' off your generosity. I thought I'd take a day or two away from the delicious table you lay, so's not to make a habit of it."

Smiling, Eve reached out a coaxing hand. "I wouldn't

mind if you made a habit of it. Matter of fact, I'd like that a lot."

Preacher sighed and roused himself. He joined Eve and they ambled off toward the southern edge of the large encampment. There they found the peaceful vista of a moonlit, rolling sea of grass that stretched out before them to the south, east and west. Eve sighed languidly and took Preacher's right hand in both of hers.

"It's so tranquil out there. You'd never know those savages are lurking out in the dark."

Preacher shrugged. "I don't reckon they are. They were Blackfoot. That means they were loaded up with that hokum of Iron Shirt's. When we killed a passel of 'em, they had to think the medicine failed 'em. They get spooked at that, so it's likely they'll go off an' lick their wounds."

"I hope you're right."

They stood silently for a long while then. After the stillness grew strained, Eve started haltingly. "About the other night. The . . . kiss. It was—it was brazen of me. But . . . I— I think it was . . . wonderful."

She did a step turn and faced Preacher, her arms wide. He paused only a moment before he reached out and drew her into a firm embrace.

Iron Shirt stood before his lodge and scowled as Quinton Praeger and his two associates rode through the rings of lodges that made up this large encampment of Blackfoot, Cheyenne and some Pawnee who had left their country to the east to join in the battle against all whites. The Sioux would come to him soon. He believed that in his heart. Which intensified his displeasure at the return of these renegade white men.

"They should stay away," he confided to Bent Trees who stood beside him.

A ghost of a smile flickered on the face of Bent Trees. "We could *make* them stay away."

Iron Shirt put a restraining hand on the forearm of Bent Trees. "The time is not right to do away with them as yet, my friend. We must get the last of the weapons they promise, the powder and balls, the caps. Without them, we cannot win."

"I heard about Talking Cloud. Will he stay after the new ritual?"

"I do not know. If not, we lose eight hands of warriors. It would weaken us."

"The Cheyenne and the Sioux?" Bent Trees made the common plains sign of a slash across the throat to signify the Lakota.

Iron Shirt nodded. "They'll come. Not all, as we had hoped. Cloud Blanket has taken his people away."

Eyebrows elevated, Bent Trees pointed out the obvious. "If Talking Cloud leaves us, then we will be too weak for the final battle."

A sudden flare of anger darkened the face of Iron Shirt. "No we will not. We will drive the whites past the Big Water river. My spirit guide tells"—a shaft of reality pierced his mind when he reminded himself of the source of his spirit wisdom—"me this is true."

Bent Trees grunted. "Would that he told me the same."

Startled by this lack of faith, Iron Shirt blurted, "You doubt my vision?"

"No—no. Only I think you should fast and visit with your spirit guide again. *We* do not know him. We have not heard him speak. Our strength, our faith, comes from you."

Iron Shirt put a hand on his friend's shoulder. "Perhaps you are right. I will think on it. First we must impress on our white friends the need for more rifles."

After another three long, satisfyingly uneventful days, Preacher guided his fledgling soldiers to the spot selected by

Lieutenant Colonel Danvers. It was situated on a nice promontory overlooking a deep valley and the ringing peaks of the Bighorn Mountains. Tents went up with many joyful sounds of relief. Even in their permanent situation, Preacher noted, the civilians kept to themselves, erecting their spare wagon covers for tents. A surveying crew set up and began to lay out the fort. Gus Beecher started to assemble his smithy, leaving his family shelter to his wife and daughters to prepare.

With the only direct, easy approach up a draw and along the wide, sloping finger of land that led to the site, the main gate would be there. Also the only stockade. That bothered Preacher. He left the details of their camp to Three Fingers Norris and Antoine Revier and went in search of Danvers. He found the commander with the surveyors, in shirtsleeves, gesturing with wide, emphatic swings of his arms. When Danvers completed his vehement discussion, he turned to find Preacher patiently waiting.

"Pardon me, Colonel. I figgered now was the time to remind you of a few things. You may want to put up a stockade all around this place. Look there, over my shoulder. That's a mighty high peak back there. I know it's kinda steep. Even so, hostiles could come sweepin' right down there and behind this wall. That'd trap you folks in back of your own device. Then there's the water. This spine is pure granite. I don't think you can dig a well. More likely a cistern would be the best you can do. A big pit, blasted out of the rock, an' covered over could give you a good supply of rainwater and snowmelt. But not enough for year 'round. An' for trees to make buildings and yer stockade, you can see that outside that little stand over there, the nearest are out of range of your best riflemen. They'll have no protection."

Lieutenant Colonel Danvers gave Preacher a long, cool look up and down as though inspecting a tramp discovered in his back yard. "Your job with the Army is ended, Mr. Preacher. I have these problems in mind and can handle them adequately. If you so choose, you may leave."

Preacher's eyes narrowed slightly, and he pursed his lips to keep his true feelings from being spoken. "Is that your final word on this?"

"It most certainly is. Now, if you will excuse me?"

"Well, then, b'god, I jist might pull out after all. Me an' my friends."

Danvers hastily informed Preacher, "Oh, but there is work for them if they wish to remain."

Close to loosing the iron grip on his anger, Preacher responded tightly. "I think I can answer for them. Thanks, but no thanks." With that, he stomped off.

Preacher felt duty-bound to explain his decision to Eve Billings. He went to her and stood, hat in one hand, over his heart, and informed her of his decision to leave the next day for his favored country in the Colorado Rockies. Eve's eyes went wide when she understood what his rambling phrases meant.

"Oh, but you can't," she protested. "You have helped us so much. We would never have made it without you, dear, dear Preacher."

And that was part of it, too, although a small part, Preacher told himself. He was beginning to feel entirely too fond of this wisp of a girl. No, he corrected himself, this stalwart young widow—and her children. Why, hell, he had no use for children. Even those he had sired among the Indian camps mattered not a jot to him. At least not until they grew old enough to go hunting, trapping and fishing with him. Nope, the settled life held no appeal to him. Only how to tell Eve that in a gentle way?

"Er, the colonel don't want me around anymore. He as much as told me to pack my saddlebags and haul out of here."

"You are your own man, aren't you? He is bound to protect civilians within the range of the fort. You could . . . could join us and he would be obliged to put up with you."

"No—no, ma'am . . . er, Eve. I couldn't do that."

"And why not?" Eve spun on one heel and called loudly. "Charlie, Charlie Billings, come here at once." When the boy arrived, she gave him clear, quick instructions. "Go find Mr. Warner and Mr. Tate. Bring them here. Mr. Beecher, too. Tell them it is very important."

"Yes, ma'am," Charlie replied and scampered away.

Preacher tried to derail her juggernaut. "Now, Eve, there's no call to cause a fuss."

Eve gave him an impish, though determined, look. "It's not a fuss I'm figuring on. You must be convinced that we need you here, to teach us things to help us survive when we set off for Oregon Country again."

"Shoot, anybody can do that for you. Don't have to be me. The way I figger it, I've got about enough time to git back to the High Lonesome, stock up on supplies, then make it to my winterin' place and settle in."

Equally stubborn, Eve Billings put her hands on her hips and leaned toward Preacher. "Are you always this selfish? Don't you ever consider giving others a helping hand?"

Preacher bent even closer. "Nope. I al'ays had to make do for myself. An' I've observed that those folks who get ahead in this world have done the same."

"Why, that's awful. It's so un-Christian."

"I don't recall layin' claim to bein' a Christian."

Shocked by this admission, Eve arched her eyebrows. "For shame, Preacher!" Then her mind exploded with a realization. "Are we . . . are we having our first fight, Preacher?"

Suddenly robbed of his self-defensive pique, Preacher abandoned his aggressive stance and began to chortle. "By dang, I think yer right. Looks like that's what it is."

Relaxed, and no longer feeling threatened, Eve joined Preacher in his laughter. He reached out for her and put one arm on her shoulder. They remained in a chaste, semi-embrace when the wagon-train leaders stormed up.

Beet-faced, Gus Beecher made the first complaint. "What's so all-fired important to take me away from settlin' in? I've my smithy to finish. We've a cave to dig, and sod walls to put up, a sod roof to add." Then he cocked a gimlet eye at Eve Billings. "Or is it that the Widow Billings has chosen now to announce her engagement?"

Scandalized, Eve covered her mouth with one hand for a moment before she spoke. "What stuff and nonsense, Gus Beecher. Preacher is talking about leaving." She went on to relate what he had told her of the confrontation with Lieutenant Colonel Danvers and his decision to leave.

That changed the tone of the men, except for Gus Beecher. "He can go any time he wants, for all I care."

Hiram Tate saw it differently. "Preacher, you can't leave us like this. There's so much we need to learn. And, how can we ever get along with Colonel Danvers?"

"I reckon much like porcupines make love—very carefully." Then Preacher blushed slightly and nodded toward Eve. "If you'll pardon my language, ma'am. As to goin', I figger I'm free to do so when I take a mind."

Isaac Warner made an open plea. "You'll leave us helpless. Look at all you've done so far. We've learned how to make better time, how to effectively fight Indians, better ways to cook for the noonin'. Oh, so many things. An' there must be more. How to better track and take down game, what to avoid on the trail. Such things make you a gold mine to us. Please, at least take a day or two to think it over. We haven't much left, but we can pay you for your advice. Won't you at least give it fair consideration, Preacher?"

Erasing the scowl on his high forehead, Preacher spoke quietly. "I'll think on it some. No promises, mind, but I'll let you know."

20

By mid-morning the next day, the surveyor and his crew had driven stakes to set out the dimensions of the stockade and its headquarters. Also the corral and two outbuildings. Favorably noting this rapid progress, Lieutenant Colonel Danvers ordered felling crews to be detailed to cut down trees in the thick stands of pine down near the base of the finger-like promontory. Hearing of this, Gus Beecher came to the colonel and, toadying up as was his want, offered his services to forge hinges for the gate, along with bolts, spikes and other iron products as needed, at a reasonable price of course. To his credit, Danvers let his face show his distaste for the man, though he did hire him on a by-the-job basis.

The colonel learned of three men among the civilians who had sawmill experience. He interviewed them and, satisfied, hired them at once. "You are to inspect, set up and operate the portable saw that accompanied us from Jefferson Barracks. I expect a preliminary report by this afternoon." He soon learned the full extent of the bad news.

Shortly after two o'clock that afternoon, the three sawyers came to Danvers. The eldest, Tom Quigley, who had been a foreman, revealed the results of their studies. "The blade made it through nice as can be. Same for the other parts. The belts could stand a good oiling an' they'll be supple again. Only one problem."

"What is that?"

Quigley wiped a damp brow. "How are we goin' to power the saw? That blade has to be movin' a fair clip to cut through wood, especially green wood."

Danvers scowled at this setback. "I was given to understand that everything necessary had been included. Surely, you've overlooked something."

"Nope. Not a blessed thing. Oh, it's all there, disassembled and the parts numbered. Ya see, Colonel, this mill was designed to be run by a waterwheel."

Suspicion registered on the face of the colonel. "There was no wheel with the saw parts."

"Nope, we have to build it. The metal fittings are all there," Quigley informed him.

"How's it all operate?"

"Well, Colonel, there's this big ol' flywheel that attaches to the spline of the waterwheel, and a little one that goes on the shaft of the saw blade. The problem is we've got to have a water source to use it."

Danvers slapped the gloves he carried in his left hand against his outer thigh. "I am constantly beset with obstacles. Why is that, do you suppose, Mr. Quigley?"

Quigley ducked his head in embarrassment. "I wouldn't rightly know, sir, bein' I ain't been in the Army. But, from those I know what have been, it seems that's the way of it, Colonel. If it ain't one thing goin' wrong, it's six others."

Lieutenant Colonel Danvers produced a warm, genuine smile, the first, save those he gave to Eve Billings, he had ever given to one of the settlers. "Quite right, Quigley, quite right, indeed. That has been the bane of my existence since I attended the military academy. Not once has anyone put it so succinctly. But that's not my immediate problem. Why did those idiots in the Quartermaster Corps provide us with a water-powered sawmill when we were coming into this god-forsaken country?"

Quigley shrugged. "It is mountainous, sir. Maybe they thought you'd find a waterfall, which would be dandy for this kind of mill."

Danvers grunted. "Those fools have never seen beyond the west bank of the Potomac, let alone the real West. Can you convert it to a treadmill?"

"Not easily, nor likely, Colonel. Best bet is we dam up that creek down below to build pressure and put the mill wheel in the spillway."

Danvers seemed doubtful. "Can that be done?"

"Easy as can be. Your engineer officer an' someone with knowledge of artillery could do the figgers and draw up what's needed. The surveyors could lay it out."

"Then, get to it. I'll assign the men you asked for to your supervision. We need that mill operative as soon as possible. By all means, long before winter."

Preacher decided to take one more look around at the operation Danvers had put in motion before making his final decision. What he saw only convinced him further of the folly of the entire project. The fellers had moved a good three-quarters of a mile from the site of the fort. Well out of range of covering fire, the only protection they had came from half a dozen Dragoons assigned to them. Already the detail assigned to limbing the logs and dragging them down to the area of the stockade had run into trouble.

Dragoon horses, unaccustomed to working in harness, rebelled against the strangeness of heavy loads that pulled against their necks. They clashed into one another, reared, whinnied and occasionally balked. For most of their journey, they remained out of rifle range from the fort as well. Preacher found Captain Dreiling watching the neophyte lumberjacks through field glasses.

Preacher addressed him in a low, confidential tone.

"Jist betwixt you an' me, Edward, this is one hell of a mistake. Those fellers out there are as exposed as a baby's bare bottom on birthin' day. You're all near a thousand miles from any other soldiers, jist about as far from any white man. Supply will be difficult, impossible in winter, and the colonel's plans for water are nonexistent, or plum silly at best."

Dreiling turned to Preacher. "Are you wound down now, my friend? For all the good it'll do, I agree with you absolutely. Putting a fort here, on this impossible plateau, in the middle of Indian country, is what I call downright suicidal."

Preacher shrugged. "I told the colonel he'd be wise to make a large cistern in the middle of the fort area. That'd give you a reliable supply most of the year. If he ran that stockade around the whole place, it would even be safe to draw water durin' an attack, too."

Dreiling brightened over that. "A cistern would work? Tell me about it."

For the next half hour Preacher enlarged his idea. Although in conclusion he returned to his main theme. "The smartest thing to do would be to get clear the hell away from here and set up somewhere else."

Later in the afternoon, Preacher had opportunity to point out to Lieutenant Colonel Danvers all he had discussed with Captain Dreiling. The colonel barely suppressed his irritation. He did make one concession.

"All right, Mr. Preacher. I'll agree with you on one point. I have been studying the approach routes to the site. I'm ordering other palisades to be erected along the south and west faces. I've come to the conclusion that without them we are entirely too exposed. I'm certain that the sheer walls to the east side will take care of any threat from that direction."

"I'd give that second thought, too, Colonel. 'Cause even if the walls are sheer, including being too steep to climb safely, unless they're completely concave, there won't be no such word as *can't* in the heads of Injuns fixed on climbin' up here."

"I'll consider it, but it won't be at the top of my list of priorities."

"Mayhap it had better be, Colonel. Because I'm sure it's on their minds." With a slow movement, Preacher raised his arm and, like the Specter of Doom, pointed a long finger at the figures of some forty mounted Cheyenne and twenty-five Lakota warriors watching in ominous silence from the hill-tops in the near distance.

Eve Billings could not believe the emotions that surged through her. At one moment, a girlish giddiness flooded her. The next, she sank into deep shame that she could imagine such a thing so soon after poor Howard's death, only to find herself awash with gloomy despair that she would never have what she so dearly wanted. Then euphoria surged again. She would hum old ballads, put a dance step in her walk, a sparkle in her eyes and a silly smile on her lips. Abruptly she broke off her self-examination to give Charlie's shoulder a hard squeeze.

"Charlie, sit still. I'm trying to cut your hair evenly all around."

"I don't want my hair cut," replied Charlie in a surly tone. "I want it to grow long so I can braid it."

Amazement washed over Eve's face. "Why, Charlie, whatever for?"

Charlie's lower lip came out in a pink crescent of pout. "Indian boys have their hair braided."

"Charles Ryan Billings, your hair is as auburn as mine, and your complexion as fair. You are not an Indian boy."

Conscious of having gone entirely too far, Charlie could not meet her eyes. He inspected his feet, which in gratitude and relief, Eve saw were now covered. Although by moccasins he had acquired who knew where. "I wanna be."

"What put that notion in your head, son?"

"I've been thinkin'. Indian boys get to ride and hunt and fish and swim whenever they want to. Preacher's told me so." Then he cut his dark eyes to his mother. "Preacher also told me that Indian boys' folks don't spank them."

Eve studied her son, conscious that he had aged beyond his years, yet remained emotionally a little boy. "Have you done something you think you might be spanked for?"

Shock registered on Charlie's face. "No! Yes. Er . . . I mean, I don't know."

"Do you want to tell me about it?"

"I can't. I promised. It's a secret. Between him an' me." Whenever Charlie Billings suffered from guilt feelings, he spoke in short, incomplete sentences.

"Who? Preacher?"

"No, Mom. Not him. Someone . . . secret."

One hand on her hip, Eve shook her head in resignation. She would learn about it sooner or later, she knew with a mother's certainty.

A week went by with the logging detail required to go farther from the rudimentary fort each day. The present party of eighteen, twelve loggers and six guards, had only ridden out of sight when Preacher heard the thin, high keen of a war cry, followed by the muffled pop of gunfire. Quickly, he ankled his way across the crudely marked-out parade ground. He went directly to the large tent located in the center of an area that would become the future headquarters.

He brushed past the sentries and strode straight to the

desk behind which sat Lieutenant Colonel Danvers. "Sorry to bother you, Colonel, but from the sound of it, your loggers are gettin' attacked."

Voice almost a squeal, Danvers bounded from his chair. "What! That's impossible. They have an escort."

Had the situation not been so serious, Preacher would have laughed out loud. "I don't think that means much to half a hundred Cheyenne."

Before Danvers could work up a reply, a mounted man thundered up to the tent. He shouted through the canvas. "Colonel—Colonel, we're under attack. Injuns are swarmin' all over us."

"Here?" Danvers mouthed rhetorically.

The wild-eyed Dragoon, his face slicked with fear, sweat, and mottled with dust burst through the flap. "It's the detail, sir. There must be a hunnerd Injuns."

Surprising to Preacher, Danvers responded quickly. "Borden," he snapped to the commander of Company A. "Assemble your men. Form a relief column. Extra cartridges for all. Be ready to ride in five minutes. Mr. Preacher, will you scout?"

Preacher stifled a groan. "I reckon so, Colonel."

Dust and powder smoke boiled up from beyond the near swell on the breast of the Bighorn Mountains. Preacher ignored the rough trail already cut into the soil and took the most direct route. Streaming behind him in a column of twos, Preacher noticed with satisfaction, the Dragoons pounded hard over the ground. Seven minutes later, they came upon the rear of the left flank of a two-sided Cheyenne attack.

Startled Indians in the grass turned at the sound of pounding hooves. Two of them started to swing their rifles into line as Captain Borden bellowed, "Echelon left and right, draw carbines . . . aim . . . fire!"

Four warriors went down before a scythe of lead. Three others took wounds that disabled them. Preacher noted that a

Dragoon sergeant had learned his lessons well. He skidded his mount to a halt and covered the injured Cheyennes with his revolver. Preacher faced front in time to drive the buttplate of his Hawken into the face of a snarling brave.

"Pour it on, boys! Help's come," sang out the voice of Lieutenant Gresham of Company B.

Gresham had been in charge of the logging detail, Preacher recalled. Quickly he cut his way toward the stalled wagons, his hand filled now with a Walker Colt. Gresham reared up and fired at a warrior who lunged from the back of his pony toward Preacher. Preacher's .44 ball reached his attacker at the same time as Gresham's .54-caliber Hall carbine round. In the next second, the complexion of the battle changed entirely.

With a hundred-twenty Dragoons rushing down on them, the forty-three remaining Cheyenne warriors lost interest in their no longer easy prey. They abandoned the attack and raced through the waving grass, to disappear down a draw. Odd, Preacher thought to himself, he could swear he had seen some Blackfoot among them. The two tribes had been enemies for hundreds of years. Preacher would have never believed he would see them fighting side by side.

The Cheyenne might listen to the message of Iron Shirt, but Preacher could not believe even such a powerful prophet could weld a lasting alliance. Yet, he felt certain he had seen a Blackfoot pattern on a shield and in the decoration of a feathered lance. When the last warrior had left the field, Preacher trotted Tarnation over to Lieutenant Gresham.

"You lose any men?"

"No, thanks be. Not that they didn't try damned hard. We're going to have to take a larger escort."

"It'd be smarter if you didn't go out at all. I've talked myself blue in the face tryin' to get Colonel Danvers to see that. Don't do much good, but I'll try again."

"I wish you luck. And . . . ah . . . thanks for gettin' the relief here so fast."

"You're welcome. Ain't your fault you've got yer neck stuck out a mile. Next time, you might not be so lucky."

Back at the fort, Preacher stormed directly into the head-quarters tent to confront Lieutenant Colonel Danvers. So exacerbated had he become, his face bore the likeness of a thundercloud. He found himself forced to stand in impotent silence while Danvers dallied over an inconsequential report. When at last the colonel glanced up indifferently, Preacher used every bit of will to curb his temper.

"Colonel, according to what those fellers in Washington City writ to me, I was to advise you in all matters regarding the frontier, including Injun fighting techniques and the habits of the tribes. For the last two months, that is what I've been tryin' to do. Only you seem determined to ignore what I say.

"Now, unlike me, these boys has got to do as you say." Preacher paused, then delivered his suspicions in clear and cogent speech. "What I wonder is why you remain so blind to the formidable danger everyone is being subjected to? Don't you care? My point is, we have hostiles where there were none when I left for Jefferson Barracks. That could be exceedingly costly in the lives of these young men."

Put off balance by Preacher's erudite delivery, Danvers gaped a moment before he waved a hand in easy dismissal. "They volunteered for the Army, every man jack of them. As for my lack of surprise, I must say that after all, I didn't expect the savages to come down and greet my troops with open arms. I learned that from you on the way out here. It is something we all have to take in stride, or get out of the game. Now, is there anything of importance you have for me?"

Preacher bit off his furious reply. "I want to scout that raiding party, see where they're goin' and what they're up to."

"That's quite all right with me. Be ready to make a complete report when you return. And leave at least one of the other scouts for duties around the fort."

An hour later, Preacher and Antoine Revier left the fledgling fort. They traveled light, with only what their saddle-and possibles-bags could carry. Once clear of the finger of land and out of sight of the fort, the wilderness swallowed them. To some, the silence and vastness would be intimidating. Not so the mountain men, for Preacher and Antoine, a welcome blanket of tranquillity settled over them.

They picked up the trail of the fleeing Cheyenne easily and began to follow it. Conscious that they were being watched every inch of the way, Preacher had an intense itching sensation between his shoulder blades.

21

Preacher and Antoine trailed along behind the war party at a leisurely pace. That way it took two days to catch up. Preacher saw the first sign of the hostiles. The point and part of the shaft of a feather-decorated lance seemed to float on the horizon. Within a few strides, a mop of black, braided hair rose into view. A single eagle feather protruded upward from the back of the head. Preacher made a sign to Antoine Revier and they reined in their mounts.

Preacher cupped his chin in one hand. "We've found 'em, right enough. Now what are we gonna do with them?"

"I figger you've got an idee or two up yer sleeve, Preacher. Me, I could use a nice snooze between now and full dark."

"Right. We eat now and wait 'til nightfall to move in closer."

After staking out their horses to graze, the two mountain men leaned against their saddles, which they propped against the thick trunk of an ancient oak. They gnawed on strips of softened jerky. Cold biscuits and a pot of beans, provided by Eve Billings, filled out the meal. Preacher's jaw continued to work on a slender wild onion he had pulled from a bunch that grew nearby, he pointed in the direction taken by the Cheyenne.

"Them fellers ain't gonna throw out a welcome blanket for us. So, I figger we need to get in real close tonight and find out what they're talkin' about. Get the lay of the land, so's to speak. Then we can decide what to do."

Antoine washed down beans with cold water from the creek. "Suits. I ain't exactly anxious to go mix in with them. How's yer Cheyenne?"

"Good enough, though a mite rusty. I reckon I can make out what they're sayin' among themselves."

"Good. How's it feel to be away from those soldier-boys an' on yer own for once?"

Preacher heaved a long sigh of relief. "I ain't felt this good in three months. Jist about got the stink of white folks out of my lungs. Why is it there's so many of them has such an aversion to keepin' clean? A good Injun nose could smell 'em comin' a good quarter mile away."

Antoine snorted, amused at the image he had created. "Can you imagine the mess it would make in a crick if all them soldiers, an' the pilgrims, took a bath every night?"

Preacher wrinkled his nose. "Never thought of it that way before. Might be you're right. All that soap and stench floatin' downstream would tell an Injun jist where to look. No matter, it's good to be out here. Now I'm gonna pull me a tomcat and catch a few winks."

Only the pale, frosty light of the stars broke up the black blanket of a moonless night later on when Preacher and Antoine fastened their horses to ground anchors and eeled through the tough, wiry grass to within twenty feet of the Cheyenne camp. Low, small lodges had been set in a semicircle around a large, central fire. Preacher extended his spyglass and swept the rows of seated men.

Sure enough, he was not pleased to note, there was more

than one Blackfoot among the Cheyenne. One of them stood before the assembly and harangued them in their language. His Cheyenne was imperfect, and Preacher found it hard to understand. What he did make out alarmed him.

"When Iron Shirt and our people join you and your cousins, the Lakota, it will be easy to kill all the white men on the bluff. Then we will sweep across the plains with rifle and firebrand and drive the rest out of the country of our brothers forever." He paused to strut proudly in front of the rapt Cheyenne.

"In two sun's time, all of the Iron Shield Society will join us here and the massacre will soon follow. Those who died in the attack on the wagons did not have strong enough faith in the medicine of Iron Shirt. Look about you. The faces you see are of those who, like you, believed. With strong hearts like yours, we cannot fail."

Preacher had heard enough. He tugged at the sleeve of the hunting shirt worn by Antoine Revier. When Antoine cut his eyes to Preacher, the latter motioned for them to draw back. Cautiously they began to move away from the Cheyenne camp. They made it halfway to their horses without incident. Then, as he crawled past a large sage bush, Preacher found himself looking at five pair of coppery knees.

Slowly he raised his gaze to take in the warriors, all of whom competently held modern rifles, pointed directly at him. He froze and sucked in a deep breath. From beyond the obscuring brush he heard the soft voice of Antoine Revier. "Preacher, dang me, but I think we're caught."

Preacher's heart rate increased rapidly, driven by the fight or flight reflex, as adrenaline pumped into his system. Suddenly he lashed out at the nearest pair of legs.

Thrashing sounds across the sage told Preacher that Antoine had chosen to resist also. Preacher had the Cheyenne warrior off his legs in no time. He snatched up the dropped rifle and used it clublike to knock the knees from under another brave. Then the other three jumped him.

Preacher fought silently, and with a controlled fury that left one Cheyenne with a broken jaw. Another warrior came at him from the front, prepared to do a kick to Preacher's face. Preacher dodged and slapped the leg to the side. Then he came upright and split the upper lip of the unprepared Indian. Grunts and the soft impact of fist against flesh told him Antoine was holding his own. A knee to the groin toppled the bleeding Cheyenne.

Preacher started to follow up with a knockout punch, only to have his arms grabbed from behind. A sturdy warrior held him tightly while the last of the group kicked him in the belly. Stomach juices burned their way up Preacher's throat. He gagged and retched while he struggled to free himself.

It did little good. The next instant, blackness washed over him and pain erupted in his head from a blow with a rifle butt. His knees went slack and he hung from the grasp of the Cheyenne who held him.

Preacher and Antoine Revier came to in the center of the Cheyenne camp. Spread-eagled and staked to the ground, they had been stripped of their clothing and moccasins. A tidal surge of pain churned in Preacher's head. Through it, he vaguely heard a stirring beyond his bare feet. A blurred figure came into view and Preacher tried to blink his eyes into focus.

When the image came clear, it turned out to be a man Preacher recognized. "Swift Bear," he grated rustily in Cheyenne. The effort caused him another tsunami of pain.

"It is truly you, White Ghost?"

"Yes, it is, Swift Bear. Yer warriors caught me fair and square." With that admission, Preacher set out on a plan that had only begun to form in his mind. It was one he hoped would save their lives. After another hard swallow, he began to bargain.

"You know me, Swift Bear, an' you know I do not lie."

"That is so. What is it you wish to talk about lying there on the ground?"

Preacher stalled a moment. "Glad you mentioned that. I would feel better about it if I was sittin' upright, so I could talk like a man, instead of a deer laid out for dressin'. Could you do that, Swift Bear?"

After due consideration, the Cheyenne war chief nodded in agreement. "Since it is you, I shall allow it. Release his arms."

Now he was getting somewhere. When the rawhide thongs had been severed, Preacher flexed his fingers to restore feeling, and levered himself up into a sitting position.

Preacher made a nod of his head and proceeded politely. "White Ghost thanks Swift Bear. Now, what you've got here is two fellers who have been friend to the Cheyenne for many winters. Why, I even took me a Cheyenne wife, had two sons by her. 'Cept she got took off by sickness."

"The white man's curse," Swift Bear provided.

"Yep. Smallpox. Nothin' could be done about it. But, my boys are being raised as Cheyenne in the band of Cloud Blanket. It is as the Great Spirit sees best. What I'm gettin' at is that since we're friends, more or less, maybe you would cut us loose and let us go on our way?"

"We are a war party. And I have a band of my own now. I no longer listen to the words of Cloud Blanket."

Preacher cocked a brow. "You two at odds? That's a shame. What happened?"

"Cloud Blanket turned away from the Iron Shield Society."

"What is that?"

"A new warrior society, with powerful medicine. It was brought to us by a Blackfoot shaman."

"Oh, yes, Iron Shirt." Preacher cocked a brow and continued shrewdly. "But Iron Shirt does not speak for the Cheyenne, now that I know for a fact. An' I don't think he speaks for Swift Bear."

Swift Bear curled his lower lip outward a moment before replying. "We follow him in the great battle."

"What fight is that?"

"To rid our land of the white men. Iron Shirt leads us in that."

"But he doesn't tell you what to do with a friend."

"No. That is so. True though it is, I cannot simply release White Ghost. You were spying on a war camp."

Preacher put on an unhappy expression, then brightened with a show of hope. "There is a way, though, isn't there?"

A brief smile showed Swift Bear followed Preacher's logic. "You could . . . fight your way free."

"You mean, take on the whole mess of you?"

Swift Bear shook his head. "No. If you could fight your way past ten warriors, you could go on your way in peace."

"What about my friend? He looks a mite worse for wear. Could I fight for his release, too?"

Considering that a while, Swift Bear finally made answer. "You would have to better four hands of men for that." At Preacher's unhappy expression, he added. "Or you could fight one man to the death."

"I would have to fight any man you send against me?" At the nod from Swift Bear, he went on. "If I win, me an' my friend go free and unharmed?"

"That is so. And if you do not defeat my choice, let us hope you both die like men."

"What weapons will we use?"

"That will be decided by the council tonight."

Preacher had another, vital question to ask. "Who will I fight?"

Swift Bear remained silent, let his gaze roam over the gathered warriors. Then he made a gesture that summoned an important-looking Blackfoot. The two spoke too quietly for Preacher to hear. When they had decided, Swift Bear turned back to Preacher.

"I have asked my brother, Three Horses, who he thinks should uphold our honor. He has suggested that it would be fitting for Tall Bull to claim your scalp. Tall Bull is a Blackfoot, one who has taken the way of Iron Shirt and is immune to the weapons of the white man."

By the slightest value of intonation, Preacher managed to keep sarcasm out of his voice when he replied dryly, "Well, then, I don't think pistols would be a fair choice for weapons. I need at least a little chance to win."

"You will learn of our decision tomorrow. When the sun is high, the fight will begin."

Preacher and Antoine spent an uneasy night. In the chill mountain air, they soon found themselves stiffening and had to clench their jaws to keep their teeth from chattering. Tied to the trunks of a pair of saplings, they could not even lay out full-length to sleep. When morning came, their muscles had grown knotted and sore.

Thoughtfully, Swift Bear had ordered them cut loose and, while food was brought to them, they worked out the kinks. They were kept under control by rawhide tethers around their waists. Preacher ate with his usual appetite; a stew made of some sort of meat he could not identify. Then he began to exercise lightly.

Relentlessly the sun climbed the sky while Preacher continued to stretch, bend and run in place. All the while, he tried to think through a strategy to insure he won. When he worked up a light sheen of sweat and his muscles seemed as smooth in operation as usual, he stopped and sat beside Antoine.

Lacking tact, Antoine brought up one of several old acquaintances who had undergone such a challenge. "Remember ol' Kip? He had to fight for his life one time like this. Against the Arapaho, I believe. Too bad it kilt him."

"Now, that's a fact. How about French Jake, though? He came through it missin' only three fingers of one hand. Gives a feller real inspiration, that does."

Antoine had more encouragement. "How about ol' Jim Bridger? Seems he ran afoul of some excitable Paiutes. They was fixed to torture him and burn him alive, only he talked them into a fight, best man wins all. Now, you know the Paiutes is sneaky. He had to fight three men before they kept their word. Killed all three Jim did. With only a couple light cuts on his arms."

"Not to mention a slice on one cheek that near tooken out one eye."

Antoine cut a slantways glance at Preacher. "You sound like you're regrettin' this fight already."

Preacher slid his gaze to the whiskered face of his companion. "Now that you mention it, maybe I am."

"You want out of it?" probed Antoine.

"I want out of here. An' the only way to do that is go through with a fight."

Antoine offered a crumb of hope. "You coulda said no."

"An' we'd been killed on the spot. Nope, that's not for this child. I plan on livin' a whole long time after this affair."

"We've had some good times, haven't we, Preacher?"

"You goin' softhearted on me, Antoine?"

"Not me, *mon ami.* I was . . . only thinking."

"About what?"

Antoine sighed heavily. "We both know of more men that failed to get through such an ordeal than those who did. I feel responsible in a way. It is as though if I had not been along, you might have gotten away."

"Nonsense, my friend. You did not cause this. I failed to keep careful watch. They found us and nabbed us, an' here we are. But I think I've figgered a way out for us. It would be crazy to expect that I'll not get hurt some in the process."

Sincerity radiated from the respectful expression Antoine wore. "By *le bon Dieu,* Preacher, you have more sand than any ten men I know. God go with you."

Preacher swallowed hard at the lump that had suddenly appeared in his throat. "Thank you, Antoine."

Before they expected it, the time arrived for the mortal combat. Down the slope a way, the Cheyenne and their tenuous allies gathered in a large, loose circle around a bare spot of ground. Swift Bear and four of his warriors came for Preacher. Two of them escorted Antoine Revier while the other pair accompanied Preacher. To muttered insults, Preacher's captors shouldered a path through the crowd and delivered him to the center. Then they released the tether and stepped back.

A loud clamor rose as Tall Bull stepped through the ranks of spectators. His name suited him to perfection. He towered well over six feet, with thick muscles and tree-trunk legs. His hands were the size of a grizzly's paws and his head would not fit the largest hat size. He had Preacher by five inches and a good fifty-five pounds. Swift Bear came forward and handed each man a knife and a tomahawk. Relief coursed through Preacher when he found that the weapons were his own. Then the Cheyenne chief stepped back and motioned for the contestants to face him.

"This is a fight to the death. You will use no other weapons than those given you. If you lose both, you may use hands, feet, and teeth. It is in the hands of the Great Spirit, and up to your skill, to decide who will win."

With that, he melted back into the inner ring of onlookers and raised his arm. "Let the fight begin."

22

Warily, the two fighters circled, intent on studying each other's strengths and weaknesses. Tall Bull, with the advantage of size and weight, struck first. His tomahawk whistled loudly in a roundhouse swing. Preacher lithely sprang out of the way. Instantly he retaliated with a flick of his left wrist.

The keen edge of his Greenriver knife bit into flesh over the left eye of Tall Bull. A sheet of blood washed over the lid and obscured his vision. In the instant of hesitation that caused, Preacher lashed out with his war 'hawk and lightly nicked Tall Bull over the left hipbone. A heavier stream of blood flowed down the Blackfoot's leg. The spectators raised an angry roar.

Tall Bull stumbled twice, then flexed his knees and coiled his body for another attack. He came in straight, tomahawk whirring in a silvery blur before his face. Knife held with the edge up, he feinted for the proper opening and drove the blade forward. Preacher jumped high in the air and brought his 'hawk down on the haft of the one in the hand of his adversary.

Sharp pain radiated up the arm of Tall Bull and he nearly

dropped his tomahawk. Then he shifted his weight and spun in a full circle. When he saw the hated white man again, he let out a howl and swung his knife with all his force. The stroke split Preacher's buckskin shirt from his left hip to his right shoulder. A thin ribbon of blood oozed from the chest of Preacher. Off balance from his effort to avoid the deadly steel, he stumbled over his own feet.

Down Preacher went, but not before Tall Bull charged forward and sank the sharp edge of his tomahawk into the thick muscle of Preacher's upper chest. By immediately going slack the blade did not cut through bone or pierce a lung. Preacher hastily rolled to one side. He recovered before Tall Bull could follow up his advantage. Panther quick, Preacher smacked the Cheyenne in the gut with the flat of his blade.

Groaning, Tall Bull doubled over. Preacher sacrificed a chance to get in another blow to return to his feet. Slowly, a plan began to form in his mind. Swinging rapidly in a figure-eight, Preacher made the blade of his 'hawk a continuous blur between them. Inexorably he edged Tall Bull backward, toward a large, old tree. Eyes fixed over the shoulder of Tall Bull, Preacher gauged his distance. When he had the Blackfoot in the proper position, he feinted to his left, then whirled right and ran around the slower-moving Tall Bull.

Seeing an opening, Tall Bull rushed in. His arm raised above his head, he was prepared to split Preacher's skull. The moment his opponent committed himself to the blow, Preacher dropped flat on the ground. Unable to arrest his motion, Tall Bull buried his tomahawk in the tree trunk up to the haft. Swiftly, Preacher cut a line across the exposed belly of Tall Bull, which released a river of blood.

Tall Bull choked back a howl of pain while he struggled to free his weapon from the wooden vise. Suddenly aware that Preacher was on the way up, momentary panic seized him. Unable to free his war 'hawk, Tall Bull abandoned it for his knife, which he changed to his right hand.

Making a shrewd surmise, Preacher tossed away his own

'hawk and shifted to his Greenriver. This gesture brought the first sound of appreciation from the spectators. Preacher stepped in and began to circle. Awkward and uncertain, his reservoir of cunning and strength bleeding out through his wounds, Tall Bull did likewise. Grimly, the fight went on.

Steel clashed on steel as Preacher parried an overhand thrust. Pain flowed through his chest like fire. Both men danced back and circled again. Tall Bull moved slower, his shoulders drooped and his head canted forward. He gasped in great drafts of air and vigilantly sought an opening. At last he sensed a flaw in Preacher's defense. With a deep grunt he lunged forward on his right leg and drove the tip of the blade toward Preacher's belly.

All at once, the knife in Preacher's hand showed up where it should not be. It deflected the blade of Tall Bull as Preacher spun away out of danger. Loss of his target sent Tall Bull stumbling to one side, bent over and vulnerable. The wound in Preacher's shoulder stung mightily as he tried to reverse his swing and plunge the Greenriver into the soft side of Tall Bull.

Having missed his lunge, Tall Bull knew the cold loneliness of desperation. Slowly he calmed his racing emotions. In sudden inspiration, he bent lower and snatched up a handful of dust and pebbles. Recovering his balance, he turned and hurled the contents of his hand into the face of Preacher.

Blinded, Preacher dropped low and did a forward roll. After two turns he crashed into the legs of the onlookers and, before Tall Bull could close on him, snatched a remembered gourd of water from between the nearest Cheyenne's legs. Quickly he poured the contents over his head and blinked his vision clear as he came to one knee. He managed it in time to keep from having Tall Bull's knife buried in his back.

Slowly Preacher yielded to the relentless pressure of the heavy, muscular warrior who had crashed into him. He shifted his feet and used the momentum of Tall Bull to throw the Blackfoot over one hip and send him crashing into the Cheyenne spectators. Immediately, Preacher regained his equilibrium and lashed out a foot.

His kick caught Tall Bull in the side of the head. Instantly groggy, Tall Bull momentarily lost sight of his opponent. Seizing his chance, Preacher dove in and made a quick slash that cut the throat of Tall Bull, who dropped to the ground, where he died before the gasping Preacher. A long, stunned silence followed.

Frowning, Two Moons stepped forward to clasp forearms with Preacher. "You have won fairly, White Ghost. Take your friend, your weapons and horses and ride out in peace. You will not be harmed."

Preacher and Antoine made the return trip to the fort in a day and a half. They paused only to dress Preacher's wounds and to rest their mounts. Preacher had grown feverish by the time they came in sight of the partly erected palisade. He rejected the suggestion made by Captain Dreiling that he see Major Couglin. Like most mountain men, he was wary of the medical profession.

"You never hear a pill-roller say he's *doing* medicine. They're all the time *practicin'*, which says to me they ain't got it right yet," he growled at the Dragoon officer's repeated insistence. Instead, he sent Antoine Revier and Three Sleeps Norris to find some special moss, leaves and spiderwebs.

When Eve Billings heard of his condition she came at once to the lean-to where Preacher lay. His forehead was dew-slicked with perspiration, and he had sunk into an uneasy sleep. His dry lips parted and he muttered unintelligible words. Eve knelt at his side and dabbed his mouth with a water-soaked cloth. Preacher moaned and shuddered reflexively.

Gibberish spilled from his tongue. "Ubbajubba."

By that time, his companions had returned with their shopping list filled. Eve looked up at them in an appeal. "Why didn't he go to the Army doctor?"

Three Sleeps answered her. "Stubborn fool won't have no truck with a doctor. Says a Cheyenne medicine man can cure a feller faster. An' a shaman won't cut anything off."

Secretly, Eve agreed. She saw as hopelessly medieval the popular assumption that amputation was the solution for nearly everything that would not respond to bleeding. Yet, Preacher obviously had an infection. The inflamed skin around the wound, the steady ooze of yellow matter from the broken scab pointed to no other possibility.

"We brought the things Preacher wanted." Antoine Revier offered the reed basket to Eve for her inspection.

What she saw made her nose wrinkle. "Do you know how to mix these?"

Revier, the half-French, half-Delaware mountain man answered eagerly. "Yes, ma'am. More or less that is. If Preacher was awake, he'd know the exact amount. We'll jist add a dab of this and a drop of that until it starts to pull the pus outta that wound."

A bullfrog croak came from the supine Preacher. "I am awake, dammit. Now listen." He went on to give the proportions of each ingredient.

Antoine mixed them while Eve hovered over Preacher. Then the jaunty son of a *voyageur* grew serious while he poured whisky over Preacher's wound and scraped away all of the scab with his knife. Next came the poultice, which Antoine packed deeply into the cut. Finally, while Three Sleeps lifted Preacher's shoulder and Eve held his head, Antoine bound the wound with a folded strip of cheese cloth he had purchased off Hattie Honeycutt, then wrapped a thin, thoroughly wet strip of well-boiled buckskin over that.

"There," he pronounced over his ministrations. "That should start to draw right nicely by this evening. Tomorrow, he'll be up and sassy as ever."

Not at all convinced, Eve asked, "Are you sure?"

Antoine considered it. "By noonin' time, at least."

Decidedly uneasy, Eve made an offer. "If you don't mind, I'll watch over him part of the evening, give you two a rest."

"Fine with me," Three Sleeps agreed. "I'm sure Preacher would rather wake up lookin' at your face instead of one of ours."

Regardless of the assurances given by Three Sleeps Norris, three days passed before Preacher awoke from his septic delirium and made conscious note of his surroundings. He forced a delighted smile, though too weak to sustain it long, when he found Eve Billings dutifully at his side with a damp cloth ready to salve his fevered brow. That his mind had not suffered became immediately clear.

"How long?" he asked.

Eve fought back the tears of joy and relief that formed in her hazel eyes. "Three days. You . . . you were very sick."

Preacher made little of it. "Weren't nothin'. A li'l bout of sweats is all."

"Preacher you nearly burned up with fever. Dr. Coughlin wanted to bleed you. I told him I'd take a shotgun to him if he tried."

Lips curled in a feeble smile, Preacher expressed his gratitude for that. "An Army sawbones is good for only one thing. Makin' a feller worse off." His voice gained strength and a gentle warmth. "Thank you for lookin' out for me, Eve. I'm much beholdin'."

"No thanks needed. Call it . . ." Go on, say it, her mind told her. "Call it a labor of love." Then she stumbled on. "Your friends took turns with me, watching over you." Eve reached out and wiped Preacher's brow a final time.

A week went by before Preacher walked abroad unaided in the fast-growing compound. The first floor of the headquarters had been completed, along with a long, low, warehouse sort of building for the quartermaster. First to go up, Preacher had pointed out to him by Antoine Revier.

"He has some near quality whisky," Antoine advised.

"Beer," Preacher corrected. "One beer is about all I think I can handle."

"*Très bien!* Then let us go and get it now, before you change your mind, or your nursemaid comes along and forbids it. *Allez vite!*"

Two more weeks went by before Preacher pronounced himself as fit as before the fight. He looked back on the duel with Tall Bull as he surveyed progress on the fort. He had not intended to kill the big Blackfoot. He had used the ploy of throwing aside his 'hawk in furtherance of that. But a Blackfoot was a Blackfoot. When Tall Bull threw the dirt in his face, Preacher knew he might not leave this circle of warriors alive. So, all bets were off.

Old news, Preacher thought as he discarded his reflections and watched the last of the split logs being hammered into place on the second-floor roof of the headquarters. Somehow, panes of glass had survived the arduous trek to this promontory and amateur glaziers were gingerly fitting filled sashes into the lower floor's windows. The front stockade had been completed, Preacher saw with relief.

It consisted of a double palisade of foot-thick pine trunks, sharpened on the tops with a two-foot space of rammed earth between. Running the length of it, a five-foot-deep battlement had been installed, to provide for firing from the wall. The huge gates had been hung and now moved ponderously on thick iron hinges. Fully a third of the outer defenses extended along the west face. Some ten feet inside the main gate, a pounded ramp of dirt and granite boulders provided access to a platform of the same material at the top. The battalion's three-pound field piece could be hauled up there to give covering fire. It stood now beside a flagpole which had been erected in front of the headquarters building in a circle of whitewashed rocks. More of the chalky stones marked out the parade ground and walkways to and from the buildings.

"Danvers must have these poor devils working day and night," Preacher observed to Eve.

"Yes, he does. I overheard some of the soldiers talking. They said the colonel was setting a record in minor infractions' punishment. The men who break minor regulations receive extra duty details after retreat—whatever that means."

Preacher turned an amused smile on her. "I think that's when they fire off the little cannon and haul down the flag."

Perplexity lined Eve's brow. "Oh, yes. But, why do they call it 'retreat'? Isn't that running from the enemy?"

Preacher shrugged. "Same word, diff'rent meanings. That's the Army for you." They laughed together.

"You're coming to supper tonight?" Eve asked.

Chuckling, Preacher spread his hands in submission. "A team of a dozen mules could not keep me away."

Something had gone decidedly wrong with the alliance between the Blackfoot, Cheyenne and Sioux, as it often did in such meldings of one-time enemies. The Cheyenne had been slow in coming in. Three large bands, including that of Cloud Blanket, had refused to join at all. The Sioux had sent only token numbers from the Brule, Oglala and Teton subtribes. Notable among those absent were the members of Red Cloud's band. As a result, the planned great uprising did not happen on schedule. Iron Shirt fumed over it. At last he decided to take out his anger on the nearest whites.

Accordingly, he stormed into the lodge occupied by Praeger, Gross and Reiker. He studied them in silence a moment, smelled their sudden outbreak of fear. What puny creatures, he thought to himself.

"Where are your wagons of rifles? Where's the powder?"

"On the way, Iron Shirt," Praeger managed calmly.

Iron Shirt spat into the fire. "That is not good enough. We hold back and waste our energy in races and gambling. This war cannot begin without the weapons you promised. When will they be here?"

Coldly Praeger responded. "I don't know any more than you do. Besides, the other tribes have not come in as you expected. When the warriors get here, the guns will be here also. What you need is another show of big medicine. I think I might have just the thing."

Intrigued, Iron Shirt leaned toward the broad-shouldered, lean white man, his eyes fixed on the knife scar. "What is that?"

"Give me time to get everything rigged up. Then, tonight at the dances, tell everyone that you are going to do a most potent dance. A spirit dance that will do wondrous things, like nothing they have ever seen. Use the dance you worked out last month, the one you were going to use as a victory dance when the white soldiers are destroyed."

Plentifully shrewd for all his lack of sophistication, Iron Shirt's eyes held a gleam of anticipation. "What is it I am going to make happen?"

"Tell them that you will make stars rise from the ground up into the sky."

Uncertain, Iron Shirt blurted, "Can I do that? I mean, what are you going to do to make it happen?"

Praeger gave him an enigmatic smile. "Wait and see. I promise you it might even have you wetting your loincloth."

Praeger and his associates, along with Soures and three henchmen spent the rest of the day well beyond the large encampment of Blackfoot, Cheyenne and Sioux. They had the last tube in place shortly before dark.

Praeger headed for the rear of one wagon. "We'll fix something to eat out here. No sense in going back and drawing attention to ourselves, then having to come back after dark. Someone might follow and spoil the whole show."

"You've got it all figgered out, Mr. Praeger," Blake Soures

said, sincerely complimenting his boss. "Those Injuns'll think the world's comin' to an end, sure enough."

Morton Gross raised a cautioning hand. "We do not want to terrify them into running away. This exercise is merely for the purpose of reinforcing the magical powers of our great prophet, Iron Shirt."

Aaron Reiker added his own praise. "Still, it was inspired of you to have ordered these pyrotechnics and to have had them shipped out here."

Praeger fought back a smirk. "We'll soon see, won't we?" He began to take food from a large woven reed basket and pass it around.

Two hours after darkness fell, Quinton Praeger roused himself. "Better get ready. That's the drum beat for Iron Shirt's fancy dance. It'll take about twenty minutes, then we let go the first shell."

When the time came, Praeger touched the glowing tip of a length of slow match to the short fuse near the bottom of a fiberboard tube. With a dull thud, a whoosh and a hissing roar the projectile leaped into the night sky. It burst when it reached the apex of its arc, showering the sky in smoky red streamers. By then the second star shell was on its way.

This one erupted in green and white, with bright spots at the end of streamers of smoke that crackled and popped as their internal fuses burned down to the small charges. Most of the fireworks Praeger had arranged for consisted of three-pound star bursts. For the finale, he had something special. Following a simultaneous discharge of six star shells, he and his associates ignited and launched five aerial reports.

Discs of white appeared one after another in the sky, each followed by a violent blast and an accompanying shock wave. When the awesome sound of the last one rolled away across the hills, Quinton Praeger heard the cackle of Blake Soures.

"That'll have them savages dribblin' in their drawers for certain sure. What a hell of a show, Mr. Praeger. I'd call it brilliant."

* * *

Those in the camp did not share the enthusiasm of Blake Soures. Unable to contain them, the guards stood helplessly by while the pony herd stampeded. Many of the warriors abandoned their immense pride to hide, shivering under their bison robes. Some fell to the ground, stupefied, in superstitious veneration. The Great Spirit truly spoke through Iron Shirt, others exclaimed to their neighbors.

Slowly the pandemonium subsided. Shaken to his core by the dreadful display, Iron Shirt had no words for those who gradually came to reaffirm their allegiance. He could only grip their forearms and nod and mumble. The coldly analytical part of his mind eventually asserted itself. Whatever the white men had done, it had restored his power over these fractious tribes.

He turned, smiling, to his most trusted subordinates, Two Moons and Bent Trees. "Trust me, my friends. With this great medicine, the mighty battle really will come."

23

Preacher had become downright itchy-footed. Another week had gone by and still no major attack by the hostiles. There had been skirmishes against wood and water details, the fellers had been shot at from a distance and the newly erected sawmill had been thoroughly riddled with .54 caliber balls on two occasions. Preacher considered the damming of the swift little creek and the locating of the mill on its banks below the obstruction to be the height of stupidity.

"Even dumber than buildin' this fort out where it's exposed to ever'thing," he had been heard to opine frequently. At least one of his worries seemed to have somewhat worked its way to a solution.

Every day, more of the pilgrims settled in to rest and wait out the year at the fort. Spring, they declared, would suit them fine to move on. They had listened to his tales and those of his companions about winter in the high country. None among them felt hearty enough to endure exposure to the elements in wagon boxes. Well and good, Preacher figured. It gave him more time to ponder on why the Blackfoot and their allies had not attacked in force.

An exception to the settling down of the immigrants was the subtle campaign still waged by Eve Billings and Isaac Warner to get Preacher to commit to leading them through the wilderness. It manifested itself again that evening at a supper presided over by Eve and Rebecca Warner. After a satisfying meal featuring roast venison, Isaac Warner sopped the last of a rich brown gravy from his plate with a delicate, yeast-raised bread roll, leaned back and patted his fledgling potbelly.

"Yessir, I've come to see spring as the ideal time to move on. We can learn a lot in the meantime, and the animals will certainly be more fit."

Preacher accepted a cheroot from the wagon captain which he tipped toward his benefactor before he lighted it. "Couldn't do a better thing. By then, it might be this fuss with the Injuns will be ended."

Isaac touched a burning ember to his own cigar. "Only one thing is left undone, then. We will still be in need of a guide, competent scouts, that sort of thing."

Preacher tried to be evasive. "When word gets around about this fort, there'll be all sorts of folk drop by. You can find someone easy."

Warner was not to be put off so easily. "Fact of the matter is, myself and the committee are set on it bein' you and possibly your friends, Revier and Norris."

"Nope. Ain't possible. Soon's this Injun ruckus is over with, I'm on my way to the Shinin' Mountains."

"We can pay well. If not all in advance, then when we reach the Oregon Country."

Shaking his head, Preacher made to leave. "Sorry, Mr. Warner. I ain't in the guide business. I leave that to them that enjoys it." He gave his thanks for the good meal and walked away.

Eve excused herself and quickly followed. When she caught up to Preacher she scurried around his broad-shouldered frame and halted in his path. Every bit the auburn-haired image of determination, she came right to the point.

"Preacher, for the life of me, I don't know what you have against leading us to the Northwest. Mr. Warner said we could pay well. Forgive me for being far too bold, brazen even, but let me tell you this. Along with the monetary reward we can give you, there can be other, more pleasant rewards, if you agree."

Stifling a groan born of inner turmoil, Preacher put his big hands on her tender shoulders. "Eve . . . Eve, what's a body to do? By jing, the truth is, I'd plow an' plant a garden for one of your smiles. For a kiss, I'd do handsprings from here to the Grand Tetons. If . . . if I heard you right, for that, I'd take on those Blackfoot single-handed and whup them all. But I can't—I won't let myself be harnessed up and put in charge of a wagon train. I'm sorry. I know I'll regret it tomorrow. Only it's jist the way I am."

Disappointment registered in Eve's hazel eyes. "That's the longest, and most eloquent, speech I've ever heard you make. I'm sorry over your stubborn refusal, but I think I can understand. You've always been a free soul. Any sort of harness, and I'm afraid that includes matrimony, would only chafe. But, now that I've said it, Preacher dear, the offer remains open. Good night."

Five double hands of Lakota warriors had set up a camp near their Cheyenne cousins. In spite of their earlier promises, they had failed to join with the Blackfoot for a large raid on the soldier-place. Iron Shirt went to visit them, his patience at an end. They welcomed him warmly enough and, after the customary meal, got down to serious talking.

"We are coming. It has been decided, and we will be there," Spotted Horse, the Lakota's principal war chief stated patiently.

Iron Shirt barely held his impatience in check. "Yes, but when?"

Spotted Horse made a gesture of indifference with his bead-decorated turkey-wing fan. "When we get there. Why are you in such haste, Iron Shirt? Going to war requires deliberation and careful planning."

That loosed a spill of heated words. "The planning is done; there is nothing difficult about it. We must not let this soldier-place be built. Like all white men, once they come, they never leave. Do you want all of your bison killed? The soldiers will do that. They shoot them for trophies. As you know, I have three tame white men in my village. They tell me this is a true thing."

Spotted Horse nodded sagely. "I have been told they scratch the ground, tear up the grass to put in seeds."

"Yes, they plant for food, like the Navajo," Iron Shirt spat in disgust. "We must attack this evil place and burn it to the ground."

Spotted Horse pursed his full lips, then nodded curtly. "It is agreed. We will come at the next moon."

Exasperated, Iron Shirt sprang to his feet. "No! It must be now. We leave for the soldier-place with tomorrow's sun. Meet us there."

For want of something to do, Preacher rode out with Lieutenant Judson of Company C the next morning on the water detail. The youthful officer, Preacher was willing to bet he did not shave more than every other day, had matured considerably since their encounter with the Pawnee. Lines had appeared on his forehead and cheeks, where none had been before. He didn't talk as loudly, nor move with nervous energy like a youngster in his teens. Privately, he shared Preacher's opinion of the water situation. With construction nearly complete at the fort, he felt secure in bringing up the subject to the mountain man.

"Our engineering officer, Major Vickers, has completed his tests for building a cistern. I for one will be glad when we don't have to come out every day to water the horses. For some reason, I can't shake the prickling sensation that Blackfoot eyes are watching my every move."

Preacher chuckled deep in his throat. "That outlook'll keep you alive a whale of a lot longer than some others I could mention."

Vickers read Preacher correctly. "Colonel Danvers certainly does have an optimistic attitude. Not that I'm criticizing, of course."

"Ain't for me to be bearin' tales, Tom. Right now, I'm jist an unemployed scout."

"Then why do you take these risks like the others?"

Preacher rubbed his square chin. "Keeps my edge keen. Fastest way to get yourself kilt in the High Lonesome is to take to thinkin' you're nice and safe."

"Is it really that wild out here, Preacher?"

"It is at times. Thing is, you never know for certain when those times have come around. Injuns is moody, and changeable. The closer you are to them, the more they give you cause to play guessin' games."

Lieutenant Judson cast a nervous glance around the hillside above the creek bed. "And we're mighty close to them down here."

"Yep. There's three Cheyenne watchin' us now, right up in them pines." Preacher jutted his chin to indicate the direction of the observers.

Tom Judson jerked as though wasp-stung. "I'd better alert the others."

A restraining hand went to his arm as Preacher drawled in a low voice. "Nope. I wouldn't get all stirred up and make 'em think we're the hostiles. If they had any thought to lift our hair, they'd not let me get an eye on 'em."

Judson cut his eyes to Preacher's face. "How can you be so sure?"

"I ain't. But I've jist never seen warriors sit their horses right quiet like that an' then attack."

"What should I do then?"

Preacher did not even hesitate. "We'll jist mosey right slow along the crick, tell the watering detail as we go. No hurry. Them Cheyenne ain't gonna leave until after we do."

Half an hour later, Lieutenant Judson heaved a heavy sigh of relief as the watering detail rode away from the creek. He reported their discovery to the Battalion Sergeant Major upon their return. BSM Muldoon doubled the number of the second detail to take horses out for water.

"It's Injuns now, is it?" Muldoon developed a faraway look in his blue eyes. With a limited supply of old John Barleycorn, his nose had lost much of its ruddy glow. He had leaned down some, also. Preacher noted the changes approvingly. Fat might be all right for a politician, but a man on the spare side moved faster in a fight.

"Three Cheyenne. One of them was a mere boy."

"But Mr. Judson said he never laid an eye on them, sure an' he did."

"*I* saw them, that's all that mattered, Muldoon."

"Right ye are, Preacher."

Preacher changed the subject. "Judson says the engineer is about ready to blast out a cistern."

"That he is. By all the saints, they're goin' at it backward as usual. What I mean is, what are we to do with all these winders in place? One mistake in the amount of blasting powder an' we'll have glass flyin' all over the inside o' this room, we will."

Preacher laughed. "Board them up, Sergeant Major."

Muldoon cocked his head to one side. "Ye ever see how fast a chunk of rock moves with a big bang behind it?"

"Ummm. You've got a point. All you can hope for is none of them powder men has got three thumbs."

"You goin' out with the new detail?"

"No. I've had an invite to take nooning with Eve Billings. She's promised something special."

Merriment twinkled in the eyes of BSM Muldoon. "Sure an' ye've the sound of a man that's been already caught."

A twinge radiated from the area of Preacher's heart. "Not in the least. I've been alone, on my own, for too many years to change my ways."

Laughing, Muldoon turned back to his paperwork. "Now, that'll be the day, it will."

Bored by lack of something destructive to do, Blake Soures and three of his henchmen decided to pay a visit to the cutler's store at the new fort. They had a hanker to try out some of the whiskey the government-contracted civilian merchant had in stock. They rode inside the stockade shortly after noon the same day, having noted the watering detail on the way.

"Somebody's mighty stupid around these parts," opined Eden Dillon. Yellowed, snaggy teeth made an unhealthy slash in the lower part of his mouth. "They ain't gonna git no water outta rock."

Blake Soures nodded agreement. "The thing for our Indian friends to do is catch them out in the open, watering horses. Be a regular slaughter."

They dismounted at a freshly built, raw, yellow pine tie-rail and looped reins. With his accustomed swagger, Soures led the way into the saloon side of the sutler's store. There, the first thing he saw was a large sign in bold, black, capital letters.

HARD LIQUOR SALES PROHIBITED
TO ENLISTED AND NCO
PERSONNEL
(OFFICERS and CIVILIANS ONLY)
by Order of
Lt. Col. Danvers, Commanding.

Soures pointed it out to his subordinates. "Well, lookie here. Aren't you glad you didn't sign on to wear one of those pretty blue uniforms?"

Pete Price leaned toward Blake Soures. "I betcha we found out who thought up puttin' this place on a finger of rock."

"It ain't natural, that's what." Dillon was put out. "Not right to get between a man an' his whisky. Downright barbarian."

From behind the bar, a jovial-faced man urged them toward the planks. "Seein' as how none of you gentlemen are soldiers, step right up and enjoy a drink."

While the four outlaws settled themselves at the bar, the barkeep poured into large, fish-eye shot glasses. With a deft flick of his wrist, he distributed them to his new customers. "You're new here, so first round is on the house."

Soures answered him with a big grin and a hearty voice. "Now, that's mighty nice. Much obliged, my good man." He had listened intently to the conversations of Quinton Praeger and his associates and now often made a conscious effort to mimic their speech mannerisms when he addressed strangers.

With a good-natured smile, and a wink, the barkeep informed them, "The next one'll cost you double."

Soures eyed the man over the rim of his shot glass, which he had raised to his lips. "Sounds like a place I know of down in the French Quarter of New Orleans."

Entermann, the sutler, gave Soures an expression of innocence. "I've never been in N'awlins."

They shared a laugh and Soures downed his whisky. A moment later, Preacher entered the saloon. He came up short on the threshold and eyed the strangers with immediate suspicion. To the best of his knowledge, there wasn't a white man within two hundred miles. Except, of course, the ones rumored to be with Iron Shirt. Preacher broke his momentary freeze and crossed the plank floor to the far end of the bar.

From there, he could keep an eye on all four hard-faced men. For their part, they wasted little time before turning cold, killer's eyes on Preacher. Their threatening demeanors sent warning jangles along the arms of the mountain man. Ordinarily, he did not wear his pair of Walker Colts inside the fort, only he'd had no time after returning from the water detail to remove them, because of his noon invitation from Eve. Sight of these four set his fingers itching to close around the butt of at least one .44. When they had made clear their awareness of his presence, Preacher seized the main chance.

"You fellers is new around here. Might I ask what brings you to Fort Washington?" Recently, Danvers had grandiosely named his small compound after the Father of His Country.

Constantly on the prod, Pete Price made a snotty reply. "You might ask, but you won't get any answers. So, butt out."

Even more on guard, Preacher tried calming words. "Now, now. That's hardly the way to answer a polite question. Seein' as how I'm the unofficial welcoming committee, I only sought to make you feel at home."

"We don't need a welcome," snapped Soures. "Who are you to be pokin' your nose into our business?"

"Folks call me Preacher."

Thought of the thousand dollars in gold bonus for killing the mountain man named Preacher galvanized Blake Soures. His hand sped to his sash and the butt of a .60-caliber pistol while he shouted to his underlings.

"We got us a thousand dollars, boys! Get him!"

With his outside holsters, Preacher beat all four easily. A Walker Colt filled his right hand and he had the hammer falling before the speediest, Pete Price, could clear the barrel of his long single-shot pistol from his belt. A thunderous clap announced the detonation of the powder load in one chamber of Preacher's Colt.

A powerful fist slammed into the lock plate of Price's pistol and rammed it painfully back into his gut. He doubled over painfully and his finger reflexively twitched. An accomplished shootist, Pete Price had cocked the cumbersome firearm before drawing it clear. As a result, another loud blast filled the room and Price blew a fist-sized hole in his left thigh. He went down shrieking in agony while blood spurted from his femoral artery. Now, Preacher had only three to contend with.

Hot lead cut a painful path across the top of Preacher's left shoulder. An instant later the Walker spoke again. Its message went to a wooly-faced hard case with mean little pig eyes and a smoking pistol in his left hand. He had fired too soon, Preacher noted. The muzzle was still high. He learned of his mistake when the messenger of death split his breastbone and ripped a hole through his left lung.

Preacher went to one knee, the .44 Colt erupting a third time. Glass tinkled when the ball shattered the chimney of a wall-mounted coal oil-lamp, after it exited the back of the head of surly Eden Dillon. Preacher cut his eyes to Blake Soures, who had taken refuge behind the bar.

Intent on making the perfect shot, Soures did not recognize the dreadful image of the Grim Reaper crouched before him in the person of Preacher. A fourth ball fluttered through the air with the leathery rustle of the death angel's wings. The lead pellet smacked through the bar front and ended in the hinge of Soures' right elbow. With a howl and a curse, he propelled himself backward, fumbled left-handed with the pistol in his waistband and drew it.

By then, Preacher had the fourth piece of frontier trash to deal with. Their weapons fired as one. Preacher immediately flattened out on the floor.

"You got him! You got him, Earl!" Soures shouted as he came full upright in time to hear the bad news.

"No, I didn'," Earl gargled out through the blood welling in his throat. "He . . . got . . . me."

Horrified, Soures cut his eyes to the floor. He focused at once on the black hole that formed the muzzle of Preacher's

Walker Colt. Flame blossomed in that darkness, then a stunning agony seared through the chest of Blake Soures. He fired his pistol blindly. The slug put a shower of splinters in the face of Preacher, who fired his second Colt into the exposed gut of his would-be killer. Soures died before he hit the floor.

"Damned unfriendly fellers, I'd say," Preacher offered to a bug-eyed Hyman Entermann.

"B'God, Preacher, you are faster than a scalded cat."

"I've worked at it a mite. Now, I think I'll have me a beer. Gun-fightin' gives me a thirst."

A moment later, the Provost Marshal, Captain Preston, and three of the afternoon guard detail rushed into the sutler's store. "What's going on here?" the officer demanded.

"Nothin' now," Preacher answered laconically.

"How did these bodies get here?"

Preacher took a pull on his beer and made a sour face. "Preston, I swear, you don't have a sensible question to ask. What you should be findin' out is who started the shootin'." His annoyance rang in his voice.

"Well . . . who did start the shooting?"

Nodding toward the jumble of broken and spilled bottles and the body sprawled among them, Preacher spoke simply. "That one there did."

With almost a simper in his prim, disapproving voice, the Provost Marshal declared, "Brawling is prohibited in this establishment or anywhere at Fort Washington. Brawling with firearms is a flogging offense."

"You won't be floggin' this mother's son."

Captain Preston gauged the man he addressed. "Oh? And why not?"

"Take a look around you, Captain Preston. There's four of them here. An' they were ready for me. An' I've got five loads left for this revolvin' pistol here."

Hyman Entermann interrupted. "It was self-defense, Captain. This one back here said they would be paid a thousand dollars gold for killing Preacher. Then he went for his gun. Preacher beat him. End of story. Now please have your men remove this filth from my establishment."

Preacher beamed at the bantam rooster attitude of the sutler. "Yer a good man, Brother Entermann."

"There'll be an investigation," Captain Preston grumbled darkly. Then he made a curt gesture to the guards.

Preacher had the last word. "Don't count on it."

Three days later, Preacher awakened as usual an hour before dawn. He pulled on a long-sleeved flannel shirt against the morning chill and stretched out the kinks. He struck flint to steel, ignited the hat-sized fire he had laid out the previous night and put on water to boil for coffee.

He was working on his second cup in the pearly light of a peaceful dawn when the Blackfoot, Cheyenne and Sioux attacked.

24

Lieutenant Brice had the water detail for the Company horses. He kept in mind everything Preacher had told his friend, Tom Judson. For one thing, he never looked directly at anything in the shadows of the trees that grew along the gorges that formed the watershed for Goose Creek. Although he could not put a name to it, Brice had a particularly active itch between his shoulder blades.

It came as no surprise to him, then, when his roving gaze picked out feathers where there should be none. Neatly trimmed feathers at that. Controlling his urge to draw his Dragoon revolver from the saddle holster and fire, he brought up the nose of his drinking horse and ambled over to his platoon sergeant.

"Sergeant Mcancy, pass the word quietly for the men to prepare to draw and fire a cylinder load into those trees over there on my command. Then we get these horses the hell away from here."

"May I ask what it is, sir?"

"Indians, Meaney. Too damned many of them for us to hold off on our own. I have me an itch that tells me they are all around the fort."

Sergeant Meaney nodded his understanding. "I have a sore gut that tells me the same, sir."

"Very well. Be careful about it, don't let the savages suspect we know they are there."

Throughout their exchange, Lieutenant Brice used all his will to keep from looking at the spot where he had seen the feathers. Now he rode with a tense back to the location, expectant of an arrow at any second. He reached the far end of the formation, told Corporal Grange about the hostiles and then looked back over the detail with every show of boredom.

To his satisfaction, he saw every man had his hand near or on the sheepskin covers of his pistol's holster. "All right, men . . . do it now!"

His own Dragoon pistol came free, and he had the hammer back before the muzzle centered on the area where the feathers had been before. "Fire!"

A thunderous roar swelled up in the creek bed, as twelve Dragoons emptied six rounds each from their pistols. Immediately they smoothly changed weapons. Lieutenant Brice stood in his stirrups.

"Back to the fort at the double. . . . Hooo!"

With exceptional skill, the platoon had the entire company's horses on the move and up and out of the creek bed before the hidden Blackfoot could recover from the blazing curtain of lead delivered by the Dragoons. They came on soon enough. Whooping and yipping, all of the Indians broke from concealment and splashed across the creek. In the lead, Red Elk, a Cheyenne, raised his rifle and fired blindly.

His bullet cracked over the heads of the trailing soldiers. It only served to move them faster. Thinking quickly, Lieutenant Brice put Sergeant Meaney at the head of the string of horses and turned back to hastily form a rear guard. The crackle of their pistols drowned out the war cries of the Blackfoot. The sudden, unexpected conflict triggered a premature opening to the battle.

While the Dragoons raced for a small sally port near the corral inside the stockade, a long line of Blackfoot warriors whipped their horses to a gallop on the long, steep slope beyond the fort to the west.

Fully a hundred Blackfoot warriors swept down the steep slope to the west of Fort Washington. An equal number of Cheyenne charged toward the main gate. Behind them loomed the Sioux. Frantically, the sentries labored to swing closed the gates. A bugle blared hysterically. Dragoons on fatigue details dropped their brooms and pitchforks and ran for their Hall carbines. Others spilled from their tents, drawing suspenders over their long-sleeved underwear. Half a dozen ran for the cannon. Preacher made for his lean-to to recover his rifles.

"Knew they would be comin'," he shouted to Three Sleeps Norris, headed in the same direction from their cookfire.

Three Sleeps spat a quid of tobacco from his mouth. "Damn right. Jist a matter of time."

Lieutenant Colonel Danvers's adjutant stood in the middle of the parade ground and bellowed orders. "Companies A and D to the west wall. Companies B and C to the north wall. Get that cannon moving!"

Dust boiled up inside the compound as Dragoons dashed back and forth, uncertain as to whether they should dismount and man the walls or form as skirmishers for a future counterattack. Gradually the officers calmed and directed them. Rifles crackled from outside.

Return fire started at once. Preacher heard Captain Dreiling's firm voice steadying his troops. "Hold your fire until they're well within range. Hold fast, men. Take careful aim. Ready . . . fire!"

A swath of lead balls flung thirty-five Cheyenne warriors from their saddles. "Reload . . . take aim . . . fire."

* * *

Two Moons had the contentment of a man whose dream had come true. He fully believed again in the medicine of Iron Shirt. Now that they traveled down the long-promised warpath to drive out all whites, the Blackfoot war chief banished all doubts. His warriors would be in the second wave to dash down the high mount. They had been given the honor of scaling the wall and fighting the soldiers hand to hand. The first surge, made up of braves from Iron Shirt's band, who were supposed to give covering fire, had already ridden half the distance to the high, pole barricade. Two Moons reflected on the past moon of difficulties.

It had taken a lot more effort than Iron Shirt's white men had expected. Not an easy task to get a warrior, proud of his individual feats of bravery, to work as part of a *team.* Even now the white man's word tasted strange in the mouth of Two Moons. What was a *team,* and what made it a better way to fight? Why was it superior to the way we have fought since the ancestor days? Where is the honor to be won if everyone holds back to shoot at the enemy from behind rocks and from the protection of gulley banks?

There was little glory in counting coup on a dead man. That was for boys beginning their seasons as warriors. Two Moons recalled the time when his sap ran fresh and hot. He had gone on a raiding party against the Cheyenne. They had stolen horses and ridden away without a scratch. The Cheyenne followed them. When the Red Top people came up to them, they offered challenge. A younger Two Moons had ridden out ahead of the line of his Raven Society brothers and shouted insults at the Cheyenne. He had exposed his manhood and waved it in the faces of the enemy while he told them what he would do with it when they had been conquered. Then he had charged directly at them, an arrow nocked and ready. The Cheyenne stared at him as though frozen.

Two Moons shot one Red Top warrior in the chest, then struck another with his bow. Two perfect coups, and right in front of his brothers! A line of fire ran across the point of his shoulder as a Cheyenne lance barely grazed him. He whirled and rode back, then all the Blackfoot charged.

The Cheyenne fought like Dark Spirits. One of them had a white man's fire-stick—no, a rifle—the older Two Moons corrected himself. With it, he killed two of the Blackfoot. Yet, when the fighting ended, Two Moons and his brothers rode away victorious, dripping scalps tied to their bows, and with more Cheyenne horses than they had started with. Now, the Red Top people fought with them, not as enemies. How the world had turned upside down. Two Moons shook his head in wonder.

From the tree line north of the fort, Spotted Horse could hear the solid thuds when the high gates swung together. The soldiers would be protected now, he thought. How foolish, the Lakota leader thought, for a man to lock himself inside a small place to fight. Only the clear, open plains suited a warrior's soul. Beyond him, on the narrow shelf that jutted out from the base of the foothills, the Cheyenne, led by Red Elk, raced toward where the soldiers waited. The *Sahiela*—the Cheyenne—our cousins, are brave and they fight well. Yet, only our braves can match the ferocity of the Blackfoot. Spotted Horse spat as he thought the word for their traditional enemy. How is it that we come to fight beside them?

Because of the medicine of Iron Shirt, he acknowledged unwillingly. He had seen with his own eyes men who died, even though they had been given the protection of Iron Shirt's medicine. Not all of our people agree, he recalled, mindful of the young hothead, Red Cloud. He had maintained that the medicine was fake. He had agreed with Cloud Blanket of the Cheyenne, and strangely, the elders agreed and stayed out of this fight. He himself had only changed his mind at the last minute. Gunfire erupted along the wall before him and the two sides joined. Spotted Horse readied his pony. Their time would come soon.

* * *

Red Elk pushed his pony to a full gallop and loosed one arrow after another at the high wall of the fort. Never had they fought against such a thing. He doubted that arrows would do much damage against the thick forest of lodgepole pines that had been lashed together across their path. What a strange way to fight, he mused. Who would want to hide behind a barrier three times the height of the tallest man?

Where was the honor in that? From beside him, one of the rifles given them by Iron Shirt barked, and as the smoke cleared, Red Elk saw a white soldier rear up and fall backward. Maybe they had a chance after all. It would be their job to keep the blue-coats busy while their cousins, the Lakota, rushed forward and scaled the walls. Such a strange way to fight. Yet, Iron Shirt had assured them all that it had come to him in a dream. One small thought nagged at him: the Blackfoot have been our enemies since the grandfather times: why do they share their medicine with us now? He would soon see how it worked, of that he was certain.

From his vantage point outside headquarters, Battalion Sergeant Major Muldoon could see little of the hostiles. Here and there feathers and painted faces revealed frantic action beyond the walls. Farther back, more ranks of savages could be seen on the slope that overlooked the fort.

He turned to the young headquarters lieutenant next to him. "Sure an' it's just like Preacher said it would be. Th' heathen devils have got themselves up on that hillside and can look right down in here. If they knew a jot about artillery, we'd all be dead ducks, we would."

A tightening of jaw muscles gave clear indication of the effect of those words on the youthful subaltern. For all *he* knew, the Indians might well have a battery of field pieces. So far, none of the savages they had engaged conducted their battles like Indians were supposed to fight. For some reason, they used standard military tactics. That made it downright scary. From the next words spoken by Muldoon, he might have been reading the lieutenant's mind.

"Of course, when they be pressed too hard, they have always fallen back on their every man for himself ways and flung themselves at us with total disregard for their lives or those of their unit. That's when the advantage falls to us. Ye'll be sein' that here, I've no doubt, sor."

Shouted curses came from the parapet behind the wall and the rate of fire increased. "There's more of 'em coming!" Arrows sailed over the defenses to land harmlessly on the parade ground.

BSM Muldoon touched the edge of the shiny black bill on his cap in salute. "If ye'll excuse me, sor, I must go and take a better look. Th' darlin' colonel will need to know."

A surge of relief passed through the lieutenant, and he made no offer to accompany Muldoon. "Right, you do that, Sergeant Major."

A flight of twenty-five arrows slammed into the ground all around, their colorful fletchings so many evil blossoms. Muldoon did not even flinch from them, instead he strode through their pattern with a light word on his lips. " 'Tis a fine day for a stroll through the flowers, it is."

Not being paid to defend the fort, the immigrant men armed themselves and formed a protective screen around their portion of the inner compound. Not surprisingly, when the call for the men to rally had come, Charlie Billings had taken up his light rifle and started off. Eve caught her son by the scooped back of his overalls.

"Where do you think you are going, young man?"

Talking over one shoulder, Charlie explained himself.

"They called for all the men to arm themselves. There's Injuns out there attacking the fort."

"That did not include ten-year-old boys. You can do your best service by staying here and reloading for me, if the Indians get inside."

Charlie's face clouded. "Aw, Mom."

"No arguments. The matter is closed. Besides, I thought you liked the idea of being an Indian."

His stubborn streak flaring, Charlie answered hotly. "That's different. These are bad Injuns. *Hostiles.*"

Eve would not be swayed any more than her son. "I want you to watch your sister in the meantime. And," she added to soften her refusal, "I think it would be wise for you to carry your rifle with you while you do."

Charlie brightened. "Sure, Mom."

When Charlie and Anna departed for the soddy that had been built for the family, Eve lifted her eyes to the heavens. "Dear God, don't let anything happen to them."

Preacher and Three Sleeps reached a portion of the revetment over the gate before the Cheyenne came into range. Both shared in the dismay of the lieutenant. Never had they seen such control and order among charging hostiles. Someone had found a way to train them and make it stick. At least for the present. Pick off a couple of war leaders and that would quickly change, he reasoned.

"There's hundreds of them, Preacher."

"Yer right, Three Sleeps. And more yet to come. D'ya notice they're fightin' like soldiers?"

"Yes, and I don't like it."

Three Cheyenne had ridden well inside range. Preacher took aim on one, Three Sleeps sighted on another. They fired a fraction of a second apart and the targets left the backs of their ponies for the Spirit World. Quickly, the mountain men reloaded. Preacher popped the last one at forty yards. Some twenty-five yards from the stockade, an irregular line of broken rocks and fair-sized boulders had been left behind by the Dragoons when the fort grounds had been cleared.

Preacher had cautioned Lieutenant Colonel Danvers about this slip in planning and had, as usual, been ignored. He pointed them out now to Three Sleeps as Cheyenne braves, who had ridden double, slipped from behind their friends and taken cover in this manmade barrier. "I told the colonel about those rocks. They'll hide a Cheyenne right enough."

An increased rate of fire from the west told Preacher of the arrival of even more hostiles. He took a quick look over the parade ground and saw the six Dragoons still trying to get the cannon in place. He shook his head.

"Ain't any of those dummies ever heard of a horse? That's half a ton of metal they're tryin' to carry on their backs. A couple of horses would pull that gun up the ramp in no time at all."

"There's a right way, and a wrong way, and—"

Preacher's sigh cut off Three Sleeps. "Yeah, I know, the Army way."

From the tree line came the foulest of Lakota curses. *"Hu ihpeya wicayapo!"*

Preacher's scowl held a bushel of misery. "Aw, damn, the Lakota have got in this thing, too. Well, one thing certain, they ain't gonna use *me* like a woman."

"Not this chile, neither," Three Sleeps readily agreed.

Eighty-five Lakota warriors, painted and ready for war, rode out of the trees. Three Sleeps saw a brown shoulder between two large rocks and snapped a shot. A howl answered him and the now bloody shoulder disappeared. While he reloaded, he offered his observation to Preacher.

"It don't get much nastier than this."

"Right as rain, Pard. An' I got a feelin' it's gonna get worse before it gets better."

* * *

Being senior, by time in grade, Captain Dreiling commanded the defenses over the main gate. He watched with even greater trepidation than Preacher when the Sioux showed themselves and began the charge down the length of the promontory. Protectively, the Dragoons on the parapet had crouched down when the Cheyenne had taken positions in the rocks and begun a sniping duel. Now he found himself forced to go along the double rank of defenders and whack rumps with the flat of his saber to get the troops up to fire at the new hostiles.

"All right, ladies, this is not a quilting bee. Get loaded, get up and prepare to fire by volley. The Sioux have come to pay us a visit." Funny, he did not feel the least bit sarcastic. At the bottom of it, he knew himself to be every bit as scared as the greenest Dragoon out there.

There had to be one in every unit, and Private Finney was the one in Company C. "But, Cap'n, if we do that, those other Injuns will potshot us for sure."

Captain Dreiling ground his teeth. "Why do you think there are two ranks of you? The kneeling rank covers the rocks, the standing one fires on the approaching hostiles. Make ready, men, they are almost in range."

How vastly different from exercises in tactical defense of fortified installations taught at the Academy, Edward Dreiling mused as dust and powder smoke drifted across the ground below. There had been no bullets or arrows snapping past then. If anyone received serious injuries it was due to carelessness or stupidity. These red men swarming out there wanted to kill those in the fort.

From what he had been told they would not stay their hand if appealed to for quarter. The Indians knew no such civilized concept as taking prisoners for exchange. This day there would be many deaths.

Will I be ready for it? his mind mocked him.

25

By noon, two heavy, concerted charges by the hostiles had been repulsed. Preacher munched on a wedge of cornbread, passed out by the women of the sheltering wagon train, and examined the powder-smeared faces of the young Dragoons. To his relief and satisfaction, he saw only expressions of determination. They had gotten over their initial fear. Some of them had even gotten up a game of mumblety-peg. Now, if luck held, the Injuns would not think of the concave wall to the east of this finger of land. Preacher lifted a gourd pitcher to his lips to wash down the cornbread with water. It had tasted good. Someone had thoughtfully cooked bits of bacon into it.

Years of fighting Indians and living in the wilderness had conditioned Preacher to take advantage of food whenever the opportunity presented itself. He ran the tip of his tongue across his teeth and reached for one of two flaky biscuits that remained on his tin plate. When he lifted it, a pink-centered slice of roast venison appeared beneath. He nodded at his plate and spoke to Antoine Revier.

"Maybe we ought to fight Injuns ever' day. Those folks are sure feedin' us nice."

"The venison came from *you know who*," said Antoine, who gave Preacher a poke in the ribs.

"Aw, git off my back, Tony."

A sudden stir broke out at the junction of the north and west walls. "They're comin' again!" BSM Muldoon bellowed. "Dragoons, stand to your arms."

Iron Shirt had lost his patience. So many warriors should have overrun that small number of soldiers long ago. They had followed orders well, at least until the volume of fire had rained down from those cursed walls increased to a steady roar. Then they forgot what they were supposed to do and went back to the old ways. He decided that a display of courage was needed. Taking up lance and rifle, he gathered his closest, most loyal followers and set out to lead the next attack.

First he harangued the warriors. "We must take this fort before the sun goes to sleep in the west. We cannot fail. Do you see that small knoll? If we do not carry the walls this time, I will be on the top, to make medicine and renew your spirits. One way or another we will kill all of the soldiers before darkness."

Revived, the Blackfoot, Cheyenne and Sioux formed new lines and made ready to attack. At the signal from Iron Shirt, they threw themselves at the walls again. For many, it took supreme effort to blank out the images of their dead brothers and friends, men who were now supposed to be protected from the white men's bullets.

Battalion Sergeant Major Muldoon had worked through the noon hour. At his direction, two sets of compound pulleys had been rigged at the top of the pounded earth ramp. Muldoon strung ropes through them and attached one end of each piece to the carriage of the three-pound cannon. The other ends, he gave to mounted Dragoons.

"Bend them around the pommels of yer darlin' saddles, if ye will. When I give the word, set off at a walk toward the stables."

Private Mallory scratched his chin. "But the stables ain't built yet, Sergeant Major."

One thing that had not changed during the journey here had been the woeful lack of intelligence on the part of Mallory. His patience already frayed by rampaging hostiles, BSM Muldoon got right up in the face of Mallory. "Sure an' they ain't gonna get built, ye idiot, unless we get this darlin' cannon into action and drive them hostiles off. Now, *do as I say.*"

Wooden pulleys creaked and taut ropes thrummed as the weight of the cannon came on them. Step by persistent step, the half-ton weapon rolled toward the base of the ramp. The lines vibrated wildly when the wheels started up the incline. Then one cord, which had been exposed too long to sun and heavy dewfall, snapped with a loud report.

Like a whiplash, it hummed through the air and viciously struck the rump of the horse ridden by Mallory. The animal uttered a very human squeal of pain, reared and dumped its dull-witted rider to the ground.

Muldoon exploded. "Damn yer black heart an' empty head, Mallory. Ye come a thousand miles and still can't keep yer seat. Harris, git over here with that horse an' another rope."

After another twenty minutes, the small field piece had been dragged into place. Quickly the crew milled around it, rammed home a bag of powder, a wad and a fist-sized ball. They all stepped back smartly and stood rigidly in a position of attention.

"Prick . . . prime," the gun captain commanded. Then he lowered a slow match over the touch hole. The little cannon went off with an ear-splitting roar.

The small, round projectile screamed through the air, to burst ten feet above a cluster of Blackfoot. Hot, smoldering shrapnel slashed into them and their horses. Shrieking, they went down together in a heap.

"Reload."

Out came a water-soaked brush, to clean the bore, then

the loader placed another bag in the muzzle and the rammer drove it down to the breech. Next came a cloth patch, and another ball. The gun crew stood back and the piece barked again. Shrieking, the ball lobbed over the wall slowly enough to be almost visible from the side.

It burst above another clutch of Blackfoot warriors. The defenders' volume of fire increased, and confusion washed over the stunned Indians.

Although Lieutenant Colonel Danvers thought it better to have one of the mountain men on each of the completed walls, Preacher did not agree. If left together, their disciplined fire and superb, long-range marksmanship would have a devastating effect on the hostiles. Accordingly, he took Three Sleeps Norris and Antoine Revier to the west wall, where the Blackfoot had concentrated.

They began knocking riders from their horses at seventy yards. Perplexed, the Blackfoot soon gave evidence of their doubt. The medicine of Iron Shirt had failed them. Only twenty-five of the seventy who were supposed to do so ran forward to throw braided horsehide ropes over the barricade. Almost at once, three of them stumbled and went down from the well-placed shots of Preacher and his companions.

Preacher made an observation about their stubbornness. "They's still got it in their heads that our bullets can't hurt them. We've gotta make them think otherwise."

Norris nodded. "You know, once an Injun's got somethin' in his head, it takes billy-be-damned to knock it out of there."

By then, six of the attackers had scaled to the top of the wall. Preacher reached out and smashed one in the head with the butt of his Hawken. The Blackfoot fell away without a sound. Then the little cannon opened up.

Its first round stunned to immobility fully a hundred of the enemy. Seven of them died along with their horses. None of them had ever experienced anything like it. The second detonation ignited fear in the hearts of many of the more prudent among the Cheyenne and Sioux. Wisely, they broke off their attack.

When the third projectile killed one and wounded seven Sioux, a general exodus began. Warriors streamed from the field, eyes wild with open fear that not even their enormous pride could suppress. Within ten minutes not a single warrior remained within rifle range of Fort Washington.

"Well, that looks like it put the fear of the Almighty into them," opined Preacher. When he reported to Lieutenant Colonel Danvers, he summed up with an ominous statement. "They'll be back. Maybe not today, but give 'em time to whup up some more medicine an' they'll be on our doorstep bright and early tomorrow."

Preacher kept his plans to himself. He had a strong hunch that Lieutenant Colonel Danvers would strenuously disapprove of what he had on for tonight. Accordingly, he, Antoine and Three Sleeps left the fort quietly, by way of the sally port near the corral, well after dark. Lights out had been sounded by the trumpeter and the fort had settled in for sleep. Out on a small knoll to the west, a big bonfire blazed.

Preacher correctly judged that Iron Shirt would be whipping up more medicine. He'd have to, the mountain man reasoned, after the disaster of today's attack. The heartbeat throbs of the big medicine drum reached Preacher's ears as they headed toward the first target, their aim to create confusion and dread among the allies of the Blackfoot. For that purpose he had selected the Lakota encampment first.

With the soldiers bottled up in the fort, and their cousins the Cheyenne close by, the Sioux had not bothered with a night watch. Only the usual herd guards had been placed to prevent their ponies from straying. Preacher found one of them easily. The youthful Brule sat quietly on his pony, eyes fixed on the stars. His lips moved silently.

No doubt he's making a poem for a gal friend, Preacher speculated as he crept up close to the unaware sentry. He had approached from downwind so not even the piebald animal gave warning as Preacher raised up in the tall grass and swung with the flat of his tomahawk blade.

A soft clang came as fine steel met hard head. The teenaged Sioux slumped forward onto the neck of his mount and twitched slightly. Preacher sprang forward and dragged him from the pony. With rawhide thongs he bound the youth, gagged him and left him in a shallow draw. Quietly, he moved on in search of another guard.

Three Sleeps Norris all but blundered into the first of the herd watchers on his side. He surged up out of a gully and found himself not three feet from the broad, bronze back of a Sioux warrior. He recovered quickly enough and brained the warrior with a pistol barrel.

One less to worry about. Gliding on moccasins through the grass, Three Sleeps continued to skirt the horses. He had nearly completed his third of the circuit when he came upon another guard. This one showed wide-eyed surprise at suddenly being confronted by a white man.

"Wa—" he blurted a moment before Three Sleeps silenced him with a hard fist to the jaw. The brave went slack, then heaved himself upward from the ground.

Three Sleeps rapped him back into quiet with the flat of his tomahawk. In no time he had the Sioux bound and gagged. Then he started back, to cover the same ground and make certain he had gotten them all.

Antoine Revier slithered, belly down, through the grass. A chubby, moon-faced youth lounged against a tree trunk. His hand went constantly to his mouth and Antoine realized he was eating something. The French-Delaware cut to his right to circle the herd guard and came upon him from the rear. In the end it became all too easy.

Gnawing on the hind leg of a roast rabbit, the drowsy, fat, young man could not have heard the last trump due to his sensual absorption with food. Antoine's left arm circled his neck and choked off the air. Surprise caused the Sioux to suck fragments of flesh into his lungs. He began to choke and thrash.

Antoine silenced him with a doeskin bag of damp sand taken from the creek. The hapless sentry would have a lump the size of his fist on his head the next morning, provided he didn't strangle on his meal. The brave tied tightly and dragged out of sight into some brush, his assailant ghosted away into the night. There would be at least one more, Antoine thought grimly.

By prearrangement, the trio of mountain men met back at the spot where they had separated. Each had taken out two of the young watchmen. Being careful not to raise an alarm, they started to cut out ponies from the herd. When they had what Preacher estimated to be between twenty and thirty, they eased them away from the rest and headed toward the Cheyenne camp.

When they had come a safe distance, Antoine Revier whispered softly to Preacher, "I can understand, you bein' right friendly with the Cheyenne, why we'd not do any permanent damage, but why spare them cutthroats. The Lakota are bad news."

Preacher answered him readily enough. "Also they are allies of the Cheyenne, and considered to be cousins from sometime in the far-off past. No sense in riling them too much. Thing is to get them to break this alliance with the bloodthirsty Blackfoot."

"Well and good. Preacher, but for me, I'd as soon kill 'em all," Three Sleeps offered.

Preacher tendered his assurances. "I think we'll have us some fun this way."

When they drew close to the Cheyenne camp, Preacher and his friends slipped onto the backs of three ponies and whipped the others up into a gallop. Whooping and caterwauling, they soon turned the gallop into a stampede. Jolted out of their ruminations on lush sweet grass, the animals bounded toward the camp.

Pounding in among the lodges, the ponies created havoc. Warriors, dopey with sleep, struggled into loincloths and stumbled out into the path of the horses. Meanwhile, Preacher, Three Sleeps and Antoine overturned several hide tents and set more afire. Only a few stray arrows challenged them. Howling with laughter, they rode well beyond the Cheyenne village to where they had left their own horses.

Dawn brought back the warriors, boiling with anger this time. After a night of medicine dances, their faith had been restored in Iron Shirt and his Iron Shield ritual. The insults the Sioux and Cheyenne had endured at the hands of Preacher and his friends had not turned them from the alliance. Rather it had stiffened their resolve. They hurled themselves at the stockade with total disregard for personal safety. Braided horsehide lariats snaked over the pointed poles of the outer wall and found purchase on some.

"They're comin' up the walls!" shouted a nervous lieutenant in Company D.

"Shoot 'em off," Preacher grunted.

Fire arrows joined the arsenal of the Blackfoot. The smoking, flame-tipped, shafts whirred over the palisade and thudded into the ground. Two landed on the roof of headquarters, only to be extinguished quickly by the soldiers stationed there, at Preacher's suggestion, for that purpose.

Three Sleeps pointed in the direction of headquarters. "Those fellers are gettin' riled some."

Preacher inclined his head. "Let's hope they don't have too many of those."

With the scalers repulsed, the hostiles drew back a little and the battle became a protracted exchange of gunfire. Using all the speed they could, the Blackfoot and their allies reloaded and fired at the men on the walls.

Lieutenant Colonel Danvers called together the company commanders of Company A and D. "We can sweep them from in front of the gate with a counterattack."

Captain Bronston of Company D scratched at a bald spot on his head. "Do you think that's wise, sir? Once we're exposed, the massive force on the west could flank us and roll us up right smartly."

"Mr. Preacher assured me that when something went wrong for the savages, they would break off an assault and scatter. I'm confident they will do the same now."

Bronston had a ready reply. "Yes, sir, but haven't you noticed that they are fighting in a disciplined manner for once. It is as though someone has introduced them to tactical concepts. If that's the case, they will attack."

"We need to find that out, don't we? Prepare your companies for a counterattack, gentlemen. The gun crew has come up with grapeshot loads from fifty-four-caliber balls we have in reserve. We can cover you with the cannon."

"Yes, sir. Sabers, sir?"

Lieutenant Col. Danvers considered Captain Bronston's suggestion a moment. "Yes, I think so. Leave your carbines behind."

It had been a facetious offering and the response took Bronston by surprise. Still, he replied quickly. "But the Halls offer us our best firepower."

"Your men cannot hold both in their hands at the same time. You'd only get off two shots at best. Pistols and sabers, Captain Bronston." He turned away.

* * *

Ten minutes later, the sally port swung open and the two companies charged out and around the flank of the Cheyenne and Sioux positions. Sabers gleamed in the sun as they descended on the unsuspecting hostiles. Only a few reared upward and fired their rifles at the fast-approaching Dragoons. Pistols barked, and those who resisted died where they stood.

Keen edges flashed deadly light as the Dragoons hacked and slashed their way through the massed forces of warriors. Faster than Captain Bronston imagined, the flank turned back on itself and Indians fell to both sides, wounded or dead. Word of the attack raced through the warriors. It took little time to rally the Blackfoot to come to the aid of their allies.

By that time, the Dragoon charge had come level with the main gate. With a roar of encouragement for the beleaguered, the Blackfoot swarmed around the corner of the stockade and rushed toward the soldiers. Arrows and rifle balls flew toward the mounted troops. Still they prevailed. With a sharp roar, the cannon detonated. Thin shrieks filled the air as the insubstantial leather sheath stripped from the improvised grapeshot. The balls rippled as they passed in front of the Dragoons. At once, some of the men among the Blackfoot began to scream in agony.

Captain Borden, who commanded the counterattack, raised his saber above his head. "Turn about! To the rear . . . Hooo!"

Back through the disorganized hostiles they rode. More of the Cheyenne and Sioux suffered from the pistols and blades in the hands of the Dragoons. Ahead of them, the sally port swung open and the troops streamed toward it.

Fighting dragged on into the afternoon. Preacher offered his opinion of the counterattack. "They lost eight Dragoons kilt an' another eleven wounded. Damn waste of time, I say."

Around three o'clock, nature intervened to disrupt the plans of Iron Shirt. Huge towers of black thunderclouds billowed up in the northwest. They moved swiftly across the Bighorns. Lightning flashed and crackled through the heavy air. The first sheet of rain swept over the finger of land toward Fort Washington at three-ten.

In seconds it turned to a solid downpour. Visibility shrank to mere feet. The three-pounder became inoperative. Already short on ammunition, the hostiles hunkered in the chill deluge and engaged in only desultory return fire. Another benefit the way Preacher saw it, the drencher softened the bow strings of the warriors, which rendered them useless.

Silently, they began to stream away from the walls of Fort Washington. Disappointed in this reversal, the Blackfoot, Cheyenne and Sioux did not even cast glances back at their relieved enemy. When the last of them plodded out of range, a shrill, worried voice came to Preacher's ears.

"Anna! Anna! Charlie, have you seen Anna anywhere?"

"No, Mom," Charlie Billings called back, sudden guilt burning his face red. "Where was she?"

"I . . . I don't know. I left her at the cave with you. When the storm came up, I thought she would surely stay."

"She's not here now."

Eve Billings saw Preacher on the wall and hurried to the stairs that led upward. Worry creased her brow when she approached the mountain man. "Preacher, Anna is missing. I can't find her anywhere."

"We'll look." Preacher grated the words out.

Twenty minutes later, every corner and nook of the fort had been searched without results. Preacher brought Eve the bad news.

"I don't know how, or why, but somehow Anna has gotten out of the fort."

"Oh, my God. You have to find her."

Despite the visions Preacher had about the appeal of a sweet-faced, blond little girl to a Cheyenne or Sioux warrior, he spared Eve that torment. "I'll do ever'thing I can. Don't you worry. It may take a while, but I'll turn over mountains to find her."

26

Not until Preacher passed well beyond the ground churned up by the Indians did he find any sign of Anna Billings. He suspected that she had become terrified of the constant fighting and later the crackling lightning and the boom of thunder. Somehow, in the midst of the furious storm, she had managed to slip away. The small door in the sally port had been found partly open. It stood to reason that the eight-year-old had drawn the latch and left the fort by that means. Preacher's major concern centered around the very good chance that she had been seen by some of the stragglers among the Indians and taken captive.

He found it encouraging when he came upon her small shoe prints in the mud, at a right angle to the direction traveled by the retreating hostiles. It did not eliminate the possibility of her capture. She could have escaped from her captors, Preacher speculated. If so, they would be coming after her. The wind diminished slowly as he followed her sign. Preacher quickly recognized the terrain. Her trail led down into the valley where Goose Creek ran through, made swift and turbulent by the dam and water wheel.

Preacher swung Tarnation northward to stay with her steps as they led toward the mill. He surmised that the small building there had been her goal. Ahead of him now, he thought he saw a frilly, lace-trimmed collar and flaxen head. He urged Tarnation to a faster pace. Satisfaction glowed in Preacher's chest when he pushed through the tall grass and saw Anna on the bank of the treacherous stream.

Calmly, she went about unlacing her shoes. She was going to cross, Preacher realized. The creek bank looked insubstantial and slippery. He drummed heels into Tarnation's flanks. The hooves squished noisily in the sodden turf, the thump of their impact muffled. Not enough, though.

Anna looked up wide-eyed at picking up sounds of the rapid approach. Unable to recognize Preacher in the low light from an overcast sky, she saw only a huge horse looming over her, remembered the charging Indians, and panicked. With only thought of escape in her mind, the girl sprang to her feet and took a step toward the water. A second later, the saturated soil of the bank gave way under even her slight weight.

With a thin scream, Anna Billings toppled forward into the stream fully clothed. Swollen by the rain, Goose Creek ran swiftly. Anna wailed in terror as the current swept her quickly downstream.

Preacher shouted encouragement as he skidded Tarnation to a halt. "Anna! Hold on. I'm coming."

He took time only to shuck his heavy holsters and Walker Colts, his hat and moccasins. Then he dove into the roiling water. Anna's fair hair formed a dim halo on the surface as she was whirled away.

"Get on your back," Preacher shouted. "Try to float."

Anna tried, failed, and went under. She came up sputtering. "I can't. My dress pulls me down," she wailed. "Please help me."

Preacher drew closer with powerful strokes. "Take off your dress."

A deeper look of horror came on Anna's face. "I c-can't. I don't have a petticoat."

Preacher was barely over an arm's length from her. "Do it anyway. That thing could suck you under for good."

Small fingers tugging at the stubborn buttons, Anna undid her dress far enough to allow its sodden weight to drag it free from her body.

Two more strokes and Preacher reached her. He slid an arm under both of hers and across her bare chest. "Now we've gotta get out of this current."

One-armed, he pulled at the turbulent water at an oblique angle to that of the stream. It soon became hard work. Preacher strained until the cords in his neck stood out like whitened ropes. To his gratitude, Anna did not try to fight the water. He noted progress when a large rock flashed past. Preacher recognized its shape and knew it to be close to the near-side bank.

A few more stout pulls, legs scissoring to provide thrust, and Preacher felt mud and sand beneath his toes. He relaxed and stood upright. Gasping breath he sized up their situation. Anna clung to him like a monkey. Staggered by the rush of water and his burden, Preacher made unsteady progress to a bar of pebbles and sand that extended into the creek. Once there, he put the girl down.

"You've only one shoe. Best that you take it off 'stead of limpin'."

Tears welled in Anna's eyes. "Thank you, Preacher. You saved me."

Preacher looked down, embarrassed. "It was me scared you into the crick in the first place."

"Did . . . did your horse run away?"

"No. He'll stay where I dropped the reins. We'd best be movin', get you a blanket."

When the naked Anna was wrapped warmly, Preacher handed her up onto the back of Tarnation, then mounted behind her. The girl gave not even a single backward glance at the stream that had come so close to claiming her life.

On the way, Preacher swung Tarnation down into a gully to keep off the skyline. They rounded a bend in the ancient, eroded riverbed and came face-to-face with five grim-visaged Cheyenne warriors.

"Oh-oh, missy, it looks like we've jumped into some trouble," Preacher told Anna calmly while he lifted and shifted her to one side to put her behind him.

Correctly reading Preacher's intention to fight, the Cheyenne raised their weapons. Preacher tensed and drew both of his Walker Colts. His intention was to weaken the Cheyenne enough to crash through and make a run for it. The fight was about to begin.

Then, at the last moment, an older warrior drifted down the shallow bank. He raised his right arm in a commanding gesture and called to his fellow Cheyenne.

"Hold! Do not attack this man. I know him well. He is a friend."

He trotted forward then and greeted Preacher. "Ho, White Ghost, it seems that you are always helping little children."

Preacher recognized him at once. "Cloud Blanket, you look the same as when I last saw you."

Cloud Blanket turned in his saddle so the other Cheyenne could hear his words. He spoke in his own tongue. "I made you my brother when you rescued my little son and daughter from that bison stampede on our hunting grounds that summer long ago."

Preacher smiled and replied in the same language. "I remember it like it was yesterday."

Cloud Blanket gestured to the five warriors. "These men scout for my band. I am moving far to the east because of the unrest among our people."

"If you are talking about the fightin' at the fort, I can understand. What's your fix on what's gotten the tribes so stirred up?"

Cloud Blanket scowled. "It is the doing of one man. Iron Shirt. I will come and talk about it with you over coffee."

It all started with a misunderstanding at the main gate. Private Masters, on sentry duty, saw Preacher approaching with an Indian at his side. He drew the obvious conclusion.

"Corporal of the Guard, Post Number Two. Chief scout returning with a prisoner. Looks like he's found the girl, too."

When Lieutenant Colonel Danvers received word of that, he left his office hastily and went to meet Preacher. Two privates and a nervous Corporal Penny stood around a mounted Indian, weapons leveled. Before Preacher could explain, Danvers burst onto the scene.

"Corporal Penny, escort the prisoner to the guardhouse."

"Yes, sir."

Preacher protested at once. "Now, hold on a minute. This man is my friend. He's not a hostile."

"He's an Indian, isn't he?" Danvers replied.

Eve Billings, tears of relief on her face, came up then to relieve Preacher of Anna. She stopped short, astonished at the figure who sat his horse in front of her. "Why, that's the Indian I told you about, Preacher. He's the one who watched us from a distance." To Danvers, she added, "He's friendly right enough. He smiled and waved to me every time."

It was time for introductions, Preacher felt. "His name is Cloud Blanket. This is Miz Billings. An' this is . . ."

Charlie Billings came forward and raised his right hand in the sign of greeting and peace. *"Heyota,* Cloud Blanket."

Shock registered on the face of Eve Billings. "Charles Ryan Billings, you . . . you *know* this Indian?"

"Oh, sure. He's my friend, but it's supposed to be a secret.

Back in the other mountains he came to me and taught me how to track game. That's why I always done so good."

"Did so well," Eve corrected automatically.

"He gave me these moccasins, too." Charlie beamed with pride in his friendship.

Lieutenant Colonel Danvers interrupted the domestic scene. "He is still a hostile prisoner, and I want him removed to a secure place at once."

Preacher's dander rose. "An' I say hell no. 'Fore you lock anyone up, Colonel, we'll all jist ride out of here and leave you to the mercy of the real hostiles."

"You can't do that. It's desertion in the face of the enemy. I'll have you shot for that."

Eyes narrowed alarmingly, Preacher pinned Danvers with a burning gaze. "You may try, Colonel, but you'll have a damn hard time doing it." He raised himself in the saddle. "Antoine, Three Sleeps, grab yer gear. We're gettin' out of here," he shouted.

After two tense minutes, the mountain men appeared with their horses loaded. The Arapaho warriors came with them. Without another word, Preacher and Cloud Blanket in the lead, they left the fort by the open main gate. After they departed, Danvers looked around and spotted BSM Muldoon.

"Sergeant Major, take a horse and follow them. I want to know every detail of what they are up to."

"Yes, sir."

Beyond the ridge that overlooked Fort Washington, Preacher halted the small party and made a fire for coffee. While it brewed, he listened to what Cloud Blanket knew of Iron Shirt. His conclusions, arrived at over the first cup of heavily sweetened brew, surprised Preacher.

"I believe that there is more behind this than a moon-struck holy man. There are three white men who go wherever Iron Shirt goes. They do not have kind faces. They are the ones who bring the rifles."

"I'll have to look into that. A while back I thought I had run into the whites that was supposed to be runnin' with Iron Shirt." He went on to relate the run-in with Blake Soures, including a description of the outlaw leader.

Cloud Blanket nodded thoughtfully, then brightened at the portrayal of Soures. "That is the man who brought the wagons with the rifles. He is like the rattlesnake."

"*Was,* Cloud Blanket. I killed him."

"He will not be missed by me or any of my hand."

"I'm gonna have to go get a look at these other whites you tole me about."

"You are not going back to the soldier lodges?"

"No. Let that damned pompous Danvers sweat a bit. The others can go back in a couple of days, if they want. That'll help some."

"While you are gone, my braves and I will not be able to protect the foolish soldiers, but we will try."

They drank another cup of coffee and Cloud Blanket described to Preacher how to find the war camp. They parted as friends.

BSM Terrance Muldoon and his three-man detail returned to Fort Washington to report. They remained unaware that they had been allowed to get close enough to hear what was being discussed. Nor, after hearing Preacher speak in Cheyenne, did Muldoon wonder why the conversation had been in English. Doubtless he would have been furious to learn that it had been done that way for his benefit.

"So, Mr. Preacher is going off to look for some nonexistent white renegades who are supposed to be aiding the hostiles that attacked us? Do you suspect, Sergeant Major, that he intends to join them?"

BSM Muldoon bristled. "Certainly not, sor, an' that's a

fact. Preacher may be a lot of things, dependin' on how ye see him, but he's not disloyal, not a bit, sor."

"I want a detail sent off to trail our Mr. Preacher. Lieutenant Judson will lead it. I know how you dislike garrison duty, Sergeant Major, so I am sending you along as ranking noncom."

"And the purpose of our going after him, if I may ask, sor?"

"I want you to bring him, and the others who deserted us, back here."

Muldoon raised an eyebrow. "To be punished, is it, sor?"

"No, to tell us what we need to know to defeat these hostiles."

"Ye think they'll be comin' back, do ye, Colonel, sor?"

"You can count on it, Sergeant Major. As soon as they lick their wounds and get in a proper frenzy." Then he turned his attention to a dispatch he had to write to his superiors back East.

After a three-days fast, hard journey, Preacher and his friends, none of whom seemed eager to return to the fort, reached the war camp deep in the Bighorn Canyon region. It had been up and down mountains all the way. Mostly up, as Preacher saw it. At noon of the last day, Preacher reined in and pointed to the crisp-edged imprints of iron wagon wheels.

"There's no question that there's white men with that biggest Blackfoot band. They're close, too. I think we need only get close enough to take a peek, then git on back."

"Sounds right," agreed Three Sleeps.

Antoine cast one eye at an odd angle. "You reckon the colonel will thank us for what we find out?"

Preacher ran long fingers through his long, dark, sandy hair. "I doubt he knows the words, Tony. We'll ease up on these-here hostiles after dark and see what we can see."

Late that night, what they saw, though they had no names

for them, were Praeger, Gross and Reiker. Preacher watched their activity for a while, then came to the conclusion that the Blackfoot and their allies were making preparations to return to Fort Washington. He nudged Three Sleeps in the ribs and whispered in his ear.

"I think we got what we came for. We'll ease our way out of here and head back in the morning."

Except for Lieutenant Judson and BSM Muldoon, the detail that followed Preacher consisted of men so inept that they made their presence painfully obvious. So lulled did they become, that they had not the slightest awareness of being watched. Early the next morning, they blithely walked their horses directly into imminent danger.

When the large war party of Blackfoot attacked, they took the Dragoons entirely by surprise.

27

Arrows flew in a dark cloud out of the grass along the trail left by Preacher. Three Dragoons died before a one could fire a shot. The hostiles, who had left early to return to the fort, had come across the sign of white men and decided upon an ambush. The sight of the Dragoons had been entirely too tempting.

Lieutenant Judson acted correctly and promptly. "Dismount. . . . Form a circle with your horses. Every other man, return fire."

The only trouble was they saw nothing to shoot at. Another flight of deadly shafts rose from the concealment of waving grass and thick brush. Instinctively, the Dragoons aimed at the places where the arrows first appeared. Several cries of pain rewarded them. Mounted warriors came from a tree line along one ridge and charged toward the circle of horses. Had the Blackfoot waited only a short while longer, they could have caught all of the birds in their nest.

*　*　*

It turned out not to be so. From a distance, Preacher and the men with him heard several muffled reports. The mountain men cocked their ears and concentrated a moment.

"It sounds like carbines to me," opined Preacher, who pronounced the word *car-bines*.

Three Sleeps agreed. "That it does. Now, what you suppose?"

"Figger Colonel Danvers sent some people after us."

Antoine joined in. "An' they got theyselves in trouble." He ended with a cackle.

Three Sleeps Norris turned to Preacher. "Should we go help 'em out?"

Preacher pretended to ponder that a moment. "I don't see why not."

The Arapaho in their wake, they set off at a brisk canter. From the faintness of the sound, Preacher reckoned they had a good twenty-minute ride.

A lot can happen in twenty minutes. Terribly outnumbered, the eighteen-man patrol died by ones and twos. Blackfoot swarmed around the improvised shelter, the horses targeted indiscriminately, along with the Dragoons. One beast, shrieking in pain from a neck wound, broke the grip of the soldier holding it and ran out among the charging hostiles.

That opened a gap which allowed a dozen Blackfoot to dash through. With lance and tomahawk, they began to slash at the Dragoons from terribly close quarters. BSM Muldoon saw Lieutenant Judson go down, a lance rammed through his belly. The unfortunate Private Mallory died a second later, his body draped over that of his officer.

"Poor, stupid lad," Muldoon said aloud as eulogy for them both.

Then his ears heard something he could not believe. Gunfire! And coming from beyond the press of savages. It could only be Preacher and those he had taken with him. Relief flooded Muldoon as he shot a screaming Blackfoot full in the face from two feet away. Another of the Dragoons died while he cocked the hammer to take out a hostile.

Three mountain men and six Arapaho warriors charged down on the backs of the triumphant Blackfoot. Their rifles cracked at the best possible range and nine Blackfoot died. Preacher unlimbered one of his Walker Colts and shot two more before the hostiles could react and turn to face this new threat.

Wounded, one of them thrashed in the grass. Preacher aimed at a fourth target. He knew his chances to be good; he hadn't missed yet. His evaluation of his marksmanship proved accurate. His .44 ball slammed into the skull of a warrior who swung a war club at the head of BSM Muldoon.

Preacher's action did not prevent Muldoon from being hit, but turned the strike into a hard, glancing blow. Believing the spirits had turned on them, the surviving Blackfoot fired a few final arrows, those without mounts were hoisted up by comrades on horseback and the warriors streamed off over a notch in the ridge to the south.

Stunned by the rap on his head, Muldoon looked slowly around himself to discover he had come out of the fray as the sole survivor. "Jesus, Mary, an' Joseph, sure an' I'm glad to see you, Preacher, that's a fact."

Preacher also totaled the grim score. "How'd this happen to you?"

"Devil take it, lad, they got us entirely by surprise, they did. Didn' know there was any heathen about 'til they shot arrows at us from the grass, an' then more of the bastids come out of the trees, shootin' better rifles than we have. It was a terrible slaughter, it was."

Preacher tried for understatement. "I can see that."

"All me poor lads. Even lame-wit Mallory, an' our darlin' lieutenant. The colonel's not going to like that, he's not."

"No doubt. Tell me something, Muldoon, you seemed to put a note in your voice when you mentioned the colonel. Was it the knock you got on your head, or something else?"

Muldoon's grimace of pain turned to a sour expression. "You've got the heart of it, Preacher, sure an' you do. I've not seen nor heard anything certain, but I do have some worries about the darlin' colonel, I do. He's been writin' a lot of dispatches of late. Only they aren't to Gen'ral Ferris, or the War Department. I've yet to see to whom he addresses them, but it's certain sure it's not anyone in our chain of command."

"There's more?" prompted Preacher.

"Aye, that's the big an' little of it. It's about his attitude toward the men, Preacher. The way he sent us out here, an eighteen-man patrol into hostile country, with not a fare-thee-well. An' orderin' that counterattack back when the heathens had the fort surrounded. It's almost as though he wants us to get killed off to the last man jack of us, it is. But, a commander leads his men, inspires them, an' protects them, too. It can't be."

That awakened dark suspicions in the mind of Preacher, although he had to put them aside for the present and look into it all later. Muldoon had suffered a hard, messy blow to the head, which cut his scalp and raised a knot. Time that was taken care of.

"You know about those things more than I, Sergeant Major. Now, let me get a good look at that wound of yours." After some gentle probing and prodding, Preacher satisfied himself the skull remained intact and pronounced his verdict. "You'll recover. But with your patrol wiped out, and no way to get back alone, it might be best for you to ride with us."

BSM Muldoon's eyebrows elevated. "Yer not goin' direct to the fort?"

"Nope. This ambush tells me we haven't finished our business here. We need to get a look at this Blackfoot messiah, Iron Shirt, up close and personal. Find out what hold he has on these Injuns."

"When will that be?"

"Tonight," promised Preacher.

Preacher's little band made careful observations of the routine engaged in by Iron Shirt. In this case, two large bands of Northern Cheyenne, won over by news of the near success at the fort, prepared for the ritual. Late that night, after the immersion, fire-walking, feasting, drumming and singing ended, would be ideal for what Preacher had in mind, he told the others.

Once they had pulled back far enough from the camp, Preacher revealed his intentions. "Antoine an' me are gonna go in there and stir 'em up some. Leave some real scary things for Iron Shirt. If we're lucky, he'll begin to doubt his own medicine."

"Such as what?" BSM Muldoon asked.

Preacher brushed off the question. "Oh, some things we gathered up earlier today."

The hearty band had ridden west of the ambush scene to avoid any contact with hostiles that might happen by. Preacher and Antoine had hunted during part of the afternoon, using bows with all the skill of an Indian. Part of what they took, they ate. Some portions of the animals had been put away for later use. Preacher knew exactly what he wanted, and had used the last hours of daylight to paint plains-Indian pictographs on strips of rawhide. He took those, and the animal parts, with him when he and Antoine slipped away to the Blackfoot encampment at around two o'clock in the morning. A heavy overcast made the ground a pool of ink.

They entered the sleeping war village silently. Only the soft scuff of moccasins on hard soil indicated their movement. Preacher worked his way to the center of camp, then located the ideal spot.

With Antoine standing guard in front of the entrance to the lodge of Iron Shirt, Preacher placed a headless skunk on the ground. Next came a fresh deer heart, to which he affixed one of the pictograph strips. Those were the symbols for Iron Shirt's name, he had explained when he painted them. Beside that, he left the severed testicles of the same deer, with signs on the rawhide for White Wolf takes these from Iron Shirt.

Satisfied with his nocturnal display, Preacher signaled to Antoine and the mountain men slipped out of camp. Once beyond any chance of apprehension, they both threw back their heads and made the wailing sounds associated with the spirits of those who had been blinded and mutilated and could not journey to the Other World. Not too surprisingly, no one stirred in camp until daylight.

Shortly after the uproar that heralded the discovery of Preacher's handiwork, the hostiles broke camp and rode off to the southeast, in the direction of Fort Washington. Preacher's stalwart band followed at a discreet distance.

Over the next several nights, Preacher continued to pay ghostly, taunting visits to the band of warriors. On the fourth night, he edged in close to two teenaged boys, along as apprentice warriors and assigned as herd guards. After a round of ordinary talk about which girl in their village they thought the most beautiful, one lad brought up a subject that Iron Shirt's fury prohibited from being talked of openly.

"My older brother has seen the bad medicine that appears in camp these last nights. This White Wolf has powerful medicine. My brother thinks maybe more strength than Iron Shirt. Men have tried to kill White Wolf before, yet he lives, while our warriors die by the white man's bullets. My brother is thinking of taking me and returning to our village."

The other boy agreed. "Yes, that is a wise thing."

From his careful observation of the furtive glances the warriors made in all directions when they left their low war lodges, and now this indication of unrest, Preacher decided that an aura of bad medicine and even fear hung over the entire camp. His work had been well done.

A quick count of those in the war camp the next morning informed Preacher that some twelve or more had abandoned the cause. Earlier that day he had watched the three white men in camp set off southeast with Cheyenne guides, well ahead of the rest. Cloud Blanket had been right, and Preacher would tell him so. A big stir came when Iron Shirt learned of the defections.

He called the warriors together, most of them already mounted to continue the ride. "They are women! They shame the name Blackfoot. I have had a vision. We will make a mighty raid on the soldiers we have fought before with our Cheyenne and Sioux brothers. This time we will be victorious! I have strengthened the medicine that protects you. Nothing of the white man's can harm you."

From his vantage point, Preacher grinned at the craftiness of this fraudulent medicine man. As if he did not plan all along to go back to the fort. He decided upon one more visit to this uneasy war camp that night.

They came in the darkest part of the night. Preacher and his companions burst into the gathering of lodges from ten different points of the compass. Whooping ferociously, a torch spluttering in one hand, Preacher bent low to set fire to a six-foot-high lodge. Then he made for another one.

Not far away, one of the Arapaho, Gourd, overturned another and shot the occupants. Three Sleeps Norris trampled mounds of supplies and set them ablaze. Antoine Revier hurled cases of ammunition and bundles of arrows into the central fire. The enemy swirled all around them, unwilling to fire their rifles for fear of hitting a friend.

In the mad gyration of the swift raid, Preacher eventually came face-to-face with Iron Shirt. Preacher's right-hand Walker Colt bucked first and the ball smacked into the chest of his enemy. Iron Shirt went down in an eyeblink. Elated, Preacher signaled for the others to leave. They had accomplished much more than he had expected. Firing their weapons behind them, the mountain men, Arapaho, and BSM Muldoon quickly faded into the dark.

28

To Preacher's astonishment, the warriors did not disband after the death of Iron Shirt. Nor did they take time to mourn the loss of their leader and elect a new one. Rather, some set out immediately, with Cheyenne braves acting as guides, in search of those who had done the damage. The rest continued toward the fort.

Preacher soon learned the reason. Iron Shirt was alive! Obviously sore as hell, he moved slowly and sat his pony warily. Surrounded by a hundred Blackfoot warriors, the medicine man was unreachable. Knowing where the hostiles were headed, Preacher urged all speed to the fort. Muldoon concurred.

Mid morning remained markedly cool two days later, when the sentry's voice rang out from the gate. "Corporal of the Guard, Post Number Two. Visitors at the gate."

Bustling over on sore feet—he'd joined the Dragoons to ride, not to walk—Corporal Collins found three men confronting the guard. They were dressed like dandies. Nevertheless, he addressed them politely enough. "Good morning, gentlemen. May I inquire as to your business at Fort Washington today?"

Quinton Praeger took the lead. "We must see your commanding officer at once."

Collins blinked. "What about?"

"It is a matter of great urgency."

Following regulations, Corporal Collins did not give an inch. "If you tell me what it is, I can convey the information to Colonel Danvers."

His patience growing short, Praeger put heat in his words. "It is a matter of life and death."

Amused by the man's pomposity, Collins let his eyes go wide. "Oh, that's what it is, eh? The colonel will want to hear that, I'm sure."

Praeger flared. "Damnit, man, the country west of here is full of roving bands of hostiles. Tell him that, and tell him that Quinton Praeger and two associates are here to see him at once."

Corporal Collins scratched one ear. "I reckon you fellers didn't see the bullet scars on the wall. We've done whipped the savages and sent them running."

Praeger regained his control and fixed the insolent corporal with a frigid stare. "No you didn't. Because all the Indians we saw were headed this way. Tell that to your Colonel Danvers."

"Uh . . . yes, sir, right away, sir."

When Lieutenant Colonel Danvers learned of their presence, he had the three men ushered into his office. He waited a moment to insure that no prying ears lingered beyond the door then turned on Praeger, Gross and Reiker with a face suffused by hot fury.

"What in the name of God are you doing here?" he demanded.

Praeger took a step forward, asserting his control. "The whole thing is coming apart. Preacher is alive."

"I know that. But he's gone now, I dismissed him and he went away."

Praeger's words struck Danvers like lead pellets. "He went right to the war camp of Iron Shirt. He's worked some sort of savage mysticism that's nearly driven Iron Shirt out of his mind. He told me after the first little gifts were left that Preacher wants his balls. It's true what I told your corporal. The Blackfoot, Cheyenne and Sioux are on the way here. But if we don't get a war started soon, it will all blow up in our faces."

Danvers fumbled for words. "That's . . . terribly disturbing. What do you expect me to do?"

"I want you to have these Dragoons attack the peaceful Cheyenne at once, the ones who did not join Iron Shirt. That's sure to bring about the desired reaction and satisfy our friends back East." He paused, looked around the headquarters and at the palisades beyond.

"Apparently you did too good a job on this fort. By now I expected to find all but you dead. The troops are in much too good shape. Looks as if they could fight their way through any number of Indians."

Instinctively Danvers stood up for his men. "My Dragoons had to fight their way out here. Naturally they gained experience."

Praeger closed with Danvers in two rapid steps. He tapped a long forefinger on the colonel's chest. "Let me remind you that *they* are the ones who are supposed to lose. The whole program is poised to fall into place. But . . ." He raised the finger and tapped Danvers again. "It will take a massacre and an Indian war to clear the land of the savage vermin."

Choking on his anger, Lieutenant Colonel Danvers turned partly away. Why had he ever thrown in his lot with these insufferable scoundrels? Desperately he tried to disassociate himself from this distasteful part of their plot. "I am only taking orders. I am not a participant in anything beyond the military involvement, of which, I'll remind you, I took no part in the planning. I suggest you leave forthwith, before any fighting begins, if you value your hides so much." With that, he showed them out of his office.

Preacher's valiant band arrived at Fort Washington the next day. The Blackfoot, Cheyenne and Sioux came right behind. Once more, the fort was very active. From the round-top knoll where he had made medicine, Iron Shirt observed the frantic activity within the walls through a brass telescope given him by Quinton Praeger. He could not mask his surprised reaction when he recognized three particular faces. He lowered the glass and turned to Two Moons.

"The Great Spirit smiles on us. The man Praeger and his nurselings are inside the fort. We can now sweep all of our enemies away in one battle. Then all the plains will burst out in flame."

For his part, Two Moons would have preferred to be spared Iron Shirt's rhetoric. Cunning and intelligent, Two Moons had long ago accepted that the great medicine of Iron Shirt was a fake. Men died at the hands of the whites not because they had lost faith, but because they had been shot. What sat foremost in the mind of Two Moons was the swiftness with which Iron Shirt had turned against their benefactors. Praeger, who wanted to be called Star Child, had brought them the fine new rifles, the barrels of powder and boxes of caps. For that he deserved praise, not death. He kept all that to himself as he replied to his leader.

"We have them trapped right enough. Why have they come here?" Two Moons inquired.

"Why do the white men do many stupid things?" Derisive laughter followed that suggestion.

"Iron Shirt, since they know of our plans, it cannot be for protection. It may be they came here to betray us."

Iron Shirt's face darkened at that. "Then they shall die slowly."

Quinton Praeger withdrew into a dark rage when he learned of the death of Blake Soures. He took his fury to the saloon in the sutler's store only half an hour before the Indians swarmed down the length of the narrow finger of land to the stockade that surrounded Fort Washington. There he observed the three, buckskin-clad men who had ridden in earlier in the day. They gulped down prodigious drafts of beer and wiped their lips with the backs of their hands. When the Blackfoot and their allies appeared, the sutler spoke from behind the bar to one of them.

"Well, Preacher, looks like you brought us more company than we wanted."

"I coulda told ya they were on the way, if you'd've asked," came the reply. "Boys, we'd best be gettin' to the walls. Those Injuns ain't here for a bison feast."

Jolted by this revelation and driven by a blind desire for revenge on Preacher, Praeger went in search of Heck Driscoll, one of Soures's lieutenants, who managed the wagons. He found him near the stables.

"Driscoll, I have a job for you. I've located this troublemaker, Preacher, and I can point him out to you. I want you to kill him. Do it up on the wall, so it will look like the savages did it."

Driscoll hitched his belt and produced a confident grin. "I can handle that all right." With that, they set off to find Preacher.

Like a cataract's roar, gunfire greeted them as they approached the wall. From outside came the challenging reports of Praeger's nice new rifles. Praeger winced involuntarily at the thought of being shot at by them. He quickly located the lean, broad-shouldered man in buckskin and pointed him out to Driscoll. The renegade gave a curt nod and moved off toward the access stairs.

Preacher first became aware of Driscoll when the mountain man moved abruptly and a tomahawk blade swished past his ear. The haft struck his right shoulder and Preacher turned, expecting to find a warrior had scaled the wall.

Not so. He faced another white man, one he vaguely recognized. His carefully planned blow gone astray, Driscoll sought to recover. Before he could lift the 'hawk, Preacher hit him in his exposed gut. Driscoll dropped the tomahawk and bent double. Air rushed from Driscoll's lungs, to be quickly stopped when Preacher kneed him in the face.

Dazed, Driscoll went to one knee. The fighting around them had grown so intense that no one noticed as Driscoll slid a knife from its sheath. Concerned with holding off the Indians, Preacher did not have time to play by the rules. He simply drew a .44 Colt and blew a hole through the head of his assailant. Heck Driscoll did a backward half gainer off the parapet.

Then enlightenment settled on Preacher. The dead man had been with the others in the Blackfoot war camp. He'd handed out rifles and ammunition from the rear of a wagon. That meant the other whites must be here. He knew them by sight, and vaguely recalled that someone had given him names: Praeger, Gross and Reiker. Behind him, the firing slackened and the first assault by the hostiles broke off. Preacher went in search of the men behind this uprising.

He found Quinton Praeger with surprising ease. Shunning the hypocrisy of fighting his Indian allies, Praeger had returned to the saloon. Preacher came upon him there.

Arctic chill coated the words Preacher spoke in a slow drawl. "I reckon you're the one they call Praeger. You're responsible for stirrin' up this Injun ruckus. An' I reckon you know who I am. For what it's worth, yer errand boy didn't get the job done." Preacher's lip curled in contempt. "I hate a stinkin' white renegade more'n I hate a Pawnee. Are you going to do it the easy way an' give up?"

From outside they heard sound of renewed attack. This time it came from the west. Praeger responded with a bravado he did not feel. "That'll be the day."

Preacher had come willing to oblige. "Do you want it inside or out?"

Praeger did not reply. Instead, he fired with a concealed pistol from under the table. The sneak's aim was off because of the extreme angle, so all that hit Preacher was a shower of splinters. The flattened ball moaned past. Responding in a manner totally unexpected by Praeger, Preacher dove over the table at him.

They spilled out of the chair together. Preacher rammed Praeger's head against the floorboards repeatedly until a small cloud of dust hung around the battered renegade. Drops of blood from Praeger's split scalp formed a halo around his head. His eyes glazed and Preacher eased up, came to his feet.

He soon found that Praeger had more than one card up his sleeve. Lightning quick, Praeger grabbed for the butt of another of his short-barreled .60 pistols. He found himself not fast enough.

Preacher filled his hand with a Walker Colt and shot his enemy in the right shoulder. The Deringer went flying. His gun hand made inoperable, Praeger made a try with his left. To his surprise, he got the pistol free and fired a shot that creased the outside of Preacher's right thigh. That did not prevent Preacher from shooting the corrupt land speculator through the heart.

Hyman Entermann stared at Preacher a moment. "There's another of them out back in the chicksale."

Preacher nodded his thanks and left the saloon. He found Morton Gross at the outhouse. The chubby renegade fumbled to button his fly as he exited the small building. Preacher's words froze him.

"I killed Praeger not a minute ago. I'd gather you are the one called Gross. It sorta fits," he added parenthetically.

"I . . . I don't know who you mean. My name is Pembrook." His slight hesitation over the name put the lie to his words.

Preacher took note of it. "I don't care what you call yerself. You rode in with a piece of renegade white trash named Praeger, who's been stirrin' up the Blackfoot, Cheyenne and Sioux. I'm here to take you to justice in front of Colonel Danvers, or bury you. The choice is yours."

In the next tense second, Morton Gross made the biggest mistake of his life. Instead of surrendering, he grabbed for his pistol. He cleared it of his coat and had the hammer back when Preacher drew and fired his Walker Colt. The .44 ball struck Gross in a rib, which flattened it and deflected it from his heart, though it did terrible damage to his left lung. Eyes wide, he blinked slowly and sagged to the ground. Preacher stepped close and kicked the gun away.

"Where will I find Reiker?"

"I . . . don't know. You must be Preacher, right?"

"That's what they call me."

"I know . . . I'm going to die. I . . . just want . . . to do something . . . on the plus side of . . . the ledger . . . before I do."

"Go on, I'm listenin'."

Blood bubbled in pink froth on the lips of Morton Gross. "Watch out . . . for your Colonel Danvers, Preacher. He's in on . . . this thing of Praeger's."

Preacher bent close. "You're sure of that?"

A breathy word answered him. "Yes." Then Morton Gross shuddered and died.

"Dang. That went too fast. I sure would like to know where Reiker is," Preacher said over the dead man.

"He's right here." The voice came from behind Preacher, like the crack of a whip.

A violent crash and a rumble came from beyond Aaron

Reiker. Unlike the previous time, the Blackfoot warriors did not try to scale the wall. Instead, they rode forward, attached several ropes to a series of spike-topped lodgepole pines in the palisade and rode fast away from the wall. With as many as eight horses per upright, the log barricade strained and at last gave away. The rammed earth behind cascaded down from sheer gravity.

Preacher tensed and made ready to spring to one side. He fully expected to get a bullet in the back at any second. Instead, Reiker started toward him, talking as he came.

"I saw Quinton's body. And now I see you have disposed of Morton as well. Saves me the trouble, I suppose. I should be grateful and let you go. Our Indian friends will finish you readily enough." Reiker paused and sighed. "But then, coward that he was, I imagine Gross told you more than you should know. You've more lives than an alley cat, Preacher, and you might get away from the Blackfoot. So, you see, I don't have any choice."

While the overconfident Reiker rambled, Preacher's expectations soared. Braced for evasion, he used flexed knees to power his next move. With a loud, piercing yell, he jumped straight into the air and spun, bringing a Walker Colt ahead of him. Lacking the precise position of Reiker, his first shot missed.

Lithe as a cat, Preacher came down on the balls of his moccasined feet as he eared back the hammer. Reiker's ball caught Preacher by surprise, and burned like hell's fire along the left side of the rib cage. Had he been standing still, he would have died. It put Preacher's second shot off so that it only cut a chunk off Reiker's right hip-bone.

Reiker stumbled to his left, to the protection of the outhouse. A stench came from the interior that told of frequent use. A fastidious man in dress and decorum, Reiker wrinkled his nose. Over it all, though, hung the coppery odor of violent death. Cautiously he peered around one corner.

Surprise puckered his lips when he saw no sign of

Preacher. Where could he have gotten to so quickly? Reiker searched the entire area behind the sutler's with his eyes. Confident that Preacher had left, there being no hiding place, he came from behind the small structure and started back toward the saloon. The door to the outhouse creaked on leather hinges at his back.

"Behind you, Reiker."

He made a valorous try, spun from left to right, so his pistol would come in line first. Preacher let him complete his turn before he pumped a .44 ball into the center of Reiker's chest. Gagging, Reiker sank to his knees. His pistol discharged. The ball punched through the door of the toilet. Feebly he reached for another pistol.

Preacher shot him again. This time the ball put a black hole at the top of the bridge of Reiker's nose. Preacher stepped into the clear.

"Got to remember to tell Entermann to do something about that smell," he muttered. He sighed and set to reloading his Walker Colt. With this accomplished, all he had left was Iron Shirt and the aroused Indians.

29

With the wall almost breached, Preacher busied himself in an effort to get some of the young Dragoons to pull the three-pound cannon to the top of the dirt platform. Lieutenant Colonel Danvers confronted him there.

"Do you mind telling me where Mr. Praeger and his associates happen to be?"

Mincing no words, Preacher told him. He concluded with a fateful remark. "An' before one of them died, he told me you are mixed up in this dirty little business."

Danvers's eyes went wild. Froth formed at the corners of his mouth as, heedless of his condition and surroundings, he drew his Dragoon revolver. "That's a damned lie. Soldiers! I'm arresting this man as an Indian sympathizer. Disarm him and lock him up in the guardhouse."

Moving swiftly, Preacher knocked both privates aside and pulled his Walker Colt. Danvers had already triggered his Dragoon pistol. The shot went somewhat wild, to punch a hole through Preacher's left shoulder, which caused him to drop his Colt. Danvers took aim again.

In the next instant, a Cheyenne lance split the heart of

Lieutenant Colonel Danvers. It had been hurled by Cloud Blanket, who dropped from the roof of the headquarters building to land beside Preacher. They embraced in the Cheyenne manner.

"Now all we have to do is kill Iron Shirt and this first-cousin-to-a-skunk alliance will fall apart."

Cloud Blanket appeared saddened. "Yes. I always knew it would come to that. Though I will not be the one to spill his blood. Here, that shoulder needs caring for."

While Cloud Blanket bound Preacher's shoulder, he offered advice on the best means of finishing Iron Shirt. Preacher listened intently. Around them, the battle raged on. Once the cannon had been moved into place, as Cloud Blanket packed the wound with a poultice, the assault on the weakened portion of the wall ended quickly.

Little respite came for the defenders. No sooner had the Blackfoot withdrawn from the west stockade than the Cheyenne and Sioux flung themselves at the north face. They used the same tactic of tearing down the wall. Another section broke away and the dirt buffer rumbled into a loose ramp. Up it plunged the Sioux warriors.

With the fortifications about to fall, the desperate young Dragoon gunners manned the cannon, firing in a flat trajectory now. When they ran out of prepared grapeshot, they dumped loose balls down the barrel and double wadded it. Preacher reappeared on the parade ground with his French Le Mat sporting rifle. Aching from wounds in both shoulders, he fought his way through a group of Sioux who had breached the wall and now swarmed onto the parade ground. BSM Muldoon saw him coming and helped clear a path with some well-aimed shots. After a solid smack to the kidneys of one warrior, which sent torrents of pain through Preacher's body, he gained the parapet.

Eyes straining against the haze of smoke and dust, Preacher at last located the Blackfoot prophet. This was going to hurt him almost as much as it would Iron Shirt, he thought as he knelt and put the buttplate of the rifle to his shoulder. True to his word, Iron Shirt made medicine on the little round-top knoll. His body twisted and jerked in the gyrations of his ritual dance around a blazing fire. Taking careful aim, Preacher touched the set trigger, then put a fingertip on the release tang.

The Le Mat let go with a terrible bark at the front end and a ferocious bite at the back. Preacher's face screwed up in a response he could not suppress. Two long seconds passed; then Iron Shirt looked up sharply as the ball cracked over his head. Moving like an aged weakling, Preacher reloaded. Again he took aim.

With another punishing report, the Le Mat fired again.

Iron Shirt staggered, sagged, toppled. He hit the ground and lay there, his limbs twitched in agonized reflex for three long minutes, then he lay still. A gusty sigh of relief came from Preacher.

It had worked as he'd expected. Although much smaller, the .36-caliber ball had markedly more velocity and better sectional density than a .54 round so that it cut through the links of chain mail and pierced the heart of Iron Shirt. Word of the messiah's death traveled fast. Suddenly, the allies fell silent on the battlefield. Cloud Blanket appeared at Preacher's right. He raised his bloodied lance to command attention.

"My brothers, your false prophet, Iron Shirt, is dead. His medicine was not good against the long gun of White Ghost, who took his life. Stop the fighting and go home. Live there in peace with the white men, who will leave this place in the Moon of Painted Leaves. There will be no fort in this place."

Slowly, his message sank in. Their heads bowed in perceived defeat, the warriors turned away from Fort Washington and began to leave the area in small groups. Within an hour they had all passed out of sight.

* * *

After the warriors had left the field and order had been restored, Eve and her children came with some of the others to where Preacher sat under a single oak that had been spared by the builders, deadening the ache of his wounds with a jug of good rye.

Not one to defer to any man, Eve spoke what they had on their minds. "Preacher, we were wondering what you had in mind for the next few months?"

Preacher took a long pull and smacked his lips. The liquor probably was not good for the healing process, he knew, but by the time he got well into the second jug, he wouldn't give a damn. "Well, I'm gonna write a report on what happened here, to go with that Captain Dreiling. You know, the one whose gonna lead these soldier-boys back come September. My friends, Antoine an' Three Sleeps, will scout for them."

Eve pushed him further. "Yes, but what about you?"

"Me? I'm gonna take myself off somewhere quiet, where I won't see no Injuns or pilgrims or soldier-boys for a long, long time, an' jist plain heal up."

Eve's expression revealed that he had just slammed a door on what she wanted so desperately to know. Gathering her resources, she relented for the moment. "Actually, I wanted to ask you about a more immediate future. I would be pleased if you would take supper with my children and myself."

Preacher beamed up at her. "Well now, I think that could be managed. I'm tired of all this backslappin' that's gone on over me shootin' Iron Shirt. A little quiet supper sounds fine."

After the meal, with Charlie and Anna asleep for the night, Preacher and Eve talked earnestly and quietly for a while. Then they took a stroll to the small cabin set aside for Preacher.

Early the next morning, Preacher emerged from the low log structure. He yawned and stretched as much as his wounds would allow, then glanced back through the open door as he made his way to the nearest cook fire and pot of coffee.

He had a big grin plastered on his face as he made an announcement to the unseen person within. "Well now, I'll allow as how I jist might find that quiet place I want to rest up in somewhere in the Northwest Territory."

WAR OF THE
MOUNTAIN MAN

Dedicated to

Tommy & Emily Ruth Ervin

What man was ever content with one crime?
Juvenal

I had rather live with the woman I love in a world full of trouble, than to live in heaven with nobody but men.
Robert G. Ingersoll

1

"I don't like the idea of the kids on the ocean," Smoke said. "By God, I just don't."

Sally faced him from across the table in the house in the high-up country of Colorado. "Smoke, there is a new treatment available in France, and Louis Arthur has got to have it. We've been to the finest doctors on this continent. They all say the same thing."

"Sally, I'm not arguing that. I want what is best for Baby Arthur. But why do all the children have to go? My God, they'll be gone for more than a year."

She smiled at him. Smoke Jensen and Sally never had the hard, deadly quarrels that so many couples suffered. They were both reasonable people of high intelligence, and each loved the other. "The exposure to a more genteel climate— and I'm not talking about the weather—will be good for the older children. They need to broaden their horizons."

Smoke laughed as he picked up his coffee mug, holding it in one big, flat-knuckled hand. The laughter was full of good humor and did not contain a bit of anger or scorn. He stuck out his little finger. "They gonna learn how to hold a coffee cup dainty-like, with their little pinkies all poked out to one side?"

Sally laughed at him. "Yes. You heathen."

Smoke chuckled and rose from the table, picking up Sally's cup as well as his own. He walked to the stove, a big man, well over six feet, with broad shoulders, huge, heavily muscled arms, and a lean waist. He walked like a cat. His presence in a room, any room, usually brought the crowd to silence. His eyes were brown and could turn as cold as the Arctic. He was a ruggedly handsome man, turning the heads of ladies wherever he traveled.

He was Smoke Jensen. The man some called the last mountain man.

Smoke was the hero in dozens of dime novels. Plays had been written and were still being performed about his exploits. Smoke, himself, had never seen one. He was, without dispute, the fastest gun in the West. He had never wanted the title of gunfighter; but he had it.

There was no accurate count of how many would-be toughs, punks, thugs, thieves, and killers had fallen under the .44's of Smoke Jensen. Some say fifty; others said it was closer to two hundred. Smoke didn't know. As a young man, scarcely out of his teens, he had ridden into a mining camp taken over by the men who had killed his wife and baby son and had wiped it out to the last man.

His reputation had then been carved in solid granite. Smoke had become a living legend.

He had met Sally, who was working as a schoolteacher, and they had fallen in love. Together, working side by side— even though she was enormously wealthy, something Smoke didn't find out until well after they were married—they carved out a ranch in Colorado and named it the Sugarloaf.

For three years Smoke dropped out of sight, living a normal, peaceful life. Then he had to surface and once more strap on his guns in a fight for survival. He stayed surfaced. He would not hunt out a fight, but God help those who came to him trouble-hunting. As the western saying goes: Smoke could point out dozens of his graveyards.

Their coffee mugs refilled, Smoke sat back down at the table and they both sugared and stirred. Sally laid her hand on his. "Roundup is all over and the cattle sold, right, honey?"

"Yes. And it was a good one. We made money. Now we're rebuilding the herds, introducing a stronger breed, mixing in some Herefords. What'd you have on your mind, Sally?"

"I'd like to go with the children. . . ." She put a finger on his lips to stop his protests before they got started. "But I'm not. I know what the doctors said. And I'm never going to set foot on a ship again. But if we stay here, rattling around in this house, we'll both go crazy with worry. Let's wait until we receive the wire that the ship has steamed out, and then take a trip. Just the two of us."

"That's a good idea. The boys can run the spread; no worries there. You got some special place in mind?"

"Yes. It's a friend I went to college with. She and her husband just moved to Montana. They live near a small town about thirty miles from Kalispell. She's married to a doctor and they have a small ranch. I'd like to see her. She was my best friend."

"Suits me. We'll take a trip up there. It'll do us both good to get away, see some country, and meet new people. We'll take the train as far as it goes and then catch a stage."

"No," Sally shook her head. "Let's put the horses in a car and ride in, Smoke. It'll be worth it to see the expressions on their faces when we ride in."

"Sidesaddle?" he kidded her, knowing better.

"You have to be kidding!"

Smoke was with her. "All right, honey. But we're going to be heading into some rough country. I've been there. Cousin Fae lives not too far from there. We can take the train probably to Butte. That's wild country, Sally. Some ol' boys up there still have the bark on. And that's Big Max Huggins's country."

She smiled, but the curving of her pretty lips held no humor. "That's one of the reasons we're going, Smoke."

He laughed. "I was wondering if you were going to get around to leveling with me."

"You know this Max Huggins?"

"Only by name. We've never crossed trails."

She stared into her coffee cup.

"Sally, this town your friends have settled near . . . it wouldn't be Hell's Creek, would it?"

"Yes."

Smoke sighed and leaned back in his chair. "Then they didn't show a lot of sense. Hell's Creek is owned—lock, stock, and outhouse—by Big Max Huggins. It's filled with gunfighters, whores, gamblers, killers . . . You name it bad, and you'll find it there. Why did they settle there?"

"Robert—that's Vicky's husband—befriended an old man who took sick while visiting back east. Robert was just setting up his practice. Years later, he got a letter from an attorney telling him the old man had died and left him his ranch."

"And Big Max wanted the ranch?"

"Yes. But mostly he wants Victoria."

The next morning, Smoke rode into town and checked with Sheriff Monte Carson.

"What can you get me on Hell's Creek and a man named Big Max Huggins?"

Monte snorted. "I can tell you all about Big Max, Smoke. We got lead in each other about ten years ago."

"Over near the Bitterroot?"

Monte nodded his head.

"I remember that shoot-out. Is there any kind of law in Hell's Creek?"

"Only what Big Max says. Oh, there's a sheriff up there. But he's crooked as a snake's track and so are his deputies. I hear the governor keeps threatening to send men in to clean up the town, but he hasn't done it yet. Why the interest in Hell's Creek?"

"Sally has some friends who live near there. We're going to visit them. I'd sort of like to know what I'm riding into."

"You're riding into trouble, Smoke. Hell's Creek is a haven for outlaw gangs. In addition to Big Max's gang—and he's got forty or fifty men who ride for him—there's Alex Bell and his boys. Dave Poe, Warner Frigo, and Val Singer all run outlaw gangs out of Hell's Creek. The only way that town is ever going to be cleaned up is for the Army to go in and do it."

"Damn, Monte, it's 1883. The wild West is supposed to be calming down."

Monte shifted his chaw. "But you and me, Smoke, we know better, don't we?"

Smoke nodded his head. "Yeah. There'll be pockets of crud in the West for years to come, I reckon."

"Any way you can talk your missus out of takin' this trip?"

Smoke just looked at him.

"I do know the feelin'," Monte said. "Women get a notion in their heads, and a man's in trouble, for a fact. When are you and Sally pullin' out?"

"Probably in about a week. Who else do you know for sure is up there?"

"Ben Webster, Nelson Barlow, Vic Young, Dave Hall, Frank Norton, Lew Brooks, Sid Yorke, Pete Akins, and Larry Gayle. Is that enough?"

"Good God!" Smoke said, standing up. "You just named some of the randiest ol' boys in the country."

"Yeah. And believe you me, Smoke, they'll be plenty more up there just as good as them boys I just named. You're gonna be steppin' into a rattler's den."

"They do sell .44's up there, don't they?" Smoke asked dryly.

"Probably not to you." Monte's reply was just as dry.

2

That night, lying in bed, Sally said, "We don't have to go up there, Smoke. I don't want you to think I'm pressuring you in any way. Because I'm not."

"You think a lot of this friend of yours, don't you?"

"Like a sister, Smoke. She's had a lot of grief in her life and I'd like for her to have some happiness. She's overdue."

"Want to explain that?"

"She lost two brothers in the Civil War. Her mother died when she was in high school. Then in her second year of college, her father died. She worked terribly hard to finish school. Took in ironing, mended clothes, worked as a maid, anything to put food in her mouth and clothes on her back. I'd help whenever I could, but Vicky is an awfully proud girl. She and Robert had one child . . . that lived. Two others died. She can't have any more. Their daughter Lisa is ten."

Smoke waited for a moment, his eyes on the dark ceiling. "Finish it, honey. Tell it all."

"This Max Huggins trash has threatened Lisa several times, to get to Vicky."

Smoke thought about that. For about five seconds. He

turned his head, his gaze meeting Sally's eyes. "We'll start packing up some things in the morning."

On the day they received the telegram from Sally's father, informing them of the steamer's departure, Smoke rode around their ranch, checking things out and speaking to the hands. His crew was a well-paid and tough bunch, who to a man would die for the brand. Some of them had been outlaws, riding the hoot-owl trail for a time. Some were gunfighters who sought relative peace and found it at the Sugarloaf. All were cowboys, hardworking and loyal.

"I still think you ought to take some of the boys with you, Smoke," his foreman grumbled. "Them's a hard bunch up yonder."

Smoke rolled a cigarette and handed the makings to his foreman. "You boys are needed here. There are still lots of folks who would just love to burn me out if they got the chance."

"They won't," the foreman said quietly.

"You boys take care of the place. You know where I'll be and how to reach me. We'll see you when we get back."

Smoke and Sally pulled out the next morning, Smoke riding a midnight-black gelding he called Star, and Sally on a fancy-stepping mountain-bred mare who could go all day and still have bottom left. Smoke led a packhorse with their few pieces of luggage and supplies.

They headed east, toward Denver, where they would catch the train. Sally had much experience with trains; Smoke had ridden only a few of them, preferring to travel in the saddle.

The beautiful woman and the handsome man turned heads when they boarded in Denver. And the whisper went from car to car: "That's Smoke Jensen! See them guns? He's killed a thousand men."

Smoke signed a half-dozen books about him and patiently answered the many questions that were asked of him, mostly by newcomers to the West, men and women making their first trip from the East.

One mouthy preacher lipped off one time too many about violent men who lived by the gun. Smoke finally told him to shut his mouth and mind his own business. The preacher's mouth opened and closed silently a few times, like a fish out of water. Then he sat back down and shut up.

They changed trains in Cheyenne and headed northwest, and Smoke had to endure yet another new bunch of pilgrims with a thousand questions.

"My, my," Sally said during a lull in the verbal bombardment. There was a twinkle in her eyes. "I didn't realize I was married to such a famous man."

"Bear it in mind," Smoke said with a straight face. "And the next time I ask for a cup of coffee, you quick step and fetch it."

Sally leaned over, putting her lips close to his ear, and whispered a terribly vulgar suggestion.

Smoke had to put his hat over his face to keep from busting out laughing. Sally was every bit the lady, but like so many western women, she could be quite blunt at times.

A fat drummer twisted in his seat and asked Smoke, "Will we see any Indians this trip? I've never seen an Indian."

"We might see a few," Smoke told him, aware that everyone within hearing range had their ears perked up. "But the tribes have pretty well been corralled. What we'll more than likely encounter—if anything—is outlaws working the trains."

"Outlaws!" a woman hollered. "You mean like . . . highwaymen?"

"Yes, ma'am. Once we cross over into Montana Territory, the odds of outlaws hitting trains really pick up. Especially this train," he added.

"What's so special about this train?" the lippy preacher asked.

"We're carrying gold."

"Now, how would someone such as you know that?" the preacher demanded.

Smoke ignored the scarcely concealed slur upon his character. "I saw them loading it, that's why."

"Well," the preacher huffed. "I'm certain the railroad has adequate security."

"They got an old man with a shotgun sitting in the car, if that's what you mean."

The preacher turned away and lifted his newspaper.

"Are we carrying gold, Smoke?" Sally asked.

"Yeah. And a lot of it. And not just gold. We're carrying several payrolls, too. For the miners."

"What are the chances of our getting held up?"

"Pretty good, I'd say. If I had to take a guess, I'd say we're carrying about a fifty-thousand-dollar payroll—all combined— and maybe twice that in gold. Be a juicy haul for those so inclined."

"They wouldn't dare attack this train," she kidded him. "Not with the famous Smoke Jensen on board." She punched him in the ribs.

"Your faith in me is touching." He rubbed the spot where she had punched him. "In more ways than one."

The day melted into dusk and then full dark, the train chugging on uneventfully through the night. The passengers slept fitfully, swaying back and forth in their seats to the rhythm of the drivers on the tracks.

Smoke sensed the train slowing and opened his eyes. Being careful not to rouse Sally, he stood up and stepped out into the aisle, making his weaving way to the door. He stepped outside and stretched, getting the kinks out of his muscles. On instinct, he slipped the leather thongs from the hammers of his six-guns.

Smoke leaned over the side and saw the skeletal form of the water tower ahead, faintly illuminated by the dim light of a nearly cloud-covered moon.

Through the odor of smoke pouring from the stack of the

locomotive, Jensen could almost taste the wetness in the air. A storm was brewing, and from the build-up of clouds, it was going to be a bad one.

He looked back at the lantern-lit interior of the car, the lamps turned down very low. The passengers, including Sally, were still sleeping.

The train gradually slowed and came to a gentle halt, something most experienced engineers tried to do late at night so the paying passengers wouldn't be disturbed.

Smoke caught the furtive movement out of the corner of his eyes. Men on the water tower. With rifles.

One big hand closed around the butt of a .44. He hesitated. Were they railroad men, posted there in case of a robbery attempt? He didn't think so. But he wasn't going to shoot until he knew for sure.

He saw the brakeman coming up the side of the coaches and Smoke called to him softly just as he dropped to the shoulder. "My name's Jensen, brakeman. Smoke Jensen. There are armed men on the water tower."

The man's head jerked up. "They damn sure ain't railroad men, Smoke. And we're carryin' a lot of gold and cash money."

"That's all I need to know," Smoke said. He leveled a .44 and knocked a leg out from under one gunman crouching on the water tower. The man fell, screaming, to the rocky ground.

Another gunman, hidden in the rocks alongside the tracks, opened fire, the slugs howling off the sides of the cars.

Smoke yelled, "Get these pilgrims down on the floor, Sally." To the brakeman, who had hauled out a pistol and was trying to find a target, he called, "How far to the next water stop?"

"Too far," the man said. "We got to water and fuel here or we don't make it."

"We'll make it," Smoke told him, pulling out his second .44 and jacking back the hammer.

One outlaw tried to run from the darkness to the locomotive. Either the engineer or the fireman shot him dead.

"How far is this payroll going?" Smoke asked, crouching down.

"All the way to the end of the line, up in Montana."

He knew the end of the line, at that time, was near Gold Creek. They would change trains before then. Smoke plugged a running outlaw and knocked him sprawling; but it wasn't a killing shot. The man jumped up and limped off. "Why in the hell doesn't the railroad put guards on these payroll shipments?"

"Beats me, Smoke. But I'm damn sure glad you decided to ride my train for this trip."

The pounding of horses' hooves punctuated the night. The outlaws had decided to give it up.

"Let's see what we got," Smoke said, shoving out empties and reloading as he walked over to the man he'd knocked off the water tower.

The man was dead. He'd landed on his head and broken his neck. He walked over to the man the engineer had shot. He was also dead. The third man Smoke had dropped was gut-shot and in bad shape, the slug blowing out his left side, taking part of the kidney with it. He looked up at Smoke.

"You played hell, mister. What's your name? I'd like to know who done me in."

"Smoke Jensen."

The man cussed. "Val sure picked the wrong train this time."

"Val Singer?" Smoke asked.

"Yeah. You know him?"

"I know him. Me and him . . ." Smoke broke it off as he looked down at the man. He was dead, his eyes wide open, staring at the cloudy sky. He looked over at the brakeman. "I winged another. Let's see if we can find him."

But he was gone. Smoke tracked a blood trail to where the outlaws had tied their horses. "He made the saddle. But as bad as he's bleeding, he won't last long. I must have hit the big vein in his leg."

The fireman walked up, his face all dark with soot. "Lem, you wanna toss them bodies in the baggage car and keep on haulin'?"

"I ain't having that crud in with me," the guard to the gold shipment said, walking up. He had not taken part in the fight because in case of an attempted robbery, he was under orders not to open the doors to anyone. "Toss 'em in with the wood and tote 'em that way."

Smoke shrugged his shoulders and helped wrap the men in blankets and carry them to the wood car. Back in his seat, Sally asked, "You suppose we'll have any more trouble?"

Smoke pulled his hat brim down over his eyes and settled down for a nap. "Not from that bunch," he said.

They changed trains in southern Idaho, staying with the Union Pacific line. This run would head straight north. End of track would put them about a hundred and fifty miles south of their destination.

The news had spread up and down the line that Smoke Jensen was on the train, and crowds gathered at every stop, hoping to get a glimpse of the West's most famous gunfighter. Smoke stayed in the car while the train was in station. He had never sought publicity and didn't want it now.

No more attempts were made to rob the train during the long pull north.

At end of track, Smoke off-loaded their horses while Sally changed from dress to jeans.

Packhorse loaded, they rode into the small town and purchased a side of bacon and some bread, a gaggle of kids and dogs right at their heels all the way.

"Right pleased to have you in town," the shopkeeper told them. "Sorry you can't stay longer. Things liven up quite a bit when you're around, I'd guess, Mr. Jensen. Be good for business."

"It usually is for the undertaker," Smoke told him, and that shut him up.

Smoke signed his name to a half-dozen penny dreadfuls, then he and Sally hit the trail, pointing their horses' noses north.

A young would-be tough, two guns tied down low, stepped out of the saloon and watched the Jensens ride out of town. He pulled his hat brim low, hitched at his guns, and said, "Huh! He don't look so tough to me. It's a good thing he didn't get in my way. I'd a called him out and left him in the street."

The town marshal looked at the kid, disgust in his eyes, then shoved the punk into a horse trough, guns and all, and walked away, leaving the big-mouth sputtering and cussing.

Smoke and Sally made their first camp alongside a fast-running and very clear and cold little creek. It didn't take either one of them very long to bathe. They knew it was time to exit the creek when they began turning blue.

They were up before dawn. After bacon and bread and coffee, Sally strapped on her short-barreled .44, and then they were in the saddle and heading north.

They were both ready for a hot bath and food they didn't have to cook over a campfire when they topped a ridge and looked down on a little town just south of Flathead Lake.

"Well," Sally said, straightening her back. "It has a hotel."

"Yeah," Smoke said with a grin. "And I'll bet they change the sheets at least once a month."

She smiled sweetly at him. "I'll bet they change them for me."

"Oh, yes, ma'am!" the desk clerk said, paling slightly as he checked the names on the register. "The feather ticks was just aired out and we'll get fresh linen on your bed pronto. You bet we will, Mrs. Jensen."

"And make sure the facilities are clean," Sally told him.

"Oh, yes, ma'am. I sure will."

The room was clean and it faced the street. Smoke laid

out clean clothes and shook out and hung up one of Sally's dresses while she bathed. He looked out the window and was not surprised to see a crowd gathering on the boardwalks below their room. Neither was he surprised to see the sheriff and two deputies among the gawking people. The desk clerk had not been slow in running his mouth.

He bathed and shaved while Sally got herself all fixed up, then dressed in a dark suit, white shirt, and string tie. He strapped on his .44's and they went down to the dining room for an early supper.

Smoke got a shot of whiskey from the bar for himself and a glass of wine for Sally, then rejoined his wife in the dining room. The sheriff approached them.

"Mind if I join you for a moment?" the lawman asked respectfully, his hat in his hand.

Smoke pushed out a chair with one boot.

"Coffee, Marie," the sheriff ordered.

"Nice little town, Sheriff," Sally said, taking a sip of wine.

"Thank you, ma'am. And it's peaceful, too."

Smoke knew his cue when he heard it. "It'll stay peaceful, too, Sheriff. We're here to rest for the night and then we'll be moving on."

"Nothin' is peaceful around you for very long, Jensen," the sheriff said. "You attract trouble like honey does flies."

"We don't have any trouble in the town near where I live," Smoke rebutted. "Hasn't been a shot fired in anger in a long, long time."

"How do you manage that?"

"We get rid of the troublemakers, Sheriff. It's really very simple."

"You run them out of town, eh?"

"We usually bury them," Sally said.

The sheriff cut his eyes to her. Strong-willed woman, he reckoned. Man would be hard-pressed to hold the reins on this one, he figured.

He'd of course seen them riding into town, her astride that mare and packing a pistol. Way she carried it, the sheriff figured she knew how to use it. And, more importantly, would use it.

"There's some pretty randy ol' boys in this town, Smoke. Some of them would like to make a reputation. I thought I'd warn you."

"The only way they're going to get to me, Sheriff, is if they come into the lobby of this hotel and call me out while I'm reading the newspaper, come in here while I'm eating and call me out, or try to backshoot me when I'm pulling out in the morning."

"And if they call you out? . . ."

"Then I guess the local undertaker is going to get some business, Sheriff."

"The one that'll more than likely try to crowd you is called Chub. He's a bad one, I'll give him that. He's killed a couple of men and wounded a couple more in face-downs. He's quick, Jensen."

"I'll bear that in mind, Sheriff."

The sheriff drank his coffee and eyeballed Smoke. Wrists as big as some men's forearms. And his upper arms; Lord have mercy! The man had muscle on top of muscle. The sheriff had heard of Smoke Jensen for years, but this was the first time he'd ever seen him. And as far as the sheriff was concerned, it was a sight that he'd not soon forget.

The sheriff pushed back his chair and stood up. "See you, Jensen. Ma'am."

"See you around, Sheriff," Smoke told him just as the waitress put their dinner in front of them.

"Smells good," Smoke said.

"Then you'd better enjoy it, mister," a small boy said, walking up to the table. " 'Cause Chub Morgan told me to tell you he was gonna kill you just as soon as you got done eatin'."

3

Smoke looked at the boy. "You go tell Chub I said to calm down. When I finish eating and have my brandy, I'll step outside to smoke my cigar on the boardwalk. I get testy when people interrupt my dinner."

"Yes, sir."

Smoke gave the boy a coin. "Now get off the streets, boy."

"Yes, sir."

But Smoke knew he wouldn't. The boy would gather up all his friends and they'd find them a spot to watch. A shooting wasn't nearly the social event a good hanging was, but it would do. Things just got boring in small western towns. Folks had been known to pack lunches and dinners and drive or ride a hundred miles for a good hanging. And a double hanging was even better.

"Who is Chub Morgan, honey?" Sally asked.

"I have no idea, Sally. But I'll tell you what he's going to be as soon as I finish my food."

She looked at him. "What?"

"Dead."

Smoke had his coffee and a glass of brandy, then bought

a cigar and stepped outside. Sally took a seat in the lobby and read the local paper.

It was near dusk and the wide street was deserted. All horses had been taken from the hitchrails and dogs had been called home. Smoke lit his cigar and leaned against an awning support.

He had played out this scene many times in his life, and Smoke knew he was not immortal. He'd taken a lot of lead in his life. And he would rather talk his way out of a gunfight than drag iron. But he was realist enough to have learned early that with some men, talking was useless. It just prolonged the inevitable. Smoke also knew—and had argued the belief many times with so-called learned people—that some men were just born bad, with a seed of evil in them.

And there was only one way to deal with those types of people.

Kill them.

Smoke puffed on his cigar and waited.

A cowboy rode into town and reined up at the saloon. He dismounted, looked around him, and spotted Smoke Jensen, all dressed in a black suit with the coat brushed back, exposing those deadly .44's.

The cowboy put it all together in a hurry and swung back into the saddle, riding down to the stable. He wanted his horse to be out of the line of fire.

After stabling his horse, the cowboy ran up the alley to the rear of the saloon and slipped inside. Everybody in the place, including the barkeep, was lined up by the windows.

"What's goin' on?" the cowboy called.

"Chub Morgan's made his brags about killin' Smoke Jensen for years. He's about to get his chance. That there's Smoke Jensen over yonder in the black suit."

The cowboy pulled his own beer and walked to the window. "You don't say? Damn, but he's a big one, ain't he? What's he doin' in this hick town?"

"Him and his wife rode in a couple hours ago. She's a

pretty little thing. Right elegant once she got out of them men's britches and put on a proper dress. Packs a .44 like she knows how to use it."

"Jensen doesn't seem too worried about facin' Chub," the cowboy remarked.

"Jensen's faced hundreds of men in his time," an old rummy said. "He's probably thinkin' more about what he's gonna have for breakfast in the mornin' than worried about a two-bit punk like Chub."

"Chub's quick," the cowboy said. "You got to give him that. But he's a fool to face Jensen."

"Yonder's Chub," the barkeep said.

Smoke, still leaning against the post, cut his eyes as a man began the walk down the street. As the man drew nearer, Smoke straightened up. He held his cigar in his left hand, the thumb of his right hand hooked under his belt buckle.

"He's gonna use that left hand .44," the cowboy said. "Folks say he's wicked with either gun."

"Reckon where his wife is?"

"Foster from the store said she was sitting in the lobby, readin' the newspaper," the barkeep said.

"My, my," the cowboy said. "Would you look at Chub. He's done went home and changed into his fancy duds."

Smoke noticed the fancy clothes the punk was wearing. He'd blacked his boots and shined his spurs. Big rowels on them; looked like California spurs. His britches had been recently pressed. Chub's shirt was a bright red; looked like satin. Had him a purple bandana tied around his neck. Even his hat was new, with a silver band.

Smoke waited. He knew where Sally was sitting; he'd told her where to sit, with a solid wood second-floor support to her back to stop any stray bullet. Not that Smoke expected any stray bullets from Chub's gun. He doubted that Chub would even clear leather. But one never really knew for sure.

Smoke watched the man approach him and, for another of

the countless times, wondered why a man would risk his life for the dubious reputation of a gunfighter.

"Jensen!" Chub called.

"Right here," Smoke said calmly.

"Your wife's a real looker," Chub said, a nasty edge to the words. "After I kill you, I'll take her."

Smoke laughed at the man. Chub's face grew red at the laughter. He cursed Smoke.

Smoke was suddenly tired of it. He wanted a good night's sleep, lying next to Sally. He hadn't ridden into town looking for trouble, and he resented trouble being pushed upon him. He was just damned tired of it.

"Make your play, punk!" Smoke called.

Chub's hands hovered over his pearl-handled guns. "Draw, Jensen!" he shouted.

"I don't draw on fools," Smoke told him. "You called me out, Chub, remember? Now, if you don't have the stomach for it, turn around and go on back home. I'd rather you did that."

"Then you a coward!"

Smoke waited, his eyes unblinking.

"You a coward, damn you!" Chub hollered. "Draw, dammit, draw!"

Smoke's cold, unwavering eyes bored into the man's gaze.

"How's it feel to be about to die?" Chub called, trying to steel himself for the draw.

"I wouldn't know, Chub," Smoke's voice was calm. "Why don't you ask yourself that question?"

The sheriff and his two deputies watched from the small office and jail.

"Now!" Chub yelled, and his hands closed around the butts of his guns.

Smoke drew, cocked, and fired with one fluid motion. A draw so fast that it was only a blur. Blink, and you missed it.

The .44 slug took Chub in the center of the chest, knocking him off his boots and down to his knees in the dusty street. His hands were still on the butts of his guns. The guns were still in leather.

"Good God!" the cowboy said. "I never even seen him draw."

The sheriff and his deputies stepped out of the office just as the boardwalks on both sides of the street filled with people.

Smoke stepped off the porch and walked to the dying Chub. He held a cocked .44 in his right hand.

Sally had risen from her seat to stand at the window, watching her man.

Chub raised his head. Blood had gathered on his lips. His eyes were full of anguish. "I . . . never even seen you draw," he managed to gasp.

"That's the way it goes, Chub," Smoke told him just as the lawman reached the bloody scene.

Chub tried to pull a pistol from leather. The sheriff reached down and blocked the move.

"Bastard!" Chub said. It was unclear whom he was cursing, Smoke or the sheriff.

A local minister ran up. "Are you saved, Chub?"

"Hell with you!" Chub said, then toppled over on his side. He closed his eyes and died.

The sheriff looked at Smoke. "Now what?"

Smoke shrugged his shoulders as he punched out the empty and reloaded. "Bury him."

Smoke and Sally rode out before dawn. The hotel's dining room had not even opened. They would stop along the way and make breakfast.

"Why do they do it, Smoke?" Sally broke the silence of the gray-lifting morning.

Smoke knew what she meant. "I've never understood it, Sally. Men like Chub must be very unhappy men. And very shallow men. Let's get off the trail and follow this creek for a ways." He changed the subject. "See where it goes."

The creek wound around and lead them to the Swan River. There they stopped and cooked breakfast. "Fellow back at the hotel said the Swan would lead us right to Hell's Creek. We may as well stay with the river. There are two more little towns between here and Hell's Creek. He said it was right at a hundred miles."

"You've been in this country before?"

"Not right here. It's all new to me. But you can bet the news of the failed train robbery has reached Huggins by now."

"You think any of those men recognized you?"

"I doubt it. But the news of our heading north reached Huggins the day after we boarded the train in Denver. But I doubt he knows we're heading for Hell's Creek."

"I'm sorry I pushed this on you, Smoke."

"You didn't push anything on me, Sally. You want to visit an old friend who's in trouble. That's your right. And anybody who tries to prevent you from doing that is wrong. If they try to stop you, they'll answer to me. It's as simple as that."

She leaned over and kissed him on the cheek. "Everything will always be black and white to you, won't it, honey? No gray in the middle."

"I know what's right, and I know what's wrong. Lawyers want to make it complicated when it isn't. We'll see your friend and her husband and help them work out their problems."

"Legally?"

Smoke munched on a piece of crisp bacon. "Depends on whether you interpret legal by using common sense or what a lawyer would think, I reckon."

* * *

Smoke and Sally followed the river north. Two days later they crossed the river and rode into a small village located on the east side of the Swan. There was no hotel in the village but there was a lady who took in boarders. Smoke and Sally got them a room and cleaned up.

The town marshal was waiting on the front porch of the boarding house when Smoke stepped out for some fresh air while supper was being cooked.

"Mr. Jensen," the marshal said respectfully.

"Afternoon," Smoke replied, then waited.

"I got to ask," the marshal finally said. "You in town trouble-huntin'?"

"No. You can relax. I don't hunt trouble. Me and my wife are just passing through."

The marshal sighed. "That's a relief. I thought maybe you was on the prod for Jake Lewis."

"Who is Jake Lewis?"

The marshal looked startled. "One of the men who survived that shoot-out you had some years ago. Over to that minin' camp on the Uncompahgre."

It was Smoke's turn to look startled. "I didn't know there were any survivors."

"Only one that I know of. Jake Lewis. And you shot him all to hell and gone. There was fifteen men in that camp. You killed fourteen of them. Jake lived. He hid in a privy 'til you rode out."

"It's news to me, Marshal. I know he wasn't one of the men who raped and killed my wife and killed our baby. I know that for a fact."

"No, sir. He sure wasn't. He joined up with Canning and Fetter later. Jake's brother was known as Lefty. You killed him in the shoot-out."

"I have no quarrel with Jake, Marshal. You can tell him that."

"Why don't you tell him, Mr. Jensen? It would sure set his mind to ease."

"Where is he?"

"Down at the saloon."

Smoke stared hard at the marshal, wondering if he were being set up.

The marshal picked his thoughts out of the air. "I run a clean town, Mr. Jensen. I don't take no payoffs from nobody and never will. This ain't no setup. But I got to warn you that Jake is armed, and he ain't drinkin'."

"What you're telling me is that you don't know what he might do, right?"

The marshal exhaled slowly. "That's about it, Mr. Jensen. He may throw down on you. I just don't know."

"But you want it settled one way or the other?"

"Yes. Jake's been livin' with this for a long time. Lately, it's been eatin' at him. When he heard you was on the rails, comin' north, he about went out of his mind with worry."

"Does he know Big Max Huggins?"

"I got to tell you that he does. He spends some time up in Hell's Creek."

"So he hasn't changed his ways much, right?"

"He ain't never caused no trouble around here. You know how it is, Mr. Jensen. I ain't got no warrants on him."

The marshal's authority ended at the edge of town.

Sally had stepped out on the porch to listen. Smoke turned and met her eyes. "Be careful," she said. "I'll save a plate for you."

Smoke nodded and slipped the hammer thongs from his .44's. He stepped off the porch and looked at the marshal. "You walk with me. If this is a setup, I'll take you out first."

"That's fair. If this is a trap, it ain't one of my doin'."

Smoke believed him, and he told him so as they walked up the street to the village's only saloon.

"Does Big Max ever get down this far south?"

"Not no more," the marshal said. "I killed one of his men several years ago and got lead in another one. I ain't the fastest man around with a gun, but I shoot straight."

"That's the most important thing. His men stay out of your town?"

"That's it. I allow any man one mistake. He leaves after the second one. Or he stays forever."

Smoke smiled, finding that he liked this blunt-talking marshal.

They stepped up onto the short boardwalk, walking past a dress shop, a gunsmith, and a large general store. The marshal pushed open the batwings and Smoke stepped into the saloon right behind him.

Jake Lewis stood alone at the bar. The other customers had taken tables. Smoke stared at the man, trying to place him. But the shoot-out at the old silver camp was years behind him, and he could not remember Jake Lewis.

Jake had brushed back his coat, exposing a pistol, the holster tied down. Smoke was curious about that. If the man wanted no trouble, why get set for it? Smoke concluded that Jake was wearing a hide-out gun. Maybe a sleeve gun. Shake his arm and the gun falls into his hand.

Smoke walked to the bar and ordered a beer. Jake turned mean little eyes on him. Jake was no lightweight. He'd hit a good two hundred pounds and looked to be in good shape. About forty years old, Smoke figured.

"You lookin' for me, Jensen?" Jake broke the silence.

"Nope."

"Just happened to ride into town and take a room, hey?"

"That's right."

"I wish I could believe that."

"Believe it. I got no quarrel with you, Jake."

"I wish I could believe that, too."

"You can. The silver camp was long ago. You weren't part of the bunch who killed Nicole and the baby. They're all dead. I know that for a fact."

"I damn near died, Jensen."

"That was your problem. You should have picked better company to run with."

"You sayin' my brother was no good?"

"You walk through a barnyard, you're going to get crap on your boots."

Someone in the seated crowd laughed at that.

Jake's face flushed. "Lefty was a good man."

"He wasn't good enough," Smoke told him.

Jake ordered a drink and sipped at the bourbon. He set the shot glass down and said, "I'm glad you showed up. We can settle this thing once and for all."

"There is nothing to settle, Jake. Nothing at all."

"I think there is. I sure do think that."

"I'm sorry to hear it."

Jake took another small sip of whiskey. "Momma took Lefty's dyin' pretty hard."

"I'm sorry for your mother. Not for Lefty. You keep walking around something, Jake. Get to it. I've got supper waiting at the boarding house."

"Don't crowd me, Jensen."

Smoke chuckled and Jake gave him a queer look. "I came in here to tell you that I wasn't trouble-hunting, and instead of being happy about it, you want to give me a bunch of lip. That shooting in the silver camp was ten years ago, Jake. I wouldn't have known you if you walked in my front door wearing pink tights and totin' a rose between your teeth."

All the men in the room had them a laugh at that. Jake's face tightened and flushed deeper.

"Big Max is waitin' for you up at Hell's Creek, Jensen," he said, grinding his teeth together in anger.

"Yeah? It figures that trash like you would end up rubbing elbows with trash like Huggins."

The crowd fell silent.

Jake slowly turned to face Smoke. "You know what I think, Jensen?"

"I'm not even sure you're capable of thinking, Jake. I think you're about as smart as a rock."

Jake curled one big hand around his glass and downed his

whiskey. "You're a big man with them guns on, Jensen. What are you with them off? Can you bare-knuckle fight, gunfighter? Or do you have to let them .44's do your talkin' for you?"

"There's sure one way to find out, Jake. Providing you have the stomach for it." Smoke walked toward the man, stopping well within swinging distance.

"We take off our guns together?" Jake asked.

"Just as soon as you get rid of that hide-out pistol you're packing."

Jake grunted and nodded his head. "It's in my sleeve."

"I know it."

Jake shook his arm and the derringer fell out onto the bar. Together, they took off their gunbelts. They faced each other.

"I'm gonna stomp your face in, pretty-boy," Jake bragged.

"I doubt it," Smoke told him, pulling on a pair of leather gloves to protect his hands and to hit harder. He knocked the man down with a quick, hard right.

Smoke stepped back, took a sip of his beer, and said, "You going to lay on the floor all evening, Jake? Come on, hurry up. I have supper waiting for me."

With a roar of rage, Jake jumped to his boots and charged.

4

Jake swung a big fist and Smoke ducked it, at the same time driving his right fist into Jake's gut and stopping him with the blow. Jake backed up and caught his wind.

With a curse, Jake came at Smoke, swinging both fists. Jake was a brawler, Smoke knew then, relying mostly on brute strength with little finesse about him. But he could be dangerous, Smoke reminded himself, if he landed one of those powerful fists.

Smoke danced back, forcing the big man to come after him, using up his wind swinging wildly and cussing.

Smoke saw a chance and took it, popping Jake smack in the mouth with a combination left and right. The blows brought blood and one tooth was knocked out, to roll and bounce on the sawdust floor.

With a howl of rage, Jake charged, both fists flailing, the blows catching Smoke on his arms and shoulders and doing no damage. Smoke back-heeled Jake and sent the man tumbling to the floor. He could have ended the fight right then, by kicking Jake in the mouth. But Smoke stepped back. He felt no anger toward Jake; but, then, he didn't especially feel sorry for him, either. He proved that by knocking Jake down just as soon as the man got to his boots.

It was another combination, both blows connecting to the jaw of Jake Lewis this time and knocking him back against the bar. Jake grabbed a bottle of whiskey and hurled it at Smoke. Smoke grabbed the bottle, popped the cork and, with a grin at Jake, took him a sip.

"You son of a . . ." Jake choked back the obscenity. He leaned against the bar, catching his breath.

"You want to quit, Jake?" Smoke asked. "You say so, and we'll have a drink together and call the fight over, with no hard feelings."

"Take him up on it, Jake!" the marshal said. "The man's bein' more than fair."

"You stay out of this," Jake yelled at the marshal. He looked at Smoke. "To hell with you, Jensen!"

Smoke shrugged his shoulders. "Whatever you say, Jake." Then he threw the bottle of whiskey at Jake, the bottle striking the man in the face and busting, spewing whiskey all over Jake and momentarily blinding him.

Smoke stepped up to him and began hitting Jake in the face, his big work-hardened fists like huge hammers as they pounded the man again and again. Jake's nose was broken, one eye closing, his lips smashed to pulp, and his jaw swelling. Smoke pounded the man with more than a dozen blows, then stepped back.

Jake wiped the blood and whiskey out of his eyes and reached down, pulling up his pants leg and jerking a knife out of his boot. "Now, Jensen, you get your guts spread all over the room."

The marshal jerked iron and jacked back the hammer. "Drop the knife, Jake," he warned. "This is a fair fight and it's one that you wanted. You either drop the knife, or I'll kill you."

With a disgusted snarl, Jake tossed the knife to one side.

"Now you made me mad, Jake," Smoke told him. "Now

you get what you've probably had coming to you for a long time." Smoke walked toward the man, his big hands clenched.

Jake lifted his fists and decided to use what boxing skills he had. He swung a roundhouse blow at Smoke, which would have knocked Jensen to the floor had it connected. Smoke grabbed the wrist with both hands, turned to one side, and Jake found himself flying through the air. He crashed through a front window and bounced off the boardwalk.

Smoke stepped out the batwings and was all over Jake.

Smoke hit the man twice in the belly, doubling him over. He grabbed Jake behind the head and brought his face down and his knee up. The knee connected squarely, and what was left of Jake's nose was now spread all over his face.

Smoke backhanded Jake, knocking him off the boardwalk and into the horse-crap by the hitchrail. One startled horse kicked Jake in the butt and sent him rolling and squalling into the middle of the street.

Smoke didn't let up. He had given the man a chance to not fight at all. Jake turned it down. Then Jake had shown his true colors by pulling a knife. To hell with him!

Jake staggered to his feet and feebly raised his fists. Smoke looked at the beaten man with blood dripping from his face and lowered his fists. He turned his back to Jake Lewis and walked back into the saloon. Jake sank to his knees in the street and tried to get up. He could not.

"Couple of you boys go out there and toss him into a horse trough," the marshal ordered. "Then I'll tell him to get the hell gone from town and don't come back." He looked at Smoke. "You'll have to kill that man someday, Jensen. You know that, don't you?"

"I hope not," Smoke said, then ordered a mug of cool beer.

"You will," the marshal stated flatly. "You humiliated him, and men like Jake can't live with that. It eats on them like a cancer."

Smoke drank half his beer. "He'll have to come looking for me if he wants a killing. As far as I'm concerned, it's over."

Smoke drained his mug and walked back to the boarding house. He needed a hot bath.

The man and wife rode out of town before dawn the next morning and made camp at noon. Sally heated water for Smoke to soak his hands in to keep down the swelling.

They stayed in camp for two days, relaxing, fishing, and behaving like a couple of kids. They walked through the woods, went skinny-dipping in a creek, and loved every minute of it. The swelling went down in Smoke's hands, and they packed up and pulled out, heading north toward Hell's Creek, following the Swan.

Two days later they rode into a small town at the south end of a lake. They were a couple of hours ride away from Hell's Creek. Their welcome in the town was slightly less than cordial. When they tried to check into the small hotel, they were told all the rooms were taken.

"Is there a boarding house?" Sally asked.

"It's full, too," the desk clerk at thc hotel told them.

"Must be a convention in town," Smoke said dryly looking around him at the deserted hotel lobby. "Sure are a lot of people stirring about."

Sally tugged at his sleeve. "Let's go, honey. We can camp outside of town."

"You don't know how the game is played, Sally," Smoke told her. "The word's gone out on us from Big Max. These people hcrc are scared to death of him. I've seen a few western towns buffaloed before, but this one takes the prize for being full of cowards."

The desk clerk refused to meet Smoke's eyes.

Smoke spun the register book around and inspected it. The hotel was nearly empty.

Smoke dipped the pen and signed them in. He tossed money on the counter. "That's for your best room. Give me the damn key," he told the clerk.

The clerk hesitated, then with a slow exhalation of breath he handed Smoke the room key.

"Thanks," Smoke told him. "Would you recommend the food in the dining room?"

"Yes, sir," the clerk said wearily. "I would. Dinner is served from five to eight."

"Thank you. You're a nice fellow."

Five minutes after checking in and finding their room, a knock came at the door. Two mean-eyed and unshaven men, both wearing deputy sheriff's badges, stood in the hall.

"You don't come into this town throwin' your weight around, Jensen," one told him. "You're goin' to jail."

"On what charge?"

"We'll think of something," the second deputy said. "And we'll see that your woman is taken care of, too."

Smoke hit him with a sneaky left. The blow snapped the man's head back and knocked him against the hall wall. Smoke backhanded the other deputy, spun, and knocked the second man down with a hard right to the mouth. He grabbed the stunned deputy he'd just slapped by the nape of the neck and the seat of his pants, propelled him down the hall, and threw him out the second-story window. The man landed on the awning, bounced once, and then rolled off, to land on the dusty street. He did not move. One leg was bent under him, broken.

Smoke ran back up the hall, jerked up the stunned and clearly frightened other so-called deputy shcriff, and gave him his exit-papers the same way. Smoke hurled him out the window, using all his strength, which was considerable. The man fell screaming, missing the awning and landing in the street on his belly, one arm bent under him. The sound of the arm breaking was nearly as loud as a pistol shot. Like his buddy, he did not move.

A crowd began gathering, looking at the two so-called lawmen and stealing glances up at Smoke, who was standing in the hall and glaring out the broken window.

"We do not wish to be disturbed," Smoke called down to

the crowd. "I'll kill the next man who bothers us." He turned and walked back to the room. He smiled at Sally. "That's how you play the game, honey," he told her.

"My, my," she said with a grin. "The things I'm learning on this trip."

"Your education is just starting. It'll really get interesting in Hell's Creek. I'll order up some hot water and you can take your bath. You tell me which one, and I'll shake out and hang up your dress."

Smoke loaded up the usually empty cylinder he kept under the hammer and walked downstairs to the clerk. The lobby was filled with people.

"Send a boy upstairs with hot water," he told the room clerk. "Lots of it. My wife wishes to bathe. And she damn well better be left alone while she's doing it."

"Y . . . y . . . yes, sir," the clerk stammered.

"Who was that trash I threw out the window?"

"Big Max Huggins men," a portly man said, stepping up. "Duly appointed deputies. By me. I'm Judge Garrison. And you're in a lot of trouble here, young man. We don't like ruffians coming into our town stirring up trouble."

Smoke slapped him. The blow knocked the man back, one side of his face reddening and blood leaking out of one corner of his mouth. The judge stumbled on a couch and fell down, landing heavily on his butt.

"So Max bought you, too, huh?" Smoke said, looking down at the scared judge, the sarcasm thick in the words. "Looks like he's got the whole damn town in his pocket."

"Not all of us," another man spoke up.

"You sure could have fooled me."

"You've brought us a lot of trouble, Mr. Jensen," another man said. "Come the morning, Big Max will be riding in here to settle up. Not just with you, but with all of us."

"Poor scared little sheep," Smoke said, looking at the knot of men. "Do you have to ask Big Max's permission to go to the bathroom?"

"Smoke," the citizen who first spoke said, "Max has got a hundred men up yonder in Hell's Creek. They's maybe thirty-five of us in town who'd stand up to them. Them ain't very good odds."

"Thirty-six," Smoke told him. "Thirty-seven counting my wife. And she's got more guts than any of you have shown me. How'd all this buffaloing come about?"

"Huggins killed our marshal and put in his own law," the citizen said. "Then he burned out or beat up anyone who tried to stand up to him. We used to have a paper here in town. The editor was killed. The minister over to the church was taken out one night and horsewhipped and tarred and feathered. Two of our women was molested by Max's men. A few of us stayed; most left."

"We're not cowards, Mr. Jensen," yet another citizen said. "We've all fought Indians and outlaws and scum. But Max has threatened our children. He ain't never come right out and done it plain. But we all got the message."

"How do you mean?"

"My little girl come home with a sack of candy. Told her ma and me that a man give it to her. Said that next, if I didn't stop bad-mouthin' Max, they might take a little walk in the woods. We got the message."

Smoke said, "You all wait right here. I got an idea." He went back upstairs and peeked in the bathroom. Sally was up to her neck in suds. "Now there is a nice sight."

She made a face at him.

"You reckon Robert and Victoria have made it known that we're coming to see them?"

"Absolutely not. I told them not to say a word about it, and they won't."

"How about the letters you've sent them? The people at the post office will be on Max's payroll."

"They were sent to Kalispell. Robert goes there once a week to see patients."

Smoke winked at her. "Good girl."

"What's up, Smoke? I know that look in your eyes."

"We're going to stay here for a time. I got an idea."

"Suits me."

Smoke shut the door and let her finish her bath. He walked downstairs. He pointed to the judge, who was sitting on a couch, holding a wet cloth to his face. "Get up," he told him. The judge got up.

"One of you men go to the marshal's office and get me a marshal's badge."

Grinning, a man ran out the door and jogged across the street. The two deputies were still lying in the street, moaning and calling out for help.

Smoke faced the judge. "Are you a real judge? Commissioned by this territory?"

"I certainly am! And I'm going to swear out a warrant for your arrest . . . you hooligan!"

Smoke popped him again, staggering the man, rocking him back on his feet. This time the judge was really scared and his expression showed it.

"Oh, you're going to be issuing arrest warrants, Garrison," Smoke told him. "But probably for the first time in a long time, they're going to be legal warrants." He turned to a man. "Go outside and get me one of those deputy sheriff's badges from that crud in the street."

"Yes, sir!" the citizen said, not able to hide his grin.

The judge began to put it all together then, and his face became shiny with fear-sweat. "You won't get away with this, Jensen," he said.

Smoke smiled at him. "You wanna bet?"

"He did what?" Big Max Huggins yelled, rising from his chair behind the desk.

"He's the marshal down at Barlow," the gunhand repeated. "And it was all done legal. Judge Garrison signed the order creating a special election and the citizens voted him in. And that ain't all. The judge also swore him in as a deputy sheriff. That was done after Jensen whupped the hell out of Bridy and Long. Tossed 'em both out of a second-story winder at the hotel. Bridy's got a busted leg and Long's right arm is broken. That's in addition to a bunch of bruises and cuts. They stove up for a long time."

Big Max Huggins nodded his big head, sat back down, and pondered these new events. Big Max did not get his name from the size of his feet, although they were large. He was large. Six-six and two hundred eighty pounds. A handsome man, Max was also vain about his looks. He dressed carefully and neatly and never missed a day shaving. He was intelligent with a criminal's cunning. He was also a very cruel man.

And right now, he was a puzzled man. "What does Jensen want?" he mused aloud.

The gunhand who had brought him the news stood in silence and shook his head.

"Jensen's got him a big fine ranch down in Colorado. He married into old New England money; his wife's as rich as a king. Or queen," he added. "Supposed to be a real looker, too. The way I hear it, the only time Jensen leaves the ranch is when he takes a notion to stick his nose into someone else's business. He ruined Dooley Hanks a couple of years back. Just like he did Jud Vale last year. Right here in this territory. Now he's ten miles away and packin' a badge. That means he's come after me. But why?"

The gunhand knew that no reply was expected. He stood quiet.

Max leaned back in his chair. "Somebody sent for him," he finally said. "But who? Had to be somebody down in Barlow."

Max stood up and reached for his guns. "Get the boys. We're riding."

The gunhand grinned. "Down to Barlow, boss?"

"Where else? I'm going to settle Smoke Jensen's hash once and for all."

5

Big Max rode into Barlow at the head of a small army. He had fifty men behind him, all heavily armed. They kicked up enough dust riding into town to put a thin cover of dirt on every storefront.

Max dismounted and walked to the boardwalk in front of the marshal's office. He turned to face his men, and the instant his back was to the office, he felt the twin barrels of a sawed-off shotgun pressing into his back.

"Move, and I'll scatter your guts all over the street, Huggins," the voice told him.

Max froze. He knew what an express gun could do. A sawed-off shotgun could literally blow a man in two. "I'm froze," he told the voice. "You Smoke Jensen?"

"That's me. Now tell your men to drop their guns in the street. Every gun they've got. In the dirt."

"And if I don't?"

The muzzle of the shotgun nudged his back. That was all it took.

Max gave the order.

Men began appearing out of stores, all of them armed

with rifles or shotguns, all of them with pistols belted around their waists.

Women came out after them, holding buckets of water and rags.

"What the hell? . . ." Max said.

"Your men created all this dust in town," Smoke told him. "So your men are going to clean it up. They're going to wash all the windows, sweep the boardwalks, and wipe down everything."

"I'll be goddamned if I will!" a gunny said, sitting his saddle.

Smoke stepped to one side and let one barrel of the express gun roar. It belched smoke and flame, and the mouthy gunhand was blown out of the saddle. He landed about ten feet behind his rearing and frightened horse, hitting the dirt in a bloody pile of torn flesh.

Holding the shotgun in his right hand, Smoke palmed one of his .44's and stuck the muzzle to Max's ear. "Give the order," Smoke told him, his voice very cold and deadly.

Max swallowed with an audible gulp. He was a hard man in a hard land and he'd known some salty ol' boys in his time. But none as hard as this man holding a .44 to his head. Smoke Jensen was death walking around.

"You boys get to cleaning," he told his men. "I'm paying you and you take orders from me. Do it."

"And drag that trash out of the street and bury it," Smoke said. He looked at a citizen who'd introduced himself as Tom Johnson. "You get some boys and gather up their guns, Tom. All of them. And take their rifles from the saddle boots. Bring them to me at the jail." He lowered and holstered his .44 and jerked Max's guns from leather. "In my office, Max. Move."

Seated, Max studied Jensen. And he was impressed. Smoke was about four inches shorter than him and probably weighed sixty pounds less, but he was a hell of a man, Max concluded. No doubt about that.

"You won the first little skirmish, Smoke," Max told him. "But you can't win the war."

Smoke poured them both coffee and sat down behind the desk. "What war, Max?" he asked innocently. "I did what I did in this town because I don't like to see citizens bullied, and I especially don't like to hear about children being threatened."

Max grunted. "There . . . may have been some incidents where my men got a little heavy-handed. But as far as I know, no kids have been harmed."

"But if you continue, Max, they will be. The odds are tilted that way."

"And you intend to do what about that?" Max challenged the gunfighter.

"For the good of humanity, I ought to just stop it right now."

"How?" Max smiled the question.

"By killing you," Smoke said bluntly.

Max studied Smoke Jensen carefully. He concluded that Smoke meant what he'd just said. He also concluded that if he was to leave this town alive, he'd better play his cards close to the vest. Very close.

Max was a cold-blooded killer. But he was an intelligent one. He knew he was sitting very close to the grave. He also knew that like himself, Smoke Jensen had been born without that one tiny cog in his psyche that prevented man from killing without remorse. But unlike Max, Smoke Jensen had landed on the side of the law. He would always defend the underdog, the poor, the right and just causes.

"Are you?" Max asked softly.

"Am I what?"

"Going to kill me?"

"Probably."

Max felt the cold touch of fear grip his heart.

"Someday," Smoke added.

Max struggled with all his might to contain the emotion of relief that flooded him. He was not accustomed to the sensation of fear. It angered him that just by looking at Smoke Jensen such an emotion could be unleashed within him.

Big Max Huggins knew this, too: Smoke Jensen had to die. And soon.

"But for right now?" Max asked.

"I don't know," Smoke admitted. "But I wouldn't press it if I were you."

"I can't buy you off, can I?"

"No."

"Women?"

"I'm married to a beautiful woman. I have never been unfaithful to her and never will be."

"You're everything I am not, is that it?"

Smoke smiled. "Oh, we're somewhat alike, Max. We just took different paths, that's all."

And damned intelligent, too, Max thought. I'm not confronting some ignoramus. "What is it, specifically, that I do that offends you so?"

Smoke laughed softly. He turned his swivel chair and pecked on the window, pointing. "You missed a spot," he told the red-faced gunhand on the boardwalk with a wet rag in his hand. He turned his attention back to Max. "Everything about you, your type, offends me, Max. You're an intelligent man; could have been a success at anything you tried to do. But you chose to be an outlaw. You've probably been a bully and a thief all your life. You like to humiliate people. You like to grind them down under your boot heel. I'm going to play a game with you, Max. You like games?"

"I'm a gambler, you know that."

"But in my game, Max, if you cheat, you die."

Sweat broke out on Max's face. Goddamn this man! He's sitting there as cool as an icehouse and talking about my death. He glanced out the window. The body of Butch had been removed and another gunhand was sprinkling dirt over the blood-soaked spot on the street. He cut his eyes back to Smoke.

"You see, Max, I don't have to work. My ranch practically runs itself. My wife is very rich. And I have a lot of money personally. Do you have any idea how many thousands and thousands of dollars in reward money I've collected over the years just by shooting wanted men?"

Max personally knew of several dozen wanted men who had gone facedown in the dirt under Smoke's guns. And there were probably a hundred more that he didn't know about. "I know you're a wealthy man, Jensen," he said grudgingly. "What kind of game do you have in mind?"

"You're going to be a solid citizen, Max. You're going to run all the trash out of your town, build a new school, a new church, a new town hall, and be a credit to this territory."

"Are you out of your damned mind!" Max almost yelled the question. "If I ran all the scum out of Hell's Creek, there wouldn't be fifty people left."

"That is a fact," Smoke acknowledged.

"You're not going to shoot me now, are you, Jensen?"

"Not unless you push me to it."

"Don't worry, I'm not." The words were bitter on the big man's tongue. He had never kowtowed to anyone in his life. Until this moment. And he didn't like it one bit.

"You want to play the game or not, Max?"

"No." Max's courage was returning after standing on the edge of death. He stood up slowly. "If you shoot me, Jensen, you're going to have to shoot me in the back. And I don't think you'll do that. I'm going to walk outside, gunfighter. I'm going to sit on the bench just outside this office and smoke me a cigar. I'm not going to bother a soul. When my men have finished mopping and scrubbing this crappy little town, we're going to ride out. We won't bother this town again. I'll give my people orders to stay clear. But if you ever come to Hell's Creek, I can't guarantee your safety. Badge or not. That's my deal." He walked out the door and sat down, pulling a cigar out of a breast pocket of his suitcoat and lighting up.

Smoke stood up and stepped outside just as Tom Johnson and several others came walking up, carrying sacks of guns taken from the outlaws.

"Put the weapons in a cell and lock it," Smoke told them.

When that had been done, Smoke locked the front door to his office and walked up the boardwalk, leaving Big Max Huggins sitting quietly and smoking his stogie.

Smoke stopped to inspect the work of Larry Gayle, the New Mexico gunslinger. Gayle turned mean eyes to him.

"I guess I'll have to kill you before long, Larry," Smoke told him.

"You'll try," Larry growled the words at him.

Smoke chuckled and walked on a few yards, stopping at the side of a gunny he didn't know.

"You ain't gonna kill me, Smoke," the man said. " 'Cause just as soon as I get done with this spit-polishin', I'm gone like the wind."

Smoke patted him on the shoulder. "Good man. Find a job and settle down somewhere. Be a good citizen."

"I ain't promisin' that. But I will get gone from wherever you is."

Smoke walked on. He stopped when he spotted Pete Akins, a gunhand he had met down in Arizona about six months back. "You going to stay on Huggins's payroll, Pete?"

"Yep." Pete put the finishing touches on a windowpane. It was so clean it squeaked under the rag.

"There's going to be a lot of blood spilled before this is over, Pete."

"For shore."

"Sorry to hear you're staying. You've never done me a harm. But if you stay, you're my enemy. I just wanted you to know that, Pete."

"You could pull out, Jensen."

"Not likely. I never leave a job unfinished."

"Me neither. Now get on out of here and leave me alone. I got winders to wash."

Chuckling, Smoke walked on. He didn't really dislike Pete Akins. But that wouldn't prevent him from gunning Pete if push came to shove.

He crossed the wide street and stopped by the side of a young man probably still in his late teens. The boy still had a few pimples on his face.

"You better haul your ashes out of here, boy," Smoke told him. "Straighten up while you've got the time."

"I'll see you in hell, Jensen," the punk told him.

"You'll be there long before I pass by, son," Smoke replied, and walked on.

He stopped by Ben Webster, who had finished his windows and was sitting on the boardwalk, smoking a cigarette. "You hire your guns, Ben, but I never knew of you working for someone as low as Big Max Huggins."

"He pays good, Smoke. 'Sides, the man who finally drops you can write his own ticket."

"You intend to be that man?"

"Yep."

"Make your will out, Ben. 'Cause when you pull iron on me, I'm gonna kill you."

Ben looked up at him. "That's a risk we take in this business, ain't it, Smoke?"

Smoke stared at the man hard. Ben finally dropped his eyes. "I don't hire my gun, Ben. Not for money."

Ben looked up. "Why then, Smoke? Why do you do it?"

"Because I have a conscience, Ben. And I've got to live with myself."

Ben spat in the street. "I don't have a bit of trouble sleepin' at night. Or in the daytime, for that matter."

"That'll make it easier when you decide to brace me, Ben."

Ben tossed his cigarette into the street and looked away.

Smoke walked on. "Sid," he spoke to Sid Yorke.

"Smoke. I ain't gonna forget this damn winder-washin'."

"Least it got your hands clean, Sid. That's probably the first time they've been clean since your mother stopped takin' a belt to your butt."

"There's always a day of reckonin', Jensen. My day's comin'."

Smoke crossed the street and sat on the bench beside Max. Now that he knew he'd live through this day, Max was beginning to see the humor in some of the toughest men in the territory washing windows and mopping up the boardwalk.

He saw Smoke watching him. "Yes, Jensen, I can see the humor in it. But have you thought about this: You've made some rough boys awfully angry at you. And they're going to be sore about this for a long time."

"They'll either get over it or come hunting me. If they come hunting me, they'll be over it permanently."

Max stared at him. "You're that sure of yourself, aren't you, Jensen?"

"I've put more than a hundred men in their graves, Max. I'm still standing."

"How many men have you killed, Jensen?"

"I honestly don't know. I would be very happy if I never had to kill another human being."

"Then quit."

"I can't."

"Why?"

"Because of people like you."

That stung the big man. His face darkened with color. He took several deep breaths, calming himself. "I never thought of myself as a bad person, Jensen. And that's the God's truth."

"You have any plans to change, Max?"

"No. And that's the truth, too. Why should I? You won't stay around here long. So I pull in my horns for a summer. So what? What have I lost? No, Jensen. Unless you kill me now, right now, in cold blood, I'll survive. Because you're going to have to come to my town to get me. And you won't last two minutes in Hell's Creek."

"You got it all figured out, huh, Max?"

"I believe so, yes."

"It promises to be an interesting summer, Max."

Max threw his smoked-down cigar into the street and

rose from the bench. "I hope I don't see you again, Jensen," he said, with his back to Smoke.

"Oh, you will, Max. You will."

Smoke sat on the bench and watched as the sullen bunch of gunfighters rode slowly out of town, being very careful to kick up as little dust as possible. Only Pete Akins raised a hand in farewell.

With a grin on his face, he called, "See you around, Smoke."

"Take it easy, Pete."

The pimply-faced boy whose name Smoke had learned was Brewer, glared hate at him as he rode past.

"You bear in mind what I said, son," Smoke called to him.

The young man gave Smoke an obscene gesture.

Bringing up the rear of the procession was a wagon, the two bone-broken deputies lying on hay in the bed, groaning as the wagon lurched along.

Tom Johnson crossed the street, leading a group of men and women, Judge Garrison among them.

"Tom, did you send those wires like I asked?" Smoke said.

"Yes, sir. Folks should start arriving in about a week. What about those people in town loyal to Huggins?"

"Tell them to hit the trail, Tom. You're the newly elected mayor."

"How about me?" Judge Garrison asked.

"You're staying, Judge. You and me, we're going to see to it that justice prevails in this part of the county. Tom has arranged for a man to come in and reopen the newspaper. He's got people coming in that include a schoolteacher, a preacher, and some shopkeepers. Barlow is going to boom again, Judge. Nice and legal."

"Young man," the judge said, sitting down on the edge of the boardwalk, "have you given any thought as to what will happen when you decide to leave?"

"Oh, yes."

They waited, but Smoke did not elaborate.

The judge sighed. "I must admit, it's a good feeling to be

free of Max Huggins." He cut his eyes to Smoke. "For as long as it lasts, that is."

"Trust me, Judge," Smoke told him, putting a finger to the side of his head. "I've got it all worked out up here." He pulled out his watch and clicked it open. "What times does the stage run?"

"It'll be here in about an hour," Tom told him.

"It turns around at Hell's Creek?"

"That's right."

Smoke smiled. "Well, then, I'll just make plans to meet the stage. Right now, I have to see about finding a deputy."

"That's not going to be easy, Smoke," the judge said. "I don't know of a single person who is qualified. Most of the ranches in this part of the county have only the hands they absolutely need to get by. There's about a dozen farmers in this area. Good people, but not gunslingers."

"Who is that prisoner in the jail? What's he being held for?"

The judge rolled his eyes. "His name is Dagonne. Jim Dagonne. He's not a bad sort; matter of fact, he's rather a likable fellow. He just likes to fight. The problem is, he never can win one. He's a good cowboy. Works hard. But when he starts drinking, he picks fights. And he always loses."

Smoke nodded his head, a smile on his face. "All right folks, let's get to work. We've got a lot to do."

6

Smoke unlocked the cell door and dragged the sleeping Jim Dagonne out of the bunk. He looked to be in his mid-twenties and in good shape, although not a big man.

"What the hell!" Dagonne hollered as Smoke dragged him across the floor and out the back door.

"Shut up, Jim," Smoke told him. He shoved him in a tub of cold water and tossed him a bar of soap. "Strip and scrub pink. I'll have your clothes washed and dried. Then we'll talk."

"Who the hell are you?" Jim hollered. "You let me out of this tub and I'll whup you all over this backyard."

"Smoke Jensen."

Jim sank into the tub and covered his head with water.

Twenty minutes later, sober and clean, wrapped in a blanket, Jim Dagonne sat in front of Smoke's desk and waited. He did not have a clue as to what Smoke wanted of him.

Smoke stared at the young man. Maybe five feet seven. Not much meat on him, but wiry; rawhide tough. Hard to tell what he looked like, with his face all banged up and both eyes swollen nearly closed, but he appeared to be a rather nice-looking young man.

"You don't have a job, Jim," Smoke finally broke the silence. "The judge said you got fired from the Circle W."

"I probably did. Joe got tired of bailing me out of jail, I reckon."

"Joe who?"

"Joe Walsh. Owns the spread."

"Good man?"

"One of the best. Arrow straight. Are you really Smoke Jensen?"

"Yes." Smoke tapped the gunbelt on his desk. "This yours?"

"Yes, sir."

"Can you use it?"

"I'm not real fast, but I don't hardly ever miss."

"That's the most important thing. You wanted anywhere, Jim?"

"No, sir! I ain't never stole nothing in my life."

Smoke reached down on the floor and picked up a bulky package. He tossed it to Jim. "New jeans, shirts, socks, and drawers in there. Go get dressed. You're my new deputy."

Jim stared at him. "I'm a what?"

"My deputy. Your drinking days are over, Jim. You're now a full-fledged member of the temperance league. You take one drink, just one, and I'll stomp your guts into a greasy puddle in the middle of that street out there, and then I'll feed what's left to the hogs. You understand me?"

"Yes, sir!"

"Fine. Get dressed and go down to Judge Garrison's office. He'll swear you in as a deputy sheriff. Then you meet me back here." He looked at the clock. "Right now, I've got to meet a stage."

* * *

"Out," Smoke told the passengers before the stage had stopped rocking. Two hurdy-gurdy girls, a tin-horn gambler, one drummer selling corsets and assorted ladies' wear, and Al Martin, a gunfighter from down Utah way, stepped down.

"You stopping here or going on to Hell's Creek?" Smoke asked the drummer.

"Hell's Creek."

"Get back in the stage. The rest of you come with me."

"And if I don't?" the gambler challenged him.

Smoke laid the barrel of a .44 against the man's head, knocking him to the street. He handcuffed him to a hitchrail, then faced Al Martin.

"You got trouble in you, Al?"

"Probably. I know you, but I can't put a name to the face."

"Smoke Jensen."

Al eyeballed Smoke, his eyes flicking from the badge to his face. The hurdy-gurdy girls stood off to one side.

"Get moving," Smoke told the driver.

"Yes, sir. I'm gone!"

He hollered at the fresh team and rattled up the street.

"I'll just have me a drink and wait for the southbound stage," Al said.

"That's fine. Stay out of trouble." He looked at the saloon girls. "You ladies get you a room at the hotel and stay quiet. You're on the next stage south. It rolls through in the morning."

They wanted to protest. But the name Smoke Jensen shut their mouths. They twirled their parasols, picked up their baggage, shook their bustles, and sashayed down the boardwalk.

"Off the street, Al," Smoke told the gunfighter.

Al tipped his hat, got his grip, and walked into the saloon.

Smoke dragged the gambler to the jail and tossed him in a cell.

"What's the charge, marshal?" the gambler called.

"Disobeying an officer of the law and littering."

"Littering?"

"You were lying in the street, weren't you?"

"Hell, man. You put me there."

"Tell it to the judge. He'll have court sometime this month."

Smoke stepped outside and rolled one of the few cigarettes he smoked a day. He lit up and smiled. It was going to be an interesting summer. He was looking forward to it.

Jim walked up, all decked out in his new clothes and with a shiny badge pinned to his shirt.

"What'd I miss?"

"Not much." Smoke brought him up to date.

"Littering?" Jim laughed. "Now that's a new one on me."

"We'll see what the judge has to say about it."

"Al Martin's a bad one. He's one of Big Max Huggins's boys. He'll try you, Smoke. Bet on that."

"He won't do it but once. Come on. I'll introduce you to my wife and we'll get something to eat."

They were halfway across the street when a dozen men came riding into town from the south, kicking up a lot of dust.

"That's Red Malone and his crew," Jim said. "He likes to ride roughshod over everybody. Owns the Lightning brand. I never worked for him 'cause I don't like him and he don't like me."

Smoke stood in the middle of the street and refused to move, forcing the horsemen to come to a stop.

"Get out of the damn street, idiot!" the lead rider yelled.

"You Malone?" Smoke asked.

"Yeah. If it's any of your business."

"There's a new law on the books, Malone. No galloping horses within the city limits."

Red laughed, and it was an ugly laugh. "I'd like to see the two-bit deputy who's gonna stop me." Then his smile faded. "Hey, you're new here. Didn't your boss tell you that me and the boys are to be left alone?" His face mirrored further confusion when he saw Jim and the badge pinned to his shirt. "What the hell's goin' on around here? You got stomped in a fight a couple of nights ago and got tossed in jail. Where is Bridy and Long?"

"Max come and got them this morning," Jim said with a grin. "They was all stove up after Smoke Jensen here tossed both of 'em out of that window up yonder yesterday." He pointed to the boarded-up window of the hotel.

Red Malone and all his men looked . . . first at the window and then back at Smoke.

"You asked what two-bit deputy was going to stop you Red?" Smoke said. "You're looking at him."

"Lemme take him, boss," a scar-faced man said. "I think I'm better than him."

Red Malone did not reply; he was studying Smoke carefully. "Heard about you for years, Jensen. You're supposed to be the fastest gun around. So what are you doing in this hick town?"

"Helping out the people, Malone. They had some bad law enforcement here. They asked me to take over."

"What'd Max have to say about that?"

"Not a whole lot, actually. And his men were too busy washing windows and mopping up the boardwalk to say very much."

Malone silently chewed on that for a moment, not really sure what Smoke was talking about. For a fact, something big had gone down here in Barlow; something that had drastically changed the town.

And that something big and drastic had a name: Smoke Jensen.

"Come on, Red!" the scar-faced man insisted. "Lemme take him." He stepped out of the saddle, handing the reins to another man.

Malone looked at the man. He wasn't worth a tinker's damn as a cowboy, but he was fast with a gun. Malone nodded his head. "All right, Charlie. It's your show."

Red Malone and his crew lifted their reins and moved to the other side of the street.

"Watch my back, Jim," Smoke said.

"You got it."

"I been hearin' about you for fifteen years or more Jensen," Charlie said. "I'm sick of hearin' about you. Makes me want to puke."

Red Malone cut his eyes to a rooftop. Tom Johnson stood there, a rifle in his hand. Marbly from the general store stepped out of his establishment, also with a rifle in his hands. Benson from the blacksmith shop appeared to Malone's right, a double-barrel shotgun in his hands. Toby from the hotel appeared on a rooftop, carrying a rifle.

The town was solidly behind Jensen, for sure.

Malone turned to his foreman. "John, we're out of this fight. Look around you. Pass the word."

John Steele looked. More townspeople had stepped out of their businesses and homes, all of them carrying weapons. John softly passed the word: Whatever happens between Jensen and Charlie, we're out of it.

Smoke stood relaxed in the center of the street. He had not taken his eyes off of Charlie.

The scar-faced gunny stood with his legs apart, body tensed for the draw. "You ready to die, Jensen?" he called.

"Not today, friend," Smoke said. "You got anything you want me to pass along after you're gone?"

Charlie cursed him.

"As a legally appointed deputy sheriff of this county, I am ordering you to surrender your guns, Charlie. There will be no charges filed against you if you do that."

Charlie laughed at him.

"You were warned," Smoke said softly.

"Draw!" Charlie yelled, and his right hand dipped down, the fingers closing around the butt of his pistol.

He felt something heavy and hard strike him in the chest. Charlie was on his back in the street, the sun-warmed dirt hot through his shirt. A shadow fell over him. Through the mist that had suddenly covered his eyes, he could see Smoke Jensen standing over him, a pistol in his hand, held by his side, the hammer back.

Charlie fumbled for his gun. He was astonished to find it was still in leather.

"I never seen anybody that fast," John Steele said to his boss. "It was like the wind."

"Yeah," Red reluctantly agreed.

The rest of Malone's bunch, all hard cases in their own right, sat their saddles quietly. They were all brave men, loyal to the brand, and all good with a gun. But they wanted no part of Smoke Jensen. Not face to face, anyway.

"You should have stayed in the bunkhouse today Charlie," Smoke told the dying man.

"You! . . ." Charlie gasped the word. Then he closed his eyes and died.

Smoke holstered his .44 and walked over to Red Malone. "No trouble in this town, Malone. No racing your horses and kicking up dust. No discharging of firearms. No foul language outside the saloon. Any of your crew gets drunk, you take them home, or me or Jim will put them in jail and the judge will fine them. Is all that understood?"

Hate leaped out of Red Malone's eyes. No one talked to him like that and got away with it.

He stepped out of the saddle without replying and turned his back to Smoke. A hard hand fell on his shoulder and spun him around, almost jerking him off his boots. Smoke Jensen stood staring at him, eyeball to eyeball.

"I asked you a question, Malone. I expect a reply."

Red noticed that Smoke had slipped on leather gloves. "I'll give you a reply, gunslinger," Red said. "and here it is."

Red swung a big fist. Had it connected, it would have knocked Smoke off his boots.

It didn't connect.

Smoke sidestepped and planted one big fist in Red's belly.

The air whooshed out of the man as he stumbled back. Smoke stepped in and popped him on the jaw with a left, following that with a right. Red fell back against a hitchrail. He shook his big head and cussed Smoke.

"Anytime you've had enough, Red," Smoke told him, "you just holler quit and that's it."

"I run this end of the county, Jensen," he said, his lips peeled back in an animal-like snarl.

Smoke answered him with a sneaky left that snapped Red's head back and bloodied his mouth. Smoke stepped back and waited.

A thin middle-aged cowboy sat his saddle and cut his eyes to John Steele. He whispered, "The boss better uncle, Steele. Jensen's givin' him a chance. If he don't, Jensen'll beat him half to death."

"I got twenty dollars that says you're wrong, Sal," John replied.

"You're on."

Red faked with a left and connected against Smoke's jaw with a right. The punch hurt. Smoke stepped back and shook his head. Red pursued him out into the street, grinning through the blood on his mouth.

Smoke ducked a punch and hammered a right over Red's kidney, following that with an uppercut to the man's mouth. Blood leaked from Red's lips.

Red backhanded Smoke in the face and charged, trying to grab him in a bear hug. Smoke danced to one side and hit Red twice in the face with a left and a right.

Red slipped a fist through and busted Smoke on the jaw, but the punch had lost a lot of steam. Smoke hit him with another combination, belly and jaw, then tripped the man, sending him sprawling to the dirt.

Red came up with a fistful of dirt and hurled it at Smoke, trying to momentarily blind the gunfighter. But Smoke had been raised by mountain men, and he knew all the tricks and then some. He ducked under the dust cloud and rammed Red in the belly with his head, both hands around the man's hard waist. Smoke drove him into a hitchrail. The hitchrail broke under the impact and Smoke released the man just in time to see Red fall into a horse trough.

Smoke stood on the outside of the trough and hammered Red's face into a bloody mask. Red lost consciousness and slipped down into the water, bubbling.

Smoke stepped back, found his hat, and put it on just as John Steele and several others were frantically pulling their boss out of the trough before he drowned.

"Drag him over to the jail and dump him in a cell," Smoke ordered.

"I'll be damned if I will!" Steele shouted at Smoke.

Jim walked up and laid his pistol across the back of the foreman's head, and it was Steele's turn to fall into the trough, face first.

"Drag both of them to jail," Smoke ordered. This time, no objections were forthcoming. The Lightning brand crew dragged the boss and the foreman across the street and into the jail, depositing both of them in a cell.

John Steele opened his eyes and glared hate at everybody. Red Malone snored and bubbled on his bunk.

"Gimme my twenty dollars," Sal said.

John dug in his damp pockets and threw a double eagle at the man. "Here's your damn money. And here's something else: You're fired!"

"Suits me," Sal said, slipping the twenty-dollar gold piece into his vest pocket. "I'm tarred of listenin' to your big mouth a-flappin' anyways."

"The next time I see you, Sal, you better be ready to drag iron."

The thin bowlegged cowboy lifted his eyes and stared at the foreman. Smoke knew that look; he had worn it himself, many times: It was the look of a very dangerous and very confident man. Smoke smiled, thinking: I've found another deputy.

"You best think about that, John." Sal's words were softly spoken and ringed with tempered steel. "I've helped bury a lot better men than you."

John spat through the bars and cursed him.

Smoke caught Jim's eyes and tapped the star pinned to his shirt, pointing at Sal. Jim grinned and nodded his head in agreement.

Smoke stepped outside and faced the Lightning crew. "You boys can have your drinks at the saloon, buy your to- bacco and needs, or whatever else legal you came to town to do. Make trouble, and you'll either join your bosses in there"— he jerked his thumb toward the jail—"or join Charlie in a pine box. The choice is yours."

"We're peaceful, Smoke," a hand said. "But this here is a friendly warnin' to you, and don't take it the wrong way. When you let Red outta there, he's gonna be on the prod for you. And right or wrong, we ride for the brand."

"That's your choice to make. Now, clear the street and drag Charlie off to the undertaker."

Jim and Sal stepped out onto the boardwalk. Smoke turned to the just-fired puncher and said, "You know any- thing about deputy sheriffing?"

"I've wore a badge a time or two."

"You want a job?"

"Might as well. Seein' as how I done been fired from cowboyin'."

"I have to warn you: It's going to get real interesting around here."

Sal hitched at his gunbelt. "I 'spect it will. Makes the time pass faster, though."

"Lemme out of here, you son of a bitch!" John Steele hollered.

7

"I've had your suit pressed," Sally told him. "We're going to a party tonight."

"Oh?"

"Yes. The ladies of the town are giving us a party. They're all quite taken with you and want to meet you up close."

Smoke rolled his eyes. "I can hardly wait."

Red Malone had woken up and had joined John Steele in bellowing from their cell.

"What are you going to do about that?" Sally asked.

"I can either shoot them, hang them, or cut them loose. What do you suggest?"

"They probably deserve the former. The latter would certainly quiet the town considerably."

"Lay out my suit. I'll go speak with Judge Garrison."

"Oh, let's bond them out," the judge said. "All that squalling is giving me a headache." He smiled. "We'll set the bond at a hundred dollars apiece."

"A hundred dollars!" John Steele recoiled from the bars and screamed like a wounded puma.

"Relax, John," Malone said. The man's face was horribly

bruised, both eyes almost swollen shut, his lips puffy, and his nose looked like a big red beet that an elephant had stepped on. He took a wad of still-damp greenbacks from his pocket and carefully counted out two hundred dollars, passing the money through the bars.

Smoke took it and infuriated the man by counting it again.

"It's all there, you son of a . . ." He choked back the oath and stood gripping the bars, shaking with anger.

"Sure is," Smoke said cheerfully. He unlocked the door and waved the men out. "You boys take it easy now. And come back to Barlow anytime, now, you hear?"

The rancher and his foreman did not reply. They stomped out and slammed the door behind them. Smoke sat at his desk and chuckled.

Smoke suffered through the party given by the good ladies of Barlow. He answered the questions—from both men and women alike—as best he could, and ate fried chicken and potato salad until he felt that if he ate another piece, he'd start clacking and laying eggs.

Walking back to the hotel—they had now been moved to the best room in the place, the Presidential Suite, which included a private water closet—Sally said, "Max Huggins had pretty well beaten these people down, hadn't he, honey?"

"Yes. And that first day in town, I came down hard on them—probably too hard. It's easy for someone ruthless to cut the heart out of people. It's ridiculously easy. Max is a smart man as well as a ruthless one. He went after the children of the townspeople. That shows me right there how low he is."

"You'll have to kill him, won't you, honey?"

"Me, or somebody. Yes."

Sal walked up, making his rounds, rattling doorknobs and looking up dark alleyways.

"Quiet, Smoke," the small man said. "I figure it'll be that way for three, maybe five days. Until Red gets back on his feet. And then he'll come gunnin' for you."

"I expect he will, Sal. I doubt if the man has ever received so thorough a beating as he got today."

"Smoke, he ain't never even been whipped before this day. And that's the God's truth."

"Walk along with us, Sal. Tell me about him."

"I ain't from this part of the country, Smoke. I was born in Missouri and come west with my parents in '50, I think it was. They settled in Nebraska and I drifted when I was seventeen. Most of my time I spent in Colorado and Idaho. That's how come it was I knowed who you was. I didn't come to this area until last year. I was fixin' to drift come the end of the month anyways. I just don't cotton to men like Red Malone and John Steele. I'll tell you what I know about him and about Max Huggins. I was told that Malone come into this area right after the Civil War. He was just a youngster, maybe nineteen or so. He carved him out a place for his ranch and defended it against Injuns and outlaws. Built it up right good. But he's always been on the shady side. Lie, cheat, steal, womanize. I was told his wife was a decent person. She bore him one son and one daughter, and then she took off when it got so Red was flauntin' his other women in her face. He's got women all over the country."

Smoke stopped them and they sat down on a long bench in front of the barber shop.

Sal pulled out the makings and asked Sally, "You object, ma'am?"

"Oh, no. Go right ahead. I'll take a puff or two off of Smoke's cigarette."

Sal almost dropped the sack at that. He kept any comments he had to himself. Strong-willed woman, he thought. Probably wants the vote, too. Lord help us all.

Sal rolled, shaped, licked, and lit up. "Red's daughter is a right comely lass. But Tessie is spoiled rotten, has the manners of a hog, and the morals of a billy goat. Melvin is crazy. Plumb loco. He likes to hurt people. And he's fast, Smoke. Have mercy, but the boy is quick. And a dead shot. But he's nuts. His eyes will scare you, make you back up. He's killed maybe half-a-dozen men, and they weren't none of them pilgrims, neither. Red's good with a short gun, but Melvin is nearabouts as fast as you, Smoke. And I ain't kiddin'.

"Naturally, just as soon as Big Max come into the area, him and Red struck a deal. Max would own the law enforcement of the county—and it's a sorry bunch—and control the north end of the county, and Red would control the south end. Red didn't have no interest in runnin' this town. He just wanted his share of the crooked games up in Hell's Creek, and his share of the gold and greenbacks taken in robberies. In return, he'd see that no one come in here with reform on their mind. So that means, Smoke, that you got to go. There ain't no other way for Red and Max to keep on doin' what they're doin'.

"Big Max, now, that's another story. Bad through and through. He's run crooked games and killed and robbed folks and run red-light houses from San Francisco to Fort Worth and north into Canada. He's a sorry excuse for a human being. I'd be happy to kill him if for no other reason than to clear the air for other folks."

"I can see why Max settled here," Smoke said.

"Sure. Wild country. One road runnin' north and south, one road runnin' east and west. No trains yet. Proper law ain't reached this part of the territory yet." He smiled, then added, " 'Cepting in this little town, that is."

The next morning, Smoke escorted the gambler he'd jailed to the stagecoach office. Jim fetched the hurdy-gurdy girls from the hotel.

"You might eventually get to Hell's Creek," Smoke informed them all. "But it won't be by going through Barlow."

"This ain't legal," the gambler protested.

"Sue me," Smoke said, and shoved the tinhorn into the stage. He looked up at the driver. "Get them out of here."

"Yes, sir!" The driver grinned and yelled at his team.

Smoke began his walk to the hotel to deal with Al Martin. The gunfighter had sent a boy to tell Smoke he wasn't about to be run out of town.

"How are you gonna deal with this guy?" Sal asked.

"He wants to stay in Barlow," Smoke replied. "So I'm going to let him stay."

"Huh?" Jim looked at Smoke.

"Forever," Smoke said tightly. "If that's the way he wants it."

Al Martin was lounging on the boardwalk in front of the hotel, having an after-breakfast cigar.

"He's quick," Sal told Smoke. "With either hand. I've seen him work."

Smoke had no comment about that.

Al Martin tossed his cigar into the dirt and stepped out into the street.

"You boys get out of the way," Smoke told his deputies.

Sal and Jim stepped to one side.

Al brushed back his coat, exposing the butts of his .45's.

"One more chance, Al," Smoke called, never breaking his stride. "You can rent a horse at the livery and ride south."

"I'm headin' north," Al returned the call.

"Not through this town," Smoke told him.

"You don't have the right to do that."

"I'm doing it, Al."

Joe Walsh, the owner of the Circle W, had left his ranch early with two of his men, to buy supplies in Barlow. The men stood in front of Bonnie's Cafe and watched. Joe had heard of Smoke Jensen for years, but he had never seen him until now.

He was very impressed by this first sighting. He'd heard

of what had happened to Red, and that amused him. If any man had a beating coming to him, it was Red. And Max Huggins. But Joe wondered if Smoke was hoss enough to take the huge Max Huggins.

"Last chance, Al," Smoke called. "I am ordering you to leave this town immediately."

Smoke stopped about forty feet from Al.

"You know where you can stick that order, Jensen."

"Then make your play, Al," Smoke said calmly.

Al went for his guns. He got both barrels of the .45's halfway out of leather before Smoke drew. Smoke shot him twice, in the belly and the chest, the slugs turning the man around and sitting him down in the street, on his butt.

"Holy Mother of Jesus!" Joe Walsh whispered the words.

"He's so quick it was a blur."

His hands shook their heads in awe.

Smoke walked up to Al Martin. The gunfighter looked up at him. "Melvin's quicker, Jensen," he pushed the words past bloody lips. "You'll meet your match with the kid."

"Maybe. But you'll meet your Maker long before that happens."

Al fell over on his side. "Cold," he muttered. "Gimme a decent buryin'," he requested. "One fittin'a human being."

"I would," Smoke told him, his words carrying to both sides of the street, "if you were a decent human being."

"Bastard!" Al cursed him.

"That's a hard man yonder," Joe told his hands. "Probably the hardest man I ever seen."

Al Martin died cursing the name of Smoke Jensen.

Smoke punched out the empty brass and reloaded just as the combination barber/undertaker came walking up.

"What kind of funeral you want him to have, Sheriff?" he asked.

"Whatever his pockets will bear," Smoke told him. "Bring his guns and personal items to the office."

"Them's right nice boots he's wearin'," the man said. "Be a shame to waste that leather."

"Whatever," Smoke said. He walked over to the cafe and stepped up on the boardwalk.

The rancher stuck out his hand. "Joe Walsh," he introduced himself. "I own the Circle W."

Smoke took the hand.

"Good to have some decent law enforcement around here." He looked across the street at Jim Dagonne and grinned. "How'd you get him off the jug?"

"I told him I'd stomp his guts out and feed what was left to the hogs if he ever took another drink."

Joe laughed. "He's a good boy. I would have rehired him in a day or two, but I think he's better off in what you got him doing." He looked at Sal. "That's a good man, too."

"I think so."

"Watch your back when you ride out in the county. Red Malone don't forget or forgive. I'll tell the wife you're in town. You and your missus come out to the ranch anytime for dinner. We'd love the company."

"I'll do it."

Smoke had sized up the rancher and thought him to be a good, hard-working man. And one who would fight if pushed. Probably the reason Red and Max had left him alone. His hands wore their guns like they knew how to use them . . . and would.

Sal walked over. "The undertaker said Al had quite a wad on him. He's gonna hire some wailers and trot out his black shiny wagon for this one. He said the weather bein' as cool as it is, Al can probably stand two days. Ought to be a new preacher in town by that time."

Smoke nodded. "You and Jim watch the town. I'm going to lay in some supplies and take a ride. I'll be gone for a couple of days, getting the lay of the land."

"Watch yourself, Smoke. Red's probably sent the word out for gunhands."

Again, Smoke nodded. "You and Jim start totin' sawed-off shotguns, Sal. Any gunslicks that come in, either move them on or bury them."

"You got it."

"I'll see you in two or three days."

Smoke rode out of the valley and into the high country. The high lonesome, Old Preacher had called it. It pulled at a man, always luring him back to its beauty. The valley was surrounded by high snowcapped peaks, with the lower ridges providing good summer graze for the cattle.

Smoke had checked out the boundaries of the Lightning spread at the surveyor's office, and he carefully avoided Malone's range. Keeping Mt. Evans to his right, Smoke rode toward Hell's Creek. He wasn't concerned about Sally's friends being worried about their not showing up. By now, everyone in the county knew Smoke was in Barlow. He only hoped the doctor and his wife had sense enough to keep their mouths shut about their being friends with Sally.

He rode up to a farmhouse and gave a shout. A man in bib overalls came out of the barn and took a long look at Smoke. Then he went back in and returned carrying a rifle.

"If you be friendly, swing down and have some coffee," the farmer called. "If you've come to make trouble for us, my woman and my two boys have rifles on you from the house."

"I'm the new marshal at Barlow," Smoke called. "The name is Smoke Jensen."

"Lord have mercy!" the farmer said. "Come on in and put your boots under our table. The wife nearabouts got the noonin' ready to dish up."

"I'm obliged."

The fare was simple but well-cooked and plentiful, consisting of hearty stew made with beef and potatoes and carrots and onions, along with huge loaves of fresh-baked bread. Smoke did not have to be told twice to dive in.

Not much was said during the nooning, for in the West, eating was serious business. The farmer told Smoke his name was Brown, his wife was Ellie, and his boys were Ralph and Elias. And that was all he said during the meal.

After the meal, Ellie poured them all coffee and Smoke brought the family up to date on what had taken place in Barlow.

The farmer, his wife, and his sons sat bug-eyed and silent during the telling.

"Lord have mercy!" Brown finally exclaimed. "You whupped Red Malone. I'd give ten dollars to a seen that!"

Smoke imagined that ten dollars was a princely sum to Mr. Brown.

"I stopped going into Barlow because of the hoodlums and the trash, Mr. Jensen," Ellie said. "And I certainly wouldn't be caught dead in Hell's Creek."

"I can understand that, Mrs. Brown," Smoke said. "I surely can."

"I take the wagon and go into town about once every three months," Brown said. "We're pretty well set up here. I got me a mill down on the crick, and we grind our own corn and such. Haul my grain and taters into town come harvest, and we get by."

"You got neighbors?"

"Shore." He pointed out the back. "Right over the field yonder is Gatewood. Just south of him is Morrison. And beyond that is Cooter's place. Just north of me is Bolen and Carson. We done that deliberate when we come out. In twenty minutes of hard ridin', we can have twelve to fifteen guns at anybody's house."

"Smart," Smoke agreed. "Has Max Huggins given any of you any trouble?"

Man and wife cut their eyes to one another. The glance did not escape Smoke.

Ellie sighed and nodded her head.

"Yeah, he has, Mister Smoke," Brown said. "His damned

ol' gunhands has ruint more than one garden and killed hogs and chickens. They killed the only milk cow Bolen had, and his baby girl needed that milk. His woman had dried up. The baby died."

Smoke drew one big hand into a huge fist. "Who led the gang that did it?"

"Vic, they called him."

"Vic Young," Smoke put the last name to it. "I know of him. He's poison mean. Rode into a farmyard down in Colorado and shot a girl's puppy dog for no reason. I haven't had any use for him since I heard that story."

"Man who would shoot a girl's puppy is low," Elias said.

"He's got him a widow woman he sees about five miles from here," Brown said softly.

Both boys grinned.

"Does he now?" Smoke said.

"Be fair and tell it all," his wife admonished him gently.

"You're right, mother," Brown said. "I'm not bein' fair to the woman." He looked at Smoke. "Martha Feckles—that's the wider's name—does sewin' for them painted ladies in Hell's Creek. She's a good woman; just got to make a livin' for her and her young'uns, that's all. This trash Vic, he come up to her place one night and—" he paused, "well, took advantage of her."

"He raped her, Mister Smoke," Ralph said.

"Hush your mouth," Ellie warned him.

"No, it's all right, ma," Brown said. "Let the boy tell it. Mister Smoke needs to know, and these young folks know more about it than we do."

"He beat her up bad, Mister Smoke," Ralph said. "Miss Martha, she's got her a daughter who's thirteen—Elias is sweet on her—"

"I am not neither!" Elias turned red.

"Shut up," the father warned him. "You are, too. Ever time you get around her you fall all over your big feet and bleat like a sheep. Tell it, Ralph."

"This Vic, he told Miss Martha that if she didn't go on . . . seein' him, he'd do the same to Aggie."

"I ought to kill him!" Elias said, considerable heat in his voice.

"Hush that kind of talk!" his mother told him. "The man's a gunfighter."

"Listen to your ma," Smoke told the boy, whom he guessed to be about fifteen at the most. "You have a right to defend hearth and home and kith and kin. You leave the gun-fighting to me. Is that understood, boy?"

"Yes, sir."

Smoke rose from the table and found his hat. "I'll be riding now. You all feel free to come shop in Barlow. We'll soon have us a newspaper and a schoolteacher and a preacher. I thank you for the meal." He reached into his pocket and pulled out a double eagle. Before Brown could protest, he said, "Buy some ammunition with that. It's going to get real salty in the valley before long."

8

Smoke rode over to the Widow Feckles's house and made a slow circle of the grounds around the neat little home before riding up to the gate and swinging down from the saddle. A girl opened the front door and stepped out onto the porch. She looked to be about thirteen or fourteen, and Smoke pegged her as Aggie.

"Good morning," Smoke said. "I'm the new marshal over at Barlow. Don't be afraid of me. I'm here to help, not hurt you or your mother."

The girl's eyes widened. "Are you really Smoke Jensen?"

"Yes, I am. Is your name Aggie?"

"How'd you know that?"

"I nooned over at the Brown farm. Thought I'd come over and say hello to you and your ma. Is she home?"

"I'll fetch her for you."

Smoke waited by the gate. A very pretty woman stepped out onto the porch and smiled at him. "Mr. Jensen?"

"Yes, ma'am."

"I'm Martha Feckles. You wanted to see me?"

"If I may, yes."

"Please come in. I've just made a fresh pot of coffee."

The sitting room was small but neat, the furniture old and worn, but clean.

"You go look after your brother, Aggie," Martha said. "And don't stray from the house."

"Yes, Momma."

When the girl had closed the door behind her, Smoke said, "Are you expecting Vic Young?"

That shook the woman. Her hands trembled as she poured the coffee. "Brown spoke out of turn, sir."

"I don't think so. I think they spoke because they're worried about you. You're in a bad situation—not of your doing—and they'd like to see you clear of it."

"I'll never be free of Vic," she said with bitterness in her voice.

"Oh, you'll be free of him, Martha. You can write that down in your diary. When do you expect him again?"

"This evening."

Smoke sipped his coffee—mostly chicory—and studied the woman. She was under a strain, he could see that in her eyes and on her face. And he could also see the remnants of a bruise on her jaw. "Did Vic strike you, Martha?"

Her laugh held no humor. "Many times. He likes to beat up women."

Smoke waited.

With a sigh, she said, "Vic's killed women before, Mr. Jensen. He brags about it. I have to protect Aggie. I have to do his bidding for her sake."

"No longer, Martha. You'll not see Vic Young again. That's a promise."

"If you put him in jail, he'll come back when he gets out and really make it difficult for us."

"I don't intend to put him in jail, Martha. I intend to kill him."

His words did not shock her. She lifted her eyes to his. "I'm no shrinking summer rose, Mr. Jensen. I was born in the West. I don't hold with eastern views about crime and punishment. Some people—men and women—are just no good. They were born bad. I'll be much beholden to you if you saw to it that Vic did not come around here again. I can mend your shirts, and I do washing and ironing. I—"

Smoke held up a hand. "Enough, Martha. Do you have friends who would take you in for the night?"

"Why . . . certainly."

"I'll hitch up your buggy, and you take the children and go to your friends for the night. You come back in the morning. All right?"

"If you say so, Mr. Jensen."

After they had gone, Smoke put his horse up in the small barn, closed the door securely, and walked the grounds, getting the feel of the place. Back in the house, he read for a time. He dozed off and slept for half an hour, waking up refreshed. He made a pot of strong coffee and waited.

Just as dusk was settling around the high country, Smoke heard a horse approaching at a canter. He stood up and slipped the hammer-thong from his .44's. He worked the guns in and out of leather and walked softly to the front door.

"Git ready, baby," a man called from the outside. "And git that sweet little baby of yourn ready, too. It's time for her to git bred."

Smoke's face tightened. He felt rage well up inside him. He mentally calmed himself. Only his eyes showed what was boiling inside him.

"You hear me, you . . ." Vic spewed profanity, the filth rolling from his mouth like sewage.

Smoke opened the door and stepped out onto the small porch. Vic crouched like a rabid animal when he spotted him.

"No more, Vic," Smoke told him. "You won't terrorize this good woman anymore."

"Who the hell are you?"

"The name is Jensen. Smoke Jensen."

Vic spat on the ground. "You rode a long ways to die, Jensen."

"You're trash, Vic. Pure crud. Just like the man you work for."

"No man calls me that and lives!"

"I just did, Vic. And I'm still living."

"Where's Martha and Aggie?"

"Safe. And I intend to see they remain safe."

"You got no call to come meddlin' in a man's personal business."

"I do when the man is trash like you."

"I'm tarred of all this jibber-jabber, Jensen. You tell me where my woman is at and then you hit the trail."

"You got any kin you want me to notify, Vic?"

"Notify about what?"

"Your death."

"Huh!" Vic looked puzzled for a moment. Then he laughed. "You may be a big shot where you come from, Jensen, but you don't spell horse crap to me."

"Then make your move, punk."

Vic was suddenly unsure of himself. He looked around him. "You alone, Jensen?"

"I don't need any help in dealing with scum like you, Vic."

"I'm warnin' you, Jensen, don't call me that no more."

"Or you'll do what, Vic? I'll tell you what you'll do. Nothing. You woman beaters are all alike. Cowards. Punks. Come on, Vic. Make your play."

All the bluster and brag left the man. His eyes began to jerk and the right side of his face developed a nervous tic. "I'll just ride on, Jensen."

"No, Vic. I won't allow that. You'd just find some other poor woman to terrorize. Some child to molest. It's over Vic. You'll kill no more women."

"They had it comin' to them!" Vic shouted as the night began closing in. "All I wanted from them was what a woman was put on earth to give to a man."

Smoke waited.

Vic began cursing, working his courage back up to a fever. "Drag iron, Jensen!" he screamed.

"After you, punk."

Vic's hand dropped to his gun. Smoke drew, cocked, and fired as fast as a striking rattler, shooting him in the belly, the slug striking the child molester and rapist two inches above his belt buckle. Vic stumbled and went down on one knee. He managed to drag his pistol from leather and cock it. Smoke shot him again, the slug taking him in the side and blowing out the other side. Vic Young fell backward, cursing as life left him.

Smoke stood over him. Vic said, "You're dead, Jensen. Max has put money on your head. Big money. He . . ."

Vic jerked on the cooling ground and died staring at whatever faced him beyond the dark river.

Smoke took the man's gunbelt and tossed leather and pistol onto the porch. He fanned the man's pockets, finding a very respectable wad of greenbacks and about a hundred dollars in gold coins. Martha would put the money to good use. He put the money on the kitchen table, along with Vic's gun and gunbelt and the rifle taken from the saddle boot.

Smoke wrote a short note and left it on the table: HE WILL BOTHER YOU NO MORE.

He signed it Smoke.

He saddled up Star and rode around to the front of the house. Smoke tied Vic across the saddle of his suddenly skittish horse and locked up the house.

Leading the horse with its dead cargo, Smoke headed north, toward Big Max Huggins's town of Hell's Creek.

It was late when he arrived on the hill overlooking the bawdy town. Lights were blazing in nearly every building, wild laughter ripped the night, and rowdy songs could be heard coming from drunken throats.

Smoke slipped the lead rope and slapped the horse on the rump, sending it galloping into the town.

He sat his saddle and waited.

He didn't have to wait long.

"Vic's dead!" the faint shout came to him as the piano playing and singing and drunken laughter gradually fell away, leaving the town silent.

Smoke watched the shadowy figures untie the body of Vic Young and lower it to the ground. He couldn't hear what the men were saying, but he could make a good guess.

Every rowdy and punk and gun-handler in the town would have known that Vic was seeing Widow Feckles. And everyone would know that she was being forced into acts of passion with Vic. And since none of the sodbusters would have the nerve to face Vic—so the gunhandlers thought; whether that was true or not, only time would tell—it had to have been the Widow Feckles who did Vic in.

Smoke kneed Star forward, moving closer to the town. "Let's burn her out!" the shout reached Smoke's ears.

"Yeah," another man yelled. "I'll get the kerosene."

Smoke swung onto the main street of Hell's Creek and reined up. Staying in the shadows, he shucked his Winchester from the saddle boot and eared back the hammer. He called, "Martha Feckles had nothing to do with killing Vic. I killed him."

"Well, who the hell are you?" came the shouted question.

"Smoke Jensen."

"Jensen! Let's get him, boys."

They came at a rush and it was like shooting clay ducks in a shooting gallery. Smoke leveled the Winchester and emptied it into the knot of men. A dozen of them fell to one side, hard hit and screaming. Smoke spun Star around and headed for the high country, leaving a trail a drunken city slicker could follow.

About five miles outside of town, Smoke found what he was looking for and reined up. He loosened the cinch strap and let the big horse blow. He took a drink of water from his canteen and filled up his hat, letting Star have a drink.

Smoke had reloaded his rifle on the run, and he took it and his saddlebags down to the rocks just below where he had tucked Star safely away in a narrow draw. He eared back the hammer when he heard the pounding of hooves. The men of Hell's Creek rounded a curve in the trail and Smoke knocked the first man out of the saddle. Shifting the muzzle, he got lead in two more before the scum started making a mad dash for safety.

Smoke deliberately held his fire, watching the men cautiously edge toward his position under a starry sky and moon-bright night. With a grin, he opened his saddlebags and took out a stick of dynamite. He had a dozen sticks in the bag. He capped the stick of giant powder and set a very short fuse. Striking a match, he lit the fuse and let it fly, sputtering and sparking through the air.

The dynamite blew and shook the ground as it exploded. Smoke saw one man blown away from behind a rock, half of an arm missing. Another man staggered to his boots and Smoke drilled him through the brisket. A third man tried to crawl away, dragging a broken leg. Smoke put him out of his misery.

Smoke put away the dynamite. Taking it along had been Sally's idea, and it had been a good one.

The trash below him cursed Smoke, calling him all sorts of names. But Smoke held his fire and eased away to a new position, which was some fifty feet higher than the old one. He now was able to see half-a-dozen men crouched behind whatever cover they could find in the night, some of that cover being mighty thin indeed.

Smoke dusted one man through and through. The man grunted once, then slowly rolled down the hill, dead. He shifted the muzzle and plugged another of Max's men through the throat. The man made a lot of horrible noises before he had the good grace to expire. Smoke had been aiming for the chest, but downhill shooting is tricky enough; couple that with night, and it gets doubly difficult.

The men of Hell's Creek decided they had had enough for this night. Smoke let them make their retreat, even though he could have easily dropped another two or three. He tightened the cinch strap, swung into the saddle, and headed south. He found a good place to camp and picketed Star. With his saddle for a pillow, he rolled into his blankets and went to sleep.

Two hours after dawn, he rode into the front yard of Martha Feckles. An idea had formed in his mind over coffee and bacon that morning, and he wanted to see how the widow received it.

"I think it's a grand idea!" she said.

Barlow had another resident.

Big Max Huggins sat in his office and stared at the wall. His thoughts were dark and violent. At this very moment, that drunken old preacher—he was all that passed for religion in Hell's Creek—was praying for the lost souls of three of those Jensen had shot in the main street of town last night. Those that had pursued him came back into town, dragging their butts in defeat. They had left six dead on the mountain. One of those had bled to death after the bomb Jensen had thrown tore off half of the man's arm.

"Goddamn you, Jensen!" Max cursed.

He leaned back in his chair—specially made due to his height and weight. He hated Smoke Jensen, but had to respect him—grudgingly—for his cold nerve. It would take either a crazy person or one with nerves of steel to ride smack into the middle of the enemy. And Smoke Jensen was no crazy person.

What to do about him?

Big Max didn't have the foggiest idea.

Smoke had put steel into the backbones of those in Barlow. A raid against the town now would be suicide. His men would be shot to pieces. There was no need to send for any outside gunfighters. He had some of the best guns in the West, either on his payroll or working out of the town on a percentage basis of their robberies.

Max's earlier boast that he would just wait Smoke out was proving to be a hollow brag. Jensen was bringing the fight to him.

Of course, Max mused, he could just pick up and move on. He'd done it many times in the past when things had gotten too hot for him.

But just the thought of that irritated him. In the past dozens of cops or sheriffs and their deputies had been on his trail. Jensen was just one man. One man!

Max sighed, thinking: But, Jesus, what a man.

It was a good thing he'd invited those friends of his from Europe. A damn good thing. They would be arriving just in time.

The good ladies of Barlow welcomed Martha Feckles and her children with open arms. The mayor gave her a small building to use for her sewing. And Judge Garrison, now that he was free of the heavy hand of Max Huggins, was proving to be a decent sort of fellow. He staked Martha for a dress shop.

The preacher and schoolteacher had arrived in town. The newspaper man was due in at any time. Some of those who had left when Max first put on the pressure were returning. Barlow now had a population of nearly four hundred. And growing.

The jail was nearly full. Each time the stage ran north, Smoke jerked out any gamblers, gunfighters, and whores who might be on it and turned them around. If they kicked up a fuss, they were tossed in the clink, fined, and were usually more than happy to catch the next stage out—south.

A deputy U.S. Marshal, on his way up to British Columbia to bring back a prisoner, was on the stage the morning a gunslick objected to being turned around.

"There ain't no warrants out on me, Jensen," the man protested. "You ain't got no right to turn me around. I can go anywheres I damn well please to go."

"That's right," Smoke told him. "Anywhere except Hell's Creek."

Amused, the U. S. Marshal leaned against a post and rolled himself a cigarette, listening to the exchange. He knew all about Hell's Creek and Big Max Huggins. But until somebody complained to the government, there was little they could do. He knew the sheriff, the city marshal, and all the deputies in Hell's Creek were crooked as a snake. But the outlaws working out of there never bothered anyone with a federal badge, and as far as he knew, there were no federal warrants on anyone in the town—at least not under the names they were going by now.

"Git out of my way, Jensen!" the gunny warned Smoke.

"Don't be a fool, man," Smoke told him. "You're in violation of the law by bracing me. I don't have any papers on you. So why don't you just go to the hotel, get you a room, and catch the next stage out?"

"South?"

"That's it."

"I'll rent me a horse and go to Hell's Creek."

"Sorry, friend," Smoke told him. "No one in this town will rent you a horse."

"Then I think I'll get back on the stage and ride up yonder like my ticket says."

Smoke hit him. The punch came out of the blue and caught the gunny on the side of the jaw. When he hit the ground, he was out cold.

Jim and Sal dragged him across the street to the jail.

"Slick," the U.S. Marshal said. "Against the law, but slick."

"You going to report what I'm doing?" Smoke asked.

"Hell, no, man! But I can tell you that the word's gone out up and down the line: You're a marked man. Huggins has put big money on your head. And I'm takin' enough money to bring in some mercenaries from Europe."

"Are they in the country?"

"As near as the Secret Service can tell, yes. Two long-distance shooters, Henri Dubois and Paul Mittermaier, are on their way west right now. Our office has sent out flyers to you. Oh, yes. We know what you're doing here. We can't give you our blessings, but we can close our eyes."

"Thanks. Dubois and Mittermaier—Frenchman and a German?"

"Yep. And they're good."

"I don't like back-shooters. I'll tell you now, Marshal: If I see them, I'm going to kill them."

"Suits me, Smoke. Good hunting." He climbed back on board the stage and was gone.

Smoke turned to Jim and Sal, who had just returned from the jail. "You hear that?"

They had heard it.

"Pass the word to all the farmers and ranchers. Any strangers, especially those speaking with an accent, I want to know about. You boys watch your backs."

Sal spat on the ground. "I hate a damned back-shooter," he said. "These boys are gonna be totin' some fancy custom-made rifles. I see one, I'm gonna plug him on the spot and apologize later if I'm wrong."

"You know what this tells me?" Smoke asked. "It tells me that Max is in a bind. What we're doing is working. We can't legally stop and permanently block freight shipments to Hell's Creek. But we can hold them up and make them open up every box and crate for search. And I mean a very long and tedious search. It won't take long for freight companies to stop accepting orders from Hell's Creek."

Jim and Sal grinned. "Oh, you got a sneaky mind, Smoke," Sal said. "I like it!"

"The last freight wagons rolled through a week ago," Jim said. "There ought to be another convoy tomorrow, I figure."

"OK," Smoke said. He looked at Sal. "You get a couple of town boys. Give them a dollar apiece to stand watch about two miles south of town. As soon as they hear the wagons, one of them can come fogging back to town for us. Everything going north has got to pass through here." Smoke smiled. "This is going to give Max fits!"

The men grinned at each other. One sure way to kill a town was to dry up its supply line. Big Max was not going to like this.

Not one little bit.

9

"Some of the boys is grumblin' about you puttin' up money on Jensen's head and then lettin' them foreigners come over here," one of Max's gunhands complained.

Max spread his hands. "I put up the money, Lew. Anybody who nails Jensen gets it. As far as Dubois and Mittermaier are concerned, they're old friends of mine. I sent for them long before Jensen entered the picture. Besides, they are much more subtle in their approach than most of those out there." He waved his hand. "You and I, of course, could handle it easily. I'm not too sure about the others."

The outlaw knew he was getting a line of buffalo chips fed him, but the flattery felt good anyway. "Right, Big Max. Sure. I understand. What do I tell the boys?"

"Tell them . . ." Max was thinking hard. "Tell them that we must be careful in disposing of Jensen. If we draw too much attention to us, the government might send troops in here and put us all out of business."

"Yeah," Lew said. "Yeah, you're right. They'll understand that, Max. I'll pass the word."

After Lew had left, Max leaned back in his chair. What next? he thought. What is Jensen going to do next?

"What are y'all lookin' for?" the teamster asked.

"Contraband," Smoke told him. "Unload your wagons."

The teamster paled under his stubble of beard and tanned skin. "All the wagons? Everything in them?"

"All the wagons, everything in them."

Griping and muttering under their breaths, the men unloaded the wagons, and Smoke and Jim and Sal went to work with pry-bars. With his back to the teamsters, Smoke pulled a small packet from under his shirt and dropped it in a box. "Check this box, Sal," he said. "I'll be opening some others."

"Right, Smoke."

After a moment, Sal called out, "Marshal, I got something that looks funny."

Smoke walked over. "The box says it's supposed to have whiskey in it. What's that in your hand?"

"Durned if I know." He handed the packet to Smoke.

Smoke had found the contents way in the back of the safe in the marshal's office. It was several thousand dollars of badly printed counterfeit greenbacks.

Smoke opened the packet. "Hey!" he said, holding one of the greenbacks up to the sunlight. "This looks phony to me."

A teamster walked over. "What is that?"

"Counterfeit money," Smoke told him. "This is real serious. You could be in a lot of trouble."

"Me!" the teamster shouted. "I ain't done nothin'."

"You're hauling this funny money," Smoke reminded him.

"Well, that's true. But that phony money sure as hell ain't mine."

"Oh, I believe you," Smoke eased his fears. "But this entire shipment is going to have to be seized and held for evidence."

"Marshal, you can have it all. Me and my boys work for a living. We're not printing no government money."

"Is this shipment prepaid?"

"Yes, sir. Everything sent to Hell's Creek is paid for in advance. That's the only way the boss would agree to do business with them thugs up yonder."

"So you and your men would prefer not to do business with those in Hell's Creek?"

"That's the gospel truth, Mr. Jensen. There ain't a one of us like the run past Barlow."

"All right, boys. You're free to turn around and head on back. We're sorry to have inconvenienced you."

After the wagons had gone, the men nearly broke up laughing as they stood amid the mounds of boxed supplies. Wiping his eyes, Smoke said, "Sal, go get some wagons and men from town. We've got to store all this stuff."

"Bet Max is gonna toss himself a royal fit when he hears about this," Sal said. "This here is food and supplies for a month."

"Yeah. I figure they have probably a month's supplies left on the shelves. After that, things are going to get desperate in Hell's Creek."

Sal headed back to town and Jim said, "You know, Smoke, Max can't let you get away with this. His men would lose all respect for him."

"Yeah, I know. This may be the fuel to pop the lid off. What's the latest on Red Malone; have you heard?"

"Not a peep. I 'spect he's still recovering from that beatin' you gave him."

"He's got to have a meeting with Max. They'll get together and try to plan some way to get rid of me."

"No way to cover all the trails up to Hell's Creek. There must be a dozen, and probably a few more that I don't know about."

"Oh, I wouldn't try to do that. But I was thinking: Red has to buy supplies and he buys them in Barlow. It would be too time-consuming and costly to go anywhere else. Marbly hates Red. He never did knuckle under to him. He told me himself he still has the right to refuse service to anyone."

Jim smiled. "Oh, now that would tick Red off. He'd go right through the ceiling."

Smoke chuckled. "I'm counting on it, Jim. I am really counting on it."

"He did what?" Big Max roared, jumping up from his chair and pounding a fist on his desk.

The outlaw Val Singer repeated what he had heard.

"That's why the damn supplies didn't arrive yesterday," Max said, sitting down and doing his best to calm himself. "Jensen . . . that low-life, no-good, lousy . . ." He spent the next few moments calling Smoke every filthy name he could think of. And he thought of a lot of them.

Big Max shook himself like a bear with fleas and took several deep breaths. What to do? was the next thought that sprang into his angry mind.

Thing about it was, he didn't know.

"Burn the damn town down," Val suggested.

"They'd rebuild it," Max said glumly.

"Grab some of their kids, then."

"I have been giving that some thought, for a fact. But we'd have to be very careful doing it, Val. Very subtle."

Val smiled, a nasty glint in his eyes. "That daughter of Martha Feckles is prime. She could pleasure a lot of us."

Big Max had thought of Aggie a time or two. For a fact. Something ugly and archaic reared up within him when he thought of Aggie.

He could envision all sorts of perversions, all with Aggie in the lead role . . . with him.

"I'll think about it," Max said, his voice husky.

Days passed and there was no retaliation from either Big Max or Red Malone. And that worried Smoke. To his mind, it meant that Max and Red were planning something very ugly and very sneaky. He warned everybody in town to keep a careful eye on their kids, to know where they were at all times. He warned the women to never walk alone, to plan shopping trips in groups. He visited everyone who lived just outside of town and warned them to be very, very careful.

He rode out into the county, visiting the small ranchers and farmers, repeating his message of caution at every stop.

"What do you think they're gonna do, Mr. Jensen?" Brown asked. Smoke had stopped in for coffee.

"I don't know, Brown. I wish I did so I could head it off. Whatever Max does, and probably Red Malone, too, is going to be dirty. Bet on that."

"Would the army come in if we was to ask them?"

"No. This is a civilian matter. I can't tell you who told me this, but I was told that the government is going to turn its back and let us handle it the way we see fit."

"That seems odd. I mean, why would they?"

"I've worn a U.S. Marshal's badge a time or two, Brown."

Smoke had worn a marshal's badge before, but that didn't mean the government owed him any favors. He hoped Brown wouldn't push the matter, and the farmer didn't.

"If we got to go clean out that bunch at Hell's Creek, or if we got to ride agin' Malone and his bunch of trash, you can count me and all my neighbors in, Smoke."

Smoke smiled. "The word I got is that you farmers won't fight. That you're scared."

"You believe that?"

"Not for one second, Brown. I got a hunch you're all Civil War veterans."

"We are. Gatewood and Cooter fought on the side of the South, rest of us wore blue. But that's behind us now. We seldom ever talk about it no more. And when we do, it ain't with no rancor. Funny thing is, we never knowed each other during the war. We just met up on the trail and become friends. But don't never think we won't fight, Smoke. Some hoodlums along the trail thought that. We buried them."

They chatted for a while longer and then Smoke pulled out, heading back to Barlow. He had him a hunch that Max Huggins had already sounded out Brown and Cooter and the other farmers in that area. Max was no fool, far from it, and he had guessed—and guessed accurately—that tackling that bunch would be foolhardy. Like most men of his ilk, Max preferred the easy way over the hard.

He pulled up in front of his office and swung down, curious about the horses tied to the hitchrail. He did not recognize the brand.

He looped the reins around the rail and stepped up on the boardwalk. The door to his office opened and several men filed out, one of them wearing the badge of sheriff of the county.

"You Jensen?" the man asked, a hard edge to his voice.

"That's right."

The man held out his hand. "I'll take your badge, Jensen. I name my deputies."

"This badge is legal, partner. Judge Garrison swore me in and he has the power to do it. So that means that you can go right straight to hell."

The sheriff shook a finger in Smoke's face. "Now let me tell you something. . . ."

Smoke slapped the finger away and his hand returned a lot harder. He backhanded the crooked sheriff a blow that jarred the man and stepped him to one side.

"Don't you ever stick your finger in my face again," Smoke warned him. "The next time you do it, I'll break it off at the elbow and put it in a place that'll have you riding sidesaddle for a long time."

Sal and Jim had stepped out of the office, both of them carrying sawed-off shotguns. It made the sleazebag sheriff's deputies awfully nervous.

"Come on, Cart," one of his men said. "I told you this wouldn't work."

Smoke laughed. "You have to be Paul Cartwright. Sure. I

remember reading about you. You served time in California for stealing while you were a lawman out there. Get out of this town, Cartwright."

"Come on, Cart." One of his men pulled at his sleeve.

"I'll be damned if I will!" Cart blustered. "I'm the sheriff of this county. And no two-bit gunslinger tells me what to do."

He took a swing at Smoke, who in turn grabbed him by the arm and tossed him off the boardwalk and into the street. Smoke jumped down just as Cart was grabbing for his gun. He kicked the .45 out of his hand and jerked the man to his boots.

Then he proceeded to beat the hell out of him.

Every time Cart would get up, Smoke would knock him down again. The editor of the paper had grabbed his brand-new, up-to-date camera and rushed out of his office in time to see Smoke knock Cart down for the second time. He quickly set up and began taking action shots.

Cart was out of shape, and Smoke really didn't want to inflict any permanent injuries on the man. He just wanted to leave a lasting impression as to who was running things in Barlow and the south end of the county.

The editor, Henry Draper, got some great shots of Cart being busted in the mouth and landing in the dirt on his butt. Jim and Sal thought it very amusing. Cart's deputies failed to see the humor in it. But they stayed out of it mainly because of Jim and Sal and the express guns they carried.

Joe Walsh and several of his hands rode into town just as Smoke was knocking Cart down for about the seventh time. The rancher sat his saddle and watched, amusement on his face and in his eyes.

The county sheriff staggered to his boots, lifted his fists, and Smoke decked him for the final count. Cart hit the dirt and didn't move.

Smoke washed his face and hands in a horse trough, picked up his hat, and settled it on his head. He looked up at

Cart's deputies and pointed to the sheriff. "Get that trash off the streets and out of this town. And don't come back. You understand all that?"

"Yes, sir," they echoed.

Smoke jerked a thumb. "Move!"

The deputies grunted Cart across his saddle, tied him in place, and rode out.

"You do have a way of making friends, Smoke," Joe said, walking his horse over to the hitchrail and dismounting.

"Let's just say I leave lasting impressions." Smoke smiled the reply, shaking the rancher's hand.

"What a headline this will make!" Henry said. The editor of the *Barlow Bugle* grabbed up all his photographic equipment and hustled back to his office to develop the pictures and write the story.

"Stick around," Smoke told Joe. "We'll have some coffee in a minute." He looked at Sal. "When did Cart get here?"

" 'Bout an hour ago. He was full of it, too. He had me and Jim plumb shakin' in our boots."

"I'm sure he did," Smoke said, noticing the wicked glint in the man's eyes. "I can tell that you haven't recovered yet."

"Right," Jim said, grinning along with Sal. "They're runnin' scared, Smoke. All of them up at Hell's Creek. Cart said that Big Max can't get a freight company to haul goods up to them. He's tryin' to get goods pulled in from that new settlement to the west of him . . . Kalispell; but the marshal over there told him to go take a dump in his hat. Or words similar to that."

Joe Walsh and his men laughed out loud, one of the hands saying, "Me and the rest of the boys talked it over, Smoke. When you need us, just give a holler. We'll ride with you and you call the shots."

"I appreciate it. Max won't stand still and get pushed around much longer. I expect some retaliation from Hell's Creek at any moment. Unfortunately, I don't have any idea in what form it might be." He told them all what he'd been doing that day, riding and warning those in the south end of the county . . . or as many as he could find.

"A man who would harm a kid is scum," Joe said. "I suggest we keep a rope handy."

A crowd had gathered around and they heatedly agreed.

Smoke let them talk it out until they fell silent. "You watch your children, people. Tell them not to leave the town limits. Not for any reason. Always bear in mind that we're dealing with scum. And these people have no morals, no values, no regard for human life. Adult or child. The farmers in this part of the county are breaking ground and planting. And they're doing it with guns strapped on. I don't want to see a man in this town walking around without a gunbelt on or a pistol stuck behind his belt. It's entirely conceivable that Max and Malone may even try to tree this town. If they do that, we want to be ready. Any woman here who doesn't know how to shoot, my wife will be conducting classes." He smiled. "She doesn't know that yet, but I'm sure she'll be more than willing to teach a class."

"You better watch out, Tom," a good-natured shout came out of the crowd. "Ella Mae learns to shoot, she's liable to fill your butt full of birdshot the next time you come home tipsy."

Tom Johnson grinned out of his suddenly red face. Tom liked his evening whiskey at the saloon.

"You're a fine one to talk, Matthew," the blacksmith yelled. "I 'member the time your woman tossed you out of the house with nothin' but your long-handles on."

The crowd burst out laughing and went their way. It was good laughter, the kind of laughter from men and women who had decided to make a stand of it. To not be pushed around and taken advantage of by thugs like Big Max Huggins.

"That laughter is good to hear," Joe said. "These folks have been down for a long time. I'm glad to see them back on their feet and standing tall." He paused to finish rolling his cigarette and light up. "And you're responsible for straightening their backbone, Smoke."

Smoke had been curious about something, and he figured now was the time to ask it. "Why didn't you do it, Joe?" he asked softly.

"Wondered when you'd get around to asking that. It's a fair question. Me and the wife left right after roundup three years ago. Took us a trip to see San Francisco. Spent all summer in California. Up and down the coast. The kids is all growed up and in college back east. We left right around the first day of May and didn't come back until late September. Hell, Smoke, it was all over by then. Big Max had built Hell's Creek, him and Red Malone was in cahoots around here, and Big Max's outlaws had cut the heart right out of this town."

He dropped the cigarette butt into the street and toed it dead. "I spent the next year just protecting my herds and my land. Red tried his damndest to run me out. But I wouldn't go. I lost . . ." He looked at one of his hands. "How many men, Chuck?"

"Four, boss. Skinny Jim, Davis, Don Morris, and John."

"Four men," Joe said quietly. "Good men who died for the brand. When Red finally got it through his head that I wasn't gonna be run out—and I can't prove it was Red doing it—he backed off and let me be."

"No way you can prove it was Red?"

"No. Not a chance. And I tried. That's on record at the territorial capitol. I raised some hell about it, and that, and with me and the boys fighting the night riders brought an end to it. They all wore hoods. Don't all cowards wear hoods or masks? I never was able to get a look at any of them." He smiled. "But I did recognize their horses. Unfortunately, that won't cut it in court." His eyes darted toward Sally as she stepped out of the hotel. "My wife is looking forward to you and your missus coming out. But I told her let's get this situ-

ation with Red and Max taken care of first, then we'll social-
ize."

"Yeah. My leaving town now, for any length of time,
would not be wise. Hey! I got an idea. How about a community dance and box supper?"

Sally walked up. "You took those thoughts right out of
my head, honey. Hi, Joe."

"Ma'am," the rancher touched the brim of his hat. "I
think that's a good idea."

Smoke's grin turned into a frown.

"What's the matter with you?" Sally asked.

"It's not a good idea."

"Why not?" she asked.

"It would mean too many people would be leaving their
homes unguarded. That might be all it would take for Max or
Red to burn someone out."

"Oh, pooh!" Sally said, stamping her foot.

"Smoke's right. I didn't think about that. Must be getting
old. Max and Red wouldn't pass up an opportunity like that.
And we couldn't keep it quiet. It'd be sure to leak out."

Smoke began smiling again.

"Now what?" Sally asked.

"I know how to have the dance and avoid trouble—at
least for the farmers and ranchers."

"How?" Joe asked. "What about Red and Max?"

"That's just it. We'll invite them."

10

Joe Walsh rode back to the ranch, chuckling as he went. Smoke Jensen was not only the slickest gunhandler he'd ever seen, but the man was damn smart, too.

There was no way a western man was going to turn down an invitation for a box supper and a dance with some really nice ladies. And both Max and Red would know that if anyone's place was torched that night, the fires could be seen for miles and there was no way either of them would leave Barlow alive.

"Slick," the rancher said. "Just damn slick."

"I had my mind all made up to not like Smoke Jensen," one of his hands said. "But I sure changed my mind. He's a right nice fellow."

"Yes, he is, Curly. I had my mind all made up to dislike the man. I figured he'd be a cocky son. Shows how wrong a man can be."

"I can't wait for this shindig," another hand said. "Been a long time since we had a good box supper and dance."

"Be a damn good time to put lead in Max Huggins and Red Malone too," Curly said. Curly and Skinny Jim had been close friends.

"Be none of that, Curly," Joe cautioned his hand. "Not unless they open the ball. Too much a chance that women and kids would get hit."

"I hate both them men," Curly replied. "With Jensen leadin' the pack, we could ride into Hell's Creek and wipe it out. I don't see why we don't do that."

"It might come to that, Curly," Joe said. "For sure, a lot of blood is going to be spilled before this is over."

"Just as long as the blood spilled comes out of Max Huggins and Red Malone and them that ride for them," Curly said. "I don't wanna die, but I'll go out happy if I know I got lead in Max or Malone."

Joe cut his eyes to the puncher. I'm going to have to watch him, the rancher thought. He's let his hate bubble very nearly out of control.

Sally and the ladies of Barlow met with the editor of the paper and designed and had printed dozens of invitations. Smoke made certain that Max Huggins and Red Malone received an invite.

Max stared at his invitation for a long time, being careful not to smudge the creamy bond paper. "What's Jensen doing this time?" he questioned the empty office. "He's got to have something up his sleeve." Then it came to him: If he attended this shindig and there was any trouble caused by his men, Max and Red would be gunned down on the spot, shot down like rabid skunks.

The big man was filled with grudging admiration for Jensen. Slick. Very, very slick. If he and Red didn't attend, Jensen and the others would be put on alert that something was going to happen out in the county, and it would be open season for any Lightning rider or gunhand from Hell's Creek caught out after dark.

He sent one of his bodyguards to fetch Val Singer, Warner Frigo, Dave Poe, and Alex Bell to his office.

"Me and Red will be attending this shindig," he informed the outlaw leaders. "And there better not be any trouble out in the county. You hold the reins tight on your boys . . . and I mean tight."

"It might be a trap," Val pointed out.

Max shook his head. "No. I don't think so. The people of Barlow are going to let off a little steam, that's all." He waved the invite. "This is their way of insuring that they can do so without fear of any trouble." He eyeballed them all. "And, by God, there isn't going to be any trouble. Those are my orders. See that they are carried out."

Red Malone had recovered from his beating at the hands—or fists—of Smoke Jensen. He stared hard and long at the invitation. He laid it on his desk and stared at it some more.

Was it a trap? He didn't think so. But he had a week to nose around and find out for sure.

"We goin', ain't we, Daddy?" Tessie asked, looking and reading over his shoulder.

Red turned his head and stared at his daughter, all blond and pretty and pouty and as worthless as her brother, Melvin. He loved them both—as much as Red Malone could love anything—but realized he had sired a whore and a nut.

"I don't know," he told her.

She pouted.

"Stop that, girl. You look like a fish suckin' in air."

Tessie plopped down in a chair and glared at him. "I got me a brand-new dress I got outta that catalog from New York, and I ain't had no chance to wear it. Now I got a chance to wear it and you tell me we might not go."

Red sighed. "Where's Melvin?"

"Same place he always is: shootin' at targets."

The boy was good with a gun, Red thought. Fast as a snake. But was he as fast as Jensen? Maybe. Just maybe the boy might do one thing in his life that was worthwhile: killing Smoke Jensen.

"Come on, Daddy!" Tessie said. "Let's go to the dance and have some fun."

Red stared at her, wondering whom she was bedding down with this time around.

The girl had more beaus than a dog had fleas.

"Pooh!" Tessie said. "I never get to do anything."

Except sneak out at night and behave like a trollop, Red thought. "I said I'd think about it," he told her. "Now go tell the cook to get dinner on the table. I'm hungry."

She sat in her chair and pouted.

"Move!" Red yelled.

She got up and left the room, shaking her butt like a hurdy-gurdy girl.

Red sighed and shook his big head. The only thing he regretted about his wife leaving him was that she didn't take those damn kids with her.

"Max has accepted," Sally told Smoke, holding out the note from Hell's Creek. "This came on the southbound stage a few minutes ago."

Smoke read the note and smiled. "One down and one to go. No word from Red yet?"

"No. Nothing."

"Smoke!" Jim's sharp call came from the outside. "Melvin Malone ridin' in. You watch yourself around this one. He's crazy as a skunk."

Smoke walked to the door and stepped out, after removing the hammer thongs from his .44's. He'd heard too much about Melvin to be careless around him. He watched the young man swing down from the saddle, being careful to keep the horse between himself and Smoke.

Smart, Smoke thought. He's no amateur.

Melvin stepped up on the boardwalk, studying Smoke as

hard as Smoke was studying him. Melvin was about six feet tall and well built, heavily muscled. He was handsome in a cruel sort of way. He wore two guns, the holsters tied down. The spurs he wore were big roweled ones, the kind that would hurt a horse, and Melvin looked the type who would enjoy doing that.

"Jensen," the young man said, stopping a few feet away. "I'm Mel Malone."

"Nice to see you, Mel. What's on your mind?"

Killing you, was the thought in Mel's head. He kept it silent. Big bastard, Mel thought. Big as them books made him out to be. "My pa said to give you a message. We'll be coming to the dance and box supper."

"Well, I'm glad to hear that, Mel. Yes, sir. Sure am. You be sure and tell Red I'm looking forward to seeing him again. He is feeling all right, now, isn't he?"

The young man stared at Smoke for a moment. Was Jensen trying to be smart-mouthed? He couldn't tell. "Uh, yeah. He feels just fine."

"That's good. Your sister Tessie makes a pretty good box supper, does she?"

"My sister couldn't fry an egg if the hen told her how," Mel replied. "But the cook can fry chicken that'll make you wanna slap your granny." Why the hell was he standing here talking about fried chicken with a man he was going to kill? He stared hard at Smoke. Fella seemed sort of likable.

Smoke chuckled. "Well, some women just never get the knack of cooking, Mel. Tell Red to take it easy now." Smoke turned and walked across the street, leaving Melvin alone on the boardwalk.

Feeling sort of stupid standing on the boardwalk all by himself, the young man wandered over to the saloon for a drink.

Sally watched it all from the window and she smiled.

"Smoke handled that just right," Jim said. "There wasn't nothing else to be said, so he just walked off leavin' Melvin standing there lookin' stupid. Which ain't hard to do, 'cause he is."

"But good with a gun," Sally remarked, watching the young man push open the batwings to the saloon. "I can tell by the way he carries himself. He walks a lot like Smoke."

"He's almost as fast as Smoke, ma'am. But not quite as good. But he's a dead shot, I'll give him that."

Sally felt just a twinge of worry that she quickly pushed aside. She had known what Smoke was when she met and later married him. She had long ago accepted that wherever he went, there would be men who would call him out. The West was slowly changing, but it would be years before gunfighting was finally banned.

When Melvin left town, Smoke was leaning up against an awning support watching him go. Smoke raised a hand in farewell. Melvin looked at him, then cut his eyes away, refusing to acknowledge the friendly gesture.

Smoke walked back to the office. Sally had just finished cleaning and straightening it up. "What do you think of Red's son, Smoke?"

Smoke poured a cup of coffee and sat down at his desk. He sipped and said, "He's crazy and he's cruel. I'll have to kill him someday."

Little by little, in small groups, Red's hands began drifting back into town for a drink or a meal or to buy this or that. So far, Red had not tried to buy any supplies from Marbly. The rancher was going to be in for a rude shock when he did.

Red's hands caused no trouble when in town. They had all noticed that every man in town was packing iron: the bartender, the editor of the *Bugle*, the store clerks . . . everybody. And they promptly took that news back to Red.

Red digested that bit of information with a sigh. "Then that's it, John," he told his foreman. "We've got to make a move and do it quick, before the town really gets together and runs our butts out of the country. And they'll do it eventually. Believe me."

"Before the dance, Red?"

Red shook his head. "No. After it. Maybe a week after it. Max has got some long-distance shooters comin' in from Europe. They was invited to come in here for a hunt long before Smoke Jensen showed up. They should be here this week. Early next week at the latest. We'll get things firmed up with Max after the party."

"Take Jensen out first?"

"I don't know. I think it'd be better to start working on the townspeople. I just don't know. Whatever Max decides to do, we got to back him up. That's the deal we made and I always keep my word." He looked around him and sniffed, a look of distaste crossing his face. "What in the name of God is that horrible smell?"

"The cook is tryin' to teach Tessie how to cook. Tessie is fixin' supper, so I'm told."

"Oh, my Lord. I'll eat with you boys tonight. What the Sam Hill is she cookin', skunk?"

"Fried chicken."

"She must have left the feathers on.

Henri Dubois and Paul Mittermaier were blissfully unaware of what was taking place in Barlow and Hell's Creek. They had seen the sights of St. Louis and were now ready to board the train west.

What they did not know was that they were under surveillance by agents of the U.S. Federal Marshal's office. They knew of the situation building in Barlow and Hell's Creek, and they also knew that with just a little help, Smoke Jensen would handle it and they would not have to get directly involved. The marshals sent a wire to the nearest town to Barlow, and the message was forwarded to Smoke Jensen by stage.

Smoke opened the envelope and read: Mercenaries left

St. Louis this a.m. No charges against Dubois or Mitter-maier. They are unaware of what is taking place in your area. Watch your back and handle situation as you see fit.

It was unsigned, but Smoke had a pretty good idea what federal office had sent it.

He showed the message to Jim and Sal. Neither man could understand why Smoke was smiling. Jim asked him.

"They have to come right through here, boys." He walked to a wall map and put his finger on a town south of them. "This is rail's end. From here to Barlow is either by horse-back or stage, and I'm betting they take the stage."

"And you got what in mind?" Sal asked.

"Any trouble that happens out in the county, you boys handle it. Starting day after tomorrow, I've got to meet the stage."

"I wonder what he's got in mind?" Jim asked Sal after Smoke left the office.

"Be fun to watch, whatever it is."

"You reckon the Frenchman and the German will see the humor in it?" Jim asked with a grin.

"Somehow I doubt it. I really do."

"The saloons are runnin' out of whiskey," Max was in-formed. "And the boys is gettin' right testy."

Max took a long pull on his stogie. "Yeah, and I had me five boxes of cigars on that shipment Jensen seized, too. So what else is new? I can't find any freight haulers to handle our orders. The only option we have is some outfit out of Canada, and by the time all the red tape is over with, it'll be six months before we get any supplies."

Alex Bell shifted in the chair. "Max, the boys ain't gonna stand still for this very much longer. They all got cash money to spend and nothin' to buy. The women is raisin' holy hell 'cause the boys is unhappy. Somethin' has got to pop, and damn soon."

Max Huggins's little empire was crumbling at the edges and he didn't know what to do about it. For the umpteenth time since Jensen entered the picture, the thought that he should pull out entered his brain. And for the same number of times, the thought galled him; but with each revival of the thought, the intensity of the sourness was somewhat lessened as common sense fought to prevail.

"I'll talk to the boys," he finally said to Alex. "Damnit!" he cursed, pounding a fist on the desk and scattering papers. "He's just one man. Just one man! He's not a god, not invincible. There has to be a way."

"There is," Alex said. "Me and Val and the others been talkin'."

Max waited, staring hard at the outlaw gang leader.

"Wipe the town out. Kill every man, woman, and child. It can be done, and you know it."

"Damnit, Alex," Max said, struggling to maintain his patience with the gang leader. "This is 1883, man. The country is connected by telegraph wires and railroads. Ten years ago, I would have said yes to your proposal. But not now. I think the press would pick it up, and the public would be up in arms and all over us. We'd have federal marshals and troops in here before you could blink."

"Fires happen all the time, Max," Alex pointed out. "We pick a night with a good strong wind and that town would go up like a tinderbox. You think about that."

"The people would still remain, Alex."

"Maybe not. Maybe not enough of them to do any good. Lots of folks die in town fires. And charred skin don't show no bullet holes. By the time the newspapers got 'hold of it, them folks would be rottin' in the ground and nobody could do nothin' about it."

Max jabbed out his cigar in an ashtray. With a slow expelling of breath, he said, "We may have to do that, Alex. It's a good plan, I'm thinking, but very risky." He stared hard at the outlaw. "Have you ever killed a child, Alex?"

"Yeah. I gut-shot a kid durin'a bank stickup; sqalled like a hog at butcherin' time. I shot him in the head to shut him up. I shot half a dozen or more ridin' with Bloody Bill Anderson. All the boys has. It ain't no big deal."

Max nodded his head in agreement. He had killed several children—accidentally and deliberately—during his bloody life. And as Alex had stated: It was no big deal. He had no nightmares about it. They got in the way, they were disposed of. It was all a matter of one's personal survival.

The plan that Alex was proposing would have to be very carefully worked out. There could be no room for error or miscalculation. And the men involved would have to be chosen carefully, for if word ever leaked out, nationwide condemnation would be certain to follow—quickly. It was a good plan, but very chancy. Very chancy.

"What do you think, Max?"

"It would take a lot of planning, Alex. And the men would have to be chosen carefully. The ones who don't ride on the raid must never know what took place. Now, then, is that possible?"

The outlaw and murderer thought about that. Slowly, he shook his head affirmatively. "Yeah. Forty men could pull it off. Any more than that would be too many. Most of the men here would keep their mouths shut about it. Out of the whole bunch, maybe ten might blab later on."

"Dispose of them now, Alex," Max gave the killing orders. "Once that is done, we start planning on destroying the town."

Alex rose with a grin on his face. "My pleasure, boss."

11

Something nagged at Smoke as he walked through the town. He walked up and down the streets, on the boardwalks wherever they were, on the dusty paths where they had not yet been built.

Something was wrong, and Smoke could not pull it out of his brain. Then it came to him. The town lacked adequate water barrels for bucket brigades in case of fire.

Swiftly, he walked back to his office and sent Jim out to round up Tom Johnson, Judge Garrison, and several others in the town.

"What's the drill in case of fire?" he asked bluntly, as was his way.

"Why . . ." Tom looked puzzled. "There isn't any."

"There will be by dark. Judge, alert the people. I want water barrels by every store and every house; buckets placed nearby. And I want those barrels to stay full at all times. We have an old pumper down at the livery stable. See that it's checked out and the hoses inspected for leaks. Benson," he looked at the blacksmith, "you're in charge of the fire brigade."

The blacksmith nodded his head. "You're thinkin' Max might try burning us out?"

"That's exactly what I'm thinking. I'll start rounding up volunteers to clear out the brush and other cover that surrounds the town. I'll ride out to Joe's place and see if he'll lend us some hands to help. Check out and destroy any place where sharpshooters could hide and pick us off. Get on it now, Sal."

The man quietly left the room.

"Max would do it, too," Judge Garrison said. "He told me when he first confronted me that if I didn't do exactly as he said, he'd pick out a child and kill her in front of me. I didn't like what I was doing, but I figured it was the only way to save some children's lives."

"I understand, Judge." Smoke leaned back in his chair. "If we can get most of this done by the dance night and keep a close eye on Max to check his reaction, we can know pretty well that he had burning us out in mind. Then he'll have to come up with another plan."

"He will," Judge Garrison said. "The man is totally and utterly ruthless."

"What are you gonna do with them mercenaries when they step off the stage, Smoke?" Jim asked.

"Oh, welcome them to town, Jim," Smoke said with a smile. "Roll out the red carpet."

That afternoon, Smoke met the southbound stage and was pleased to see it was full, with several men riding on top. The driver handed the mailbag to Marbly's wife—who was the town's postmistress—and seeing there were no passengers departing Barlow, he hollered his team forward.

Those men perched precariously on top gave Smoke some extremely dirty looks as the stagecoach pulled out. Its next stop would be a way station some fifty miles south, where it would change teams, another stop near Salmon Lake for food and a fresh team, and then on into Missoula, some one hundred twenty-five miles from Barlow.

"Stage was full today," Mrs. Marbly noted, handing Smoke a letter posted from Kalispell, addressed to Sally Jensen, the Grand Hotel, Barlow, Montana Territory. "That means some are giving up on Hell's Creek."

"That it does, ma'am," Smoke said. "Those were all gamblers riding on top. The inside was filled with saloon girls. When the gamblers and the wilted roses start leaving a town, it's like they say about rats leaving a ship. It's about to sink."

"Good riddance to bad rubbish, I say," Mrs. Marbly said. "I'm not an evil-hearted person, Marshal Jensen. My motto is if you can't say something good about a person, don't say anything at all. But that motto has been sorely put to the test by those hooligans and trash up at Hell's Creek. If God were to strike them all dead, I would dance on their graves, Lord forgive me."

She walked back into the store. A good, decent woman who had been pushed just too far, one time too often. Smoke knew she carried a Smith & Wesson pocket .38 in her purse. And he had no doubts but that she would use it.

He took the letter back to the hotel, gave it to Sally, and waited until she had read it.

"You guessed, of course, that it was from Victoria?"

He nodded his head.

"This was posted yesterday in Kalispell—that's only thirty miles away from Hell's Creek—but it's still fast service. There have been a rash of killings in Hell's Creek. Outlaws killing outlaws. One of them managed to escape from the town and came to Robert for treatment. He told Robert that Big Max had ordered the killings. He didn't know why, but that something big was up. Then the man died. Robert—he's no fool—took the body back into Hell's Creek and told Big Max he had found the body on the road and thought it should be reported to the authorities. Big Max thanked him for being such a civic-minded person and told Robert he'd take care of it. Max knows that Robert is scared to try to leave because of the threats made against Lisa. What does it mean, Smoke?"

"Probably that Val Singer and Warner Frigo and the other gang leaders are getting rid of those they feel might not be able to keep their mouths shut once this something big goes down. So much for honor among thieves."

"And this something big is? . . ."

"Probably a raid against the town. A raid that includes killing everyone here. Sally, have the hotel pack me a bait of food. I'm going to take a little trip. I should be back by late tomorrow afternoon. I'll arrange for Jim and Sal to meet the stage in case Dubois and Mittermaier should arrive; but I think it's still a couple of days early for that."

"Where are you going, honey?"

"To get the one thing this town needs, Sally." He grinned. "A doctor."

Smoke had checked the land office and knew where the Turner spread was located. He spared his horse, resting often, and rode into Big Max Huggins's country well after dark. He avoided the town by several miles and pulled up at what he hoped was the Turner spread about ten o'clock.

He circled the house to see if they kept a dog and was relieved to find they did not. Smoke picketed Star and slipped up toward the house. He flattened himself against the woodshed when the front door opened and a man stepped out. The man closed the door behind him and stood in the front yard, breathing in the cool night air.

"Dr. Turner?" Smoke called softly.

The man spun around, startled.

"Take it easy, Doctor," Smoke said. "I'm friendly. I'm going to walk toward you, both my hands in plain sight. OK?"

"Who are you?" the doctor demanded.

"The name is Jensen. Smoke Jensen." Smoke walked closer.

"Hold it right there!" the doctor warned. "I have a gun."

"No, you don't," Smoke replied, stepping closer. "And even if you did, it's doubtful you'd know how to use it."

Smoke stopped a few feet from the man and stared at him.

"If you're Smoke Jensen, tell me about yourself."

"My wife's name is Sally. We live in Colorado on a spread we named the Sugarloaf. My wife went to college back east with your wife, Victoria. Sally calls her Vicky. Vicky lost her parents while she was in school and had to work very hard to get through. You have one child that lived, Lisa. Your wife can't have any more children. Sally got a letter from Vicky today, telling us about the recent killings in Hell's Creek and the outlaw who staggered up to this ranch and told you about it. You got this ranch by befriending an old man who was visiting back east. You . . ."

"Enough." The doctor held up a hand, visible in the faint light of a quarter moon. He smiled and stuck out the hand for Smoke to shake it. "Welcome to our home, Mr. Jensen."

Smoke shook the hand. "We don't have much time, Doctor. Things are going to blow wide open around here very soon, and you and your family have got to get clear. Let's go in the house and talk."

Lisa was in bed, asleep. Vicky was introduced to Smoke. She stepped back and inspected him, good humor in her eyes. Smoke liked her immediately. He would reserve judgment on the doctor.

"Sally always could pick them," Vicky said. "You are one hell of a man, Smoke Jensen."

"Vicky," her husband said in a long-suffering tone.

Smoke laughed. "Relax, Robert. Sally can occasionally let the words fly herself. I can see why these two were friends at school."

"How about some coffee and something to eat, Smoke?" Vicky asked.

"That would be nice. While I'm eating, you two can pack."

That stopped them both in their tracks. Robert asked, "Pack? Where are we going?"

"Getting out of here." Smoke found the cups and poured his own coffee. Very quickly, he explained what was going on. "As far as your ranch goes, if Max burns the buildings down, you've still got the land. You don't have any cattle or any hands. You can always rebuild. You can't do anything from the grave. So pack. We're pulling out."

Smoke drank his coffee and ate a sandwich. Then he went outside and hitched up the teams to a wagon and a buggy. He helped the doctor load his medical equipment onto the wagon, then their luggage and a few possessions from the house. Lisa was awake and wide-eyed as she solemnly stared at the most famous gunfighter in the West.

"I'm surprised Lisa doesn't have a dog," Smoke said.

"I did," the little girl said, sadness in her voice. "Patches was his name. A man killed it a few months ago."

"A rather unsavory character named Warner Frigo rode up into the yard and shot him," Robert said. "It was another one of Max Huggins's little not-too-subtle warnings."

Smoke knelt down and, with a gentleness in his voice that surprised Robert and Vicky, said to Lisa, "We'll get you another dog, Lisa. It won't take the place of Patches, I know that. You'll always remember him. But you can love your new puppy, too. How about it?"

"I'd like that, Mister Smoke. I really would."

Smoke picked her up with no more effort than picking up a feather pillow and smiled. "First thing after we get you all settled is a new puppy, Lisa."

"Frigo is a bad man," the girl said. "He's awful. Only cruel people kill dogs who aren't doing them any harm."

"That's right, Lisa. That's exactly right. Don't you worry about Frigo. I'll take care of him." He set her back down and said, "Let's go, people. We've got a long haul ahead of us."

Vicky walked through the house once more, and there was sadness in her eyes. "I've grown to love this old house,

this land with the mountains and the eagles and all its vastness." She blew out a lamp, plunging the room into darkness. "I pray that Max and his hooligans will let the house
stand." She sighed and squared her shoulders. "But if they
don't . . . we'll rebuild."

"That's the spirit," Smoke told her. "But you might decide
to relocate down in Barlow."

"Why would we do that?" Robert asked.

"Because I intend to destroy Hell's Creek, that's why.

Because with the wagons they would have to come within
a half mile of Hell's Creek, Smoke wrapped the horses' hooves
in sacking when they got close. Out of habit, he checked his
guns, loading them up full. The action did not escape the
eyes of the doctor and his wife. Lisa had fallen asleep in the
back of the wagon, lying on a soft comforter and wrapped up
in a blanket, for the night was cool.

"Rumor has it you've killed twenty-five men, Smoke,"
Robert said.

"Closer to two hundred, I reckon," Smoke corrected.

"Two hundred!" the doctor blurted out. "Two hundred men?"

"Killed twenty-five when I was about nineteen or twenty,
I think I was. They raped my wife and then killed her and our
son. I tracked them down to a silver camp on the Uncompahgre and read to them from the Scriptures, so to speak."

"You were only nineteen?" Vicky breathed the question.

"Maybe twenty. I don't remember."

"So young," Robert muttered.

"Oh, I dropped my first man when I was about seventeen,
I think I was. After Pa died an old mountain man named
Preacher took me in and raised me. It was a shooting just
west of the Needle Mountains. They call the place Rico now.
Two men braced me in the trading post. Pike and another
man. Never did know his name. I killed them both."

Robert and Victoria listened in silence, their mouths open

in shock and fascination, their expressions much like one would wear while gazing at a rattlesnake.

"Me and Preacher, we rode over to what's now called Pagosa Springs—that's Indian for healing water. Two men called me out over there. Man named Haywood and another fellow who was Pike's brother." Smoke tied another piece of sacking in place. "I dropped Haywood and let Pike's brother live. I only shot him twice, in the leg and the arm.

"Me and Preacher rode on over to La Plaza de los Leones; that's on the Cuchara River. It's now called Walsenburg. You see, I was looking for the men who killed my brother and my pa. Killed seven that day and hung one. Casey was his name.

"We drifted on over to Canon City, looking for a man named Ackerman. He found us, him and five of his gang. Killed five, left one alive."

"Lord Jesus," Robert said softly. "That's thirty-three men."

"Oh, I haven't even gotten started yet," Smoke said. "Me and Preacher, we spent the winter back at Brown's Hole, then come spring we drifted out again. That summer I met Nicole and we got married. Sort of. Within a year it all fell to pieces. Bounty hunters got lead in Preacher and I thought they'd killed him. They did kill Nicole and the baby. That's when I rode up to the silver camp with hate in my heart."

"And there have been many more dead men since then?" Robert asked.

"More than I can count, Robert. They just keep coming at me. It was early spring in . . . oh, '74 I think it was. I rode over into Idaho looking for the rest of the men who killed my pa and my brother. Town called Bury. I was going by the name of Buck West."

The horses' hooves muffled, the small party moved out.

"A man called Big Jack braced me at a trading post. His partner buried him out back. I rode on. I had ten thousand dollars on my head at that time, and a lot of bounty hunters were hard after me.

"It was in Challis that two gunhands called me out in the

street. I think their names were Carson and Phillips. After I killed them, the marshal asked me to leave. I don't blame him, and I left.

"I rode into Bury with no one knowing who I really was. I was looking to kill the last of the three men who killed my pa and brother: Josh Richards, Wiley Potter, and Keith Stratton. Sally was teaching school there. I saw my sister Janey for the first time in ten years. She was Richard's mistress. She didn't recognize me right off.

"I was walking Sally back to her home when two gunhandlers braced me on the street. Dickerson and Russell. I dropped them both.

"Things turned both tragic and funny after that. Sally lost her job school-teaching and went to live in a whorehouse."

"A whorehouse!" Victoria almost shouted the word. "Sally in a whorehouse?"

Smoke chuckled. "Yep. Oh, she didn't work there. She just lived there."

"My heavens!" Robert muttered.

"Ol' boy on the SRP payroll braced me. I don't remember his name. I had to kill him. It was that day that Janey recognized me as her brother." Smoke cut his eyes and turned his head. He held up a hand for the wagons to stop.

"What's the matter?" Robert asked.

"Something out there," Smoke said.

"How do you know that?"

"Star's ears just came up. A horse is as good as a dog about warning you."

They all heard the clop of horses' hooves and watched as two men rode out of the darkness and up to their wagon.

Both of the men had guns in their hands, the hammers jacked back.

"Well, now," one said. "Ain't this a sight? The doctor and his pretty wife tryin' to slip out, and Smoke Jensen leadin' them. Look here, Jensen. Look down the barrel of the gun that's gonna kill you!"

12

All Robert or Vicky would remember in the retelling of the event was a series of roaring gunshots. What they did not know was that at the sound of the horses' hooves, Smoke had wrapped the reins around the saddle horn and filled both his hands with .44's.

And neither Robert nor Vicky had seen the third man; but Smoke had.

It was all over in two heartbeats. Three men lay dead or dying on the ground. Robert started to climb down from the wagon.

"Sit down!" Smoke's words were sharp. "Pick up those reins and whap those horses on the butt. We've got to move and do it fast."

"But those men . . ." Robert protested.

Smoke knee-reined Star up to the wagon. When he spoke, his words were low and savage. "Mister, do you want to see your wife and little girl spread-eagled on the ground, being raped, over and over again, until dawn?"

"No. Of course not! But . . ."

"Then shut up and drive this wagon." Smoke slapped one

horse on the butt and the team jumped forward, the doctor hanging onto the reins. "Go, Vicky!" Smoke shouted. "Stay on this road south. Don't get off of it. I'll catch up in about an hour. Move!"

Smoke jumped off Star and grabbed the outlaws' rifles from the saddle boots. He jerked off their gunbelts and swiftly loaded the two Winchesters and the Henry up full. "You gotta help me!" one gut-shot outlaw moaned. "I'm hard-hit."

"That's your problem," Smoke told him. "You were going to kill me, remember?"

"You're a heartless bastard, ain't you, Jensen?"

"No," Smoke replied, levering a round in each chamber of the rifles. "Just a realist, that's all. Now either shut up or die; one or the other."

He left the man moaning in the road and, leading Star, got himself into position in the rocks above the road, in the center of the curve, several sticks of capped and fused dynamite beside him. He made him a little smoldering pocket of punk to light the fuses and waited. He could hear the pounding of hooves, the riders coming hard.

He lit a fuse and judged his toss, placing the charge about fifty feet in front of the laboring horses. The dynamite blew and the horses panicked, throwing riders in all directions. Most of them landed, rolled, and came up on their boots, running for cover. Several lay still, badly hurt and unconscious.

Smoke worked the lever on the Henry as fast as he could and knocked down half-a-dozen riders. He grinned when he saw where many of the gunhands had taken shelter. He poured dirt over the smoldering punk to kill it and left his position, working his way back and then up to about a hundred yards above the road.

He lit another stick of dynamite and tossed it in the middle of a rock pile above the men, then another stick. The explosions jarred the rocks loose and sent them bouncing and crashing onto the men below.

Smoke ran for Star, jumped into the saddle, and was gone into the night. It would take the outlaws anywhere from thirty minutes to two hours to round up their horses.

When he caught up with Robert and Vicky, he halted the parade.

"What did you do back there?" Robert asked, his eyes wide. "We heard explosions and shots."

"I showed them the error of their evil ways and put them on the path of righteousness."

Vicky laughed out loud.

"In other words, you killed them?"

"Lord knows, I sure tried. We'll go on for a few miles and then stop and make camp."

"But those men of Hell's Creek . . . they'll be after us, won't they?"

"Not that bunch," Smoke assured the doctor. "I took the guts right out of them back yonder."

Five miles farther, off the road and camped in a little draw, Smoke drank his coffee and ate a cold sandwich. Lisa had tried to stay awake but finally closed her eyes and was sound asleep.

"Tell us the rest of the story," Victoria urged.

"Where was I?" Smoke asked.

"Killing people," Robert muttered.

Smoke suppressed a chuckle. He had a hunch the doctor was made of stronger stuff than he appeared. "Well, on the day in Bury that my real identity got known, I was trapped in the town. I'd just left the whorehouse talking with Sally and was coming up an alley when I was braced. That ol' boy let it be known that he was gonna collect that thirty thousand dollars that Potter and Richards and Stratton had put on my head. After I shot that fella, I told him to be sure and tell Saint Peter that none of this was my idea."

Robert was shaking his head but listening intently.

"Before I got out of that alley, another gunny braced me. I left him on the ground and got back to my horse. I put the reins in my teeth and charged the mob that was comin' up the street, led by a crooked sheriff name of Reese.

"Drifter—that was my horse—killed one with his hooves and I shot another gunhand name of Jerry. Me and Drifter scattered gunhands all over the main street of Bury, left that town, and linked up with Preacher and a bunch of old mountain men that was camped up in the mountains outside of town. Let me see . . . there was Preacher, Tennysee, Audie— he was a midget—Beartooth, Dupre, Greybull, Nighthawk— he was an Indian . . . a Crow—Phew, Deadlead, Powder Pete, Matt—he was a Negro. Matt was the youngest of the bunch and he was about seventy.

"We blew the roadbank in and trapped those in the town. Wasn't but two ways in or out, and we closed them both. We gave the citizens a chance to leave and a lot of them did. In the days that followed, before I met a bunch in a ghost town, we got Sally and the wilted flowers out and then I went head-hunting."

"How many men did you kill during those days?"Victoria asked.

"Any who tried to kill me, Vicky. A half a dozen or so, I imagine. On that day we burned down Bury and I met Richards and his bunch in that ghost town, the first man to brace me was a man called Davis. Then Williams and Cross. Then a hired gun name of Simpson faced me. Then there was Martin and a man I didn't know. Rogers and Sheriff Reese came after me. I plugged Rogers and Reese's horse crushed him. I shot Turkel off a rooftop and Dritt shot off part of my ear." He lifted one hand. "This part. I dropped three more. Britt, Harris, and Smith. Then Williams got lead in me and I blew Rogers to hell with a shotgun. Brown come up and I dropped him.

"I used my knife to pick the lead out of my leg and wrapped a bandana around it. I believe there were three more left. I plugged two and used a rifle to blow a hired gun name of Fenerty out of it."

Smoke's voice softened as memories filled him, taking him back years. Robert and Victoria could practically feel the pain of those years as they strained to hear him.

"All right, you bastards!" Smoke yelled, tall and bloody in the smoky main street of the ghost town. "Richards, Potter, Stratton. Face me, if you've got the nerve."

The sharp odor of sweat mingled with blood and gunsmoke filled the still summer air as four men stepped out into the bloody, dusty street.

Richards, Potter, and Stratton stood at one end of the street. A tall bloody figure stood at the other. All their guns were in leather.

"You son of a bitch!" Stratton screamed, his voice as high-pitched as a woman's. "You ruined it all. Damn you!" He clawed for his pistol.

Smoke drew, cocked, and fired before Stratton could clear leather.

Potter grabbed for his gun. Smoke shot him dead, holstered his pistol, and waited for Richards to make his play.

Richards was sure he could beat Smoke. He had not moved. He stood with a faint smile on his lips, staring at Smoke.

"You ready to die?" Smoke asked the man.

"As ready as I'll ever be, I suppose." Richards's hands were steady. There was no fear in his voice. "Janey gone?"

"Yeah. She took your money and pulled out."

Richards smiled. "That's one tough babe, Jensen."

"Among other things."

"Been a long run, hasn't it, Jensen?"

"It's just about over."

"What happens to all my holdings?"

"I don't care what happens to the mines. The miners can have them. I'm giving all your stock and the lands they graze on to decent honest punchers and homesteaders."

A puzzled look spread over Richards's face. He waved his hand at the carnage that lay all around them. "You did . . . all this for nothing?"

Someone moaned, the sound painfully inching up the dusty street.

"I did it for my pa, my brother, my wife, and our baby son."

"But killing me won't bring them back!"

"No. But it will insure that you never do anything like that again."

"I can truthfully say that I wish I had never heard the name Jensen."

"You'll never hear it again after this day, Richards."

"One way to find out, Jensen." He drew and fired. Richards was snake-quick but he hurried his shot, the lead digging up dirt at Smoke's boots.

Smoke's shot hit the man in the right shoulder, spinning him around. Richards grabbed for his left-hand gun and Smoke fired again, the slug striking the man in the chest. He struggled to level his pistol. Smoke shot him again, the slug hitting Richards in the belly. Richards sat down hard in the street.

Smoke walked up the street to stand over the man. Richards reached out for the pistol that had fallen from his numb hand. Smoke kicked it away.

Blood filled the man's mouth. The light began to fade around him. Richards said, "You'll . . . meet . . ."

Smoke never found out whom he was supposed to meet. Richards toppled over on his face and died.

Robert and Vicky were silent for a few moments after Smoke had finished his story.

Vicky said, "And after that?"

"I got Sally and we took off, heading for Colorado. We've been there ever since." Smoke tossed the dregs of his coffee into the night. "We best get some sleep. We still got a pull ahead of us come morning."

* * *

Smoke led the wagon and buggy into Barlow. The group was met with cheers from the onlookers. Draper was there with his camera, taking pictures.

"I must admit," Robert said, "I rather like the welcoming committee."

Sally rushed out of the hotel and the two women hugged each other. With Lisa in tow, the ladies disappeared into the hotel. They had a lot of catching up to do.

"I'm teaching the women of the town who don't know much about guns to shoot," Sally told her friend. "Classes are this afternoon. Do you have any jeans?"

"Britches?" Vicky looked horrified.

"Sure. It's a changing world, Victoria. We'll get you some at Marbly's."

"Everything's been quiet, Smoke," Sal said, walking up. He shook hands with the doctor, his eyes sizing the man up. He took note that the doctor did not wear a gun.

"Do I pass inspection?" Robert asked with a smile.

"Won't know that until the shootin' starts."

"I've done more than my share of hunting, I assure you," Robert replied stiffly.

"Deer don't shoot back," Sal said, then walked off.

Robert looked around him. The people standing around them were all friendly-looking and he had shook a lot of hands. He also had noticed that every man was armed. Every man. Including the editor of the *Bugle*. No doubt about it, the doctor thought. This town is braced for trouble.

"Mrs. Jensen told us what you were doing yesterday, Smoke," Tom Johnson said. "We fixed up an office for Dr. Turner. It's right next to his house."

Smoke grasped the doctor by the shoulder. "You and Victoria get settled in, Robert. Big doings come Saturday night." He smiled. "The town is throwing a party."

* * *

Forty-eight hours before the dance and box supper, Smoke met the northbound stage and knew he'd hit pay dirt when two nattily-dressed men stepped off to stretch their legs. They were the only two passengers on the stage. Northbound business had dwindled since Smoke had arrived in Barlow and pinned on a badge. The two men were dressed like dandies but their eyes, cold and emotionless, gave them away.

Henri Dubois and Paul Mittermaier.

Smoke had talked with the driver several days before, setting things up, and the driver nodded his head at Smoke's glance. "It's gonna be about an hour 'fore we pull out, boys," he called. "I got to change this cracked brake lever and one of the pads. Yonder's the saloon. I'll give a hoot and a holler when I'm ready to go."

The team was led away, team and coach heading for the barn.

Henri and Paul headed for the saloon. One of the Circle W hands, Wesson, had agreed to his part in the action. He walked toward the men and slammed a shoulder into the big German.

"Watch where you're goin', stupid!" Wesson said.

"Get out of my way, you ignorant lout!" the German replied.

"What the hell did you call me?" The hand faced him.

"Back off, Paul," Henri said softly.

"What's the matter?" Wesson said with a sneer. "Your buddy have to do your fightin' for you?"

Paul drew back a fist and Wesson popped him on the nose. Henri gave Wesson a blow to the jaw just as the saloon cleared, all of Joe's hands pouring out. The Circle W crew then proceeded to kick the snot out of the pair of assassins, leaving them unconscious on the street.

"Clear out," Smoke told them. "I'll see you all come Saturday night. Thanks, boys."

"Our pleasure, Smoke," Curly grinned around the words. He looked down at the unconscious and badly battered men.

"Them ol' boys won't be doin' much of anything for a week or two. Maybe longer."

The Circle W crew rode out of town.

"Now what?" Jim asked.

Smoke grinned and reached into his coat pocket, pulling out a bottle of opium-based elixir. "I bought a full case of this from a drummer last week. By the time these two wake up, they're going to be on a train, heading back east. Come on, help me drag them off the street."

They dragged the unconscious men into an alley and stripped them of their duded-up clothes, dressing them in filthy, ragged shirts and jeans. Henri moaned and tried to sit up. Smoke popped him on the noggin with a cosh he'd taken to carrying and the Frenchman laid back down.

With the two men now dressed like bums, Smoke poured a half bottle of knock-out medicine down each of their throats and placed then in the back of a freight wagon.

"Keep them unconscious," Smoke told the grinning freighters who had been more than willing to participate in the game. Anything to get rid of Max Huggins and his gang of outlaws. "When you get down to Helena, pour a bottle of the elixir down them and toss them in an empty eastbound railcar. They'll be somewhere in Nebraska when they wake up."

"Will do, Smoke," the freighter told him. "Don't worry about a thing. Man, this is more fun than I thought it'd be. We was lookin' forward to seeing a shoot-out; but, hell, this is better." Laughing, the freighters pulled out, joining other empty freight wagons on the pull back south.

"Now what do you have in the back of that devious mind of yourn?" Sal asked, unable to wipe the grin off his face.

"Let's go inspect their luggage. I want to see these fancy guns that were going to be used to kill me."

Sal whistled when Smoke opened the gun cases. Both men had seen rifles of this type before, but neither had seen one so duded-up. They were Winchester high-wall, falling block rifles. Single shot.

Smoke hefted one. The rifle had been reworked and the balance was perfect. The telescope was about two feet long, and the shells looked like either the German or the Frenchman or both had carefully and painstakingly loaded their own.

"That bullet would travel about three miles before it knocked you down," Sal said, inspecting one cartridge.

"You know," Smoke said, "most guns are tools. A man uses one snake-killing, or varmint-killing, or to protect himself or his loved ones. I've driven tacks and nails in horseshoes with the butt of my pistols. But these rifles are meant for only one thing."

"Yeah," Sal agreed, closing the lid to the gun case. "Man-killin'."

13

The people started coming into town for the dance and box supper during the middle of the day on a beautiful Saturday afternoon.

Most would spend the night camped under their wagons or in the wagon bed under canvas if it was raining. A few took rooms at the Grand Hotel.

Just before dusk, Smoke had taken his bath and dressed in a black suit, white shirt with string tie and slipped into his just-polished boots. He strapped on his guns and looked in on Sally. She had dressed in a simple gingham outfit; but with Sally, she could make a flour sack look good.

She gave her hair a final pat and turned to Smoke. "Are you expecting trouble tonight, honey?"

"Yes, I am. When Joe Walsh's crew meet up with Red Malone's Lightning crew, anything is apt to happen."

"All the crews coming in?"

"As far as I know. Joe really stripped his herds this spring, keeping mostly young stuff. So night-herding is not that essential."

"Shooting trouble?"

"No. We've taken care of that. All guns will be checked upon entering the dance area. If any object to that, they can carry their butts back home. If any trouble starts, it will be fists."

"But you and Sal and Jim will be armed?"

Smoke smiled. "Oh, yes, honey."

"This promises to be quite an interesting night."

"That . . . is one way of putting it, yes."

They walked down the stairs and were a head-turning couple, Sally a beautiful woman and Smoke a strikingly handsome man in a rugged sort of way.

They joined Dr. and Mrs. Turner in the hotel dining room for coffee.

"I will say this, Smoke," Robert said. "I find the people of Barlow a refreshing change from the hoodlums and rowdies of Hell's Creek. We both like it here."

"I'm glad you do. And I hope you decide to stay. It's going to be a growing little town."

"But you and Sally will eventually move on?"

"Oh, yes. Back to the Sugarloaf. It's home. We'll get this situation straightened out here and be back home in early fall."

"Will there be trouble tonight?" Vicky asked.

"Probably." Smoke gave her an honest reply. "But it won't be gunplay."

"Anyone from Hell's Creek made an appearance yet?" Robert asked.

"Not to my knowledge. But they'll be along. They can't afford not to show up."

They looked up, and Tom Walsh and his Circle W crew rode in and dismounted. Tom drove the buggy, sitting beside his wife. Mrs. Walsh joined the ladies in the dining room, while Smoke and Dr. Turner stepped outside to join Joe and his crew.

"All right, boys," Smoke spoke to the Circle W hands. "This is the way it's going to be this night. When you enter the dance and box supper area, you check your guns with Mrs. Marbly. The only people who will be armed will be me and my deputies. And I've appointed several special deputies for this night. Anyone who doesn't think they can abide by that rule, haul your ashes out of town."

"Suits me." Curly was the first to speak. "But it's gonna be interestin' to see you take Melvin Malone's guns offen him."

"I'll take them," Smoke replied. "Or tomorrow his dad will be burying him."

Tom Johnson, one of the special deputies, rode in from the north, just as Benson, another of the special deputies, rode up from the south end of town. Johnson said, "Big Max and half a dozen of his gunslicks coming in."

"Red Malone and his crew are just outside of town," Benson added.

"Get your shotguns, boys," Smoke said. "Line up with me on the boardwalk."

Johnson, Marbly, Benson, and Toby got sawed-off shotguns and lined up in front of the hotel, two on each side of Smoke. Jim and Sal stood a dozen yards off, one on each side of the five. They too were armed with Greeners.

Smoke knew some of the men who rode in with Max: Alex Bell, Dave Poe, Val Singer. He did not know the others with them. But he knew the breed: hired guns.

"I don't like this," Val muttered, eyeballing the shotgun-armed men on the boardwalk.

"Relax," Max told him. "It's just a show of force."

"Hell of a welcoming committee, boss," John Steele said.

"Don't nobody do nothin' stupid," Red Malone said to his men. "Them express guns would kill everybody in the whole damn street. Let's find out what's going on."

One of Red's hands was driving the buggy with the elegantly gowned Tessie. She took one look at Smoke and said, "Oohhh, I think I'm in love!"

In heat would be more like it, the hand thought. But he kept that to himself.

Tessie's exploits were known throughout the entire county—and several adjacent counties.

The crews of Max and Red swung their horses and faced Smoke and his deputies.

"Good evening, gentlemen, Miss Tessie," Smoke said. "Welcome to Barlow."

"What's the idea of all this force?" Red demanded in a loud voice.

Smoke ignored him. "It's a beautiful night, people, so we decided to move everything outdoors. The dance area is roped off, as is the box supper area. We have plenty of chairs and benches for your comfort if you didn't bring blankets to sit on. That tent set up just before you enter the entertainment area is where you will check your guns."

Smoke had stepped off the boardwalk as he was speaking, moving close to Mel Malone.

"I'll be damned if I'll check my guns!" the young man said.

Smoke jerked him off his horse, slapped him twice, ripped the gunbelt from him, and tossed guns and belt into a horse trough. He did it so quickly no one had a chance to interfere.

Smoke faced the young man as he spoke to his deputies. "Anybody who makes a grab for a gun, start killing the whole bunch of them."

Hammers were eared back on the sawed-off shotguns and the muzzles leveled at the mounted men.

"Now, hold on!" Red bellowed. Sawed-off shotguns at this range would tear them all apart.

Smoke grabbed Melvin by his fancy shirt and jerked him close. "You say one more word to me about what you're not going to do, sonny-boy, and I'll break both your goddamn arms so you'll never be able to pick up a gun again. You understand me?"

For the first time in his life, Melvin Malone knew real fear. It clutched at him, souring his stomach. He looked into the eyes of Smoke Jensen and saw death staring back at him. Death rode a fiery horse and the grim reaper wore the face of Smoke Jensen.

"Yes, sir," he said quietly. "I understand." Then rage over-rode fear and the young man made up his mind. He carried a hide-out gun behind his belt buckle.

Smoke released him. He was expecting a sneak-play from the young man and was ready for it.

Mel grabbed for his Remington over-and-under .41 derringer and Smoke hit him. Smoke's big fist smashed into the young man's face, flattening his nose and knocking him flat on his butt in the street. Before Mel could shake the birds and bells and buzzing bees out of his head, Smoke had rolled him over and clamped handcuffs tight around his wrists.

Smoke straightened up. "Take him to jail, Jim. The charge is disorderly conduct, disturbing the peace and attempted murder of a peace officer. Bond, if any, will set by Judge Garrison in the morning. That's it, people. Check your guns with Mrs. Marbly and have fun."

Smoke walked back onto the boardwalk, turned, and faced the mounted men.

Red cut his eyes to the south. A dozen men, all armed with rifles, stood in the street, blocking any escape. Max followed the glance, grunted, and then looked toward the north. Another dozen men, all heavily armed, blocked the north end of the street.

"I think," Alex Bell said with unusual restraint, "that we'uns better check our guns and get ready for the dance."

"We'll do that," Red said, swinging his gaze back to Smoke, "and there'll be no trouble in this town tonight. Not by any of my people. But you'll not try my boy on them charges Jensen."

"He'll be tried, Red. And if convicted, he'd do his time in the territorial prison. Now hear me well, all of you. The days of lawlessness are over in this town. The days of any of you riding roughshod over decent, law-abiding people have ended. Pull in your horns and act right, or die. That's the only choice I'm going to give any of you. If any of you cause trouble at tonight's festivities, I'll kill you. I'll shoot you down like a rabid skunk and drag your carcass off and stick it in the first hole I come to. And if it's the lime pit of an old privy, that'll do just fine. Now stable your horses and check your guns."

Max was the first to move. He backed his horse and rode to the livery stable, Red and the others following. And it was a silent following. Not one of them doubted that Smoke Jensen meant every word they'd just heard him say.

In the stable, Val Singer said, "I'd hate to think I had to spend eternity in a shit-pit."

"And Jensen would do it, too," Alex Bell said.

"We got to do something about Jensen, Max," Dave Poe said. "And we got to do it damn quick."

"I know. Did you boys notice anything riding into town?"

No one had.

"Then open your damn eyes!" Max snapped at them. "Look around you. You're supposed to be gunfighters, men who live by your wits. Hell, boys, there are water barrels everywhere. Full barrels. With buckets close by. This very stable is where the town used to keep their pumper. It's gone. That means that Jensen outguessed us . . . again. He guessed we might try to burn him out, and they're prepared for it.

"Did any of you see the clearing of brush that's been done around the town? And up on the ridges where a sharpshooter might hide? There is no place. Not anymore. The town is ready for an attack."

"Where is them high-priced sharpshooters from Europe that was comin' in?" Val asked.

"I don't know," Max admitted. "They should have been here by now. Unless . . ." he mused aloud. Then he shook his head. "No. Jensen had no way of knowing they were coming in. And neither one of them carries a sidearm . . . where it can be seen. He'd have no reason to pull them off the stage. I can but assume they are on their way in."

One of the gunslingers unbuckled his gunbelt and draped it over his shoulder. "Well," he drawled. "Let's go be good little boys and check our guns and dance with some real ladies, and then we'll eat some home cookin' for a change."

Smoke stood on the edge of the lantern-lighted perimeter and let Curly from the Circle W and a redheaded hand from the Lightning brand slug it out. He had no idea what had started the fracas, but as long as no guns were involved, he had told his deputies to let the men fight, but to just keep it away from the ladies.

"Anybody that would work for Red Malone would eat road apples," Curly told the puncher.

Red flattened him.

Curly jumped up, butted Red in the stomach with his head, and both of them went rolling across the dirt. Curly came up on top and proceeded to rearrange Red's face for him.

Smoke finally pulled the man off the Lightning puncher. "That's enough, Curly. He's out of it. Kill him and the matter becomes something other than a fistfight."

The blacksmith, Benson, grabbed Curly and led him off to a horse trough. Benson, strong as a grizzly bear, picked Curly up and dunked him headfirst into the trough several times.

"Now cool down, man," Benson told him. "Your sweetie's box is gonna be comin' up soon. You miss the bid on it and she'll never speak to you again." Benson was holding him by his boots, upside down.

"You do have a point," Curly sputtered. "Now turn me a-loose."

"You sure?" Benson asked.

"Damn right, I'm sure."

Benson turned him loose and Curly dropped headfirst into the horse trough.

Everybody gathered around, including Max and Red, had a good laugh at that.

Curly came up for air, sputtering and cussing.

Smoke walked to where Dr. Turner was kneeling down beside the moaning cowboy.

"He'll be all right," the doctor said. "His nose is broken and he's lost some teeth, but I can't find any broken ribs. He'll be sore for a few days. Barbaric method of settling arguments," he added.

"Beats the hell out of guns," Smoke told him.

"You have a point," the doctor conceded.

The rest of the evening went smoothly, with no more trouble. The bidding on the boxes was fast and sometimes heavy, depending on whether two young men were courting the same young lady. Smoke bid on Mrs. Walsh's box and Joe bid on Sally's, and everybody seemed to have a good time. Even Max got into the spirit of things and was laughing and telling jokes to the ladies . . . clean jokes.

After everyone had eaten and the dancing began, Max walked over to Smoke, standing in the shadows.

"You really think you've got the bull by the horns, now, don't you, Jensen?"

"Or riding a tiger."

Max chuckled. "Yes. The old East Indian proverb. I know it. And you surely must know, Smoke, that we of Hell's Creek are not simply going to give up and desert the town."

"You'd be smart if you did."

"No way, Jensen. You've backed us into a corner. We have to fight."

"If you say so."

"Innocent people will be hurt . . . killed."

"That's usually the way it goes." He turned slightly to face Max. "Take some advice, Max: Pull out. Break up your gangs and leave the country. If you stay, I'm going to have to kill you. You must know that."

"Or I'll kill you."

"A lot of men have tried that, Max. I've soaked up a lot of lead in my day. I'm still here."

"Oh, I think Melvin is as good as you are. And you'll never bring that boy to trial, Smoke."

"Maybe not. We'll have to see, won't we?"

"And maybe I have a couple of aces in the hole, Smoke."

"By the names of Henri Dubois and Paul Mittermaier?"

Max's smile was not in the least pleasant to look at. The big man sighed in disgust. He had been counting on the back-shooting pair.

"I've got their fancy rifles locked up in my office. Those two are halfway back to New York City by now. They're so doped up it'll be days before they even know who they are, much less where they are."

Max chuckled. Outlaw, killer, thief, he nevertheless had a sense of humor. And while he did not like being bested, he could still appreciate—however reluctantly—the method that was used in doing so.

"Slick, Jensen. I keep underestimating you. I've got to stop doing that. Jensen, what is the point of your interference? Is this what you're going to do for the rest of your life, stick your damn nose in other peoples' affairs?"

"I hope not, Max. To tell the truth, my wife and I came up here to visit friends. Nothing else."

"Dr. Turner and his wife," Max put it together. "I should have guessed. Sure. Who else in Hell's Creek would your wife want to associate with? So, now Barlow has a doctor and we don't. What's next, Jensen?"

"Your packing up and pulling out."

"That is something I will never do, Jensen."

Smoke shrugged his heavy shoulders. "You've noticed the cleanup around the town, the new water barrels." It was not put as a question. "You've seen where we've fixed up our pumper. And you've seen how the people are all armed and willing to stand shoulder to shoulder to fight you and Red Malone. Don't you feel it in your guts, Max? Can't you see you're not going to win this one?"

Max felt it, all right. He'd been sensing it for several days. Riding into Barlow had been depressing. The town was clean and neat, with swept boardwalks and washed windows and shrubs and flowers planted around the homes. Not like Hell's Creek, where litter was ankle-deep in some spots and the gunhands lived in shacks and tents and squalor. The stench of unwashed bodies was something one grew accustomed to in Hell's Creek. The people here took pride in their town. Here, in Barlow, there was a better class of people and good water.

Of course, that's all Hell needed.

Max's eyes flickered to the lush little body of Tessie, doing a reel with that pig-farmer's boy, Elias. His blood grew hot with perversion.

The quick glance did not escape the eyes of Smoke, who filed it away.

"I'll go down with my town," Max said, his voice husky with sudden desire. "If indeed we are to go down at all. And that certainly remains to be seen."

"Men like you never learn, Max. Civilization is fast spreading throughout the West. The people aren't going to tolerate men like us much longer."

"Us?" The statement confused Max. "Us!"

"Sure, Max. Us. I'm tolerated because I'm bringing a change to this town. When you and Red are either dead or run out of the territory, the people won't want me around. I'm a gunfighter, Max. The smell of gunsmoke lingers around me like some sort of invisible shroud. Just like the smell of perversion lingers around you."

Max's head jerked up. "What the hell do you mean by that, Jensen? Perversion?"

"You touch that Feckles girl and I'll kill you, Max. I'll

ride right into Hell's Creek and shoot you. As God is my witness, I'll do it."

"She's a woman, Jensen. She might be a child in mind, but she's got the body of a woman." Max knew he ought to shut his big mouth, but arrogance worked his tongue.

"You're pure crud, Max. I know that you lusted after both Victoria and Lisa. Tell you what, Max. I'm going to start sending out wires to a lot of law enforcement offices; I'm going to blanket your back trail and see what I can come up with. And I'm going to start with telegrams concerning child molestation and rape over . . . say, the past ten years or so. How does that grab you, partner?"

Max was thinking hard. He'd left a trail behind him, for sure.

If Jensen started digging, he'd soon put two and two together and Max would be forced to run. No question about that.

Max forced a laugh. "You do that, Jensen. My back trail is clean."

"We'll soon know," Smoke spoke the words softly. "It'll take me about a week to find out."

Max could scarcely control his wildly raging temper. He stared at Smoke for a moment and then spun on his boot heels, hollering for his men to get their gear and mount up. They were leaving.

"What's with Big Max?" Joe Walsh asked, walking up.

"I touched a festering boil," Smoke told him. "And it's just about ready to explode."

14

Over coffee the next morning in his office, Smoke told Jim and Sal and Judge Garrison what had brought on Max Huggins's sudden departure the night before.

"Let me start canvasing various law enforcement agencies, Smoke," Judge Garrison said. "I have many more contacts than you. I should have something within a week, probably in less time than that."

"Good, Judge. Get right on it, will you?"

"Immediately." The judge left the room and walked over to the telegraph office. He would be very busy for the next several days. Judge Garrison did not set a bond for Melvin Malone. He said the attempted murder charge meant he did not have to set a bond. Melvin would stay in jail.

"You're dead, Jensen," Melvin hollered from his cell. He rattled the barred door. "You're a dead man walking around and you're just too stupid to know that."

"Shut up, boy," Smoke called. "You're only making things more difficult for yourself."

"Son of a bitch!" Melvin yelled. "That's you, Jensen. Low-life, no-good . . ."

Smoke tuned him out.

"You know Red is gonna try to bust him out," Sal said.

"Sure. Once he hears no bond was set, he'll try force. Maybe as soon as tonight."

"You want us to set up cots and sleep here?" Jim asked.

"No." Smoke's reply was quick. "Red, so I'm told, likes to use dynamite. That's how he drove all those small farmers out that were settling around his holdings. He might decide to use explosives here. Too risky for us to sleep in."

"Hell, Smoke!" Sal said. "He uses dynamite, he might blow up Melvin tryin' to get him out."

Smoke shook his head. "We won't be that lucky, Sal." Smoke cut his eyes to the window in time to see John Steele riding up, the point man for several wagons, coming into town for supplies. They pulled up in front of Marbly's General Store.

"Oh, boy," Jim said. "Here it comes."

Smoke stood up and reached for his hat. "Yep," he said, heading for the door. "Storm clouds are gathering and it's about to rain trouble all over us. Let's go, boys. I wouldn't want to miss this."

The three men crossed the street just as John Steele was entering Marbly's store. They stepped up onto the boardwalk in time to hear John's shout of disbelief.

"What the hell do you mean, you little worm?" John roared. "My money is no good? My money is as good as anybody's, and by the Lord, you're going to sell me what I want."

"Get out of my store." Marbly stood his ground. "I don't want you or any of your scummy crew in my place of business. Get out, I say!"

John reached across the counter and grabbed Marbly by the shirtfront. Mrs. Marbly jerked an axe handle out of a barrel and honked it across the top of John's Stetson-covered head. John's eyes rolled back in his head and he sank to the floor, out cold. One of the Lightning hands jerked out a gun and aimed it at the woman. Smoke dusted him through and through with a .44 slug. The force of the slug knocked the cowboy to one side and into a showcase. He died among women's underthings, his head on a corset.

The townspeople reacted immediately to the shooting. The street filled with armed men. The remaining Lightning crew held up their hands in a hurry, not wanting to get plugged from every angle.

Smoke holstered his .44 and pointed to John Steele. "Drag him to jail." He looked at Marbly. "You going to press charges?"

"Damn right!" the shopkeeper said, considerable heat in his voice.

"Charge him with assault and battery," Smoke said to Sal. "Jim, get the undertaker."

Smoke stepped outside and faced the Lightning crew. "This town is off-limits to you and to anyone who works for Red Malone—including Red. I am officially banning any and all of you from Barlow. Take the word back to Red."

"Big talk, Jensen," the hand sneered at him. "I'll see your hide nailed to the wall afore this is over."

Smoke reached up and took off his badge, handing it to Marbly. "You want to try it now, cowboy? Guns or fists, it makes no difference to me."

The cowboy, who was going by the name of Dan since he was wanted in several states for cattle rustling and armed robbery, among other things, hesitated.

Smoke smiled, knowing he was giving the man no way out. It was the way of the West that when challenged, you had but two options: fight or be branded a coward. Smoke did not like the code but, in this case, felt he was justified in invoking it.

Dan took off his gunbelt and handed it to a Lightning puncher. He flexed his arms and looked back at Smoke. "You mind if I warm up a little first?"

"I don't care if you do the Virginia reel," Smoke told him, and that got a laugh from the gathering crowd, both men and women. "You probably can't dance any better than you can fight."

The crowd roared with laughter and Dan flushed in anger. "I think I'll just clean your clock," Dan said.

"Then come on, cowboy."

Dan tried a sucker punch that brought no response from Smoke. He hooked a left that Smoke blocked and tried to follow through with a right that Smoke flicked away.

Smoke jumped lightly off the boardwalk and waved Dan down to join him.

"Stand still and fight, damn you!" Dan yelled.

"Oh!" Smoke said. "I see. That's what you want. I thought you were still warming up."

The crowd loved it and roared their approval.

Dan didn't think it was a bit funny and stepped in close. Smoke rattled his teeth with a left and put a knot on his head with a right. Dan backed up, shaking his head and spitting out blood.

"I'm waiting to fight," Smoke taunted him.

Dan charged him with a shout of defiance, and Smoke stuck out a boot and tripped the man, sending him sprawling into the dirt of the street.

The Lightning cook sat his seat on the wagon and shook his head. Dan was gonna get the crap beat out of him for sure, and just as soon as that was over and done with and they got back to the ranch, Cookie was packin' up his kit and gettin' the hell gone from the Lightning brand. His oldest boy had been forever trying to get him over into Idaho to help on his horse ranch. This time, by God, he was going. Hadn't oughta a stayed this long with this pack of screwballs.

That thought had just crossed his mind when Dan got up from the dirt and went charging and yelling toward Smoke

Jensen. The cook grimaced as Smoke poleaxed the puncher with a solid right fist that turned Dan around and sent him stumbling out into the street.

As a matter of fact, the cook thought, there ain't no reason to go back to the ranch. I just got paid, I got my best clothes on, I'm wearin' my gun, and I ain't got nothin' back there no good for anything no how.

The dull smack of Smoke Jensen's fist again connecting with Dan's jaw prompted Cookie to climb down from the wagon seat and walk up toward the stage office. He had more than enough money in his pockets to get a room at the Grand and buy his ticket over to Idaho. Hell with Red Malone and his foolish boy and the whole damn crazy bunch out at Lightning.

Cookie turned in time to see Dan whip out a knife. "Stupid, Dan," he muttered. "Now Smoke's gonna kill you."

"I'll gut you, Jensen," Dan screamed his rage and frustration. He stepped closer.

Smoke reached behind his right hand .44 and pulled out a long-bladed Bowie knife. "You sure this is the way you want it?" Smoke asked him.

Dan moved closer, working the blade from side to side. He tried to fake Smoke but Jensen wasn't falling for it.

"Don't do this, Dan!" one of the Lightning crew yelled. "It ain't worth it."

Dan pressed on, curses rolling off his tongue. He swung the blade and Smoke parried it, the metal clanking as the razor-sharp knives met.

Smoke stepped in and cut Dan from earlobe to point of jaw. "Drop the knife," he warned the puncher. "Mountain men raised me. I've been knife-fighting since I was sixteen."

"Hell with you!" Dan said as the blood dripped from the cut on his face.

"I don't want to kill you, boy," Smoke told him. "Give this up."

Dan moved in and Smoke cut, his knife arm, opening him up from elbow down to hand. Dan screamed as the knife dropped from his numbed and useless hand.

"Get Dr. Turner," Smoke said to the crowd. "See what he can do with this fool."

Smoke wiped the blood from his blade and sheathed it. Turning to the Lightning punchers, he said, "You have one minute to get clear of this town. And don't ever come back."

Cookie watched from the boardwalk as the bleeding Dan was led to the doctor's office. "Told you so, boy," he muttered. "I learned fifty years ago to give mountain men a wide berth."

Cookie turned and walked into the ticket office. Idaho sure looked good to him.

Red Malone received the news of being banned from Barlow stoically. He had been expecting something like this, so it didn't surprise him.

But he was shook down to his boots at the news of John Steele being jailed. "How is Dan?" he finally asked.

"He ain't never gonna use his right arm again. Tendons was cut."

Red grunted. "Cookie?"

"He quit."

"Get my horse. I'm riding to Barlow."

"You want me to get the boys together?"

"No. I'm riding alone. Do it, Jake. I don't want to hear any arguments."

Red rode to the town limits and sat his saddle in the middle of the road. Malone was many things, but a fool was not one of them. Someone would soon spot him and take the news to Jensen. Smoke would ride out to see what he wanted.

In a couple of minutes, Jensen rode up and faced him. "Something I can do for you, Red?"

"Has bond been set for John Steele?"

"Fifty dollars. He's out, saddling his horse. He'll be along shortly."

"He hurt?"

"He's got a knot on his noggin and his pride is bruised, that's all."

Red nodded his head. "You'd a done Dan a favor if you'd gone on and killed him. A one-armed puncher ain't good for much, Jensen."

"That's his problem, Red."

John Steele came riding out, wheeled his horse up beside Red, and faced Smoke. The man was killing mad and it showed on his face, which was chalk-white with anger. Smoke knew that was the sign of a very dangerous man. A red-faced man usually meant all bluff and bluster, but one whose face was chalk-white meant he was cold inside.

"I want to see my boy, Jensen. He ain't much, I'll give you that, but he's still mine. You can have my gun and search me. Have a deputy there with us. But I want to see him."

"All right, Red. I wouldn't have kicked up any fuss at that. A father has a right to see his own. John, you ride on to the spread. Don't come back to town. I mean it. Your high handed, roughshod ways of dealing with the people of Barlow are over."

"You and me, Jensen," the foreman said tightly. "Someday, just you and me."

"Shut your mouth and clear out, John. Don't dig your own grave."

John wheeled his horse and rode away.

"Did this . . . incident with John go down the way my hand said it did?"

"What'd your hand say about it?" After listening to a brief rundown, Smoke nodded his head. "That's about it, Red."

It was obvious that Red had more on his mind than seeing his son. Smoke got the impression Malone didn't even like the boy. He might love him, but he sure didn't like him.

"Where am I supposed to buy supplies, Jensen?"

"I don't know, Red. But if Marbly doesn't want you in his store, that's his right."

"You've pushed me up against a wall just like you're pushin' Max. Don't you think we'll push back, Jensen?"

"We're ready anytime you boys want to start the tug-of-war, Red."

"Damnit, man!" Red stirred in the saddle. "My boys will have to drive teams way the hell south of here for supplies."

"There's a way you can prevent that, Red, and you know it."

"There's two ways, Jensen. And you know the other way I'm talkin' about."

"You want to try it now, Red?" Smoke calmly laid down the challenge.

Red grudgingly smiled at the man's calmness and courage. He took a deep breath and shook his head. "I reckon not, Jensen. But you can't stick around here forever. You got to leave sometime. I'll wait."

"I'm betting you won't, Red. Oh, you might; I'll give you that. But sooner or later, your daughter is going to want some pretties from the dress shop or the general store, and she'll agitate you or someone else until you drive her in. One of your hands is going to get drunk and come rip-snorting in here. You or some of your crew or your kid will get sick and have to see the doctor or the man at the apothecary shop. Any of those things could blow the lid off. And one of them more than likely will."

"You'd stop me from bringing my girl or one of my men in to see the doctor?"

"That's right, Red."

"You're a heartless bastard, Jensen!"

"Oh, I wouldn't prevent the doctor from going out to your spread. Or you could bring them to this town limit and he could treat them. But after today, unless it's for a court appearance, neither you nor any of your family or crew sets a foot in Barlow."

Red curtly nodded his head. "I got a packet in my saddle-bags for Mel. It's some readin' material and money so's he can buy himself some food from the cafe. Is that all right?"

"Suits me, Red."

Red unbuckled the straps and handed Smoke a small packet.

"You know I'll have to inspect it?"

"I know. It's a Bible, Jensen. That's the only book I could find in the house. Maybe he'll read it, maybe he won't. I reckon I should have."

"You think it's too late for that, Red?"

The rancher thought about that for a moment. "Yeah, I think it is, Jensen." He shook his head. "That don't make no never-mind. I'll deal with the devil when I meet him. Jensen, either I'm gonna kill you, John Steele is gonna kill you, Max Huggins is gonna kill you, or somebody is gonna kill you for that bounty on your head . . . and you know there is one."

"So I've heard."

"And there you sit, just as calm and unconcerned as a hog in slop."

"That's me, Red. I don't worry about things I have no control over. I don't fret about too little or too much rain. That's in God's hands. And I don't worry about what you or Max and your scummy crews are going to do. Oh, I could take control of that, Red, by blowing you out of the saddle right now. But even though I've killed lots of men, I'm not a murderer and I don't force gunplay on people who haven't pushed me. So I just wait."

"Lemme see if I can get through to you, Jensen. The people in this town are little people. You and me and Max, we're big people. Big people have always had little people under their thumb. That's what makes the world go round, Jensen. Do you understand that?"

"I hear your words, Red, and you're wrong. But you'll never see that, though. If you lived in a big city, you'd be running a sweatshop, forcing decent people to work long hours under miserable conditions for little pay. That's just the way you are, I reckon. Lots of folks are like you and Max, Red. You're born that way. I call it the bad seed theory."

"Goddamn you, Jensen," Red flared. "I came out here in late '65 when this country was wild, man, wild! I built my spread with sweat and blood, a lot of it my blood. I fought Injuns and homesteaders and hog-farmers and white trash. I scratched and clawed and chewed my way to what I got. And I'll not see it tore apart in front of my eyes. I demand respect."

"You left out a lot of things, Red. You left out that you probably came out here running from the law back east. . . ."

Smoke knew he'd hit pay dirt from the expression on Red's face. The man looked like he'd been hit with a club. He ground his teeth together so hard Smoke could hear the gnashing. Red's face turned white and he fought to maintain control.

"You always were a liar and a cheat and a thief and a womanizer. I'm told you beat your wife so often and so savagely she finally had enough and quit you. Now I add all that up, Red, and do you know what the total is?"

Red stared at Smoke. He was killing mad but smart enough to know if he dragged iron, Jensen would beat him. Red was good with a gun, but no match for Smoke Jensen.

"So add it up and tell me what you come up with, gunfighter," Red spat the words.

"Scum," Smoke said softly. "One hundred percent stinking scum."

"I'll spit on your grave, Jensen."

"I doubt it."

"Goddamn you, Jensen!" Red flared. "Who gives you the right to pass judgment on me? You're nothin' but a gunhandler. You made your money killin' people. What in the hell gives you the right to think you're better than me?"

"Oh, I don't think I'm better than you in the Biblical sense, Red. We're all going to have to stand before our Maker and be judged."

Red's face had regained much of its normal color. He wore a puzzled look as he spread his hands wide. "Then? . . ."

"Red, I could stand here and try to explain the differences between us until I fell off my horse from exhaustion. No matter what I said, I'd never get through to you. So I'll tell you this: If you're not going to change your murdering, thieving ways and try to live a decent life, if you're not going to fire the scum from your payroll and run them out of this country, I suggest you go make your peace with God. Go make out your will and leave your ill-gotten holdings to Tessie."

"Tessie! Hell's fire, man. She'd go through my money like a whirlwind. I'll leave my holdings to my son."

"He won't be around very much longer, Red."

"Huh?"

"If he beats the charges—and he probably will; Judge Garrison says the attempted murder charge is pretty flimsy— he'll come after me. And I'll kill him. Then you'll go on the prod, and I'll put you down. The way I see it, Red, any way it goes, you're looking at a grave." Smoke glanced at the packet in his left hand. "I thought you wanted to see your boy?"

"I changed my mind. I got some ruminatin' to do, Jensen. I got to think on what all you've said this day. I don't know whether you're the bravest man I ever met or just damn crazy. But if you wanted another enemy, Jensen, you just made one with me."

"See you around, Red."

"You set foot outside this town, Jensen, you better be wearin' a gun."

Smoke smiled. "I'm wearin' one now, Red."

Red shook his head and wheeled his horse, heading back to his ranch.

Smoke rode back to the jail and inspected the contents of the packet. Exactly what Red had said. He rifled through the pages of the Bible to check for a derringer or a knife, then tossed money and Bible to Melvin.

"Your dad brought you some reading material, kid."

Melvin began tearing out the pages.

"What are you doing, boy?" Smoke asked. "That's the holy Bible."

"Damn heathen," Sal muttered.

Melvin grinned. "Tell my pa thanks, Jensen. I needed something to wipe my butt with."

15

Melvin Malone was released from jail, the attempted murder charge dropped. Sal picked up the torn pages from the Bible and carefully disposed of them, muttering about heathens and those doomed to the pits of hell.

A week passed, with no retaliation from either Max Huggins or Red Malone. But the townspeople did not relax; they knew an attack was coming. They just didn't know when or how.

Smoke received an unsigned telegram telling about the further misadventures of Paul Mittermaier and Henri Dubois. It seems the pair had been arrested and jailed in Kansas City for strong-arm robbery. They told some wild tale about being beaten and drugged in a small town out west, and then waking up in an empty railroad car. They claimed they were really foreign tourists, over here to do some buffalo hunting.

The judge laughed at them and sent them off to prison for a couple of years.

Smoke sent the wire to Max Huggins.

On a warm and bright summer's day, Aggie Feckles walked into a field on the outskirts of town to pick flowers for the kitchen table.

Several hours later, Martha showed up at the marshal's office, nearly hysterical.

Smoke didn't need a crystal ball to know what had taken place. He sent a boy over to the hotel for Sally, so she could look after Martha, and began stuffing his saddlebags with items he might need when he declared war on Hell's Creek.

"We'll get a posse together," Judge Garrison said.

"No, we won't," Smoke nixed that idea. "That's what Max wants. They want a posse chasing after shadows and leaving the town undefended." He looked around him. Sally and Martha had gone over to Mrs. Marbly's. "If Aggie is still alive, I'll bring her back."

"If she's still alive?" The blacksmith, Benson, questioned.

"The lawyers have a phrase for it," Smoke replied. He glanced at Judge Garrison.

"Corpus delicti," the judge told the crowded room. "It means the facts to prove a crime. In a case this heinous—and we might as well say the word: rape—Max, if it is Max, would probably dispose of the body after the viciousness was done. He'd be a total fool to keep her alive. And Max is not a fool. Let's all hope and pray he's savoring the anticipation and has not completed the act."

Smoke walked out of the office and stepped into the saddle.

Judge Garrison followed him out. "Smoke, I've received some confirmation about Max Huggins's back trail. I was on my way over to tell you when I heard about Aggie. He's wanted back east. Mostly for rape of young girls. He then killed them. In several states."

"Do you have the warrants?"

"That'll take some time. Probably a month or better. It's a time-consuming process, Smoke."

Smoke shook his head and grimaced as he picked up the reins. "Aggie doesn't have a month, Judge. Looks like this is going to be western justice. See you."

He rode out of town, heading north.

Smoke stopped at the Brown farm and pulled the farmer off to one side, briefing him.

Brown's face tightened. "I'll try to keep this from Elias. The boy is sure sweet on that girl; no tellin' what he'd try to do. Damnit!" the man cursed. "What kind of filth would do something like this?"

Ellie brought them coffee and her husband told her what had happened.

"That poor child. How much hope do you hold out for her, Mr. Jensen?"

"Not much. Max will probably do the deed and then kill her. It's a pattern of his."

She frowned and said, "I'm a God-fearing woman, Mr. Jensen. But I have to ask this: Why doesn't society hang men like Max Huggins and others who do these terrible things? Why are they allowed to live?"

"I don't know, ma'am. It has something to do with a movement started back east. Something about the worth of a criminal's life or some such drivel as that. God help us all if it spreads out here."

They all turned at the sounds of a horse approaching. Pete Akins was coming up the road. He saw Smoke standing in the farmer's yard and turned in, closing the gate behind him. The gunfighter dismounted and walked over to the group.

"I'm out of it, Smoke," he said, taking off his hat in the presence of Mrs. Brown. "Bell and Frigo and some others grabbed the little Feckles girl and hauled her to Max Huggins. My gun may be for hire, but I'll be damned—'cuse the word, ma'am—if I'll have a part in abusin' a child or botherin' a good woman. If you want another deputy, you got one, Smoke."

"I had a hunch you'd come around, Pete. Where is Aggie being held?"

"She ain't bein' held nowhere, Smoke. She's dead. Max done his evil and give her to the men. Made me sick to my stomach. I'd ridden over to Kalispell for supplies; came back right in the middle of it. I just got out of Hell's Creek with my hide on."

"Are they planning on attacking the town, Pete?"

"If a big enough posse rides out, yeah. They got men on the ridges with signal mirrors to tell yea or nay. I figured I'd ride in and warn the townspeople."

Smoke scribbed a short note and handed it to Pete. "This will keep someone in the town from shooting you, Pete. I'm going to go show the citizens of Hell's Creek what hell is really like."

"You want some company?"

Smoke shook his head. "This is something I want to do myself. How many people pulled out with you?"

"No one, Smoke. There ain't nothin' but trash left up there. Men and women. There ain't no kids in the town. Not a one. Even that so'called minister up yonder took his turn with that poor child. When she went crazy-actin' after all the horribleness, Frigo shot her."

"You keep an eye on Elias, Brown. Hog-tie the boy if you have to."

Smoke stepped into the saddle and was gone.

The outlaw and gunslinger experienced the chill of a cold sweat as the muzzle of the .44 was pressed against his head. He'd just stepped out of the privy and was slipping into his galluses when the muzzle touched his head.

"If I think you're lying to me," Smoke's voice was as cold as the invisible grip of death that touched the hired gun, "I'll stake you out and skin you alive. Do you understand?"

"Yes, sir. Jensen?"

"That's right, punk. Did you take part in the rape of Aggie?"

"Yes, sir."

"How many more?"

"Jesus, Smoke . . . ever'body in the whole damn town. Including some of the women. She screamed and hollered until she couldn't holler no more. Went on all day. Then she went nuts in the head and Frigo shot her."

Smoke cursed under his breath. "How did you feel raping that child, punk?"

"I . . . liked it, damn you!"

"Yeah, scum like you would. They waiting for me down in town?"

"Yeah. They damn sure are. So go on down and git killed Jensen. You . . ."

He never got to finish it. Smoke buried the big blade of his Bowie into the man's back and twisted it upward with all his considerable strength. Smoke slammed the man's face first onto the ground to stifle the scream building in his throat. He wiped the blade clean on the man's shirttail and sheathed the weapon. Smoke checked his guns, loading them full, then took the dead gunny's two Remington Frontier .44's, looping gunbelt and all over one shoulder. He made his way back to his horse and circled the town, keeping to the timber until he found a good spot to picket the animal.

He changed into moccasins, slung his saddlebags over his other shoulder, picked up his rifle, and began working his way toward the town. He knew they were waiting for him because of the silence of the usually raucous place. Lights were burning, but there was no laughter coming from any of the saloons.

And Smoke was determined that before he left that night, there would be no cause for joy in the town for a long, long time. If he could, he was going to destroy as much of Hell's Creek as possible.

He paused for a moment, listening. The old mountain man, Preacher, his mentor, had taught him many things, including patience. Smoke heard the faint jingle of spurs coming up the weed-grown alleyway. He pressed against the building. When the man drew close, Smoke hit him in the face with the butt of the rifle. The man dropped like a stone faint moonlight glistening off his bloody and broken face.

Smoke walked on to a corral. He didn't want to hurt any animal, they could not choose their owners. He silently slid open the bars. When the action started, the horses would find the opening and bolt. He did the same at two other corrals. He glanced at the huge livery stable and decided to leave it alone. Men were probably lying in wait for him in there.

He slipped around to the back of a saloon, dug in a pocket of his saddlebags, and came out with six sticks of dynamite, taped together, already capped with a long fuse.

He softly entered through the back door. Now he could hear voices and the tinkle of glasses and beer mugs. But the conversation was low and the drinking was probably light.

Smoke thumbnailed a match into flame and lit the long fuse, placing the charge against the storeroom wall. With a smile on his face, he slipped back into the night.

Smoke planted two more charges on that side of the street before he was spotted by a man who'd stepped out of a back door to relieve himself.

"Hey!" the man shouted, turning and still spewing water.

Smoke shot him about five inches below the belt buckle. The man fell to the earth, screaming in agony.

"You'll not rape another girl," Smoke muttered, then dashed across the street, at the far end of town.

The saloon charge blew. Smoke saw one man thrown from the building, crashing through glass. He hit the street and did not move. Another man fell through the floor and onto the dusty walkway in front as the rear part of the poorly constructed building collapsed under the heavy weight of the charge.

The second and third charges blew, and chaos reigned for a few minutes as men and women poured into the street.

Smoke emptied the Remingtons into a knot of men, knocking them sprawling. He lit another charge, tossed that through a side window of a building, and dashed away. He collided with a man, recovered first, and pointed a pistol at the man's head.

"The body of the girl Aggie, where is it?" He jacked back the hammer. "And I'm only going to ask it one time."

"Sid tossed it into a backwater just off the river yonder. I swear to you I ain't lyin'."

Smoke jerked him to his feet. "Show me, you weasel. And you'd better be right the first time."

Keeping low, as the flames began licking at the dry timber of the destroyed buildings, the man led Smoke to a dry wash and from there to the slough. The naked body of Aggie was clearly visible.

"Get her, you crud," Smoke ordered, the menace in his voice chilling the man.

The man waded into the dark waters and pulled the girl to the shore.

"Pick her up and walk toward the timber," he ordered.

"But she ain't got nothin' on! That ain't decent!"

One look from Smoke's cold eyes convinced the man that he'd better shut his mouth and do as ordered.

"Where is the bastard?" Smoke heard the voice of Max Huggins plain in the night. "Find him, you fools. Find him and kill him!"

At his horse, Smoke had the man wrap Aggie's body in a blanket.

"What are you gonna do with me?" the man asked.

"Did you take a part in raping this girl? And don't lie to me."

"Yeah, I did. Ever'body did."

Smoke hit him with one big gloved fist. The man dropped like a rock.

The flames in the town were slowly being contained by a bucket brigade and one small pumper.

Smoke knew there was no point in taking the man back to Barlow for trial. Once away from Smoke Jensen's gun, the man would lie, denying any part of the rape. If a deal could be worked out, everybody in Hell's Creek would alibi for the other and nothing would be accomplished there.

Smoke left the man on the ground and picked up the slender, blanket-covered body of Aggie Feckles. Star didn't like the idea of carrying the dead, but Smoke managed to get into the saddle. He headed back for Barlow, taking a route first west, then cutting south, to throw off any pursuers. He doubted there would be many; they were too busy fighting the fires.

At a farmer's house, he borrowed a horse and tied Aggie across the saddle. He rode into Barlow just as dawn was breaking fair in the eastern skies. People began lining the streets, silently watching as he rode in, leading the horse with the body of Aggie across the saddle.

Dr. Turner came out of the hotel, where he had just given Martha a sedative, and walked over to Smoke. Smoke stepped wearily out of the saddle and gave the reins to Jim. The deputy led the animal to the stable.

A crowd began to slowly gather around.

"After they abused her," Smoke said, his words soft, "Warner Frigo shot her in the head and dumped her body in a slough."

"Pete Akins told us the rest of it," Judge Garrison said. A little bit of soap was still on his face. He had been shaving when the news of Smoke riding in reached him. "This is absolutely the most dastardly act I have seen in all my years on the bench."

"How much damage did you do in Hell's Creek Marshal?" a citizen asked.

"Burned down about a half-dozen buildings. Got lead in maybe a dozen people. I used some dynamite, and the explosions probably killed another six or seven and put that many out of commission for a time. How is Martha?"

"She's sleeping," Turner said. "Victoria and Sally are with her now. I just gave her a sedative about fifteen minutes ago. She'll be groggy when she wakes up."

"The girl was shot at close range," Smoke told him. "the slug took off about half her face. Have the undertaker do his work and then nail the coffin lid shut. Let's spare Martha that."

The doctor nodded his agreement.

"I've got to get some rest. I'll see you all this afternoon." Smoke wearily climbed the steps to their suite after asking Toby to have a boy get water for a bath.

He hung up his guns, pulled off his boots, waited in his long-handles until the tub was filled, and then took a bath. Sally came into the WC and scrubbed his back.

Smoke slipped under the cool, fresh sheets and closed his eyes. He slept deeply and soundly and dreamlessly. He awakened just after noon and was finishing shaving when the sounds of gunshots and women screaming sent him running down the hotel steps.

16

Max had not waited long to retaliate. The gunhands on his payroll and those who lived in Hell's Creek had hit the town hard from the north and were now preparing to strike again, from the south end. Several had thrown torches and two buildings were on fire; but the bucket brigades were working and the fires were being snuffed out before much damage could be done.

"Get into position!" Smoke yelled. "Just like we practiced. Move!"

The men and women of the town responded, quickly getting into battle positions on the roofs and behind shelter. The outlaws saw what was taking place and broke off the second attack before it could get started. They galloped south.

Smoke didn't need a fortune-teller to know where they were heading: to Red Malone's spread.

"Do we follow them?" Toby asked, coming out of the hotel carrying a rifle.

"Not a whole bunch of us. That's what they want. They'd set up an ambush point and nail us. Jim," he called, "saddle me a horse. Not Star. He needs a rest."

Smoke looked around. "Judge, deputize Pete Akins. Pete and Jim will stay here. Sal, come on. Let's do some head-hunting."

Sally pressed a couple of biscuits and salt meat in his hand while the hotel cook made a poke of food for the men to take with them. Smoke gulped down a cup of coffee and then was in the saddle, riding a long-legged buckskin with a mean look in his eyes.

"I know that horse," Sal said. "That's the stableman's personal ride. He's a good one."

Smoke nodded and the men were off, leaving the road just outside of town and cutting across country. From their tracks, it was clear that the outlaws had arrogantly elected to stay with the road, daring Smoke and any others to chase them.

The short cut that Smoke chose was one pointed out to him by Jim; and Sal knew it as well or better. It would cut off miles getting to the Lightning spread. It was rough country; high-up country.

The men rode the mountain trails and passes in silence. A great gray wolf watched them from a ridge. Smoke spoke to the wolf in Cheyenne, one of several Indian languages that Old Preacher had taught him. Preacher had taught him that for man to fear the wolf was downright ignorant. Preacher had said that he'd never known of a man being attacked by a wolf unless that man was threatening the wolf or got too close to a fresh kill. Either way, according to Preacher, it was the man's fault, not the wolf's.

"Magnificent animals," Sal said, looking at the timber wolf. "But they don't make good pets worth a damn."

"They're not meant to be pets," Smoke agreed. "God didn't put them here for that. Damn stupid hunters keep killing them, and the deer and elk population suffers because of it. They're part of the balance of nature. I wish the white man would understand that. Indians understood it."

The wolf stood on the ridge and watched the men pass.

Then it turned and went back to its den, where it was watching over the cubs while its mate hunted for food, which is a lot more than can be said for a great many so-called superior humans.

"There they are," Sal pointed out.

Smoke looked to his right and slightly behind him. A group of riders, tiny from this distance, rode far below them. About twenty-five of them.

"We'll be a good fifteen minutes ahead of them after we cut off up yonder," Sal said. "I know a place that'll be dandy for an ambush."

"Take the lead, Sal. I'll follow you."

The men rode down from the high country, the temperature warming as they descended from the high-up into a valley. Wildflowers had burst forth, coloring the landscape with brilliant summer hues.

Smoke was going to add some more color to the scenery: blood-red.

The two men left their horses safe within boulders and timber and, with their rifles, got into place. They were about fifty yards above the road. This was not the stage road, but an offshoot that led to and stopped at Malone's ranch, some miles farther on. They were on Lightning range.

Sal pointed that out.

"Good," Smoke replied. "Maybe they'll hear the shots and come to lend their buddies a hand. We'll lessen the odds against the town if they do."

Sal took that time to point out that should that occur, the two of them would be outnumbered something like forty to one.

Smoke grinned and patted the bulging saddlebags he'd taken from behind his saddle. "Have faith, Sal. If worse comes to worse, we'll blast our way out."

"There ain't a nerve in your body, is there, Smoke?"

"Oh, I've known fear, Sal." Smoke thought for a moment, then smiled. "Back in '69, I think it was."

Both men laughed, then sobered as the outlaws came into view, riding around a curve in the road, still too far away for accurate shooting.

"Wish we had brung one of them fancy rifles you took from them foreigners," Sal said. "We'd a sure tried it out."

Smoke eared back the hammer on his Winchester. "They'll be in range in about a minute. I'll take the left side, you take the right."

"Good," Sal said flatly. "I can recognize Ernie's horse from here. Ain't neither one of them worth a damn for anything."

"Here we go, Sal."

The men lifted the rifles to their shoulders, sighted in, took up slack on the triggers, and emptied two saddles.

The outlaws appeared confused as their horses reared and bucked at the gunfire and the sudden smell of blood. Instead of turning left or right, or retreating, the outlaws put the spur to the animals' flanks and came forward.

"Like shootin' clay pigeons standin' still," Sal muttered, and emptied another saddle.

Smoke grabbed several taped-together sticks of dynamite from the open saddlebag, lit the fuse, and tossed it down the hill. The charge landed just above the road and blew, sending small rocks hurling through the air like deadly missiles.

Through the cloud of dust raised by the dynamite, Smoke and Sal could see a half-dozen more riderless horses, the outlaws on the ground, some of them writhing in agony with hideous head wounds and broken limbs, the others lying very still, their skulls crushed by the flying rocks.

Smoke and Sal started tossing the lead around. The dozen or so outlaws left in the saddle decided it was way past time to clear out. They put the spurs to their horses and were gone, fogging it to Red's ranch.

Smoke and Sal mounted up and rode down into the carnage, to see if anything could be salvaged. Sal rounded up the outlaws' horses while Smoke stood among the dead and wounded, making certain no one summoned up the courage to try a shot at either one of them.

They had just finished tying the dead across their saddles and securing the wounded on their horses when Red Malone and his crew thundered up, raising an unnecessary cloud of dust.

"What the hell are you doin' on my range, Jensen?" the man yelled.

"I'm a deputy sheriff of this county, Red," Smoke calmly told him. "And I'm carrying out my duties as such. You interfere and I'll put your butt in jail."

Sal had worked around; he now faced Red, a rifle pointed at the rancher's chest. The action did not escape Red, and he knew if trouble started, he would be the first one dead.

But he wouldn't, couldn't, leave it alone. "You got a warrant for the arrest of these men, Jensen?"

"I saw them attack the town of Barlow, Red. Me and several hundred other people. Those alive are going back to stand trial. Now back off."

All looked up as the sound of hooves pounding against the earth reached them. Twenty men from the town reined up, heavily armed, among them Joe Walsh and a half dozen of his hands.

"The town's secure, Smoke," Benson said. "We thought we'd ride out and give you a hand."

"It's appreciated. You men start escorting these bums back to town." Smoke and Sal swung into the saddle. Smoke looked at Red. "Their trial will begin in a couple of days. You and your men are still banned from the town. Keep that in mind, Red."

"Someday, Jensen," Red warned, his voice thick with anger. "Someday."

"Anytime, Red. Just anytime at all." Smoke lifted the reins and rode away.

* * *

The funeral of Aggie Feckles was an emotional, gut-wrenching time for all. Midway through the ordeal, Martha collapsed and had to be carried back to the doctor's office. Young Elias Brown had a very difficult time fighting back his tears. Just as the earth was being shoveled into the hole, Smoke cut his eyes and looked toward the north. Plumes of smoke were billowing into the sky.

"Max is burning you men out!" he called to Brown and his friends. "Let's ride."

They were too late, of course. It was miles to the collection of farmhouses and barns and other outbuildings. Brown had been completely burned out. Gatewood lost his house, but the other buildings were intact. Cooter lost his barn and smokehouse. Bolen's house was gone, and Morrison and Carson lost barns and equipment. All the farmers' cows and hogs had been shot, the chickens scattered and trampled.

"Goddamn a man who would do this!" Brown said. He squared his shoulders and added, "That sorry son will not run me out. We'll rebuild."

"And we'll help you," Tom Johnson said.

"Your credit is good at my store," Marbly said. "For as long as it takes."

"I have money put back," Judge Garrison told the farmers. "I'm good for loans."

Sally and Victoria had ridden out in a buggy. Sally said, "Smoke, I'm going to wire our family's board of directors back east. I think it's time Barlow had a bank. I'll get the first steps in motion this afternoon."

Smoke turned and smiled at her. "Good, honey. That's a great idea."

"Your wife owns a bank?" Marbly asked.

"Her family is one of the richest families in the nation," Smoke told the startled crowd. "They own factories, banks shipping lines, railroads . . . you name it. If Sally says put a bank in Barlow, a bank will be put in Barlow." He turned to

Jim Dagonne. "Let's go pick up some tracks and see where they lead to. As if we didn't know."

But the direction the marauders took did not lead toward Hell's Creek. They went north for a couple of miles, then cut toward the northeast, toward the flathead range and the glacier country.

"What's up there, Jim?"

"Man, that is rugged country. I understand they's talk in Washington about making a big chunk of it a national park. It's about a million or so acres. And the weather is unpredictable as hell. Storms can blow in there—even in the summer, so I'm told—dropping temperatures fifty . . . sixty degrees. They's mountains in there over two miles high and impassable."

"You've been in there?"

"I've been on the edge of it several times. Continental Divide runs right through it."

"Anything between here and there?"

"Tradin' post of sorts up ahead on the Hungry Horse. Some pretty salty ol' boys hang around there."

Smoke nodded. "We'll follow these tracks as long as we can. We'll supply at the post. The nick in that shoe is a dead giveaway. That'll hold up in court."

"You plan on bringing them back?"

"Not if I can help it."

The country was so rugged and unsettled that the men could not make the trading post that day. They camped along a creek and dined on fresh fish caught with their hands, Indian style.

"Where'd you learn how to do that?" Jim asked after watching Smoke catch their supper by hand.

"I was raised by mountain men, Jim. A very independent and self-sufficient bunch."

"I've met a couple of real old men who was mountain men. I saw something in their eyes that made me back off and talk right respectful to them."

"Wise thing to do. A mountain man isn't going to take much crap from anybody."

They ate until they could hold no more, then rolled up in their blankets, using saddles for pillows, and were up before dawn, making coffee and talking little until they'd shaken the kinks out and had a cup of coffee you could float nails in.

"Who runs this trading post?" Smoke finally asked.

"Don't know no more. Man by the name of Smith used to run it. He might still. Smith ain't his real name. He's a bad one. Have to be bad to run a place like that. Got him a graveyard out back of hard cases who tried to steal from him or brace him over one thing or another."

"Fast gun?"

"Nope. Sawed-off shotgun. And he don't hesitate none in usin' it, neither. He's got the worst whiskey you ever tried to drink. I think he adds snake heads to it for flavor. And I ain't kiddin'."

"I think I'll stick with beer."

"That would be wise."

They rolled their blankets in their ground sheets and were in the saddle as the sun was struggling to push its rays over the mountains.

They followed the tracks, and they led straight to the trading post on the north fork of the Flathead River. Both men had taken off their badges, had dusty clothing from the trail, and had not shaved that morning. Both of them had heavy beards, so they were beginning to look a little rough around the edges.

"If Smith is still here, is he going to recognize you?" Smoke asked.

"Probably. But he ain't gonna say nothing except howdy, 'til he figures out what I might be up to. How are we going to play this?"

"You just follow my lead."

"I's afraid you was gonna say that."

The men put their horses in the big barn behind the long,

low trading post and unsaddled them, carefully rubbing them down and giving them a good bait of corn. 25 *ceents a skoop,* the sign said.

"Yep," Jim said. "Smith is still here. You ever seen such outrageous prices?"

"It's the only game in town, partner."

"You called that right."

Smoke lifted the right rear hoof of each animal until he found the one with the chipped shoe. He smiled up at Jim. "We found our man."

"Men," Jim corrected. "I count six of them."

Smoke straightened up and, with a grin on his face, said, "Hell, Jim, don't look so glum. We got them outnumbered."

"If that's the way you count," Jim said soberly, "I shore am glad you don't count out my payroll!"

17

The men took the leather thongs off their guns and stepped up onto the rough porch. With Smoke in the lead, they entered the dimly lit old trading post. The smell of twist tobacco all mixed in with that of candy, whiskey, beer, and ancient sweat odors that clung to the walls and ceiling hit them. They walked past bolts of brightly colored cloth, stacks of men's britches and shirts, and a table piled high with boots of all sizes. They passed the notions counter, filled with elixirs and nostrums that were guaranteed to cure any and all illnesses. Most of them were based with alcohol or an opiate of some type, which killed the pain for a while.

Smoke and Jim stopped at the gun case to look at the new double-action revolvers.

"Pretty," Jim said.

"I don't like them," Smoke said. "The trigger pull is so hard it throws your aim off. And if you have to cock it, what's the point of having one of those things?"

"Good question," his deputy agreed. "They look awkward to me." Something on the nostrum table caught his eye and he picked up a bottle of Lydia E. Pinkham's Vegetable

Compound. He read the label, blushed, and put the bottle down. "The things they put on labels. I declare."

"Sally swears by it. Says it works wonders."

"You ever tasted it?"

"Hell, no! I did taste some Kickapoo Indian Sagwa a couple of years ago, back east."

"Did it work?"

"It tasted so bad I forgot what I took it for."

Smiling, the men stepped into the bar part of the trading post and walked up to the counter, in this case, several rough-hewn boards atop empty beer barrels.

Smith flicked his eyes to Jim and they narrowed in recognition. But he said only, "Howdy, boys. What might your poison be on this day?"

"Beer," Smoke said. "For both of us."

Both Smoke and Jim had quickly inspected the heavily armed men sitting at two pulled-together tables near a dirty window at the front of the barroom.

"Hadn't been up here in a long time,"Jim said after taking a pull from his mug. "I'd forgot how purty this country is. And how chilly the nights get."

"It do get airish at times," Smith agreed. "I got fresh venison stew on the stove and my squaw just baked some bread."

"Sounds good," Smoke said. "Jim?"

"I could do with a taste. Them cold fish we had for breakfast didn't nearabouts fill me up."

Smoke and Jim took their beers to a table across the room from the arsonists and began whispering to each other, knowing that would arouse some suspicion from the men who had torched the farmhouses and barns.

It didn't take long.

"What are you two a-whisperin' about over there?" one burly man called across the room.

Smoke looked at him just as the stew and bread was being placed on the table. "None of your damn business."

The man flushed and started to get up. One of his buddies

pulled him back into the chair. "Let it alone, Sonny. They ain't worth our time."

"I ain't so sure about that," Sonny said, giving Smoke a good once-over. "I seen that face afore."

"That's Murtaugh talkin'," Smith whispered. "Watch your step, Jim. They're all bad ones."

"Now the damn barkeep's whisperin'!" Sonny yelled.

Smith turned and faced him. "It's my goddamn store, lunkhead. I'll whisper anytime I take a notion to."

"Who you callin' a lunkhead, you old goat?" Sonny hollered.

"You, you big-mouth ninny!" Smith fired back, moving toward the bar. There, he reached behind him and came around with a sawed-off shotgun in his hands. He eared back both hammers and pointed it at Sonny. "Now, then, mule-mouth, you got anything else you'd like to say to me?"

Sonny's complexion, not too good to begin with, lightened appreciably as he looked at the twin barrels of the express gun, pointing straight at him. Those around him took on the expression of a very sad basset hound, knowing that if Smith pulled the triggers, someone would be picking them up with a shovel and a spoon.

"I reckon not," Sonny finally managed to say.

"Good." Smith eased down the hammers and laid the shotgun on the bar. "That's just dandy. Use your mouth to eat and drink, and stop flappin' that thing at me."

With a scowl on his ugly face, Sonny turned away, but not before giving Smoke another dirty look.

The stew smelled good and tasted even better. The bread was lavishly buttered, and Smoke and Jim fell to eating.

"Bring us some of that stew," Murtaugh called.

"Dollar a bowl," Smith told him.

"A dollar a bowl! Hell, man, that's plumb unreasonable."

"Then go hungry."

"I'll take another bowl," Jim said. "That's fine eatin'."

"You better see the color of his money afore you dish up

anymore grub to him," Murtaugh said. "He don't look like he's very flush to me."

"You worry about your own self," Jim verbally fired across the room. "I got money, and I earned it decent."

"What'd you mean by that?" the arsonist asked.

"Just what I said."

"You sayin' I ain't decent?"

"You said that, not me. Now hush up. I'm tryin' to eat, not jaw with you."

Murtaugh gave him a dirty look. "Maybe you think you're boss enough to shut me up?"

"Just as soon as I finish eatin', mister."

"Anybody busts up furniture, they pay for it," Smith said.

"They started this war of words," Smoke pointed out. "All we did was come in for a drink and some food."

"That's right," Jim said, spooning stew into his mouth. "Sad state of affairs when a man can't even eat without havin' to listen to all sorts of jibber jabber from lunkheads."

"Now, I ain't puttin' up with no saddle-bum callin' me a lunkhead!" Murtaugh stood up. He walked across the room. "I better hear some apologies comin' out of that mouth of yourn, cowboy," he said to Jim.

Jim grinned up at him. His right hand was holding a spoon, his left hand out of sight.

Jim belched loudly. "There's your apology, big-mouth. Catch it and carry it back across the room with you."

Murtaugh cursed and swung a big fist at Jim's head. But Jim anticipated the punch and ducked it, coming out of the chair and driving his fist into the bigger man's stomach. Murtaugh bent over, gagging. Jim grabbed the man by his hair and slammed his forehead onto the tabletop. Turning the stunned Murtaugh around, and grabbing him by the collar and the seat of his britches, Jim propelled him across the room, dumping him onto the table he had just exited.

"You boys best look after him," Jim told Murtaugh's buddies. "He can't seem to take care of hisself atall."

Sonny looked around him. Smith was holding the Greener, hammers back, pointed at him.

Jim walked back to his table and looked at the spilled stew. "Get the money for this from Murtaugh," he told Smith. "It was his head that spilt it."

"I'll be damned!" Murtaugh said, and charged across the room at Jim, both fists whipping the air.

Jim picked up a chair and hit the rampaging Murtaugh in the face with it. The firebug hit the floor, on his back, and did not move. His face was bloody and several teeth had departed his mouth to take up residence on the floor.

"That does it," Sonny said, rising from his chair. He looked at Smith. "You gonna take a side in this?"

Smoke stood up, brushing back his coat, exposing his .44's. "Stay out of it, Smith. We're deputy sheriffs from down Barlow way. These men are wanted for arson and destruction of livestock. Any damage to your place will be taken care of."

"That's fair. I know Jim and you look familiar to me. Who you be, mister?"

"Smoke Jensen."

Sonny suddenly looked sick. And so did the other four with him.

"Have mercy!" Smith said.

"We ain't done nothin' to nobody and we ain't destroyed no livestock," Sonny said.

Murtaugh groaned on the floor and sat up. He blinked a couple of times and wiped his bloody mouth with the back of his hand. "What the hell's goin' on?"

"You're under arrest," Jim told him.

"Your aunt's drawers, I am!" Murtaugh's hand dropped to the butt of his gun at just about the same time Jim kicked him in the face. Murtaugh hit the floor again and this time he was out for the count.

Sonny grabbed for his gun and Smoke shot him in the belly. The outlaw stumbled backward and sat down hard on the floor, both hands holding his .44-caliber-punctured belly. He started hollering.

One of his buddies jerked iron and Jim took him out of the game with a slug to the shoulder.

The trading post erupted in gunsmoke and lead. The booming of .44's and .45's rattled the windows and shook the glasses behind the bar. Things really got lively when Smith leveled his Greener and blew one outlaw clear out of the barroom, the charge of rusty nails, ball bearings, tacks, and whatever else Smith could find to load his shells nearly tearing the man in two, picking him off his boots, and tossing him out a window.

One outlaw, gut-shot and screaming in pain, dropped his pistols and went staggering out into the other room. He died underneath the table holding five-cent bottles of Dr. Farrigut's elixir for the remedying of paralysis, softening of the brain, and mental imbecility.

When the dust and bird-droppings from the ceiling and gunsmoke began to clear the room, three arsonists were dead, one was not long for this world, and Murtaugh was again trying to sit up, blood from his broken nose streaming down his chin. The punk Jim had shot through the shoulder was leaning up against a wall, moaning in pain.

"My, my," Smith said, picking out the empties from his Greener and loading up. "I ain't seen such a sight in two . . . three years. Things was gettin' plumb borin' around here. Them no-goods really burn some folks out?"

"Five families," Smoke told him, punching out his empty brass and reloading. "All good people. I suspect Big Max Huggins paid them to do it."

"I'll talk," the shoulder-shot outlaw hollered. It was Big Max who paid us to do it. I'll testify in court. I'll tell . . ."

Murtaugh palmed a hide-out gun and shot the man between the eyes, closing his mouth forever.

Smoke slammed the barrel of his .44 against Murtaugh's

head, and for the third time in about three minutes, the out-law went to sleep on the floor.

"Gimme ten dollars for the winder and you give whatever else is in their pockets to them folks that was burnt out," Smith said. "That fair?"

"Plenty fair," Jim said. "The families will thank you."

Smoke tied Murtaugh's hands behind his back with rawhide and straightened up. "We'll help you bury this trash, Smith. Then I'll get a signed statement from you attesting to the fact that you heard that one"—he pointed to the man with a hole beween his eyes—"confessing as to who paid them. You won't have to appear in court."

"Good enough," Smith said. "Shovel's in the back. I'll get my old woman to sing a death chant for them. She's Flathead. Does a nice job of it, too. Right touchin', some folks say."

Smoke put all the guns in a sack and tied it to a saddle horn, while Jim readied the horses for travel back to Barlow. The guns and horses and saddles they would give to the farmers who were burned out. The men had about five hundred dollars between them. That would go a long way toward rebuilding the homes and barns and smokehouses.

Morning Dove was still chanting her death song as they rode away.

18

Judge Garrison read the signed statement from Smith.

"Will that hold up in a court of law, Judge?" Smoke asked.

"It will in my court," the judge said with a smile. "Besides, both you and Deputy Dagonne heard one man confess. Don't worry, Smoke. Just remember the name of the town the jury is going to be picked from."

Both men shared a laugh at that. Smoke said, "Any further word about Max Huggins's background?"

"Yes, but unfortunately, we can't use any of it. Some of the parties involved are still too frightened to testify. Others have moved away or died. While the authorities east of here know Max is guilty, they can't prove it."

Smoke thought about that for a moment. "But Max doesn't have to know that, Judge."

The judge looked puzzled for a moment, then smiled. "Of course, you're quite right."

"Let me think about how we can use that information, Judge. We've got Max bumping from side to side now, let's see if we can keep him that way."

"Good idea. I have trial scheduled to start Thursday for

those who tried to shoot up the town. I want extra security, Smoke."

"You've got it, Judge. How about Melvin Malone's case?"

"His is the first one I try. This is . . . unusual for a judge, Smoke. But I want to ask your opinion. I can put him in jail. I can put him to doing community work . . . public service work it's now being called. But putting him to work cleaning the streets is only going to anger him further. Jail? Probably do the same thing. Or I can fine him. What do you think?"

Smoke rolled a cigarette and lit up. Finally, he shrugged his shoulders. "The boy wants to kill me so bad now it's like a fire inside him. . . ."

"Is he that good?" the judge interrupted.

"I doubt it. He makes the mistake that so many would-be gunhandlers make: He hurried his first shot. I was born blessed with excellent eye and hand coordination, Judge. I was born ambidextrous." He smiled. "Sally taught me that word, by the way. The speed came with years of practice. I still practice. But I think the thing that keeps me alive—or has kept me alive all these years—is that I'm not afraid when the moment comes. I'm confident without being overly so. As to your original question . . . fine him and let him walk for all I care."

The judge nodded. "It might buy us more time, if you know what I mean."

"I do. Kill Melvin now, and Red is very likely to blow wide open. The town is growing stronger every day. In another two weeks, it would take an army to overrun it."

"That's correct. And we owe it all to you."

Smoke waved that away. "I just propped you people up, that's all. Gave you all a little talking to and jerked you around and around. You all did the rest."

The judge grinned and rubbed the side of his face. "I never thought I'd see the day when I appreciated a slapping around, but I do, boy, I do."

"See you around, Judge."

Smoke stepped out of the judge's chambers and walked the streets of town. People waved and called his name as he passed. No doubt about it, Smoke thought. These folks are going to fight for their town. And they're probably going to have it to do . . . very soon.

He walked back to the jail and stepped inside. Murtaugh started cussing him as soon as he heard the jingle of Smoke's spurs. "You'll never hold me in this cracker box, Jensen. Soon as I can get my hands on a gun, you're dead, hotshot. You're dead, and that's a promise."

Smoke did not reply.

"I know a lot of things you don't, Jensen," Murtaugh kept flapping his mouth. "A whole lot of things."

Smoke waited.

Murtaugh laughed from his cell. "Have your trials, Jensen. Let that lard-butted judge bang his gavel and hand down his pronouncements. It ain't gonna make a bit of difference in the long run."

Murtaugh lay down on his bunk and shut his mouth.

Smoke got up and closed the door to the cell block.

"Have the others had anything to say?" he asked Sal.

"They've all been boastin' about us not keepin' them for very long. I been doin' some thinkin' about that. I think someone's gonna spring them after they've been sentenced."

"From the jail, you think?" Smoke asked.

Sal shook his head. "I don't know. I'd guess so. Max or Red ain't gonna take a chance of bustin' them away from the prison wagon when they come to haul them off to the territorial prison. That'd bring too much heat on Max, and he don't want that. So, yeah. I'd say they'll make their try just after these hard cases are sentenced."

"We have until Thursday to make some plans. The judge has requested extra security, so he thinks something is in the works, too."

Pete Akins hitched at his gunbelt. "Max could have at least seventy-five men ready to ride in ten minutes. He could pull fifty more in here in two . . . three days. The folks in this town are good people, and I mean that; I never did none of them no harm and they know it. They've accepted me. But they ain't gunhands, Smoke. If you know what I mean."

Smoke knew what he meant. Most of the men were good shots with a rifle. But few of them had ever killed a man close up. They had fought in the war; but that was, for the most part, a very impersonal thing.

Smoke tossed the question out, "How many men does Red Malone have on the payroll?"

"Thirty," Jim answered it. "He pays them all fightin' wages. And there ain't no backup in none of them. They ride for the brand and that's it."

"So we're conceivably looking at anywhere from a hundred to a hundred and fifty men."

"Or more," Pete added.

Smoke paced the office in silence, deep in thought. Finally, he stopped and faced his deputies. "He's got to try to destroy the town. That's his only option. Killing me alone won't stop the movement now. He can't let Sally's people start up this proposed bank. That would bring the state and in some cases, the federal government into it . . . if anything were to happen to it."

"Maybe there's another way to look at that, Smoke," Sal pointed out. "Maybe Max wants the bank to start up. Rob the bank, destroy the town, and haul his ashes out of the area and start up somewheres else. You can bet that he has someone in this town feedin' him information."

"Who?" Jim asked.

Sal shook his head. "That I don't know. It could be anybody. The swamper over at the saloon. The bartender, a store clerk . . . anybody who's hard up for money."

"Hell, that could be any one of a hundred people," Pete said. "Lemme tell you about Max. He's sneaky. He has one ear to the ground all the time. He hears about somebody seein' somebody else's wife, he holds that over their head.

He finds out about somebody bein' wanted, say, back in Ohio, he uses that for leverage. Max can be smooth. He might have loaned someone in this town money when he first come here. Money's tight right now. Maybe they couldn't repay him like they said they would. Man, he could have half-a-dozen people in this town feedin' him information."

Smoke turned and looked out the window. It might be Jerry at the saddle shop. Lucy at the hotel. The boy down at the stable. One of the farmers scattered around this end of the county. One of Joe Walsh's hands. Then it came to Smoke; but he kept his suspicions to himself, hoping they would not prove true.

He left the office and walked over to the hotel. He sat with Sally for a long time in their suite, talking, exchanging ideas. At first she thought his suspicions to be perfectly horrible. Then, gradually, she began to agree. When Smoke left, both he and Sally wore long faces.

Smoke walked the streets, looking hard into the face of every man and women he passed. Had to be, he thought. I didn't see it at first because I wasn't looking for it. But as he spoke and waved to another citizen, heading out of town, the family resemblance was just too strong to ignore.

There it was, staring him right in the face and saying good morning to him.

"You have to be joking!" Judge Garrison said, recoiling back in his chair.

"No. I'm ninety-nine percent certain. It has to be, Judge. Look at the person."

The judge drummed his fingertips on his desk. He shook his head and sighed. "Now that you mention it, I can see it. My God. I would have never put it together. It was all a sham on this person's part."

"It had to be, Judge. Looking back, it all went down too smoothly, with no arguments."

"And you propose to do what about it at this time?"

"I don't know. From all I've learned by association, this individual does not appear to be a bad person. Rather likable, actually. Let's just sit on this for the time being, Judge. See what develops."

"Just between us?"

"You, me, and Sally are the only three in town who know or who suspect."

"You think it's just this one person?"

Smoke sighed. "I hope so. But how can we be sure?"

"We can't."

Smoke stood up and put on his hat. He told the judge about Sal's suspicions as to when an attack to free the prisoners might take place.

The judge nodded his head in agreement. "I think he's right. They wouldn't want to attack the prisoner wagon from the territorial prison; that might bring the state militia down on their heads. They'll strike here, Smoke. Bet on it. We'll just have to be ready for it."

"We'll be ready," Smoke assured him. "I'm going to deputize all of Joe Walsh's hands and Brown and Gatewood and the other farmers in that area just in case Max tries a diversion to pull me out of town."

"That's a good idea. If trouble comes—and it would be a diversion—north of town, Brown and his friends could then legally handle it. Same with trouble south of town. I'll draw up papers making them full deputies. That will make it official and part of the record."

"The trial going to be in the new civic building?"

"Yes. I expect a large crowd to attend. Oh, by the way, the Marblys' dog had puppies about six weeks ago. Mrs. Marbly said to tell you to stop by and pick one out for Lisa Turner."

"I'll do that right now. See you, Judge."

Marbly grinned at Smoke. "I'm afraid they're mutts, Marshal. But they sure are cute. Come on, I'll show them to you."

"Mutts is right," Smoke said, squatting down by the

squirming, yelping litter. "That one," he said, pointing. "The one with the patch around his eye."

"Her eye," Mrs. Marbly corrected.

"Whatever. I like that one."

"Lisa will love it. Tell Mrs. Turner she's paper-trained and completely weaned."

"Victoria will love that, I'm sure." Smoke picked up the puppy, who promptly peed all down his shirt from excitement and then licked his face to apologize, and carried the squirming mass of energy over to Dr. Turner's house.

Lisa was so happy she cried—she named the pup Patches—and ran out in the backyard to play.

Since it was not proper for a man to be alone in a house with a married woman, Vicky invited Smoke to take coffee with her on the front porch.

"I love everything about this town, Smoke," she said after the coffee was poured. "The people are so friendly and they accepted us immediately."

"Yes. They're good people. Where is Robert?"

"On a call out in the country. He left early this morning and said he wouldn't be back until late. He wanted to check on the families who were burned out."

"Anything serious?"

Vicky laughed. "Not really. One of the kids came down with chicken pock and gave it to all the other kids who hadn't as yet had it. A lot of them are having an itching good time."

Smoke grimaced, remembering his own bout with chicken pock as a boy back in Missouri.

"Are you expecting trouble when the trial starts, Smoke?"

"I won't lie to you, yes, I am. Either during the trial or just after the sentencing. Security will be tight. Are you planning on attending?"

"I . . . don't know. I doubt it. I don't want Lisa to have to hear all that—there will probably be some pretty rough language at times—and if I went, I'd have to leave her alone, and I won't do that."

"I think that's wise. Sally isn't going to attend either. I'll ask her if she'll come over and stay with you. If there is trouble, Sally—as you've seen in the shooting classes—can handle a six-shooter with either hand. And won't hesitate to use one."

Victoria shook her head. "Sally certainly has changed since our days back at school."

"Out here, Vicky, one must change. Believe me when I say that the West will be wild for many years to come. People out here resist change; they fight it. It's the sheer vastness of the West that makes laws so difficult to enforce. Here it is 1883, and there are still many areas that remain largely unexplored. Millions of acres for outlaws to run into and hide. Oh, it's getting smaller with each year that passes. Law enforcement people are being linked by telegraph and train, but the gun still remains the great settler of troubles."

"When will you hang your guns up, Smoke?"

"When a full year passes and no one comes after me looking for a reputation. When newspapers and magazines and books no longer carry my name."

Victoria smiled. "What you're saying is, you will never hang them up."

"I'm afraid that's true."

"Would you like to hang them up?"

"Very much so." He looked at her and smiled. "For one thing, they're heavy."

She laughed aloud at that, then sobered. "What value do you place on human life, Smoke?"

"The highest value I can accord it, Vicky . . . for those who respect the rights of others; for those who can follow even the simplest rules of society. I don't prejudge on the basis of what a person has contributed to our society, but whether a person has taken away from it. None of us are obligated to create fine art or music, or invent things that better mankind. We're not obligated to do anything to improve society. What we are obligated to do is not take away from it." He waved one big hand. "There is an entire subculture out there with only lawlessness on their minds. To hurt, to steal, to kill, to maim, to destroy. They don't give a damn for your rights, or my rights, or Lisa's rights to live life and enjoy it in relative safety and comfort. They want what they want and to hell with anything else. They spit in the face of law and order and decency. If those types of people get in my way, I'll kill them."

Although the day was not cool, Victoria shivered. It did not escape the attention of Smoke.

"You think I'm half savage, don't you, Vicky?" he asked.

"I don't know what my thoughts are about you," she replied honestly. "You bring Lisa a little puppy and then talk about killing human beings. You are a philosopher and yet you've killed at least a hundred men. Probably twice that number. You respect law and order, and yet carry the name of gunfighter. I think you are a walking contradiction, Smoke Jensen."

He smiled. "I've been called that, too, Vicky."

"What are you, Smoke Jensen? The Robin Hood of the West?"

"I don't know whether I'm that or that fellow who went around sticking his lance into windmills."

"Don Quixote. No, I don't think you and Don Quixote have much in common. You get quite a lot accomplished . . . in your own rough way."

"It's a rough world, Vicky. There is a saying out here: A man saddles his own horse and kills his own snakes. Now, only a few species of snakes are harmful, and a rattlesnake will usually leave you alone if you don't mess with it. But these two-legged snakes we have surrounding us right now are the vicious kind. They are capable of thinking, know right from wrong, but still want to strike out and sink their fangs into anyone who gets in their way or tries to block their lawless behavior. They have had their chance to live decently. They looked at a decent way of life and chose to ignore it. And they've made that choice dozens of times. Nobody forced them into a life of crime. They chose it willingly. As far as I am concerned, that means they gave up any right to demand compassion when they're caught. If they face me, they are going to get a bullet."

"The West frightens me, Smoke. I like the people in this town. But even they carry guns."

"Then go back east, Vicky. Go back where you have a uniformed police officer on every street corner and it's getting to be when a criminal is caught, the punishment is light or nothing at all."

"But they're human beings, Smoke!"

"They're garbage, Vicky. Rabies-carrying rats whose diseased fleas are hopping onto everyone who gets close to them."

Smoke stopped talking as a tall stranger on a painted pony rode slowly into town. The stranger cut his eyes to Smoke, sitting on the porch, and smiled.

Smoke stood up. "Time to go to work, Vicky. Max is pulling in the heavyweights now."

"What do you mean?"

"That's Dek Phillips. A hired gun from down Texas way originally."

"Why is he here?"

Smoke stepped off the porch. "To kill me."

19

Victoria gasped and put one hand to her mouth. "But . . . you're the marshal! A deputy sheriff!"

"That doesn't mean anything to men like Dek. When this is over, Vicky—the war, I mean—and Max Huggins and Red Malone are either dead or have pulled out, go on back to Vermont or wherever you came from. Maybe I'm judging you hastily. But I don't think you're cut out for the West. Excuse me now, Vicky. I got to go stomp on the head of a snake."

"You're going to arrest him?"

"I'm probably going to kill him."

"But he hasn't done anything!"

"That's right. So I'll just crowd a little bit and see what he's got on his mind. If he wants to ride on out, I'll let him. Thanks for the coffee. See you, Vicky."

Smoke walked over to his office. Sal, Jim, and Pete were standing out in front. Dek's horse was tied to the hitchrail outside the saloon.

"We seen him ride in," Sal said. "You know him, Smoke?"

"I know him. From years back. He's a no-good."

"We agree on that," Pete said. "I'd hired on for fightin' wages down in Arizona some years back. I seen Dek shoot a nester woman in the back. I drew my wages and left. But give the devil his due, Smoke. He's good. He's damn good."

"I've seen him work. Yeah, he's good. But the problem is he knows it and it's swelled his head. He stopped working with his gun years ago, letting his reputation carry him."

"By the way," Jim said. "I been hearin' shootin' every mornin' for the past week or more. From outside of town. Real faint like. Sounds like someone practicin'. Reckon who that is?"

Smoke stepped off the boardwalk. "Me," he said. He walked across the dirt street to the saloon and pushed over the batwings, stepping into the dimness.

The bar had cleared of patrons when Dek walked in. His reputation was known throughout the West, and unlike Smoke, he liked all the hoopla. Smoke walked to the bar and faced Dek, leaning against the other end of the long counter.

"Jensen," Dek said. "I hear you been throwing a wide loop here of late."

"What of it?"

"Some folks don't like it. So they got ahold of me to cut you back to size some."

"And you figure you're the man for the job, huh?"

"I figure so."

"Anybody ever tell you that you were a damn fool, Dek?"

The gunfighter flushed, then fought his sudden anger under control and smiled at Smoke. "That won't work, Jensen. So save your little mind games for the two-bit punks."

"That's you, Dek."

Dek carefully picked up his shot glass and took a small sip of whiskey, gently placing the drink back on the bar. "You've had all those books written about you. I even seen a play some actors put on about you once. Made me want to puke.

Smoke waited. He'd played this scene many times in his life. Dek was working up his courage.

The barkeep said, "Can I pull you a beer, Marshal?"

"Yes, that would be nice. Thanks, Ralph. A beer would taste good."

Dek tossed a coin on the bar. "On me, barkeep. It's gonna be his last one."

"It's on the house," Ralph said. "And I 'spect the marshal will be comin' in tomorrow for his afternoon taste."

Dek didn't like that. His eyes narrowed and his left hand clenched into a fist. Slowly, he relaxed and picked up his whiskey. Another tiny sip went down his throat.

Ralph slid the beer mug up the bar and Smoke stopped it with his hand. He took a healthy pull, holding the mug in his left hand. He wiped his mouth with the back of his hand and took several steps toward Dek.

Dek watched him, the light in his eyes much like that of a wild animal, filled with suspicion.

Smoke stopped and said, "Why, Dek?"

"Huh? Why? Why what, Jensen?"

"Why do you want to kill me?"

"That's a stupid question! 'Cause there's money on your head, that's why."

"What good is it going to do you dead?" Smoke took another few steps.

"Huh? Dead? You're the one gonna be dead, Jensen. Not me. Now you're crowdin' me, Jensen. You just stand still. Back up and drink your beer."

Smoke took another step. He was almost within swinging distance. "You got a mother somewhere, Dek?"

"Naw. She's been dead. Now, dammit, Jensen, you stand still, you hear me?"

"No wife for me to write to?"

"Naw. Why the hell would you want to write to my wife even if I had one?"

"To tell her about your death, that's why." Smoke took two more steps.

"Jensen, you're crazy! You know that? You're as nutty as a road lizard. You . . ."

Smoke hit him in the mouth with a right that smashed the man's lips and knocked him spinning. Smoke jerked the man's guns from leather and tossed them behind the bar. He stepped back, raising his fists.

"Now, Dek. Now we'll see how much courage you have. Come on, Dek. You think you're such a bad man. Fight me. Stand up, Dek. I don't think you know how. I don't think you have the guts to fight me."

Dek cussed him.

Smoke took the time to pull riding gloves from behind his gunbelt and slip them on. He laughed at Dek. "Oh, come on, Dek. What's the matter? You afraid I might kick your big tough butt all over this town in front of God and everybody? You afraid somebody might see and laugh at you?"

"That'll be the day," Dek snarled, raising his fists. "You ain't about man enough to put me down."

"We'll sure see, Dek. But there is one thing that puzzles me."

"What's that?"

"Are you trying to talk me to death?"

Cursing, Dek charged Smoke. Smoke ducked a wild swing and tripped him. Grabbing Dek by the collar and by the seat of his pants, Smoke propelled him through the batwings and out into the street, Dek hollering and cussing all the way. On the boardwalk, Smoke gave a mighty heave and tossed Dek into the dirt.

Dek landed on his face and came up spitting dirt and cussing and waving his arms.

Smoke stepped in and gave Dek a combination, left and right, both to the face, which staggered the gunfighter and backed him up, shaking his head and spitting blood.

A crowd began gathering, grinning and watching the fun. The women tried to frown and pretend they didn't like it, but from the gleam in their eyes, they were very much enjoying watching one of Max Huggins's men get the tar knocked out of him.

"Knock his teeth down his throat, Smoke!" Mrs. Marbly hollered.

"Yeah," the minister's wife shouted. "Smite him hip and thigh and bust his mouth, too, Marshal."

Dek looked wildly around him. He looked back at Smoke just in time to catch a big right fist smack on his nose. The nose crunched and Dek squalled as the blood flew. Dek backed up, trying to clear his vision.

Jensen didn't give him much chance to do that. Smoke waded in, both big fists working. He busted Dek in the belly and connected with a left to the man's ear that guaranteed him a cauliflower for a long time . . . not to mention impairing his hearing for the rest of his life.

Dek connected with a punch that bruised Smoke's cheek and seemed only to make him stronger.

Dek suddenly realized that Smoke was going to cripple him; was going to forever end his days as a gunfighter, and was going to do it with his fists, not his guns. He looked for a way out. But several hundred people had formed a wide circle around them. There was no way out. He was trapped.

"Gimme a break, Jensen," he panted the plea. "I ain't never done nothin' to you to deserve this."

Smoke almost laughed at him. The man had been hired to kill him and was now asking for a break. Dek Phillips had killed women and children and brought untold grief and suffering to many, many others. And he was asking for a break.

Smoke gave him a break. He stepped in close and with one powerful fist broke several of Dek's ribs.

Dek yelped in pain and involuntarily lowered his guard. Smoke knocked him down with a left to the jaw.

Smoke stood over him and said, "You know what I'm going to do, Dek. Are you going to lay there like a whipped coward while I kick you to death, or get up and fight?"

Dek slowly got to his boots. "You're a devil, Jensen," he panted, blood dripping from his face. "You got to come from hell." He flicked a fake at Smoke but Jensen wasn't buying it. Dek swung a looping right that Smoke ducked under and danced away.

"Stand still, damn you, Jensen!"

Smoke's reply was a right to the jaw. Even those in the rear of the crowd heard Dek's jaw break.

Smoke began to deliberately and methodically ruin the man. He gave him his overdue punishment for all the good lives he had taken over the years, and for all the misery and heartbreak he had caused.

The crowd no longer cheered. They stood in silence and watched with satisfaction in their eyes as Max Huggins's man was beaten half to death in front of their eyes. Vicky Turner stood in silence, shocked by the brutality taking place in front of her eyes. Sally Jensen stood beside her. The wife of Smoke Jensen knew fully well what her husband was doing, and she approved of it. Men like Dek Phillips could not understand compassion because they possessed none. They understood only one thing: brute force. That was the only thing they could relate to. And Smoke was giving Dek a lesson in it that he would never forget.

When Dek Phillips finally measured his length in the dirt and did not get up, Smoke walked to a horse trough and bathed his face and hands. He straightened up and said to Pete, "Tie him across his saddle and take him to the edge of Hell's Creek."

"The man is injured!" Robert Turner shouted. "He needs medical attention."

"Shut up, boy!" Joe Walsh spoke from the edge of the crowd. He had ridden up unnoticed and sat his saddle during the final minutes of the fight. "Dek Phillips just got all the attention his kind deserve." The crowd muttered their agreement with that.

Sal said, "This ain't back east, Doctor. The laws are still few out here. You're a nice fellow, I'll give you that, but you got some adjustin' to do if you're gonna make it out here. You might feel sorry for a rabid dog, but you don't try to comfort it. You just kill it. You best learn that."

His face stiff with anger, Dr. Robert Turner took Victoria's hand and left the street, walking back to his office.

Pete rode out, leading the horse with Dek Phillips tied across the saddle.

Joe Walsh told several of his hands to accompany Pete, to act as guards in case some of the scum at Hell's Creek tried to waylay him.

Smoke walked back to the hotel to bathe the sweat and grime from him and change into fresh clothing.

Henry Draper, editor of the *Barlow Bugle,* headed back to his office to write the story of how the mighty hired gunfighter Dek Phillips had fallen under the fists of Marshal Smoke Jensen. He knew he could sell the story to dozens of newspapers back east. The reading public loved it.

The crowds broke up into small groups, talking over and rehashing the fight. With each victory they were stronger as a town, becoming closer-knit. The advance party from back east was due in the next day, and soon they would have a bank. Max Huggins would continue trying to destroy them— they all knew that—but they all sensed he would fail.

And they owed it all to one man: Smoke Jensen.

Max Huggins had just come from the bedside of Dek Phillips. The horse doctor who had attended the gunfighter had said the man would probably live, but he would be marked forever. His jaw was broken, his ribs were cracked, one arm was broken, a lot of his teeth had been knocked out. And worse, the horse doctor said, Dek Phillips's spirit appeared to be broken.

"The trial will probably last two . . . three days." Val Singer broke into Max's thoughts. "It'll take a good two weeks for the prison wagon to get around to pickin' up the boys. By that time, the bank will be operatin'. We hit the bank, loot the town, lift us some petticoats and have some fun with the women, and then strike out for greener pastures. What'd you think, Max?"

Max was thinking about Smoke Jensen. For three weeks, the big man had been exercising, running several miles a day and working out. He might not be able to beat Smoke Jensen with a gun—and that was up for grabs, for Max knew he was one of the best with a short gun—but there was no doubt in Max's mind that he was the better fighter of the two.

But how much time did he have? His informant in Barlow had sent him word that Judge Garrison and Smoke Jensen were gathering up old arrest warrants on him from his days back east. Two or three weeks might be cutting it very close.

And his informant had also told him that old warrants were being looked at against Red Malone. If the authorities back east came through, the rancher would have to run with Max. And Max knew the man would never agree to do that. The man would stand his ground and die with a six-shooter in his hand. He was too bullheaded to do anything else.

With a deep sigh, Big Max turned his attentions to the group of outlaws in his office. "Yes," he said slowly. "We're out of time here. Smoke Jensen has beaten us. Red may not see it that way, but I do. Smoke has used fists and guns to bring civilization to our doorstep."

Max eyeballed the group, one at a time. Val Singer, Warner Frigo, Dave Poe, Alex Bell, Sheriff Paul Cartwright.

"We're all wanted men, maybe not under the names we're using now, but wanted nevertheless. Two or three weeks is going to be cutting it awfully close. But I understand that is the way it's going to have to be. Monies have to be in the bank before we hit the town. To hell with those in jail. If we can get them out during the raid, fine. If not, that's all right, too. Are we in agreement with that?"

They were in agreement.

"The next problem," Max said, "is where do we run to?"

Everyone had a different idea. Cartwright couldn't go back to California. He was wanted out there. Singer couldn't go east. He was wanted in six or seven states in that direction. . . . And so it was with them all.

Max waved them silent. "All right, all right! Enough. It might be best if we split up after the raid anyway. We'll pick a place to meet and divvy up the loot, and then split up. And boys," he eyeballed each of them, "I shall be personally leading this raid."

The outlaws all exchanged glances. Max had masterminded a lot of raids, but none of them had ever known him to lead one. They were curious, and Val Singer put that curiosity into words.

"I have plans for a certain lady in that town," Max said with a smile. "I want her to know a real man just once in her life . . . just before I kill her."

"Well, if you gonna be draggin' some squallin' petticoat around with you," Warner Frigo said, "I think it's best we do split up. We're gonna have enough money to divvy up to buy the best women in any crib in the world."

"Yeah," Dave Poe said. "That don't make no sense, Max. It's too risky. Once we're out of this area, when words gets out about harmin' a woman, they'll be posses lookin' for you all over the place. And you do have a tendency to stand out in a crowd," he added dryly.

"It'll die down. It always has before. Hell, don't you boys

get righteous on me. You've all raped before. Besides, you don't even know who I have in mind."

"Sure we do," Alex Bell said. "Has to be the doctor's wife, Victoria Turner."

Max smiled. "Nope. Her name is Sally. Sally Jensen."

20

The trial of the outlaws and the arsonist went off without a hitch. Judge Garrison handed down the toughest sentences he could under the law and the territorial prison was notified. The returning wire said it would be two or three weeks before the wagon could come and pick them up.

Smoke noticed the now-familiar buggy rolling out of town, heading north. He walked to the livery, threw a saddle on Star, and headed out, staying to the high ground, which oftentimes ran parallel to the road but high-up.

He trailed the buggy to within a few miles of Hell's Creek and watched as Max Huggins rode out to meet it. Max and the driver of the buggy sat for a long time on a log, talking, Huggins with one big arm around the other person's shoulder.

That night he told Sally about it. She shook her head in disgust. "Things are just never what they seem to be, are hey, honey?"

"This thing isn't, that's for sure. Problem is, I don't know what to do about it. No laws have been broken. The only thing broken will be the faith of the townspeople."

"And a broken heart when the other partner in the marriage learns of it," she added.

"Yeah. If they don't already know about it."

"I hadn't thought about that. Oh, Smoke, I just can't believe that. Just thinking about it makes me sick!"

"I'll have to face one or the other pretty soon, I reckon. And I'm not looking forward to that. Well, let's get off of it. How's the bank coming along?"

"I just got word this morning. It'll open for business next Monday morning. The money will be coming in day after tomorrow. And it will be heavily guarded."

She handed him a telegraph and let him read it. He whistled. "That's a lot of money."

"Yes. And that will be too good an opportunity for Max to pass up."

"I wish you and Victoria would get out of here, Sally. The two of you go on back to the Sugarloaf."

She shook her head. "No. I'm staying. We'll leave together, Smoke."

He had expected that answer so it came as no surprise to him. "I'd say I have two weeks before Max hits us. Maybe three. But no longer. I think those rumors the snitch carried to him about those old warrants back east has him spooked. And I'm told that Red Malone is getting jumpy, too."

She smiled at him. "The Sugarloaf will look good, won't it?"

"You bet." He got up and found his hat. "I'm going to prowl the town for a while."

"Anything wrong?"

"No. I just want to check around."

"I'm going to read. If you're late, I'll leave the lamp low."

Smoke walked down the stairs and through the lobby speaking to the night clerk at the desk. The Grand Hotel was full, for with the coming of the paper, a doctor, two lawyers and a half-dozen new businesses, the town was experiencing a growth unseen since its inception.

The saloon was doing a land-office business and had hired two nighttime waitresses and a piano player. The piano player was banging out a tune, the melody floating on the night air.

Pete walked up, spurs jingling softly. "Horse tied out of sight down by the creek," he told Smoke. "I never seen the brand before. Fancy riggin'. Rifle is gone from the boot. We might have us a back-shooter in town."

"You tell the others?"

"Goin' to now."

"OK. Watch yourself."

Pete gone, Smoke stepped back into the shadows created by the storefront and lifted his eyes, inspecting the rooftops of the buildings across the street. He squatted down and removed his spurs, laying them behind a bench on the boardwalk.

Standing up, he freed his .44's and slipped into an alleyway, walking around behind the buildings. He paused at the alley's end, staying close to the hotel's outside wall. He listened, all senses working overtime.

Smoke watched a man come out of a privy and walk into the hotel, through the back door. The lamplight inside flashed momentarily as the door opened. Smoke closed his eyes to retain his night vision. He opened his eyes and walked on, slipping around the buildings.

He angled around Martha's Dress Shoppe and came out behind the cafe. A slight movement ahead of him flattened Smoke against the back wall of the cafe, eyes searching the darkness. He caught a faint glint of moonlight off what appeared to be the barrel of a carbine—short-barreled for easier handling. Smoke waited, muscles tensed. He pulled his right-hand .44 from leather and, with his left hand over the hammer to reduce the noise, cocked it.

The man behind the gun stepped away from the building, and for an instant, Smoke could see his face. It was no one he had ever seen before. The man was clean-shaven, his clothing dark and looking neat. The man took a step, a silent one. He wore no spurs.

Slowly, Smoke knelt down, carefully stretching out on the cool ground to offer the man less of a target. "You looking for me, partner?" Smoke softly called.

The man turned and fired, the slug striking the wood of the building some four feet above Smoke's head. Smoke fired, the .44 slug hitting the rifle and tearing the weapon from the man's hands. The gunman ran back into the darkness.

"Yo, Smoke!" Sal called from the street.

"I'm all right. Stay under cover. I'm thinking this man is not alone." Smoke rolled to his left as some primal warning jumped through his brain.

Two fast shots, coming from different weapons, tore up the ground where he had been lying.

Smoke caught the muzzle flashes of one of the guns and snapped off a fast shot. The gunhand screamed as the slug ripped his belly and sent him tumbling off the roof of the saddle shop. He hit the ground and did not move.

An unknown gunhand stepped out of his hiding place behind Smoke and leveled his pistol. Jim and Sal fired as one from the main street, both slugs striking the man, knocking him off his boots.

Smoke rolled and came up on his feet, behind a tree. Both his hands were filled with .44's, hammers back. A slug ripped the night, burning through the bark of the tree, knocking chip flying. Smoke stepped to the other side of the tree and fired twice, left and right guns working. The man doubled over both shots taking him in the stomach. Smoke ran to him and kicked the dropped guns out of his reach. He knelt down beside the hard-hit man just as his deputies came running up.

"You're not going to make it," Smoke told the bloodied man. "Who hired you?"

The man grinned through his pain. "Told the boys we w

gonna be buckin' a stacked deck comin' after you." He groaned. "But the money was just too good to pass up."

"Whose money?" Smoke asked.

"You go to hell!" the man said, then closed his eyes and died.

"This one's still alive!" Sal called, kneeling beside the man who had fallen off the roof. "But not for long. I think his neck's broke."

"Hell, that's Blanchard," Pete said, looking down at the man. "I thought he was in prison down in New Mexico." He knelt down. "Come on, Blanchard," he urged. "Go out clean for once in your life. This is your last chance, man. Who hired you?"

Two dozen people, men and women, in various dress, including nightshirts and long-handles, had gathered around.

"Huggins from over to . . . Hell's Creek," the dying man gasped. "Pulled us up from Utah. We rode the train. Me and Dixson. Dee was . . . he rode over from Idaho."

"Dee Mansfield?" Smoke questioned.

"Yeah."

"That his horse down by the crick?" Sal asked.

"Yeah. He . . . Gettin' cold and I can't . . . move my hands."

Dr. Turner pushed through the crowd and knelt down, looking at the man. It was a quick look. Blanchard had died.

The doctor stood up and faced Smoke. "When is this carnage going to end, Jensen?"

"Whenever Red Malone and Max Huggins call it off," Smoke told him. He spotted the undertaker. "Haul them off," he said. "OK, folks, show's over. Let's break it up."

"No, it isn't," Tom Johnson said, walking up. "Melvin Malone just rode into town. He's calling you out, Smoke."

"Damn!" the word exploded from Smoke's mouth. "I knew that kid would cut his wolf loose someday." He punched out his empties and loaded up full. "Sal, clear the streets."

"I demand an end to this barbaric practice of justice at the point of a gun!" Dr. Turner said. "Just arrest him, Marshal. You don't have to kill him. You have the manpower to overwhelm him."

Smoke looked at the man in the dim light. "You . . . demand, Robert? Who in the hell do you think you are, anyway? Demand? Overwhelm him? How? He's come to kill, Robert, not talk. He'll shoot anyone who tries to disarm him."

"You don't know that, Smoke. That's just conjecture on your part. Law and order must prevail out here. It's past time."

"Why don't you go disarm him, then, Doctor?" Sal suggested.

"I . . . uh . . . I'm not a lawman," the doctor said, his face coloring. "That's your job."

"Yeah, right," Sal's reply was dour. "I think that was the reason I hung up a badge the last time I wore one."

Smoke turned his back to the doctor and walked away, his deputies moving with him, the crowd following along.

"He's in the saloon," Tom called. "You goin' to kill the punk, Smoke?"

"I hope not," Smoke muttered.

"There might not be any other way, Smoke," Jim pointed out.

"I know. But I can always hope."

Smoke stepped up onto the boardwalk and pushed open the batwings. The piano player stopped his pounding of the ivories when he spotted Smoke. The waitresses moved as far away from the bar as they could get. The long bar was already void of customers. Only Melvin stood there, a whiskey bottle in front of him, his right hand close to the butt of his Colt.

"Come on in, Jensen," Melvin said. "I'll buy you a drink."

"You were banned from this town, Melvin. Leave now and I won't toss you in jail."

"You'll never toss me in jail again, Jensen. Me, or anyone else for that matter."

"Boy, don't be a fool!" Smoke snapped at him. He knew that his plan to move close enough to slug the young man was out the window. Kill was written on Melvin's face, and his eyes were unnaturally bright with the blood lust that reared up within him. "I've faced a hundred young hot-shots like you. They're all dead, boy. Dead, or crippled."

Smoke could tell that Melvin was not drunk. The young man had enough sense about him to lay off the bottle before a gunfight. Alcohol impaired the reflexes.

Melvin laughed at the warning.

Smoke was thinking fast. He had been warned that Melvin was very, very quick and very, very accurate, so any idea of just wounding the young man was out of the question. When Melvin dragged iron, Smoke was going to have to get off the first shot and make it a good one.

"Boy, think of your father." Smoke tried a different tact. "Your sister. Think what your dying is going to do to them."

"Me, dying?" The young man was clearly startled. "Me? Oh, you got it all wrong, Jensen. You're the one that's going to be pushin' up flowers, not me."

"Listen to me, boy," Smoke said, doing his best to talk some sense into Melvin. "You . . ."

"Shut up!" Melvin yelled, stepping away from the bar. "You're a coward, Jensen. You're afraid to draw on me."

A coldness touched Smoke. A coldness that was surrounded by a dark rage. It sometimes happened when he was looking at death. It was a feeling much like the ancient Viking berserkers must have experienced in battle.

"I tried, boy." Smoke's words were touched with sadness. "Nobody can say I didn't try."

"And that's all you're gonna do in this fight," Melvin sneered the words. "Try to beat me. You've had a long run, Jensen. Now it's over. Now my pa can stop worryin' about his back trail and we can get on with our lives."

"All but one of you," Smoke corrected the young man.

"Huh?"

"Your life is over."

With a curse on his lips, Melvin's hands flashed to his guns and he was rattlesnake quick. But Smoke's draw was as smooth as honey and lightning fast. Melvin got off a shot, the slug blowing a hole in the barroom floor. Smoke's first shot took the young gunslinger in the belly. Melvin's second shot grazed Smoke's shoulder, burning a hole in his shirt and searing his flesh. Smoke shot the young man again, the slug turning Melvin. Still he would not go down.

Melvin lifted his left-hand Colt and fired, the slug smashing the bar. Smoke shot him again and Melvin went down to his knees, still holding his Colts.

Smoke stepped through the swirl of gunsmoke and walked to the young man. He kicked the guns from his hands and stood over him.

"I beat Blackjack Simmons and Ted Novarro," Melvin moaned the words. "Holland didn't even clear leather against me."

"They were fast," Smoke spoke the words softly.

"But you . . ." Melvin gasped. "You . . ."

He toppled over on his face and began communicating with the afterlife.

Smoke punched out his empties and reloaded. "Jim, get word to Red that he can come in and take his boy home. Just Red. Anybody else of the Lightning brand tries to enter this town, I'll toss them in jail or leave them in the dust."

The young deputy left the barroom and walked to the stable, saddling his horse for the night ride.

"Knowing Red as I do," Sal pointed out, "he just might come bustin' up here with all his hands, figuring to burn down the town."

"If he does, it'll be the last thing he'll ever do," Smoke said. He looked around the barroom. "I want ten men on guard at all times tonight. Take some water and biscuits with you when you go to the rooftops. Go home and get your rifles." He looked at the barkeep. "Shut it down, Ralph."

"Will do, Marshal. I'll clean up and then get my rifle to stand a turn."

"Thanks, Ralph."

The body of Melvin Malone was carried to the undertaker and the lamps in the saloon were turned off. The men of the first watch were getting in place on the rooftops as Smoke, Sal, and Pete walked the boardwalks of the town, rattling doorknobs and looking into the darkness of alleys.

Smoke passed Robert Turner on the boardwalk as the man was going home. The doctor did not speak to the gunfighter.

"Yonder goes a scared man," Sal said. "Something about that fella just don't add up to me."

Pete said, "I been thinkin' the same thing. He looks familiar to me, but I swear I can't place him."

"Think of Max Huggins for a moment," Smoke told the men.

"What do you mean, Smoke?" Sal asked.

"Max Huggins is Dr. Robert Turner's brother."

21

Smoke swore his deputies to silence about the true identity of Dr. Turner, then went to the hotel to catch a few hours' sleep. He was up long before dawn. Smoke dressed quietly, letting Sally sleep, then went down to the jail to bathe his face and hands and shave. He walked out onto the silent boardwalks and leaned against a support pole. Jim had arrived back in town after delivering the news. He said Red did not take the news well. Smoke sent the man off to bed and then rolled a cigarette, waiting for the arrival of Red Malone.

Just at dawn, the hooves of a slow walking horse drummed over the wooden bridge at the south end of town. It was Red Malone, and he had come alone.

Red reined up and stared at Smoke through the gray light of dawn. The man's face was hard and uncompromising. "I come to get my boy, Jensen."

Smoke jerked a thumb. "He's over at the undertaker's, Red."

"I'll get my boy buried proper, Jensen, and then you and me, we'll settle this."

"Why settle anything, Red? Your boy came to me, looking for trouble. Thirty . . . forty men heard me practically beg him not to draw. He was a grown man and he made his choice. He tossed the dice and threw craps. Bury your boy and put the hate out of your heart."

Red stared at him for a long moment. Then, without another word, he turned his horse's head and rode slowly up the street, toward the undertaker. A few minutes later Melvin was tied across the saddle of his pony, the horse carrying its owner for the last time.

As he rode slowly past Smoke, Red turned his head and said, "I'll be back, Jensen."

"I'll be here, Red."

Smoke waited until the sounds of horses had faded to the south, then walked across the street to the hotel dining room for breakfast. Red was going to work himself up into a murderous rage, then gather all his hands and attack the town. He would get with Max Huggins and work it all out. Max and his men would attack from the north, Red and his bunch from the south. Smoke was sure of it.

After breakfast, Smoke walked up and down the town's streets, telling people what he felt was coming at them. They had all felt that sooner or later they would be attacked. They took the news stoically. Benson, the blacksmith, summed up the town's feelings. "We'll be ready, Marshal."

The town braced for trouble, and Smoke went to see Dr. Robert Turner.

The doctor met him at the door. "If you're hurt, I'll treat you, Smoke; I'd do that for any man. But other than that, you are not welcome in this house."

"I see," Smoke said, standing on the small porch. "Does that include my wife, too?"

Robert hesitated. Women were held in high esteem back east, but nothing compared to the way they were almost revered out here in the wild West. "Sally is welcome here anytime, of course."

"You just don't like my barbaric ways, is that it, Doc?"

"Something like that, yes. All this killing is quite unnecessary, you know."

"No, I didn't know that, Doc. What am I supposed to do when a man confronts me with a gun? Kiss him? Let me tell you something, Doc. This will probably change over the coming years, and in a way it'll be a sad thing when it does; but out here, a coward can't make it. Now, there is a reason for that. If a man is a coward, then there is a good chance that he's also a liar and a cheat. Not always, but often that's true. You see, Doc, out here, a man's word is his bond. If a man's word can't be trusted, what good is he? So no man wants the title of coward branded on him. Too much goes with it. Are you beginning to understand what I just said?"

"Of course, I understand it. It's still stupid, primitive, and barbaric."

"Victoria home?"

"No. She went shopping."

"That's good. 'Cause I just don't believe she knows the game you're playing."

Robert stared at him for a time. The doctor's eyes were unreadable. "I don't know what you're talking about, Jensen."

"You're a liar."

Robert didn't back up. "I'm no gunhand, Smoke. And I certainly can't whip you with my fists, so I'm not going to try. Does that make me a coward?"

Smoke chuckled. "No. But I didn't call you that to provoke a fight. That's a bully's way. And I'm not a bully. I called you that to get your attention. Have I got it?"

"Yes. I believe you could say that." Robert stepped out onto the porch and waved Smoke to a chair. "What's on your mind?"

"Your brother, Max Huggins."

Robert was so shaken he missed the seat of the chair and went tumbling to the porch floor. Smoke helped the man up and into the chair. Robert was ghost-white and his hands were trembling.

"You want me to get you a drink of water?" Smoke asked.

"That would be nice. Yes. Would you?"

"Sure." Smoke went into the kitchen, pumped a glass full of water, and took it to the man.

Robert drank the glass empty and sighed heavily, as if a load had been taken from him. "How did you find out about Max?"

"By looking at the two of you and guessing. I knew someone had been leaking information out of town, so I followed you one day. Now, then, what do you intend to do about it?"

The man shrugged. "Victoria doesn't know, Smoke."

"All right. Neither Sally nor I believed she was a part of it."

"How many people know?"

"Me and Sally. Judge Garrison. My deputies."

"When the townspeople find out, I guess I'm through in Barlow, right?"

"I imagine so. You and Victoria, you're not cut out for this kind of life, Robert. The West is not for people like you. It's still plenty raw out here. You and Victoria, you both want all the pretty things that are scarce out here. Women wear gingham out here, not lace. Coming up here from train's end, me and Sally took our baths in creeks. I can't work up a picture in my mind of you and Victoria doing that. Killings are common out here, Robert. Not as common as they used to be, but people will still travel a hundred miles to see a good hanging."

The city doctor shook his head at that and grimaced in disgust.

"And then there is the little matter of your brother to take into consideration."

"Max is my brother. Can't you understand that?"

"He's also a thief, a rapist, a murderer, and God only knows what else. And accept this, Doc: I intend to kill him."

"Judge, jury, and executioner, right, Smoke?"

"Sometimes that's the way it has to be, Robert. And you're no better than Max, are you, Robert?"

"What do you mean by that?"

"There was no old rancher that you befriended back in the city, was there, Robert?"

The doctor's silence gave Smoke his reply.

"I suspected as much. Max killed that rancher and then had the letter forged. The letter you showed your wife."

"He never said, and I never asked."

"Didn't you even care?"

"Yes," the doctor's reply was spoken low. "Yes, I cared. I came out here in hopes of changing my brother, making him see that what he was doing was wrong. Evil. Our parents died two years ago, four months apart. They left quite a sizeable estate; it all came to me. Of course, they had written Max out of the will years before. I even offered Max half of the estate."

"Sally thought you were a poor struggling doctor."

Robert laughed, a bitter bark that held no humor. "Hardly. I assure you I have plenty of money."

"And Max told you he would change his evil ways and become a fine upstanding citizen." It was not a question.

"Yes, he did, and I believed him."

"All that crap you told Victoria, that she wrote to Sally, about Lisa and Victoria being lusted after by Max. All that was a lie?"

"No. No, it wasn't. He told me he wanted my wife. And he told me he would use Lisa to have her."

"And you still defend the sorry no-good? Jesus Christ, Robert, what have you got between your ears? Mush?"

"I owe him my life, Smoke. Three times, I owe him. And I owe him my family fortune."

"You want to explain that?"

"A gang of thugs set on me when I was a boy. They had knives. Max whipped them. Every one of them. Later, when I got a—a woman in a family way, her father had me cornered, with a gun. Max killed him."

Smoke looked at the man, amazement in his eyes. "You're a real swell fellow, Robert. You know that?"

Robert could not miss the sarcasm in Smoke's tone. "She was just trash. So was her father."

"You did see the child through school, I hope?"

"Of course not. Don't be ridiculous. I told you, she was trash. Anyway, she moved away. I have no idea where she and the brat might be."

Smoke took off his hat and shook his head in disbelief. Robert was as bad, in his own way, as Max. He wondered if Victoria knew about any of it. He didn't think so. At least, he hoped not, for Sally's sake. "Go on, Robert." Smoke put his hat on and leaned back in the chair, rolling a cigarette. "It's such a heartrending tale."

"Yes. It really is, isn't it?"

Smoke looked at him to see if the man was serious. He was. Smoke sighed and waited.

"The third time Max saved my life I was in college. He was on the run from the law—had been for years—but he was back east at the time. I had a rather unpleasant experience with a brother. . . ."

"You have another brother?"

"Oh, no. This was a fraternity brother at school."

"What the hell is that? Never mind. I don't want to know."

"I beat the young man quite severely about the head with a brick. It was over a woman, of course. Max finished him off for me."

Smoke was jarred right down to his boots. The good doctor, Robert Turner, was crazy. Insane. Smoke had read of people who had, or professed to have, two or three or more personalities. This was, he believed, the first time he'd ever met one of those people. He sincerely hoped he would never meet another.

"Finished him off? What do you mean, Robert?" Smoke knew exactly what he meant, but he wanted to hear the words out of Robert's mouth.

"Killed him, of course. Oh, the young man was dying anyway. Max just took the brick and beat his head in with it. I was appalled, of course. I abhor violence of any kind."

"Yeah. I can sure see that."

"It was in the dead of winter. And my heavens, but it was cold. Max took the body and threw it into the river, after tying several heavy objects to it. We're brothers, you know. Brothers help each other."

"Yeah. Right."

"It was just after that when my father got into his . . . ah . . . predicament. Max took care of that, too. Then he headed west. He always kept in touch with me, though. We're brothers, you know."

"How did he take care of your father's . . . ah . . . troubles?"

"Killed my father's mistress. She was attempting to blackmail Father. That would have done poor Mum in had she ever found out about it."

"I'm sure it would have, Robert." It's just about doing me in listening to it, he thought.

Robert sat up straight in his chair and clasped both hands to his knees. "Well, my good fellow. I certainly am glad we had this little chat. I feel so much better now that I realize what an understanding man you are." He stood up, a broad smile on his face. "I must go see my patients now. They need me, you know? It's such a nice feeling to be wanted."

Robert walked back into the house, took his doctor's bag, and got into his buggy, clucking the horse forward. Smoke sat on the porch and watched the doctor drive out of town.

"The man is nuts," Smoke said. "Crazy and dangerous. Very dangerous."

He was sitting on the porch when Vicky strolled up, her arms filled with packages. She did not seem surprised to see Smoke sitting there. He helped her with her packages, then waited on the porch for her to come out of the house.

"Are you waiting for Robert?" she asked.

"No. I had a long chat with Robert. He just left. I was sitting here . . . ah . . . sort of catching my breath after our conversation."

"Whatever in the world do you mean, Smoke?"

Smoke did not know how to handle this. He was not the type of man who relied on finesse. His way was straight ahead and get the job done.

He shook his head and stood up. "Nothing, Vicky. It was just that our conversation got a little deep for me. Medical stuff."

"Oh! Are you ill? Is Sally all right?"

"Both of us are fine. Where is Lisa?"

"Playing with a friend." She smiled. "Don't worry. The kids are well guarded."

Smoke nodded. "Vicky, could I ask you some questions without your getting angry?"

"Why . . . of course." She studied his face. "It's Robert, isn't it?"

"Ah, yeah. It is." Smoke really didn't know how to get into this.

"He's a good man, I believe. But a very strange man at times. It's . . . and please don't think I'm criticizing him or talking behind his back; I've tried to discuss this with him. . . ." She paused. "It's almost as though he is several different people in one body. Do you know what I mean?"

"Yes, Vicky, I do."

"I've been worried about him ever since we came out here. My goodness, I haven't even told this to Sally. You're easy to talk to, Smoke."

"Has his . . . ah . . . behavior been sort of odd, Vicky?"

"Why . . . yes. That's it. You've noticed it, too?"

"Oh, yeah. I sure have. He sort of . . . ah . . . rambled, I guess you'd call it, while talking with me."

She stared at him for a moment, then rose from the chair and walked to the edge of the porch. She stood for a moment, looking at the mountains in the distance. Smoke could hear her sigh. "I don't know what to do, Smoke," she said. "I don't have a penny of my own money. I am totally dependent upon Robert. He has violent mood changes. I'm frightened of him, and so is Lisa." She turned to face Smoke.

"I know he used to meet Max Huggins in town. I thought that very odd. And I have no idea what they discussed. Except . . ." she flushed deeply, ". . . me."

"And Lisa," Smoke said, taking a chance.

"Yes. Max came to the ranch lots of times. Robert would laugh and joke with him. Usually outside, away from me. But sometimes in the living room. I never could understand the . . . well, call it a bond between them."

"They're brothers, Victoria."

She fainted, falling off the porch.

22

Smoke yelled at a passing boy to run to the hotel and fetch Sally, then go to his office and tell his deputies to get over here.

The boy took off like he had rockets on his feet.

Smoke picked Vicky up and placed her on the couch in the living room. He was dampening a cloth at the kitchen pump when Sally ran in.

"What happened?"

"She fainted after I told her that Max Huggins and Robert were brothers."

"I'm surprised she didn't have a heart attack. Give me that cloth and go outside."

Smoke went outside and sat on the porch. Sal, Jim, and Pete had just arrived, out of breath from unaccustomed running in high-heeled boots. They were typical cowboys; anything that could not be done from the hurricane deck of a horse they usually tried to avoid.

"What's up, Smoke?" Pete asked.

He brought his men up to date. Judge Garrison rolled up in his buggy and joined the men in the front yard.

"That poor woman," the judge said. "She certainly has a heavy cross to bear."

"Judge," Smoke said, "can you get Robert declared insane?"

"All I have to do is sign my name to a piece of paper. He'll be taken to the state hospital for the insane."

One of Joe Walsh's hands rode up and dismounted. "Say, Smoke, I just seen Dr. Turner headin' north toward Hell's Creek. He was putting the whip to that horse of his. He was shoutin' and cussin' as he drove. Damn near ran me down. I hollered and asked him what was the matter. He said he had to get to his brother. What brother's he talkin' about? I didn't know he had any kin out here."

"We just found out that he and Max Huggins are brothers," Smoke told him.

The cowboy's eyes bugged out and his mouth dropped open. "Holy crap!"

Smoke turned to the judge. "Get all the legal action going that needs to be done, Judge. Committing Robert, and seeing to it that his estate is in Victoria's hands."

"Easily done, Smoke. I'll have the paperwork done in an hour and wire his banks back east. You get into his strongbox or files and find out where and how much. Have the papers sent to me."

Smoke walked back into the house.

Sally had opened Victoria's bodice and placed a cool cloth on the woman's head. Her eyes were open and she seemed alert. Smoke pulled a chair up close to the couch.

"I'm sorry, Vicky," he said. "But I just didn't know how else to tell you."

"It's all right, Smoke. I'm glad you did. It answers a lot of questions I had in my mind. Now I can see the family resemblance."

Smoke told her what the cowboy had seen. "Judge Garrison is going to have him committed, and we're going to get Robert's estate in your hands. I need to know where he keeps his documents, bank books, and so forth."

"I'll show you." She fastened a few buttons on her bodice and sat up on the couch.

"You best lay back down," Smoke told her.

"No." She smiled and stood up. She was steady on her feet. "If I'm to be a western woman, I've got to learn to be strong."

Smoke returned the smile. "I thought you were leaving, heading back east?"

"I'm staying," Vicky said. "I want my daughter to be raised out here. The town needs another schoolteacher, and that is what I was trained to be."

Sal had entered the room. He took one look at Vicky's open bodice and blushed. Turning his back to the woman, he said, "I sent Pete over to fetch your girl, ma'am. They'll be along directly."

"Thank you, Mr. . . ."

"Just Sal, ma'am."

Vicky buttoned up her bodice. "You may turn around now, Sal."

"Thank you. I feel sorta stupid standin' here talkin' to a wall."

"That was kind of you thinking of Lisa."

Sal blushed. "Wasn't nothin', ma'am."

"It is to me, I assure you. Well!" She patted her hair and got herself together. "I have to assume that Robert is not coming back. So I think what I'll do is this: If you all will leave me alone for a time—Sally, will you look after Lisa for a few minutes? Good, thank you—I'll have myself a good cry and then start putting my life back in order."

Sal was the first one out the door. Women made him nervous, unpredictable creatures that they were.

"Man ought to be horsewhipped leavin' a good woman like that one back yonder," Sal said to Smoke as they all walked back to the office.

Sally looked at Smoke and winked at him. "Sal, what are our plans when we leave here?"

"Why . . . I don't rightly know, ma'am. Why do you ask?"

"The county is going to need a sheriff," Smoke picked up

on what his wife was leading up to. "And you've been a fine deputy. How's about I recommend you to Judge Garrison."

"You mean that?"

"Are you interested?"

"Sure. But how 'bout these boys?" He jerked his thumb at Pete and Jim.

"Well," Smoke said with a smile, "I think Pete is going to try his hand at ranchin', seeing as how he's been tippy-toeing around the Widow Feckles, the both of them making goo-goo eyes at each other."

Pete's face suddenly turned beet-red. "I just remembered something. I got to go see about my horse," he said, and walked across the street.

"How about you?" Sal asked Jim.

"I like this deputy sheriffin'. Sure beats thirty a month and sleepin' in drafty bunkhouses. It's fine with me, Sal."

"Good. It's settled then. Judge Garrison has papers declaring the election of Cartwright to have been illegal, and the man has no more authority. He's going to post election notices starting tomorrow. And you're going to be the only candidate."

"What are you gonna do?" Sal asked, clearly startled at the rapid turn of events.

"Retire from law enforcement and hang around to see the fun. A badge is too restrictive for me, Sal. I like room to roam."

"In other words, you're gonna take the fight to them."

"Why, Sal," Smoke said with a serious look on his face "you know I wouldn't do anything like that."

"He occasionally tells tall tales, too, Sal," Sally told him

"Judge Garrison did what?" Max jumped to his feet.

"Declared my election as sheriff illegal and they had a

election down to Barlow yesterday," Cartwright said. "Sal is the new sheriff."

"He can't do that. We weren't advised of any election."

"Yes, we were." Cartwright held out a piece of paper. "One of the boys found this tacked to a tree just outside of town."

Max snatched the paper from him and squinted. "Hell, you can't read it without a magnifying glass!"

"That's sure enough the truth and that's what I done, too. It's a legal paper, telling the citizens of Hell's Creek about the election."

Max sat down and cussed. Loud and long. He wadded up the notice and hurled it across the room. He had never before been stymied at every turn, and it was an unpleasant sensation that he did not like.

"Well, you can still be town marshal of Hell's Creek."

"Big deal," Cartwright said sarcastically. "We got no protection now, Max. We don't know what's goin' on in Barlow now that your brother moved in with you. And the boys is gettin' right edgy."

"About what, Paul?"

"They're wantin' to hit the town now and get out. The bank's in place, ain't it?"

"Not yet. Monday morning is still the target date. We'll double our money if we wait until everybody there has dug up the money they've buried or pulled it out of mattress ticks. Tell the boys to calm down."

Cartwright left and Max turned in his chair, looking out his office window. His main concern right now was what he was going to do with Robert. His younger brother was getting unpredictable. He was like a goose, waking up in a new world every morning. Most of the time he was lucid, but other times he was crazy as a loon. Of course, he had always known his brother was nuts, walking a very fine line between genius—which he was—and insanity—which he certainly was.

But he was family, and family looked out for each other. As best they could, that is.

"You just sign right here, Victoria," Judge Garrison said, "and Robert's estate will be under your control."

Victoria signed and she became executor over Robert Turner's estate, thus insuring that she and Lisa would not be thrust penniless into the world.

Sal was now the officially elected and legal sheriff of the county, and Smoke had turned in his badge.

While Smoke respected the law, he was also well aware that there were hard limits placed upon it when dealing with the lawless. As a private citizen, he had shed himself of those limits. Now he could meet Max Huggins and Red Malone on an equal footing.

Smoke bought supplies at Marbly's General Store—including a sack of dynamite—and made ready to hit the trail. In addition to his .44 Winchester, he carried a Sharps .56 in another saddle boot. Two days after the election, Smoke kissed Sally good-bye and swung into the saddle. Star was ready to go; the big black was bred for the trails and was growing impatient with all this inactivity.

"I won't ask how long you'll be gone," Sally said.

"Two or three days this time around. I'll be back in time to see the bank open."

He headed north, toward Hell's Creek, to see what mischief he could get into. He had heard rumors that Big Max Huggins thought himself to be unbeatable as a bare-knuckle fighter. Smoke knew that the man could be formidable; just his size would make him dangerous. But Smoke also knew that many big men rarely knew much about the finesse of fighting, depending mostly on their strength and bulk to overwhelm their opponents.

The trick would be to catch Big Max by himself. Smoke didn't trust anyone left in Hell's Creek not to shoot him after he whipped Max—and he knew he could whip him. He'd take some cuts and bruises doing so, for Max was a huge and powerful man. But Smoke had whipped men just as big and just as tough; men who knew something about boxing.

Smoke stayed off the road, keeping to the mountain trails, enjoying the aloneness of it all. He rested and ate an early lunch above a peaceful valley, exploding with summer colors. Deer fed below him, and once he spotted a grizzly ambling along, eating berries and overturning logs, looking for grubs. Squirrels chattered and birds sang their joyful songs all around him.

Then suddenly it all stopped and the timber fell as silent as a tomb. The deer below him raced away and the grizzly reared up on his hind legs, testing the air. The bear dropped down to all fours and skedaddled back into the timber.

Smoke had picked a very secure position to noon, with Star well hidden. He did not move; movement would attract attention faster than noise.

Soon the horsemen came into view, about a dozen of them, riding through the valley. Smoke moved then, getting his field glasses out of the saddlebags and focusing in on the men, being careful not to let the sun glint off the lenses.

He knew some of them—or had seen them before. They were hired guns—hired by Max Huggins. The men were riding heavily armed, carrying their rifles across the saddle horns. Smoke could see where many of them had shoved extra six-shooters behind their belts.

The route they were taking would lead them straight to the farm complex of Brown and Gatewood and the others. Those families had taken enough grief from Huggins and Red Malone and their ilk, Smoke thought, returning to Star and stowing the binoculars.

He decided he'd trail along behind the hired guns and add a little spice to their lives as soon as he was sure what they were up to.

Smoke decided not to wait when he saw the men reach into their back pockets and pull out hoods. They reined up and slipped the hoods over their faces.

They were about three miles from the farm complex. No man elects to wear a hood over his face unless he's up to no good, but still Smoke held his fire. He was looking down at a pack of trash, that he knew. But so far they had done nothing wrong.

He left them, riding higher into the timber and getting ahead of the gunslingers. On a ridge overlooking the valley where Brown and the others were rebuilding, Smoke swung down from the saddle and shucked the Sharps .56 from its boot. He got into position and waited.

He didn't have long to wait. The raiders came at a gallop, riding hard and heading straight for Brown's farm, guns at hand.

Smoke leveled the Sharps and blew one outlaw from the saddle, the big slug taking the man in the chest and flinging him off his horse, dead as he hit the ground.

Brown, his wife, and their two sons had been working with guns close by. The four of them, upon hearing the booming of the .56, dropped their hammers and shovels and grabbed their rifles, getting behind cover. They emptied four saddles during the first charge, and that broke the attack off before it could get started. The outlaws turned around and headed back north. They had lost five out of twelve, and that had not been in their plans.

They were about to lose more.

They headed straight for Smoke's position, at a hard gallop. Smoke leveled the Sharps, sighted in, and squeezed the trigger. Another hooded man screamed and fell from the saddle, one arm hanging useless by his side, shattered by the heavy .56 caliber slug. He stood up and Smoke finished him.

The hooded raiders were riding in a panic now, not knowing how many riflemen were hidden along the ridges. Smoke lifted the Sharps and sighted in another, firing and missing. He sighted in another man and this time he did not miss. The raider pitched forward, both hands flung into the air, and toppled from the saddle.

Smoke walked back to his horse, booted the rifle, and mounted up, riding down to see if any of the outlaws on the ground were still alive. Two of them were, and one of them was not going to make it. The second man had only a flesh wound.

Smoke jerked the hoods from them and glared down at the men. "You'll live," he told the man with the flesh wound. He cut his eyes to the other man. "You won't. You got anything you'd like to say before you die?"

Brown and his family had gathered around. The sound of the galloping horses of the farmer's neighbors coming to their aid grew loud. Soon the men of the entire complex had gathered around the fallen raiders.

"How'd you know?" the dying man gasped out the question, his eyes bright with pain, his hands holding his .56 caliber-punctured belly.

"I didn't," Smoke told him. "I was having lunch on the ridges when you crud came riding along."

"What'd you gonna do with me?" the other outlaw whined.

"Shut up," Smoke said. "You get on my nerves and I might just decide to hang you."

"That ain't legal!" the man hollered. "I got a right to a fair trial."

Cooter snorted. "Ain't that something now? They come up here attackin' us, and damned if he ain't hollerin' about his right to a fair trial. I swear I don't know where our system of justice is takin' us."

"Wait a few years," Smoke told him. "I guarantee you it'll get worse."

"I need a doctor!" the gut-shot outlaw hollered.

"Not in ten minutes you won't," Gatewood told him.

"What'd you mean, you hog-slop?" the outlaw groaned the words.

" 'Cause in ten minutes, you gonna be dead."

He was right.

23

Smoke helped gather up the weapons from the dead raiders. Brown and the others in the farming complex now had enough weapons and ammo to stand off any type of attack, major or minor.

"They got their nerve comin' back here," Cooter said as they dug shallow graves for the outlaws.

"And we'll keep comin' back," the outlaw trussed up on the ground said. "Until all you hog-farmers are dead." He had regained his courage, certain he was facing death and determined to face it tough.

"You're wrong," Smoke told him, stepping out of the hole and letting one of Cooter's boys finish the digging. "Take a look at these men around you, hombre. Even without my guns, they'd have stopped the attack. I don't know whose idea this was, but I doubt if it was Max's."

The young man on the ground glared at him but kept his mouth closed.

Smoke had an idea. "Can you read and write, punk?"

"Huh?"

"You heard me. Can you read and write?"

"Naw. I never learned how. What business is that of yours?"

Smoke walked to his horse, dug in the saddlebags, and found a scrap of paper and the stub of a pencil. He wrote a short note and returned to the outlaw. Folding the paper, he tucked it into the raider's shirt pocket and buttoned it tight.

"That's a note for Big Max. You give it to him, and to him alone. I'll know if you've showed it to anyone else." That was a lie, but Smoke figured the outlaw wouldn't. "You understand?"

"You turnin' me loose?"

"Yeah. With a piece of advice. And here it is: Get gone from this country. Give the note to Max and then saddle you a fresh horse, get your kit together, and haul your ashes out of Hell's Creek. We know Max and Red are going to attack the town. That is, if the old arrest warrants on his head don't catch up with him first. And they might." Another lie. "The town is ready for the attack, hombre. Ready and waiting twenty-four hours a day. We know the bank is tempting. But don't try it; don't ride in there with them. The townspeople will shoot you into bloody rags. There's nigh on to six hundred people in and around Barlow now. Six hundred." That was also a slight exaggeration. "And there are guards standing watch around the clock, ready to give the call. It's a death trap waiting for you."

"You say!" the outlaw sneered, but there was genuine fear in his voice that all around him could detect.

Smoke jerked the man to his feet, untied his hands, and shoved him toward his horse, who had wandered back toward its master after running for a time. Pistols and rifle and all his ammo had been taken from the raider.

"Ride," Smoke told him. "And give that note to Max."

The man climbed into the saddle and looked down at Smoke. "I might take your advice. I just might. I got to think on it some."

"You'd be wise to take it. I'm giving you a break by letting you go."

"And I appreciate it." He tapped the pocket where Smoke had put the message. "All right, Smoke. I'll give this to Big Max, and I'm gone. You'll not see me again unless you come around a ranch. That's where you'll find me . . . punchin' cows."

"Are there any kids in Hell's Creek? Any decent women?"

The man shook his head. "None at all. There ain't nothin' there 'ceptin' the bottom of the barrel—if you know what I mean."

"Good luck to you."

"Thanks." The man rode north, toward Hell's Creek.

Smoke swung into the saddle. "Before you boys bury that crud, go through their pockets and take whatever money you find. You earned it."

"Don't seem right, takin' money from the dead," Bolen said.

"They won't need it," Smoke assured the man. "Near as I can figure out from reading the Bible, there aren't any honky-tonks in hell."

Big Max Huggins opened the folded piece of paper and read. He read it again and began cussing. He ripped the small note into shreds and did some more fancy cussing. All of the cussing leveled at and centered around Smoke Jensen.

The note read: MAX, YOU STUPID, HORSE-FACED PIECE OF HOG CRAP. MEET ME TOMORROW AT THE WEST SIDE OF THE SWAN RANGE BY THE CREEK. NO GUNS. I'M GOING TO STOMP YOUR FACE IN WITH FISTS AND BOOTS. COME ALONE IF YOU HAVE THE GUTS—WHICH YOU PROBABLY DO NOT HAVE, BEING THE COWARD THAT YOU ARE.

Max let his temper rage for a few moments, then began to calm himself. He sat back down behind his desk and smiled.

Max had killed men with his fists and felt very confident that he would do the same with Smoke Jensen.

This is what you've been training for, isn't it? he thought. Yes, of course it is. How to play it? The fight will be rough and tumble, kick and gouge. That isn't what you meant and you know it! he mentally berated himself.

Jensen had slighted his courage, for a fact.

Max folded his hamlike hands behind his head and leaned back in his chair. How to play it? Well, there was only one way: He would play it straight. He would go alone.

Jensen had tossed down the challenge; Jensen had implied that he did not have the courage to meet him alone. Well, he'd show that damn two-bit gunfighter a thing or two about courage.

Jensen had chosen well, Max thought. He knew exactly where Smoke would be: on the flats just above the creek. Good level place for a fight.

Max would go in alone, but he would be armed, to do otherwise would be foolish. Once there, both men would shuck their guns together, each in plain sight of the other. Then, Max smiled, I will beat Smoke Jensen to death with my fists.

Smoke camped on the flats. On the afternoon before the fight—if Max showed up, and Smoke felt confident he would—Smoke prowled the area, picking up and throwing away every stick and rock he could find. He walked the area a dozen times, looking for holes in the ground that might trip a man. He memorized the natural arena. Then, sure he had done everything humanly possible, he cooked his supper and made his coffee. He rolled into his blankets just after dark and went to sleep with a smile on his lips.

What he was doing he knew was foolish. It was male pride at its worst. But when two bulls are grazing in the same pasture, one is going to be dominant over the other, that was nature's way. And Smoke had been raised too close to the earth to attempt to alter nature's way.

The fight would really accomplish nothing of substance. Smoke knew it, and Max probably knew it, too. If he didn't then the man was a fool.

Smoke knew that what he ought to do was to kill Max Huggins just as soon as the man stepped down from the saddle. But that wasn't his way, and Max probably realized it. If Max came, and came alone, then he was going to follow the same rules.

It promised to be a very interesting fight.

Smoke was up at dawn, boiling his coffee and frying his bacon. He ate lightly, for he knew the fight might take several hours until the end, and he did not want to fight on a full stomach.

At full light he looked out over the flats, and far in the distance he saw a lone rider approaching. From the size of the man, he knew it had to be Max Huggins. He lifted his field glasses and scanned the area all around Max, to the rear and both sides. He could pick up no sign of outriders. Big Max was coming in alone.

Max rode up to the flats and dismounted. He was wearing two guns, tied down. Smoke stood up from his squat and hooked his thumbs behind the buckle of his gunbelt.

"How do we play this, Max?"

"It's your show. You call it."

"First we untie, then we unbuckle and put them over here, next to my bedroll."

"That sounds good to me."

The men untied, unbuckled, and laid their guns on the ground, next to Smoke's bedroll.

Smoke pointed to the battered coffeepot and two tin cups. "Help yourself. It's fresh made."

"Thanks. That'll taste good." Max squatted down and poured two cups. With a smile, he handed one cup to Smoke and said, "If it's poisoned or drugged, then we'll go out together."

"It's neither," Smoke said, and took a sip of coffee. "It's just hot."

The men sipped and stared at each other in silence. Max broke the silence. "How'd you put it together about Robert?"

"Family resemblance is strong. Then I followed Robert one day and saw you together."

"He's quite insane, you know." It was not a question.

"Yes, I know. What are you going to do with him?"

"I honestly don't know, Smoke."

"Judge Garrison has legal papers ordering him committed to the asylum."

Max's face hardened. "Robert will never be confined in one of those places. They're treated worse than animals in there."

"You better think of something to do with him after you're gone."

"Oh? Am I going somewhere?"

"Yes. You're either going to leave this area voluntarily, go to prison, or I'm going to kill you."

Max chuckled, then laughed out loud. "Damn, but you are a gutsy man, Smoke Jensen. If the circumstances were different, I could really like you."

"There is nothing about you that I like, Max."

Max chuckled again, and it was not in the least forced. "That's a shame. I'm going to both enjoy and regret beating you to death."

"Don't flatter yourself. I've whipped bigger and better men than you in my time."

Max cut his eyes, looking at Smoke. The man was all muscle and bone. Max upgraded his original estimate of Smoke's weight. His arms and shoulders and chest and hands were enormous. Max probably had a good sixty pounds on the man, but he guessed accurately that Smoke would be quicker and able to dance around with more grace than he.

"I'm not surprised that you came alone," Smoke said.

"I do have some honor about me," Max replied stiffly.

"Honorable men do not make war against women and children. Neither do they rape young girls."

"Aggie was a mistake," Max admitted. "But both Robert and I—we get it from our father—have hot blood when it comes to girls. It's a failing, I will admit."

Smoke wondered how many young girls had suffered and died at the hands of the man he faced. And once again the thought came to him: I ought to just shoot him.

Smoke sipped his coffee, holding the cup in a gloved hand, and stared at Max Huggins from the other side of the fire.

"I guess it's about that time," Smoke said.

Both rose as one and tossed the dregs of their coffee to the ground. They tossed the cups to the ground and walked away from the campsite. Max flexed his arms and wiggled his hands and did a little boxing shuffle with his feet.

"That's cute," Smoke told him. "Where'd you learn that? From a hurdy-gurdy girl?"

"You're going to be easy, Jensen. That's one of Jem Mace's moves."

"Somehow I think he did it better. You looked kind of stupid."

Max stepped in quickly and tried a right at Smoke's head. Smoke sidestepped, but not to the side that Max anticipated, and the left that followed the right almost jerked him off his boots when it exploded against thin air.

"Damn, you're clumsy," Smoke told him.

Max charged in and Smoke was forced to back up. Smoke knew that if Max connected solidly with that big right, it would hurt. Max drew first blood with a sneaky left that bloodied Smoke's mouth; but Smoke moved away too quickly for the right he threw to connect. Smoke's left did connect against Max's belly and it was like hitting a tree.

He danced back and let Max follow him. Neither man

had as yet worked up a sweat or was even breathing hard. Both of them knew that this fight could last a long time.

Max snaked a right that almost connected. Smoke smashed a left uppercut that jerked Max's head back and stopped him for a couple of seconds. Before he could fully recover, Smoke danced away.

Blood was leaking out of one side of Max's mouth as he followed Smoke around the flats. Smoke suspected the big man had bitten his tongue due to that uppercut.

Suddenly Max dropped his fists and charged, trying to catch Smoke in a bear hug. What Max got was a combination left and right to his face, followed by a boot to his knee that staggered him. Before he could catch his balance, Smoke had hit him twice more, both times on the face. Max felt blood running down from his nose and the sensation infuriated him. He stepped in and busted Smoke on the jaw with a hard right, and then a left to the belly that hurt the smaller man.

Smoke backed up, shaking his head, for Max had a punch like the kick of a mule.

Max sensed victory too soon, but with good reason. Never had he had to hit a man Smoke's size more than twice to put him down. He stepped closer to put the finishing touches to one Smoke Jensen, and Smoke knocked the crap out of Max Huggins.

The hard right fist connected flush on the side of Max's jaw and put the big man down on the grass. He was astonished! He wasn't hurt, just simply astounded that Jensen had actually knocked him down.

Max was further astonished when Smoke backed up, allowing the man to get to his feet. Smoke was fighting ring rules.

"Just as long as you do, Max," Smoke said after correctly reading the man's expression.

Max nodded and stepped in, raising his fists. So it was

boxing that Jensen wanted, hey! Well, he would sure oblige the man.

Both men were wary now, each of them knowing the other could do plenty of damage. They circled each other, Max with his fists held high, Smoke with his left fist held wide from his body and his right fist just in front of and to one side of his head.

He's no boxer! Max thought gleefully. Not with a stupid stance like that. Now I have him. Now I have him.

What Max got was a left fake that he brushed aside and a powerful right that barreled through and busted him flush on the mouth. He felt his lips split and the blood gush. The left that he had brushed away caught him a smashing blow on the side that hurt the big man, backing him up.

Smoke pressed in, hitting the man with a flurry of blows to the arms and shoulders as Max could do nothing but cover up until he caught his wind. And the blows were bruising.

Smoke pounded the man's arms, hurting and bruising them, taking some of the power from them. Max finally had to lower his guard and shove Smoke from him. The move got Smoke off him for a moment, but it also earned Max a smashing blow to the head.

Max saw an opening and took it, handing Smoke a one-two combination to the head. The blows popped Smoke's head back and bloodied his mouth. The left had caught him above the eye and opened a cut.

Smoke backed up, shook his head, and then plowed right back in, pressing the attack. He drove a right fist in that caught Max on the nose, and the big man felt the already injured nose break. The blood poured. Smoke didn't let up. He mashed a left and right to Max's head that rocked the big man back on his heels. Max got in a hard right that shook Smoke down to his boots, staggering him.

Max jumped at Smoke, intending to boot the man to the ground. One boot did catch Smoke on the leg, bruising the flesh but not putting him down. Smoke countered with a kick of his own that caught Max on the shin and brought a yelp of pain from the man. Smoke jumped in and blasted another left and right. The left took Max on the side of the jaw and the right hit him flush in the mouth.

Max grimly spat out part of a broken tooth and came on, both fists held high.

Smoke hit the man in the belly and took a left hook to his head for that move. Max followed the hook with a heel-drop that sent Smoke to the ground. Max tried to kick him. Smoke rolled away and came up on his boots, a hard light in his eyes.

Max had expanded the fight, moving away from ring rules with that attempted kick. If that were the way the man wanted it, so be it.

Max swung a looping right. Smoke caught the forearm and wrist and threw the man to the ground, then stepped in and gave Max a vicious kick to the kidney that brought a howl of pain from him. Smoke brought his balled fist down hard on Max's neck just as the man was trying to get up. The blow knocked him flat on the ground. Smoke went to work with his boots, stomping and kicking. One boot caught Max flush in the mouth, and the force of the kick shattered the big man's front teeth, top and bottom.

With a scream of rage and pain, Max flung out his hand and caught Smoke's jeans leg, tumbling the smaller man to the ground. Smoke rolled and came up on his boots before Max could get to his feet and apply the boots to him.

For a full minute the men stood toe to toe and slugged it out, with each of them giving and receiving about the same amount of damage. But Smoke could tell the bigger man was losing some of his power. Max was fighting with his mouth open now, sucking in air in great gasping gulps. Smoke had known nothing but hard work all his life. Max had spent the last fifteen years either sitting behind a desk planning his evil, or sitting at a poker table, cheating those who played the game of chance with him.

Smoke sent a crashing right fist through Max's guard, a punch that knocked the big man to the ground. Smoke stepped in and kicked the man in the butt just as he was trying to get to his feet. The butt-kick knocked Max sprawling, sliding facedown in the dirt and the grass.

"You know what I'm going to do, don't you, Max?" Smoke asked, standing over the man. Max tried to get to his feet and Smoke kicked him in the butt again, knocking the big man down to the ground.

"I'm going to rearrange your face, Max." Smoke walked around to the front of the struggling giant of a man. "When I get tired of hitting you, I'm going to kick your face in."

Max knew he was whipped, knew Smoke was going to stomp him into the ground. "I've had enough," the big man said, blood dripping from his mouth.

"I imagine Aggie said something along those lines, didn't she, Max?"

"She was trash! Nester trash."

Smoke kicked him in the belly with all the power he could get behind the boot. Max's body arched upward off the ground and he screamed in pain.

Smoke backed away and let the man struggle to his feet. Big Max stood before him, swaying slightly. "Fight, you sorry bastard," Smoke told him.

Max lumbered forward and walked into a straight right that he felt all the way down to his toenails. Smoke followed that with a left that turned Max's head and loosened teeth. Smoke didn't let up. He began to work on Max's belly, driving hammer blows to the man's guts. Max backed up, unable to throw a punch that would stop Smoke Jensen. He landed several punches, but they had no power behind them.

Smoke shifted his area of punishment. He began working on Max's face. The face of Big Max now began to resemble a raw side of beef that someone had worked over with a sledgehammer. His nose was flattened, one ear was swollen and pulpy, his mouth was a ruined mess, and both eyes were closing. Still Smoke Jensen continued to punish the man.

Max searched frantically around him for a weapon—a club, a rock, anything! He found nothing. Smoke had carefully cleared the area. He tried to run and Smoke pursued him, leaping onto his back and riding the man around the area like some sort of beast of burden. It was the most humiliating thing that Big Max Huggins had ever been forced to endure.

Max finally collapsed onto the ground, his strength gone. Smoke stood over him. The smaller man had taken his licks. One eye was almost closed, and blood was leaking from his nose and mouth. But he was on his boots and ready to fight.

Max heard the words: "You got a choice, Big Man," Smoke told him. "You either get up and fight, or as God is my witness, I'll kick you to death."

Max struggled up. He turned and faced Jensen, lifting his fists. Max charged in a last-ditch effort to grab the smaller man and break his back.

Smoke stepped to one side and buried his fist into Max's belly, doubling the man over and bringing a painful retching sound from his mouth. Smoke's fist struck the man on his ear and Max experienced a roaring in his head. Another fist came up, seemingly from the ground, and slammed into his battered face. That was followed by a right fist that crashed into his nose. Smoke's fist hammered his lower back and smashed into his rib cage, sending waves of pain through the man as his kidneys took the brunt of the blows.

Max was beyond mere pain. This was an agony new to him. He had been moved into a sea of solid hurt. It was nothing like he had ever experienced before. His shirt had been torn from him sometime during the fight, and his upper torso was bruised and bloody.

Still Smoke Jensen would not back off. Big Max Huggins

stood like a giant oak that was being battered by the elements, his huge arms hanging by his sides. He could not find the strength to lift them.

Smoke knocked him down and Max painfully climbed to his boots to face his tormentor. He turned in time to catch another huge right fist to his already ruined and swollen mouth.

Through eyes that were now nothing more than swollen slits, Max could see Jensen smiling at him. He had never seen a smile that savage on Smoke's face. Jensen's eyes were cold, killing cold. Max watched as Jensen measured him. He knew with a soaring feeling of relief the fight was soon to be over.

Smoke started his punch somewhere down around his ankles, and when the gloved fist exploded against his head, Max's world turned black.

The big man lay stretched out on the ground. Unconscious.

24

Smoke muscled Big Max across his saddle and tied him there. He looped Max's gunbelt on the saddle horn and slapped the horse on the rump, sending it on its way back to Hell's Creek.

Smoke packed up and headed for the high country, making camp not five miles from Hell's Creek. He had plans for that town. Smoke ached all over and his hands were swollen. He looked for and found the plants he sought, carefully picking them and boiling them in water, then soaking his hands. He stayed snug in the camp for two days, resting and eating and treating his hands until the swelling had gone down and he was ready to go.

Smoke had spent the time in the hidden camp not only resting and treating his hands and the cuts on his face, but also capping and fusing the dynamite, tying them into three-stick bombs. Star was rested and restless and eager to hit the trail.

At dawn of the third day after the fight on the flats, Smoke swung into the saddle and pointed Star's head toward

Hell's Creek. He had it in his mind to destroy that town and as many people in it as possible.

The startled gun hands who watched as Big Max's horse walked slowly up the muddy and rutted main street of Hell's Creek could not believe their eyes. They were further astonished—and some a little frightened—when they untied Max and lowered him to the ground.

To a man, none of them had ever seen a person beaten so badly as was Max.

Robert Turner snapped out of his befuddlement of the moment and slipped back into his role as doctor. He ordered Max carried to bed and ran for his bag. Robert had taken one look at his brother's battered body and knew the big man was hurt—how seriously he would know only after a thorough examination.

"Not seriously," he finally said with a sigh, leaning back in the chair by his brother's bed. "No ribs are broken that I can detect, but his face will never be as it was. Smoke Jensen did this deliberately. This is the most callous act I have ever witnessed. Jensen deliberately set out to destroy my brother's handsome looks."

Robert looked around at the outlaws. "Well, my mind is made up. I have never believed in violence, but this"— he looked down at the sleeping Max, the sleep brought on by massive doses of laudanum—"has to be avenged."

Val Singer seized the moment, guessing what this crazy galoot had in mind. "What do you plan to do about it, Robert?" he asked.

"Why . . . I plan to step into my brother's boots and lead the raid against Barlow, that's what. What do you think about that, Mr. Singer?"

The outlaw leaders had to fight to hide their smiles. Of course, they'd let sonny-boy here lead the raid. Of course, they'd go along with it. For with Max out of the picture, they could ravage the town, rob the bank, and would not have to share a damn thing with Big Max Huggins. And before they left the country, they would kill Robert Turner.

So much for honor among thieves.

"That's a damn good idea, Robert," Dave Poe said. "I like it. I really do. When do you think we ought to hit the town?"

"Tomorrow morning, just as the bank opens."

"I like it," Alex Bell said.

Smoke had left his horse in timber on the edge of town, and he worked his way up a dry creek bed, coming out behind a privy. He ducked back down as two men walked to the outhouse, chatting as they walked.

"This time tomorrow, Larry," one of them said, "Barlow ain't gonna be nothing but a memory, and we'll have had our fill of women and be a damn sight richer."

"Yeah, and we won't have to share none of it with Big Max. That's what makes it so rich to me."

Smoke listened, wondering what was going on. Tomorrow! They were going to hit the town tomorrow?

"Goofy Robert said he'd give Max enough laudanum to keep him out for a day and a half. He'd give it to him just before we pull out."

"Who's gonna kill that nut?"

"Hell, who cares? Sometime during the shootin' one of us will plug him. I've got me an itch for some of them women in that town."

"Me, too."

The men stepped into the two-holer and closed the door. Smoke made his way back up the wash, swung into the saddle, and headed for Barlow.

He stopped at Brown's house to rest his horse and to tell the farmer to warn the others about the raid the next day.

"You want us in town, Smoke?" Brown asked.

"No. I want you men to load up full and be prepared to defend yourselves in case they decide to attack you first, although I don't think they will."

"We'll be ready." He smiled, his eyes on Smoke's bruised face. "Who won the fight?"

"Big Max is still unconscious," Smoke told him with a grin.

"Glad to hear it."

Smoke mounted up and headed for Barlow. He hit the town at a gallop and yelled for people to gather around him. "It's tomorrow morning, people," he shouted, so all could hear. "The men of Hell's Creek are going to hit the town at nine o'clock, to coincide with the bank opening. Start gathering up guns and ammo, and make certain the pumper is checked out and the fire barrels are full."

He swung down from the saddle and handed the reins to the boy that helped out at the livery. "Rub him down good and give him all the corn he wants, boy." Smoke handed the boy a coin and Star was led off for a well-deserved rest.

Smoke stepped up on the boardwalk in front of the sheriff's office, while others gathered up the rest of the townspeople. Smoke stayed in hurried whispered conference with Sal, Judge Garrison, and Tom Johnson for a few minutes, until the whole town was assembled in the street.

Judge Garrison, Sal, and the mayor agreed with his suggestions, and Smoke turned, facing the crowd. "All right, folks," he said, raising his voice so all could hear. "Here it is. There is a good chance that a rider was sent out to Red Malone's spread before I slipped into Hell's Creek and overheard the outlaws' plans. Red will probably attack us from the south at the same time the raiders hit us from the north. We've got to be ready to hit them twice as hard as they hit us. Jim has already left to warn Joe Walsh and his people. I told Jim to tell Joe to stay put and guard his ranch. Red hates him as much as he hates us. So it's going to be up to us to defend this town and everything you people have worked for. That's all I have to say, except start getting ready for a war."

The crowds broke up into small groups, each group leader,

already appointed, waiting to see where they were supposed to be when the attack came.

"Tom," Smoke said, "you and your group take the inside of the bank. Take lots of ammo and water."

"Will do, Smoke," the mayor said, and moved out to get ready.

"One group inside Marbly's store. Toby, you and your people will defend the hotel. Benson's group will take the livery. Ralph, you and your bunch will fight from the saloon. The rest of them know where to be and what to do. Let's start getting ready."

Sal looked at Smoke's battered face and commented, "Need I have to ask who won the fight?"

"Big Max didn't," Smoke said, then walked toward the hotel for a hot bath, a change into fresh clothes, and to rest beside Sally.

"I'd give a pretty penny to have seen that scrap," Sal said.

"Yeah," Pete Akins agreed. "He must have hurt him bad for Max not to be leadin' the raid come the morning."

"How many men are we facing tomorrow?" the owner of the cafe asked.

"Nearabouts a hundred from Hell's Creek," Pete told him. "Maybe more than that. And all of Red Malone's bunch. We'll have them outnumbered, but bear this in mind: Them we'll be facin' is killers. Ninety-nine percent of the townspeople ain't." He looked hard at the cafe owner and at the other group leaders. "You pass the word, boys: Don't give no mercy, 'cause you shore as hell ain't gonna be gettin' none from them that attack us."

Smoke took a long hot soak in their private bath in th suite, then napped for an hour. He dressed and began clean ing his guns, loading rifle, shotgun, and pistols up full. H took his spare pistols out of wraps and cleaned and oile them, loading them up. They were old Remington Frontier .44's, and Smoke had had them for a long time. He liked the feel of them, and was comfortable and confident with them in his hands.

"Early in the morning," Smoke told his wife, "you go get Victoria and Martha and the kids. Bring them back up to this suite. We'll be up long before then—the cafe and hotel dining room is going to open about four o'clock to feed those that don't eat at home—and we'll rearrange the furniture in this suite to stop any bullet. I'll have a boy start bringing up water to fight any fires that might start. Their plan is to destroy the town, so they'll be throwing torches."

Sally sat at the table with her husband, oiling and cleaning her own guns. "Vicky doesn't know anything about pistols," she said. "But Martha does. We'll have rifles and shotguns ready. How about Robert, Smoke?"

He shook his head. "I don't want to kill him, honey. I can't justify killing a crazy person unless there is just no other way out."

"I've been reading that there is some new treatment for the mad. But insane asylums are just awful."

"I know. I mean, I've heard they are. Chain them down like wild animals until they die." He rose from the table and buckled his gunbelt around his lean waist, tying it down. "I'm going to roam the town."

Everybody was pitching in to secure the town. The new bankers just arrived from the East were nervous about the upcoming fight but doing their share in carrying water, moving barricades in place, and anything else they were asked to do. And Smoke could also read excitement in their faces.

Sal caught up with him. "Where are you going to be come the mornin', Smoke?"

"I'll be lone-wolfing it, Sal. Moving around. Did you see to it that everybody had a red bandana?"

"Everybody that will be behind a friendly gun will have

one tied around their right arm. They was a darn good idea of yours. That's gonna help keep us from shootin' our own people."

"The dust and smoke are going to be bad when it starts. So I would suggest we water down the main street just before the bank opens. What do you think?"

"Another good idea. I'm gonna miss you and Sally when y'all pull out."

"You'll handle it, Sal. And, Sal? . . ."

The sheriff turned to face him.

"Martha and Vicky and the kids will be with Sally in our suite come the morning. So you won't have to worry about Victoria."

Sal blushed and headed across the street. Smoke smiled and continued his walking tour.

The saloon had been turned into a fort, as had the livery stable and barn. Marbly's store was barricaded, and anything that might be broken had been taken from the shelves and stored in wooden boxes. Smoke nodded his approval and walked back to the hotel. The waiting was going to be hard.

"Way I see it," John Steele said to Red Malone, "we just ain't got much of a choice."

"We have no choice," the rancher said. "We both have warrants on us in other states. The town has to be destroyed, and everybody in it dead and buried in deep graves. We'll toss the bodies into the fires and burn them before we bury them. The authorities, if any show up, won't be able to prove a damn thing."

"Some of our men rode out today, right after the rider from Hell's Creek left. Said they wasn't havin' no part of killin' women and kids."

Red snorted his disgust. "We don't need them. We're better off without them."

What neither of them knew was that the hands who had left in disgust over making war against women and kids were riding toward Barlow, to join the defenders of the little town.

"After Barlow is burned out," Red said, "the outlaws will scatter to the wind. We'll ride and burn down Hell's Creek. We'll blame everything on Max's bunch. Hell, we can even say that we sided with the townspeople in trying to fight them outlaws off. We'll take some of our own men dead, for sure. We can point their graves out to the investigators as proof."

"That still leaves Joe Walsh and his crew," the foreman pointed out.

"We'll deal with them. We've got them outnumbered three to one. Soon as Barlow is done and over, we'll ride for the Circle W and clean out Walsh and his crew."

John smiled a death's-head grin. "Then we can wipe out all them damn hog-farmers and other nesters, and the valley will once again be ourn."

"Yeah." Red rubbed the stubble of beard on his jowls. "And some of them nester girls ain't that bad looking. We can have some fun with them." He laughed. "Be just like old times. . . . Hey, John, remember them days?"

John Steele joined in the laughter. The men were in high spirits as they walked out of the house to sit on the porch.

"Just let me get Jensen in gunsights," Red said. "All I need is one shot. Front or back, it don't make no difference to me."

The town of Barlow rolled up the boardwalks early that evening. Far earlier than usual. Everyone wanted to get a good night's sleep before the storm struck the next morning.

Red's Lightning hands who had rebelled against fighting women and kids had ridden in, holding up a white handkerchief—well, it was almost white—and Smoke, along with Judge Garrison and Mayor Johnson, met them in the street.

"We done quit Red," the spokesman for the group said. "We ain't havin' no part in killin' women and little kids. If you want our help, we're here."

"How do we know you weren't sent in here by Red to start shooting us in the backs come the attack in the morning?" Tom asked.

"That's a good question," the hired gun said. "And I don't know how to answer it."

"I do," Sal said, stepping off the boardwalk and into the street. "Howdy, Cobb."

"Howdy, Sal. We all right proud of you, you bein' elected sheriff and all. Me and Benny and Hale and Stacy here, we got to talkin' about that this mornin'. After that no-good from Hell's Crick come talkin' to Red this mornin' about killin' the women and kids and burnin' this town down. We couldn't do that, Sal. You've ridden some trails with us; you know we're not that kind of men. Oh, we've hired our guns out—just like you've done, for fightin' wages. But there ain't none of us ever made war agin' nobody 'ceptin' grown-up men. And we ain't about to start now. Smoke, I guess that's the only answer we can give you."

Smoke smiled and nodded his head. "It sounds good to me, boys."

"Me, too," Judge Garrison said. He wore two guns belted around his expansive waist. Two old Remington .44's—the Army model. Both guns looked to Smoke as if they'd seen some action. "There'll be stars in your crown for this, boys."

Stacy shifted in his saddle. "I don't know about that Judge. I just don't want no more black marks agin' me in the Judgment Book. The Good Lord knows I got aplenty o them already."

"You boys stable your horses and meet me in the hote dinin' room," Sal said. "Glad to have you with us."

"Right will prevail, Smoke," Judge Garrison proclaime "Sometimes it just takes an outsider to prod those oppresse into action."

Smoke looked at the .44's belted around the judge's waist. "When is the last time you fired those, Judge?"

The judge smiled. "I came out of the War Between the States a colonel, Smoke. Of cavalry. I had my law degree when I enlisted. I fought through nearly every major campaign." He smiled. "With Lee. I graduated VMI, sir."

"Then I won't worry about you, sir."

"Coming from you, that is high praise. Tell me, since I haven't had a chance to ask, how did you leave Max Huggins?"

"Unconscious and tied across his saddle."

The judge walked away, shaking with laughter. His booming laughter could be heard up and down the main street of Barlow.

25

Smoke was up and dressed for war long before dawn. He wore his customary two pistols in leather, his two spares were tucked behind his gunbelt, and he carried an American Arms 12 gauge sawed-off shotgun, a bandoleer of shells slung across his chest, bandit-style.

He and Sally had breakfast before the sun was up, and then he walked Lisa and Victoria back to the hotel, Lisa carrying her puppy, Patches, in her arms. Pete escorted Martha Feckles and the boy to the suite, and the women made ready for war.

The men tied red bandanas around the upper part of their right arms. Since there were no females among the raiders who were riding to attack them, the women dressed in their customary attire. More than a few of them, including Mrs. Marbly, Victoria, Sally, and Martha, wore men's britches.

Sal's eyes bugged out when he saw Victoria. "Lord have mercy!" he said. "What's next?"

"The vote," Smoke told him.

"You have to be kidding! Votin' is men's business. Women don't know nothin' about pickin' politicians."

"You'd be surprised," Smoke said.

Smoke walked the town, inspecting each water barrel—and there were many. He checked to see if the buckets were ready in case of fire. They were. He checked each store that was to house fighters. They were ready and willing, even if many of them were scared. Mrs. Marbly, a very formidable-sized lady, had found herself a pair of men's overalls, and when she bent over, she looked like the rear end of a stage-coach. But she handled the double-barreled shotgun like she knew what she was doing. Smoke concluded that he wouldn't want to mess with her.

Pete was still in shock after seeing Mrs. Marbly in men's overalls, bent over.

"Close your mouth, Pete," Smoke told him. "Before you suck in a fly."

Jim was stationed two miles out of town, on a ridge, a fast horse tied nearby. As soon as he spotted the dust of the raiders, he was to come hightailing it back into town and give the warning.

Smoke walked to the north end of the town and leaned up against a hitchrail. He rolled him a cigarette and lit up, wait-ing for the action to start.

He looked back up the wide street. It was void of any kind of life. The horses were stabled safely and the children's pets were in the house, out of harm's way.

Smoke watched as a water wagon rolled down the street, then back up, watering the wide street to keep down the dust. He clicked open his watch: eight-thirty. He walked on down the street, coming to a nearly collapsed old building; a relic of a business of some sort that had failed. This was the last building on either side of the street. Smoke stepped up on the porch and pushed open the door. Rusty hinges howled in protest. He stepped inside and looked in both rooms of the structure. He tried the back door, working it several times to make certain he could exit that way. There was not a window-pane intact in any frame, so he did not have to worry about being cut by flying glass. He sat down on the dusty floor and waited.

At eight-forty-five, Jim came fogging into town from his post. Smoke heard him yell, "Here they come, folks. And there's plenty to go around." He rode into the livery stable and disappeared.

Smoke eared back the hammers on the sawed-off and knelt by the window. Moments later, he could feel the vibration through the floor, the faint thunder of hundreds of hooves striking the ground.

As the pack of outlaws drew closer, Smoke stared in amazement. Robert was leading the bunch. He wore a pith helmet, the leather strap tied under his chin, and was waving a sword. God knows where he had found either article in Hell's Creek.

The raiders, more than a hundred strong, thundered into town. Smoke let Robert and a few behind him gallop past, then he gave both barrels of the sawed-off to the outlaws.

The hand-loaded charge of nails and buckshot cleared a bloody path in the middle of the outlaw horde. Smoke dropped the shotgun and jerked out his Colts, cocking and firing as fast as he could, deadly rolling thunder erupted from the small collapsing building on the edge of town. Horses began milling around, confused and frightened and riderless. Bodies lay in the street.

A wounded outlaw, his hands filled with guns, staggered up on the porch. He spotted Smoke and leveled his guns. Smoke gave him two .44 slugs in the chest and the man's days of lawlessness were over.

Smoke quickly reloaded his Colts, shoved fresh shell into the express gun, and ran out the back door, turning to his right.

"Red and his bunch are attacking from the south!" he heard the faint shout over the roar of battle.

Smoke ducked into the space between a home and a business and ran to the street. A hatless and bearded man stepped off the path and turned to face Smoke. Smoke pulled the trigger of the sawed-off, and the force of the charge lifted the outlaw off his boots and knocked him out into the street. Smoke ran to the edge of the street and gave the other barrel to a cursing raider. Blood smeared his saddle and the man hit the street, dead.

Smoke filled both hands with Colts and began emptying saddles. From the sounds of shotgun fire coming from the bank building, and the number of bodies littering the street in front of the bank, the Easterners were having a duck shoot and doing a damn fine job of holding their own.

Smoke stepped back and reloaded the pistols and the shotgun.

"Forward, men!" he heard Robert shout, the cry coming from behind him. "Slay the Philistines."

Smoke turned around. Robert was charging him on horseback, waving his sword. Smoke ducked the slashing sword that could have taken his head off and swung up behind Robert as the frightened horse reared up, dumping both men on the ground. Robert lost his sword and Smoke gave him a one-two combination that dropped the man to the ground, out cold. Smoke tore the pith helmet off and used the leather chin strap to bind Robert's hands behind his back. He used the man's belt to securely bind his ankles, then rolled the doctor under a building. Smoke picked up his shotgun and stepped back into the fray.

Two raiders, apparently having lost their appetite for any further battle, came racing up the street, heading north. Smoke stepped out and gave them both barrels of the sawed-off. Two more saddles cleared.

Smoke stepped up on the boardwalk and ran toward the center of town, reloading the shotgun as he went. He turned down an alleyway and entered the hotel through the back door, muttering curses because the rear of the building was not guarded.

Just above him, on the second floor, Warner Frigo had

kicked open the door to the presidential suite and was looking down at Lisa, huddled on the floor, holding her puppy close.

"Well, now," the outlaw said with a sneer. "Won't you just be a juicy little thing to have."

He holstered his guns and reached down for her, lust in his eyes.

"You'll hurt no more children and kill not another child's pet," Warner heard the woman say.

He looked up. Sally stood in the foyer, holding a sawed-off in her hands, both hammers eared back.

Warner's lips peeled back in an ugly smile. "I'll have you after I taste little-bit here."

"I doubt it," Sally said, then pulled both triggers. The force of the blast knocked Warner off both boots and sent him flying into the hall. He hit the hall wall and slid down to the carpeted floor. The wall behind him was a gory mess.

Smoke looked up as the shotgun went off. If anyone had tried to mess with Sally, they picked the wrong woman. He went up the stairs to check it out.

He saw Warner's body and stuck his head into the foyer. "Everybody all right in there?" he called.

"Just dandy," Sally said. "Would you please remove tha' garbage from the hall, darling?"

"Sure." Smoke dragged Warner's body down the hall and threw him out the second-story window. The downward hurtling body hit Sid Yorke and knocked him out of the saddle. The outlaw stared in horror at what was left of Warner Frigo

He looked up at Smoke, standing behind the shattere window, grinning down at him. Sid lifted his pistol, an Judge Garrison, standing in his office, fired both Remington .44's, the slugs knocking the man to his knees. The outla died in that position, his hands by his side. His hat fell fro his head. The wind picked it up and sailed it down the stree

Sal stepped out from his position just as John Steele w rounding a corner.

"Hey, John!" Sal called.

The foreman of the Lightning whirled in a crouch, both hands by his holstered guns.

"You always bragged how good you was," the newly elected sheriff said, his voice carrying over the din of battle and the whinnying of frightened horses. "You wanna find out now?"

John dragged iron. He was far too slow. Sal put two slugs in his belly before Steele could clear leather.

"I guess now you know," Sal told him.

"You sorry . . ." John gasped the words. He never got to finish it. The foreman fell off the boardwalk and landed in a horse trough.

"Have to remember to clean that out," Sal muttered.

Judge Garrison went out the back door of his office and came face to face with Paul Cartwright. The judge smiled at the man. "You used to love to lord it over me, Paul. You have guns in your hands. Use them!"

The deposed sheriff's guns came up. Judge Garrison lifted his Remington Army Model .44's, and the muzzles blossomed in fire and smoke. Paul Cartwright fell backward, dead.

The judge reloaded and walked up the back of the buildings, conviction and courage in his eyes.

"Gimme all your goddamn money, you heifer!" Frank Norton yelled at Mrs. Marbly.

Mrs. Marbly lifted her shotgun and blew the outlaw out the back door.

"Nice going, Mother," her husband said.

Larry Gayle knew it was a losing cause. He had been thrown from his rearing, bucking horse and was now cautiously making his way out of town . . . on foot. He'd find a horse. To hell with Barlow, Max Huggins, and the whole ness. There had to be easier pickings somewheres else was his philosophy.

"Going somewhere, Larry?" the voice spun him around.

Pete Akins stood facing him.

Larry lifted his Smith & Wesson Schofield .45 and got off the first shot. It grazed Pete's shoulder. Pete was much more careful with his shooting. He shot Larry between the eyes. He walked to the prostrate and very dead outlaw and looked down at him. He shook his head.

"Whoo, boy. You was ugly alive. Dead, you'll probably come back to haunt graveyards."

Ted Mercer stood facing Smoke Jensen. The outlaw felt a coldness take hold of him. His Colt was in his hand, but he was holding it by his side. Could Jensen beat him? He didn't know. He really didn't want to find out.

"You can drop that iron and walk," Smoke told him. "Change your life. It's up to you."

"You're only sayin' that 'cause you know you can't beat this."

"You're wrong, Ted."

"Your guns are in leather!"

"Drop it and walk, man. Don't be a fool."

"I think I'll just kill you, Jensen." Ted's hand jerked up. He felt a dull shock hit him in the belly, another hammerlike blow beat at his chest. Impossible! he thought. No man is that fast. No man is . . .

Smoke walked up and looked down at the dead outlaw. "I gave you a chance," he said.

Fires had been started by the raiders, but they had been quickly put out by the ladies of the bucket brigades. The plans of the outlaws were put out as quickly as the flames. Lew Brooks jumped his horse over the body of a friend and went charging between buildings. Judge Garrison stepped out and gave the outlaw a good dose of frontier justice, not from a law book but from a .44. Lew hit the ground, rolled over, and came up with a .45 in his hand. Judge Garrison imposed the death sentence on the man, then calmly reloaded and walked up the alleyway.

Jake Stringer knew that John Steele was down and dead along with several other Lightning men. He didn't know where Red Malone was. He tried to calm a badly spooked horse and climb into the saddle. But the horse was having none of that. The animal jumped away and left Jake on foot.

"Damn that hammerhead!" Jake swore. "I ought to shoot it."

"Why not try me?" Jim Dagonne said.

Jake turned. Jim's guns were in leather, as were his own. A smile creased his lips. "I enjoyed whuppin' you with my fists, Jim. Now I'm gonna enjoy killin' you."

Jim was no fast gunhand, but he was a dead shot. Jake cleared leather first and his shot went into the dirt at Jim's boots. Jim plugged the man just above the belt buckle. Jake sat down on the ground and started hollering.

Jim walked to him. He could see where the slug had exited out the man's back, right through the kidney. "You ain't gonna make it, Jake. You got anyone you want me to write?"

"I didn't even know you could write," Jake said, then fell over on his face and closed his eyes.

Ella Mae, Tom Johnson's wife, was struggling with a man who had less than honorable intentions on his mind. He ripped her bodice open and stared hungrily at her flesh. Momentarily free, Ella Mae ran to the kitchen, jerked up the coffeepot from the stove, and threw the boiling contents into the man's face.

The outlaw screamed and went lurching and staggering through the living room, finding his way out the front door, his face seared from the boiling coffee. He stumbled out into the street and was run down by another wounded outlaw trying to get out of the death trap named Barlow. The burned outlaw fell under the hooves and lay still.

Clark Hall made the bank and hurled himself through the door. He came up on his boots just in time to face several men with shotguns. He had time to say one word: "No!"

Three sawed-off shotguns roared, and Clark Hall was literally torn out of his boots and thrown out into the street.

The shooting stopped. An eerie silence fell over the town.

Smoke stepped out into the street, the Remington Frontier .44's in his hands. The moaning of the wounded drifted to him.

Judge Garrison took charge. "Gather up the wounded, and we'll patch them up as best we can and then try them. We were forced to use frontier justice to stop this, but there'll be no unauthorized hangings. From now on we go by the book."

Ralph from the saloon was dead. Shot through the head. Toby at the hotel had taken a slug through his shoulder. Several other citizens were wounded, but Ralph was the only fatality. The streets and alleys of the town were littered with dead and wounded. Guns lay everywhere one looked and riderless horses milled around, not knowing what to do or where to go.

Henry Draper came out of his office at the newspaper, wearing two huge Dragoons belted around his waist. That would account for some of the booming sounds Smoke had heard and also some of the hideous wounds he'd seen. Draper set up his camera and began preparing for shots of the carnage. This was great stuff. The newspapers back east would eat it up.

Tom Johnson had wandered the main street, counting the dead and wounded. "Red Malone's not here," he said, walking up to Smoke and a group of others.

"How about his men?" Sal asked.

"Most of them are dead. I saw two of them riding out north early on. Looked like they were clearing the country."

"You have enough to do here for three men, Sal," Smoke said. "Besides, this is personal between me and Red. I'll get him. And I'll bring him in alive if I can."

"You better find him before Joe Walsh does," Jim said. "Joe told him years ago that if he ever caught him without his private army with him, he'd kill him."

"There is that much bad blood between them?" Smoke asked. "I knew they didn't like each other. . . ."

"Man, yeah!" Jim said. "He helped found this town—Joe I mean. Him and Red don't like each other at all."

"Well, I'll be!" came the shout. "Here's that so-called preacher from up at Hell's Creek. He had him a torch and was right in the middle of it all."

"Dead?" Pete called.

"I'll say. Plugged through and through."

Smoke walked the littered street, looking at the dead and wounded. But Alex Bell, Ben Webster, Nelson Barrett, Al Martin, Dave Poe, and Val Singer were not among them. That left a lot of very bad men still on the loose, but Smoke doubted that they would ever return to Barlow.

He walked to the hotel, kissed Sally and petted Lisa's puppy Patches, then told his wife, "I'll be back. I'm going after Red Malone."

"I'll go down and help with the wounded."

"See you when I return."

As Smoke was riding out, Jim said to Pete, "I wonder if he'll bring Red in alive."

Pete spat on the ground. "Not if Red tries to draw on him."

26

Smoke rode easy, knowing there was no hurry. Red Malone was not about to run. But he wondered about Max. What would the big man do—that is, if he were still alive? Or had his renegades returned to Hell's Creek after their failure in Barlow and killed him? And that was highly likely.

Smoke rode on, keeping Star in an easy canter, sometimes walking him. But the big horse loved to run and they ate up the distance. He was soon on Lightning range and, within minutes, facing three Lightning cowboys. One of them was wearing a bloody shirt, due to a bullet graze on his arm.

"The people of Barlow are signing warrants right now, boys. Best thing you can do is just ride and keep on riding. If you think Sal and his deputies won't come out here to get you, you're flat wrong."

The cowboys looked at each other, then back at Smoke. One said, "You'll let us ride?"

Smoke jerked a thumb. "Ride on."

"I'll tell you this much," another said. "Red is alone. Except for that no-account daughter of his. But you won't take him alive."

"Thanks. But I'd hate to kill a man in front of his daughter."

One of the cowboys laughed. "Smoke, that girl is as low and mean-spirited as her pa. She don't give a popcorn poot for him. All she wants is the ranch. I believe she'd kill him herself if she got the chance."

"Thanks. I hope I don't see you boys again."

They grinned. "You won't!"

They rode out, taking trails that would skirt the town of Barlow.

When Smoke rode into the yard, Tessie was sitting on the porch. A shotgun lay on the porch floor. At the sight of him, she started bawling and squalling. As he drew closer, he could see that her dress was torn. She stopped crying long enough to expose more skin. Then she resumed her blubbering.

Smoke sat his saddle for a moment, staring at the young woman. "Where's your father?" he asked when there was a break in the hollering.

"He's dead!" she squalled. "In the house. He tried to attack me. He went crazy. I had to defend my honor!" She began a new round of wailing.

Smoke swung down from the saddle and walked up onto the porch. He really didn't know what to expect; maybe a trap. He just didn't know.

He opened the screen door and the smell of blood hit him hard. He walked through the house until he found Red, dead, sprawled in front of a safe in his study. The door was open, and greenbacks and small sacks of gold lay on the floor and in the safe.

Smoke grunted. Red Malone had been shot in the back at close range.

"Ohhh!" Tessie hollered from the front porch. "I'm shamed forever. My own father tried to assault me. Oh, the dishonor and disgrace of it all." She started blubbering.

Smoke looked down at Red. "I hate to say it, Red, but even you probably deserved better kids than you had."

He walked outside. Tessie honked her nose into a bandana and said, "What am I gonna do with this big ol' ranch? Why, I'm just a woman; I can't handle men's work."

"I certainly don't envy you, ma'am. Don't you have anybody else left on the ranch?"

"Just the cook. She's gone visitin' friends for the day. I suppose I could get her to help me bury Pa. You think he'll keep 'til late this afternoon?"

"I expect so, ma'am." Smoke stepped into the saddle.

"Are you just gonna leave me here all alone with my poor dead father? I could sure use some comforting." She batted her eyes at him. It was the most grotesque thing Smoke had ever seen—and he had seen some sights in his time.

"I'll explain to the sheriff what happened," Smoke said as he backed Star up. Damned if he was going to turn his back to this woman. "I'll sure do that."

When he had backed Star to the point where he was reasonably sure she could not hit him with the sawed-off, Smoke gave the big black his head. Star took off like the wind. The horse wasn't real thrilled with Tessie, either.

When Smoke arrived back in town, he told Judge Garrison and Sal what he'd seen out at the Lightning spread. Neither man seemed very surprised.

"She'll take every dollar from the safe, sell off the herds and be gone in a month," the judge prophesied. "And good riddance to bad baggage."

Smoke looked around. Most of the bodies had been tossed in wagons and were being hauled off to be buried in mass grave. Half the men in town were working with shovel at the gravesite.

"Wagons coming," Jim announced, pointing to the north

As the wagons neared, Judge Garrison said, "Saloon girls, gamblers, and assorted riffraff from Hell's Creek. Rats leaving a sinking ship."

"No," Smoke said. "A burning one. Because that's what we're going to do in the morning."

"Suits me," Tom said. "I'll ride with you."

"Keep moving," Sal told the lead wagon. "And don't stop until you're in the next county. And he won't want you, either, 'cause I'm fixin' to wire the sheriff and tell him about you scum."

One of the ladies of the evening, sitting in the back of the wagon, gave him a very obscene gesture with a finger.

"I'll jerk you out of that wagon and hand you over to the good ladies of this town," Sal warned her. "And they'll shave your head and tar and feather you."

The shady lady tucked her finger away and stared straight ahead.

The wagons rumbled out of sight.

"Why wait until the morning?" Pete asked. "Hell, Smoke. Let's ride up there and put that town out of its misery right now."

Smoke was curious to see what had happened to Big Max. "All right. Let's ride."

The band of men had stopped at Brown's farmhouse and asked if the farmers wanted any of the lumber in the town before they put the torch to it.

To a man, they shook their heads. "Thanks kindly, but no thanks," Gatewood said. "We just want shut of that den of thieves and whores and hoodlums."

The men rode on, Smoke, Pete, Tom Johnson, Judge Garson, and half a dozen more of the town. They were heavily armed, for no one among them knew what awaited them in Hell's Creek.

Desolation.

As they topped the ridge overlooking the town, they would all sense the place was empty, completely void of life.

"Let's check it out," Smoke said.

The men inspected every building. The town was deserted. Thre was no sign of Big Max Huggins. Smoke looked at the safe in Max's quarters. The door was open and there was no sign of forced entry. So Max had found the strength to open it and ride.

Smoke found a coal-oil lantern, lit it, and tossed it into the squalor that someone had once lived in . . . and from all indications, it had housed several women. The building was quickly ablaze. The other men were doing the same with coal-oil-soaked rags. Soon, the fierceness of the heat drove them back.

In half an hour, the town of Hell's Creek, Montana was no more than an unpleasant memory.

The men headed back toward Barlow, for a hot bath, a good meal, and some well-deserved rest. The day's events would alter their lives forever. For the good.

All that was left for Sally and Smoke were the good-bye to the people of Barlow and the ranchers and farmers out in the county. In the short time they'd been there, a lot had happened and they had discovered some friendships that would last forever.

Robert had been transferred to the territorial mental asylum and the doctors there had given him very little hope of ever recovering.

Through Sally's help, the new bank had agreed to loan Martha and Pete the money for a down payment on the Lightning spread. The two were married the day before Smoke and Sally were due to pull out.

Tessie Malone left the country the very day she sold Lightning to Pete and Martha.

Much to Sal's embarrassment, Victoria announced that the newly elected sheriff had proposed marriage to her and that she had accepted. Victoria had also accepted a position of teaching at the new school.

The other new schoolteacher in town, a cute little red-head, was making goo-goo eyes at Jim Dagonne. Bets were that he'd be roped and hog-tied before summer's end.

Smoke and Sally had said their good-byes to Joe Walsh and his wife.

The town of Barlow had been quiet for a week. Not one shot had been fired, not one fist had been swung in anger. Sal commented that it was just too good to last.

That proved true when one of Joe Walsh's hands came fogging into town, pale as a ghost and so excited he could hardly talk. He'd found Smoke Jensen's body on the trail. Sally Jensen was missing.

27

Smoke was not dead, but had the bullet that grazed his skull been one millimeter more to the right, the slug would have blown out his brains.

He was back on his feet the next day, over the protestations of the new doctor in Barlow, and strapping on his guns.

Every able-bodied man in Barlow had been on the search for Sally and her kidnapper or kidnappers. They had ridden back into town at dawn, weary. They had lost the trail.

All Smoke could remember was that he and Sally and the packhorse had ridden down the edge of Swan Lake, intending to pick up the Swan River and follow it south to the railroad. They had stopped to water and rest their horses when Smoke's head seemed to explode.

That's all he could remember.

He swung into the saddle and pointed Star's head south, intending to backtrack. He had a headache, but other than that, he felt fine.

"You're sure you don't want some help?" Sal asked.

"No. A big posse is too easy to spot. Besides, Sally will leave messages along the way; messages and markers th would make sense only to me. It's Big Max, I'd bet on that. I was instrumental in bringing down his little empire, so now he intends to destroy as much of what I hold dear as possible. See you, Sal."

Smoke rode easy, down to the south end of the lake. There he dismounted and began searching the area, using tactics taught him by the old mountain man, Preacher. He worked in ever-widening circles, on moccasin-clad feet. By midafternoon he had picked up the trail—the true one, not the one that had been deliberately left for the posse.

The trail headed north by northeast. The lead horse was carrying a heavy load. That would be Max Huggins. Smoke recognized the hoofprints of Sally's mare. If they stayed on this trail, Smoke surmised, they were heading for glacier country.

Smoke doggedly stayed with the trail, taking his time, being careful not to miss a thing. He found where they'd camped at the base of and on the east side of Mt. Evans. Sally had left three stones in the form of an arrowhead pointing toward the Flathead River.

Smoke followed, his head no longer aching and his strength having returned. He kept his fury under control—barely. He met a lone hunter, and the man took one look into Smoke's eyes and felt the chill of death touch him. The hunter backed off the trail and let Smoke pass with just a nod of his head.

The man would tell his grandkids that he had once seen Smoke Jensen on the prod, and that it was not a sight he ever wanted to see again.

On the east side of the South Fork Flathead, Max had met up with the tracks of a dozen riders. Probably the remnants of Max's gang, Smoke thought. Several miles farther, one rider had left the bunch. Smoke left the trail and circled. He picketed Star and worked his way back a bit on foot. He smiled when he saw who had stayed behind to waylay him.

It was the young man who had taken to calling himself Kid Brewer; the young man with a few pimples on his face who had made the obscene gesture at Smoke after the window-washing incident.

"Waiting for me, Kid?" Smoke called from behind the young man.

Kid Brewer whirled, his hands frozen over the butts of his tied-down guns. Smoke Jensen stood facing him, a Winchester pointed at his belly.

"You really shouldn't have taken a part in the taking of my wife, punk," Smoke told him. "Coming at me is one thing; taking my wife is something entirely different."

"Yeah," the young gunhand sneered at him. "So what do you think you're going to do about it?"

Smoke shot him. The .44 slug from the rifle struck the young man in the right elbow, knocking him down and forever crippling his gun hand. He lay on the cool ground moaning and calling for his mother.

Smoke walked down to him and placed the muzzle of the rifle on the gunhand's left elbow. "If you think I won't leave you permanently crippled in both arms, you're crazy. Talk to me, punk."

Brewer looked up into the coldest eyes he had ever seen in all his young life. They so chilled him he momentarily forgot the pain in his shattered right arm. He began talking so fast Smoke had to slow him down.

When he had finished, Smoke smashed Brewer's gun, threw him on his saddle, and when the young man had stopped screaming after the jolting pain in his arm from the toss had lessened, Smoke gave him some advice. "If I ever see you again and you're wearing a gun, I'll kill you." He slapped the horse on the rump and the pony took off at a fast canter. Brewer was still screaming when Smoke mounted up.

Smoke backtracked and once more picked up the trail. He found where they had nooned and discovered Sally had taken stones and spelled out: O K. With a smile that would have backed up the devil, Smoke swung into the saddle and rode on.

He left the obvious trail and rode up into the high lonesome, into the east slopes of the Rockies. He dismounted and took his binoculars, carefully scanning the area below him. He scanned it once, then twice, and then a third time. He picked up the thin tentacle of smoke on the third try. He studied the area below him until he felt he had found a way in. He mounted up and headed down into the valley.

Nelson Barrett was enjoying a cup of hot coffee. His pleasure abruptly lessened when he felt the cold steel of a big Bowie knife against his throat. What made it even worse was the dark stain that suddenly appeared in the crotch of his dirty Jeans.

"Talk to me, pee-pants," Smoke whispered. "And I'd better like what you have to say. 'Cause if I don't, I'll stake you out and skin you alive."

"Your woman's awright!" Nelson blurted. "There ain't nobody touched her. I swear it, man!"

"You were left here to do what?"

"Kill you!"

"Well, now. Is that a fact? What do you think I ought to do with you?"

"You let me ride, you'll never see me again, Smoke. As God is my witness, I promise you that."

Smoke took the knife from the man's throat and Nelson made a grab for his gun. Smoke jammed the big blade into the man's back and ripped upward with it. Nelson Barrett fell face-first into the small fire.

Smoke wiped the blade clean on Nelson's shirttail and poured himself a cup of coffee. He drank it slowly, then carefully put out the fire. He left Nelson where he lay and mounted up.

He crossed the Middle Fork of the Flathead River and rode into the area that would someday become the Glacier National Park. Smoke slipped into a jacket, for it had turned cold.

He plunged into a wild, beautiful wilderness. His thoughts

turned to Preacher and how much the old man would have enjoyed the beauty of this rugged, lonesome country.

Then his thoughts lost all trace of beauty and turned savage and ugly as he followed the trail of Max Huggins and his dwindling gang of thugs and punks and human crap. He thought he heard a voice from out of the dark tangle of vegetation and pulled up, dismounting. He picketed Star and moved forward, both guns in his hands.

Al Martin, Dave Poe, and Ben Webster squatted around a campfire, boiling coffee and frying bacon.

"I cain't understand why Big Max don't go ahead and take the woman," Al said. "I would have."

" 'Cause he'd have to knock her out cold to do it," Ben replied. "And that ain't no fun."

"He ought to just go 'head and shoot her," Dave opined. "She ain't never gonna be what Max wants her to be."

"I say we go on and kill Jensen, if that is him behind us, then kill Max, take his money, and have our pleasures with the woman," Al said. "There ain't nobody ever gonna find her body in this place."

Smoke stepped out and ruined the men's appetites. Both .44's belched flame and death, destroying the tranquility of the lovely forest in the high-up country.

Smoke dragged their bodies away from the fire and dumped them down a ravine. He pulled the picket pins of their horses and set them free. Smoke got Star and unsaddled him, rubbing the animal down and allowing him to graze for a time.

By that time, the bacon was done and the coffee was ready. Smoke drank and ate, sopping out the grease in the frying pan with a hunk of stale bread.

Smoke rolled him a cigarette and leaned back, enjoying the warmth of the fire. He poured another cup of coffee. If his calculations were correct, all that remained were Max, Val Singer, and Alex Bell. He moved away from the fire, laid his head on his saddle, and went to sleep.

He slept for a couple of hours, then rose and began cir

cling the camp. He found another stick message from Sally. Three sticks laid out side by side, with four sticks next to them, in the shape of a crude D. Triple Divide Peak. Had to be.

Ol' Preacher had told him about this country, as had other old mountain men, and like most outdoorsmen, Smoke retained that knowledge in his head, a mental map.

He saddled up and took a chance, cutting straight east for a time, then turning north just west of what he felt was the Continental Divide. If he was right, and Max and what was left of his gang were not too far ahead of him—and he didn't think they were—he would make Triple Divide Peak ahead of Max.

Smoke pushed Star that day, but it was nothing the big horse couldn't take and still have more to give. Man and horse traveled through country that seemed as unchanged now as it was when God created the earth.

And Smoke could not understand why Max, with his love of cities and towns, hurdy-gurdy girls and parties, had chosen to come here, into this cold and vast wilderness.

He concluded that Max, like his brother Robert, had a streak of insanity running through him.

Smoke made camp that evening between Mt. Thompson and Triple Divide Peak. He loved this country, this high lonesome, where bighorn sheep played their perilous games on the face of seemingly untraversable mountains. Where cedars grew so tall they seemed to touch the sky. Where far below where he camped, heating his coffee over a hat-sized fire, he could see herds of buffalo roaming.

It all seemed just too peaceful a place for what Smoke had in mind.

But peaceful or not, he had come to find Sally, and get Sally he would. He rolled up in his blankets and went to sleep. Tomorrow was going to be a very busy day.

Smoke was up before dawn. He did not build a fire. He watered Star and left the big horse to graze. Below him, by one of the many small lakes that were scattered like jewels in this wilderness, he had spotted a campfire. Leaving his boots and spurs behind, Smoke slipped into his moccasins and picked up his rifle. He had it in his mind that he and Sally would be riding toward the Sugarloaf come noon.

Smoke moved through the thick underbrush and damp grass like a wraith. His clothing was of earth tones, blending in with his surroundings. From his high-up vantage point, Smoke had seen the second fire. That would be where Max and Sally were camped. Max had chosen to make his stand— if that's what he had in mind—on the flat of a sheer drop-off, maybe a thousand feet above where his two remaining gunmen were camped, waiting for Smoke Jensen.

"Let us not disappoint you, gentlemen," Smoke muttered. "I do hate to keep people waiting."

"No word from any of them we left behind," Val Singer said to Alex Bell. "That means that Jensen got them."

Bell said nothing for a moment. He sipped his coffee, warming his hands on the tin cup. He was cold, he was uncomfortable, and he was scared. All along the way up into this godforsaken country, they had left good men behind them; men left there to take care of Smoke Jensen. But Jensen had taken care of them, it seemed. The man was a devil. Straight out of hell. Had to be.

"Let's get out of here, Val," he finally spoke. "To hell with Max and the woman. Let's just ride."

"It's too late," Val said, the words soft.

"What the hell do you mean?"

"Jensen's here."

Alex looked wildly around him. He could see nothing only the seemingly impenetrable tangle of brush that was all around them. "I don't see nothin'. I don't hear nothin'."

"No," the gunfighter said, standing up and working his gun in and out of leather. "You wouldn't with Jensen. But he's here."

Alex stood up, loosening his guns. "You're beginning to spook me, Val."

"We shoulda left when Jensen showed up. We shoulda just pulled out and got gone. Now it's too late."

"That's right, Val," the voice came from the underbrush. "Now it's too late."

Alex Bell jerked iron and emptied one gun into the thick brush.

Laughter was his reply.

"Come out here and fight, damn you!" Alex screamed.

A .44 slug from a Winchester doubled him over, the slug taking him just above the belt buckle. The second slug turned him around and dropped him to the cold ground. His gun fell from numbed fingers.

Val Singer had not moved. He stood tall, his right hand close to the butt of his Colt. He waited.

Alex Bell moaned on the ground. Val ignored him.

Smoke stepped out of the brush. He carried the rifle in his left hand, his right hand by his side.

Val said, "I guess we do it now, don't we, Smoke?"

"I reckon."

"No point in my sayin' I'd just ride on out and leave you be?"

"Nope."

"You're a hard man, Smoke."

"Yep."

Val cussed him.

Smoke waited, tall and tough and cold-eyed.

Val jerked iron and Smoke shot him twice in the belly once with his Colt and once with the .44 rifle. Smoke walked to the fire and poured a cup of coffee. He made a sandwich out of the nearly burned bacon and some bread wrapped in a cloth. He cut his eyes to Val Singer.

"We all make mistakes," the gun-for-hire said, his eyes pain-filled as he lay on the ground, both hands holding his punctured belly.

"Indeed you did."

"Gimme some coffee, Smoke."

"You're gut-shot. Worse thing in the world for you is liquid."

Val laughed bitterly. "I'm a good two hundred miles from a doctor. You think I don't know I've had it?"

Smoke poured Val a cup of the strong brew and handed it to him.

"Thanks," Val said. He took a sip of the brew and then screamed as the pain rose in waves.

To the west and above them, Sally had been working for several hours, rubbing the rawhide that bound her wrists against a rock. She felt the rawhide part and then, keeping her hands behind her, began to work circulation back into her hands.

Max turned to look at her. His face was a ruin. Smoke had destroyed the man's handsome looks with his fists. Madness shone in his eyes; madness combined with a burning hatred for Smoke Jensen.

"You heard the shots?"

"Yes."

"I'm next."

"I'm sure."

Max tried to smile. The broken bones in his face twisted his smile into a grimace. "I've got about an hour before Jensen can work his way up here. So I'll have you and then throw you off this cliff."

"I'm cold," Sally said. "May I scoot closer to the fire?"

"May I?" Max said mockingly. "My, how proper. Yes Sally, you may."

Sally scooted to the fire's edge. Max turned his back to her, looking down into the valley below. Sally reached around and quickly untied the rawhide that bound her ankles, but left the rawhide looped around her boots.

Alex Bell sighed once and then died.

"Well, that's the end of it," Val managed to say, his voice thick with pain. "That's the last one of us 'ceptin' Max. An' I 'spect you'll nail him, too. You gonna bury us, Smoke?"

"Nope." Smoke ate his sandwich and sipped his coffee.

"You just gonna leave us for the buzzards and the bears and the wolves?" The outlaw could not believe that Smoke really meant that.

"Yep."

"That ain't decent!"

"You're not a decent person, Singer. There is nothing decent about you."

"I was drove to a life of crime!"

Smoke laughed at him. "That's all horse-crap and you know it, Val. You chose your life willingly. So don't go out with a lie on your lips."

"I guess," the outlaw said, his voice weak. He looked around him and laughed bitterly. "All them books them folks back east write about the glamorous life on the hootowl trail. They don't know nothin'. All the outlaws I ever seen, me included, were dirty and hungry and cold and miserable ninety-nine days out of a hundred. But there ain't no point in wishin' I could change it, is there?"

"No, there isn't."

"Smoke?"

Smoke looked at him.

"You're a good man, Jensen. You got a good woman. I wish you both the best."

"Thanks, Val. You want to be buried with your boots on?"

"No. Gonna be hot enough where I'm goin'." He laid his head on the ground and closed his eyes.

Smoke waited for death to take the man.

"Max?" Sally whispered. She had taken a good-sized chunk of burning wood from the fire and stepped up behind the man. One end of the fire-brand was blazing hot.

Max turned and Sally hit him in the face with the burning wood, then jammed the blazing wood into his open mouth. Max dropped his rifle and screamed, backing up. His boot hit a rock and sent him tumbling over the edge of the cliff. He screamed for a thousand feet.

Silence fell over the wilderness.

Sally rubbed her aching ankles and wrists, then set about making fresh coffee and slicing bacon. Her man would be along in about an hour.

Smoke rode into the flats and dismounted. He held his woman in his arms for a long time. She pushed him away and expelled breath. "What took you so long?"

"I buried Val Singer. Are you all right?"

"I am now. Come on, eat. I made fresh coffee."

The sun burst out of the clouds and mist of mid-afternoon. Sally looked across the fire at Smoke Jensen. "No point in starting out now. We can wait until morning."

"Oh? You have something in mind?"

She came to him and whispered in his ear.

Smoke took her in his arms. "Now that's the best suggestion I've heard in a long time."